SUSAN KAYE QUINN

*Tiffany —
Keep following
your dreams...
until they come
true.*

THIRD DAUGHTER

Sue Quinn

Third Daughter (The Dharian Affairs, Book One)
Copyright © 2013 by Susan Kaye Quinn
December 2013 Edition
All rights reserved.

No part of this publication may be reproduced, stored in a retrieval system or transmitted in any form or by any means, electronic or mechanical, including photocopying, recording, or otherwise, without written permission from the publisher. For information visit:
www.SusanKayeQuinn.com

Cover by Steven Novak
www.NovakIllustration.com

Developmental Editing by Bryon Quertermous
www.BryonQuertermous.com

Copyediting by Sher A. Hart
www.SherAHart.com

Interior Design by Novel Ninjutsu
www.NovelNinjutsu.com

Summary

The Third Daughter of the Queen wants to marry for love, but rumors of a new flying weapon force her to accept a barbarian prince's proposal of a peace-brokering marriage.

Third Daughter is the first book in The Dharian Affairs trilogy (*Third Daughter, Second Daughter, First Daughter*). This steampunk-goes-to-Bollywood (Bollypunk!) romance takes place in an east-Indian-flavored alternate world filled with skyships, saber duels, and lots of royal intrigue. And, of course, kissing.

For Rick Daley
who will be shocked to find a romance dedicated to him

one

The cloudless night whispered sweet promises to Aniri.

Below her stone rooftop, the shadows of the forested grounds danced in the summer's breeze, their small rustlings calling to her like a lover. The sound was the perfect cover for escape into the darkness and the warm arms she hoped to find there. No one should notice her absence. Of all the guards, handmaidens, and many silent keepers of the royal household, none would venture up to her private observatory this late in the eve. But she still had to be careful. Even this close to her birthday, the Queen would not be forgiving if she was caught.

Aniri scanned the palace grounds to make sure it was clear of any witnesses. The manicured lawns were empty: the only sign of life came from the distant embassy

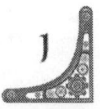

windows where gas lamps flickered and soft music trilled from late-reveling partygoers. Aniri pressed the leather eyecup of her aetherscope to her face, slowly turning the brass knobs to bring the party into focus. The instrument was meant for watching the rise of the twin full moons, but it worked well enough for spying on the Samirian ambassador and her assemblage of guests.

Their shiny new automaton was thick-legged and awkward, but the Samirian tinker's design was still clever: the steam-driven mechanical wonder actually danced, albeit just one clumsy pirouette after another. When it came to a graceless stop, the guests snapped their fingers in appreciation. The faint sound of their applause drifted over the lawn, but the party continued on. With the grounds still empty, Aniri swung her aetherscope to the forest. The broken edges of the river snaked through the darkened trees, slipped under a stone bridge, and then flowed past the red sandstone walls of the Queen's estate. A black shape darted out from under the bridge, then disappeared into the shadows between the trees.

Time to go.

She peered over the edge of the balcony. No sense in being caught by someone who snuck out for a dalliance in the dark. With the way clear, she opened the leather satchel at her feet and uncoiled the sheet she had twisted into a rope. *Always check your knots, Aniri.* Her father's voice accompanied her on every climb, but she had to wonder what he would have made of this particular one. She rechecked the knots. It would cause quite a stir if she plummeted to her death while climbing down the palace wall.

The massive stone lion that guarded the parapet served as an excellent anchor. She looped the rope around it, then stood on the edge of the wall and leaned

out over the blackness. *Loop the rope under and between your feet, Aniri. It will carry your weight.* Practical advice, but the knots would impede her progress, and speed was of the essence. She lowered herself, hand over hand, bracing her feet against the wall. A mossy spot, hidden by the dark and slick with dew, sent her silk slippers pawing rapid-fire several times before she found purchase between the giant stone blocks.

Always use the proper equipment. She took a deep breath. Her father would probably disapprove of her attire. Silk nightclothes were hardly climbing wear, and she couldn't find any plausible excuse to wear her climbing shoes to bed. Her handmaiden, Priya, was far too clever for that—and already suspicious when Aniri wanted to retire to her observatory alone. At least she had her fingerless climbing gloves, and on every climb she wore the thin, braided bracelet her father gave her. For luck. She thought he would approve.

Hand over hand, Aniri continued her descent. Halfway down, a sudden clacking broke the quiet and rose above the scrapings of her slippers on the treacherous walls. She held still against the cool stone, hands gripped tight on her rope of sheets. A lone two-wheeled surrey ambled out of the shadows of the Samirian embassy and headed toward her dark corner of the Queen's estate. Aniri held her breath and silently cursed the full two-moon night. If the carriage came much closer, the occupants would surely see her clinging to the side of the palace like a spider on her thread.

The six-hooved beast pulling the surrey slowed as it neared the giant stone statue of Devkasera. The mother goddess of ancient Dharia loomed larger-than-life, threatening the carriage with a sword and a scroll—the powers of destruction and creation—clasped in two of her six hands. The Queen loved the ancient traditions, so the goddess held a place of respect in the middle of the palace lawns. Aniri preferred the clean streets and steam-driven inventions of modern Dharia to the unwashed feet and mystic religion of her country's past, but that didn't stop her from sending a silent prayer to Devkasera—for invisibility for herself or perhaps a sudden loss of sight by the persons in the carriage.

The surrey paused at the statue, then veered right and headed for the far wall that enclosed the estate. Aniri repressed a laugh—perhaps she should pray to Devkasera to bring her birthday sooner as well. Her arms ached from holding her position, but she waited until the carriage had passed through the palace gate. Beyond it, the lights of Kartavya, Dharia's capital city, winked through the coal-smoke haze as if giving her an all-clear signal.

Her muscles rejoiced when she moved again, working her way down the last half of the wall and dropping the final two feet. From there, she scampered over the surrounding manicured hedgerows as if she had fled the palace a hundred times before. Her unbound dark hair flapped behind her, and the cool night breeze fluttered her black silk nightclothes against her skin like a thousand butterfly wings. It was the feeling of freedom breathing against her, and she had to clamp her teeth against the giggle that threatened to ruin her escape.

She slowed and picked her way through the darkened brambles of the forest grabbing at her legs. The first time, she slipped away from dinner in her normal evening attire—a midnight-black corset latched with brass clasps, a starched skirt of blood-red silk, and a sweep of silk over her shoulder for the traditional touch the Queen required. Aniri thought the dark colors would ease her escape, but

she had stuck to the needled branches like a royal pincushion. The second time, she cast aside the bodice and most of the silk, keeping only her short bloomers and camisole—essentially running through the forest in her unmentionables. That had been deliciously decadent, but also very chilly. This time, her nightclothes were proving the most suitable costume yet for midnight escapades.

She smiled and slipped through the forest like a phantom, black on black, silent and stealthy. The faint trace of coal smoke gave way to the fresh scent of leaves mixed with river mist. She breathed it deep: the lushness of it always captivated her. The Queen had imported trees and beasts from the barbarians in the north to recreate the Dharian forests long ago swept away by agriculture. Fortunately, her majesty favored the gentle animals sacred to the gods. Aniri was careful not to disturb a long-tailed bandir hanging from a branch, eyes closed and peaceful. She didn't believe the superstitions about waking one, but she couldn't afford the screech it would let loose.

Aniri broke out of the forest and onto the wet rocks bordering the river. The footbridge ahead was a silent sentinel over the constant chatter of the river. There was no sign of movement. Was she too late? But then Devesh stepped from the shadows, showing his face to the moons as if he had nothing to hide.

She skittered over the slippery rocks and flew into his arms.

"Aniri," he said, but she was uninterested in wasting precious moments with words. She shut him up with her lips pressed fiercely to his. He closed his dark, humor-filled eyes, and wrapped his arms around her. Being a courtesan, he was well-trained in courtly conversation, but the artistry of his lips moving slow yet urgent against hers made her forget her own name.

The silk of his jacket was smooth under her hands, the steel studs of his collar cool on her wandering fingertips. When she broke their kiss, the moonlight bleached the color from his Samirian diplomat attire: the deep russet brown of his jacket turned black, and the parade of buttons across his chest shone like stars against it.

Devesh smiled, and his lingering hands traced silken lines along her back. "You look... enticing this evening. Although I must admit to preferring the bloomers."

She grinned and flushed with the memory of their fevered kisses. Their grapplings were still innocent, but that night, they had ventured closer to the passion they would share one day. Her skin prickled, her clothes even now a thin barrier between his hands and her bare skin.

"Some activities require a certain type of attire," she said.

"Indeed." His smile grew. "I didn't know if you would come tonight. Sneaking out of the palace is dangerous business, and you're quickly becoming a repeat offender."

"No more dangerous than sending a note through Priya. What if she had read it?"

"I'm sure that she did." His smile was bright against his bronzed skin. "But what could she make of a poem declaring your beauty in the moonlight? I imagine she thought it quite romantic."

She no doubt did. Priya was constantly gaming the odds of one match or another at court.

"You should take care in feeding her overactive imagination." But her admonishment was weak. Devesh's kisses were like a smoky drug, leaving her hazed and blissful afterwards: three days was far too long to go without them. "If she suspects our romance is real, and not just your earnest fantasy, word could get back to the Queen. And if we're caught before my birthday, the Queen will throw you out of the embassy simply to spite me for flouting her rules."

A wild strand of her hair tangled with the evening breeze. Devesh brushed it from her face, then cupped her cheek. "A moment with you, even stolen, is worth the risk."

His words were as intoxicating as his kisses. She reached up, eager for more. Devesh slowed and deepened their kiss, taming her feverish passion with a deliberation that made her even more crazed. Waiting to be with him was like a slow torture of endless minutes. But the day was coming: she could almost taste its nearness like the mouth-watering scent of a long-hungered meal just outside of reach. Soon she would be free: free of the court, free to kiss in broad daylight, free to leave Dharia behind and find the vermin who killed her father. Devesh had promised to help her search his country until they found the men responsible. She ached for that day like she did for Devesh. Soon she would have both.

When the intensity of their kiss made her gasp for breath, she broke it and leaned against him. "Two weeks, Dev," she whispered. "Just two. And I'll be eighteen."

"I'm counting the days, my love."

His intense gaze made her suddenly shy. She turned her attention to toying with the collar that brushed his neck. "You will say yes, won't you? When I ask?"

He gently pulled her face up to look at him. "When you are free to marry for love, Third Daughter of the Queen, you had better not ask anyone other than me. I'll have to hang myself from the nearest tree or else die of a broken heart."

Her shyness was banished in a stroke. "Aren't

courtesans supposed to be the ones breaking hearts?"

"Truly," he said with mock despair. "There's nothing more sad than a broken-hearted courtesan. I would have to commit suicide just out of professional courtesy."

Her laugh was cut short by the realization that a man stood in the shadows behind Devesh, watching them with a look that would cut stone. She jerked in surprise, let out a small shriek, and only recognized the owner of the stare when Devesh turned to see.

"Queen's breath!" she exclaimed. "Janak, don't startle me like that."

"It is my job, my lady." His gruff voice and scarred, angular face held no apology. Janak was *raksaka*, the deadly protectors of the royal household for generations, known for their ability to move unseen and unheard and for their unwavering loyalty to the Queen. Less so for their tact.

"Your job is to protect me, not frighten me halfway to my grave."

His hardened face was impassive except for the small lift of one eyebrow. "Sometimes one requires the other, your most royal highness."

She glared at him. His lack of respect was less concerning than the fact that he stood before her at all. His standard all-black raksaka attire was like one long piece of light-stealing fabric continuously wrapped around his body, and he nearly blended with the forest, even now as she was looking straight at him. His soft-footed boots had served him well in tracking her unnoticed. She turned to find Devesh had retreated, restoring a proper distance between them.

"Arama, Princess Aniri." He gave her a small bow, hands pressed together with the casual greeting as if they had not just been caught in each other's arms.

She sighed. The evening was ruined, but the greater danger was that Janak would report them back to her mother. He wasn't simply raksaka, but the Queen's informal advisor as well.

"Wait for me," she said to Janak with as much royal disdain as she could muster. "Over there." She gestured with a single raised eyebrow of her own that he should stand apart by the bridge. Raksaka only retired when incapable of serving, but if he betrayed her secret, by the Queen's breath, she would seek an early retirement for him. If there were any justice in the world, he would have been retired long ago.

Janak didn't move. "Your Highness, as much as you clearly needed my assistance this evening…" He glanced at Devesh's now properly attentive form. "…I'm here to deliver a message that your presence is required in the Queen's chamber."

Aniri threw a nervous glance at Devesh. "What does my mother want at this hour?"

Janak smiled, a look that was simply bizarre on his face. In fact, Aniri couldn't remember ever having seen him smile. Until that moment, she would have said he wasn't capable of producing one.

"Prince Malik has made an offer of peace," Janak said.

Aniri blinked. "The barbarian prince?" They weren't at war with the Jungali, but a recent raid on crops and farm animals at the northern border had been bloody and brutal. Several were left dead—Dharian and Jungali both—and tensions had been raised. "I thought the Queen dispatched some of her guard to the border. And the Jungali have made reparations. What more is there to—"

"The villagers don't want reparations, your most

royal eminence," Janak said. "They want justice. And the rumors of the Jungali being in possession of a new flying weapon leave the Queen with few choices. Even an increased military presence at the border runs the danger of provoking them." He gave Aniri a withering look. "My lady might take care to learn more about the difficulties of her Queendom."

"I don't need lectures from a palace guard." But the truth was she paid little heed to the politics of her mother's court. She was Third Daughter—there had never been a need.

He bowed his head, a deference she was sure was meant to mock her. "My lady misunderstands my message. The barbarian prince has made an offer of peace. In exchange for your hand."

"What?" The horror in her voice was a beat slower than the small hairs rising on her neck. "An arranged marriage? But... he's... Jungali."

"Indeed." Janak's smile grew wider, and the panic in her chest bloomed even as she struggled to keep from giving him the satisfaction of seeing it.

She was so close to being free, so close... Her eldest sister, First Daughter Nahali, had arranged her own marriage by choosing a respectable Dharian noble: she would carry on the Queendom. Second Daughter Seledri's arranged marriage to a prince of Samir had forged another bond in the long-lasting peace between Samir and Dharia. That left her, the Third Daughter, free of royal obligation once she came of age. Free to marry for love. Free of the tightly scripted palace life that choked her like a silken gag.

It was impossible that an arranged marriage would be asked of her now. And even if it were, no marriage had ever been arranged between a Dharian and the barbarians

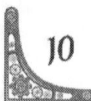

of the north. They ate with their bare fingers and killed each other with clubs—

Devesh's hand landed on her shoulder, making her jump. "Aniri, listen to me. You must refuse him." He turned her toward him, his grip growing stronger, and she winced at its strength. A scuffle of pebbles told her Janak loomed at her back. He might wish to see her forced into a duty she never wanted, but he would protect her with his life. Even Aniri didn't doubt the loyalty of raksaka to those in direct line for the crown. No matter that she was as likely to become Queen as he was.

Devesh dropped his hold on her but didn't move away. "I'm worried for you, Aniri." His voice was soft again. "I must speak to you about this. Will you be at the Queen's tea tomorrow?"

"Yes."

"Afterward, can you meet me…" He glanced at Janak. "…in the place we first met?"

They had met in the Queen's training hall, where Aniri had accepted the handsome new fencing instructor's offer of lessons even though she had fenced for years. The hall would afford them some privacy, whereas at the Queen's tea, she could hardly look at Devesh without arousing suspicions.

"I will meet you there," Aniri said softly. But an ache already stabbed her chest: a fear that somehow it might be her last time with him.

He stepped back. "Very well. Gods be with you, my lady." He bowed deeply in farewell and turned to slip away into the darkness. The shadows swallowed him along with her last chance of a carefree life. She stared after him, her stomach wrenching into knots tighter than the rope she'd fashioned to steal away to him. When Aniri had composed her face, she turned and marched to

Janak, the slick rocks by the riverside cutting into her slippered feet.

She stared up at the impassive face of her guard. Why her mother insisted Janak, of all the raksaka, attend her was beyond her understanding. It mattered little to Aniri that he had attained the highest rank among the raksaka, that he had served the Queen in many duties both at home and abroad, or that he was the Queen's most trusted advisor. He had failed in the one duty that mattered to Aniri: protecting her father from the common robbers who'd killed him. And now Janak stood there, holding in his hands dangerous knowledge about the only man she had ever loved half as much.

"You will not speak of Devesh to anyone. If you do, I will see that you serve the rest of your life guarding the royal stables."

"Trust me, your most royal eminence," Janak said coolly. "If I could convince the Queen you were anything less than a reckless menace to yourself, I would gladly fulfill my duty elsewhere. The stables would be a welcome change of scenery."

She glared at him, not sure if her threat carried any weight at all. Finally, she brushed past him, marching toward the palace without a look back. He shadowed her all the way as though he expected her to bolt for freedom and disappear into the dark after Devesh.

She only wished that were possible.

two

Aniri closed the door in Janak's face, leaving him standing outside the Queen's office. His ever-stoic expression broke in surprise as the heavy, wooden door swung shut. He was no doubt still lurking there, but he could wait to hear secondhand about her humiliation in this arranged marriage to a barbarian. Besides, she needed a moment alone to quell the pounding in her chest. While the chambermaid fetched her mother, Aniri could think of no better place to collect her thoughts than the Queen's office.

This was where mementos of her father were sequestered away.

Her mother's carved desk dominated the small room, in between the adjacent bedroom door and a gilded bookcase along the opposite wall. Aniri drifted toward the shelving. Paintings of her father sat between the treasures he brought back from his travels. She picked up a rough seashell that glinted green and purple secrets in its coiled form. It was from the isles off the west coast of Dharia and still smelled of the ocean. *Listen closely, Aniri, and you'll hear Devruna's promise of calm seas for your travels.* She had believed her father, with the wide-eyed innocence only a child can, and heard the goddess's words in the shell's soft noise.

Now, the only words she heard were his, but they eased the tightness in her chest anyway. She put the shell back in its place by a tiny statue of Devruna riding a tentacled sea creature. Next was a nubbled glass vase, heavy with sand as black as midnight, yet it sparkled in the flickering gaslamp light. The sand was from Chira, where volcanic mountains spilled ink-like lava and created shores of glittering blackness—a strangely devilish idea that entranced Aniri.

Her father would have taken her to all these places had he lived.

Her fingers trailed across the smooth shelf to an ink sketch of him reclined under a tree. He was probably no older than Devesh when the drawing was made. His face was serious as he scribbled something with an ornate feather quill. Aniri recognized it as a gift from her mother: she said he blew like a feather wherever the wind took him. His travels kept him away for weeks at a time, but he always lavished tales and treasures on his three little girls when he returned. Aniri burned with envy when her sisters were old enough to take those trips with him. She was robbed of her turn by the murderers who stole her father's life in a countryside Samirian inn.

The Queen had moved on quickly after his death. The abundance of courtesans in her court seemed to satisfy whatever needs she had for male companionship.

Aniri tried not to think of it because whenever she did, she had a difficult time keeping her tongue. At least her mother hadn't chosen another man to be king, one who might try to play father to her as well.

If Aniri had been Queen, she would have scoured Samir until she found and hung the common thieves who killed her king. Her mother never summoned a single guard. She never went to Samir to claim the body, just let them send him back in a casket. Aniri was only ten at the time, but her memory of the bells tolling her father's death was as clear as the winter sky that day.

The carved wooden door to her mother's bedroom swung open, and the Queen strode out, looking as polished as she would for tea. Her black hair was pinned into cascading curls, and a delicate gold hairpiece draped a single ruby on her forehead. Her deep purple dress was very Samirian in fashion with its gold-stitched corset and starched silk skirt, but the Queen's strict dress code required everyone at court to make some concession to traditional fashion, and she made no exception for herself. Her nod to the elaborate draped dresses of the past was a regal sweep of embroidered gold fabric over one arm. It floated in a pool that traveled behind her and somehow made her more imposing. Aniri was certain she did it on purpose, simply because everything her mother did was deliberate and well thought out.

And her people loved her for it.

The Queen stopped in front of her, coolly taking in her black silk pajamas pricked by the forest along with her scuffed and dirty silk slippers. Good thing she hadn't worn the climbing shoes; they would only have earned her more scorn in her mother's eyes. Years of discipline prevented her from smiling with that thought.

"Aniri, dear." The Queen's voice was disappointed,

but softer than Aniri expected. Her mother pulled something from Aniri's hair; a briar came free, even as a strand of hair tried to hold it. "Has Janak told you why I summoned you?"

Aniri nodded.

The Queen frowned. "I had hoped to meet you in your chambers this eve to discuss this matter. But when I found you were gone..." She took a deep breath, as if summoning her patience from some deep well—and she had to reach all the way to the bottom, in Aniri's case. "I had a feeling Janak might know where you had gone. I'm glad he returned you safely."

This wasn't the tongue lashing Aniri had expected, which for some reason raised her hackles. Perhaps because she knew what was coming next: the complete loss of her future. "I was perfectly safe the entire time, Mother."

She smiled. "Safe doesn't always mean what we think it does."

Aniri raised her eyebrows. Her mother didn't usually speak in riddles.

The Queen sighed again and drifted to her desk. Her long-fingered hands tapped the communiques there. Finally, she faced Aniri again, her arms folded to bring the sweep of golden cloth to the front, an imperious shield.

"Aniri, I know how much it meant to you, the coming of your birthday."

Meant. Past tense. Aniri's chest caved in a little. She waited for the rest.

"This attack at the border..." Her mother paused. "The people are troubled by it and impatient for a security I have difficulty providing them under the circumstances."

"Because the Jungali have developed some kind of new weapon," Aniri said flatly. She really couldn't care less about the politics, although Janak was probably right. She should have been paying closer attention. At least then she wouldn't have allowed herself to fall for a Samirian courtesan who could never be hers.

"Perhaps." Her mother took Aniri's measure with her gaze. "Or they could be simply saber-rattling. The Jungali have many internal factions, and it's difficult to know how much is bluster for their own people and how much is a true threat to Dharia. But our people would be reassured if we secured a peace treaty with the Jungali, and Prince Malik seems sincere in his offer."

For once, Aniri wished the Queen would simply be her mother. To think of her daughter first, before the country. But that would never happen, and it was foolish to wish for it. As foolish as falling in love with a courtesan.

Aniri's stomach hollowed out, as if she hung over a deep precipice with nothing but silk threads keeping her from plunging to her death. "Have you already accepted his offer?"

"No." Her mother watched her again, definitely measuring her response.

Aniri tried to keep her shock and relief to herself, but it proved impossible. "What?"

"Aniri, I am not going to arrange this marriage for you."

"I... I don't understand." Her heart was hammering now, threatening to drown out the soft raspings of silk on silk as her mother strode over to take Aniri gently by the shoulders.

She pushed back Aniri's hair, tucking the coarse and wind-blown strands behind her ear. "You are so like your

father. I know that to lock you into a marriage, even for the best intent of our country, would be like caging a wild bird. You would beat yourself bloody against the bars."

Aniri just stared into her mother's soft brown eyes. Who was this woman?

A soft smile graced her mother's face. "Don't you wonder why your father always traveled far and wide?"

"I... um... no." *My father.* Why were they talking about him? Aniri's mind spun. "Because he liked to see new things?"

"He did, but it was more than that. He *needed* to be free, to travel, to be away from the rigors of the court. And for all the peace in the Queendom, I couldn't deny him that, no matter how much I feared for his safety every time he left the palace grounds."

Aniri was confused by this turn, but hope quickly surged from the hollowness in her stomach. "So, you're saying I do not have to accept Prince Malik's offer?"

"That is precisely what I am saying." The Queen dropped her hands from Aniri's shoulders. "However, I would like you to at least consider it. Sleep on it. Give some thought to whether you can give your future to your country. Whether it's in your heart to do your duty. Or not."

And like that, the hope dropped off a cliff. "And if I say no?"

"There is no punishment." But the sigh in her voice told Aniri what she already knew: this would be the last in a long line of disappointments Aniri had presented to the Queen. Her disgrace would be final—and public. The court would know the Third Daughter of the Queen had refused her duty when it called. Her mother would lose favor with her people; they would lose faith in her strong, calm ability to run their country. But her mother would

take that burden on herself rather than force Aniri into a marriage she didn't want.

Guilt dragged hard on Aniri's shoulders.

"Prince Malik will be here tomorrow," the Queen said. "I would like you to receive his formal offer and give it serious thought. Your wishes in this will be final."

Aniri nodded. The word *final* haunted her all the way back to her room.

three

The Queen's afternoon high tea wasn't an affair for the weak of heart.

Or the sensitive in flesh.

Priya pulled painfully on Aniri's hair in an attempt to twist it into something elegant. She fished out another briar, like the one the Queen had found the night before, and made an indelicate sound as she flung it at the mirrored table in front of them. Priya herself was already dressed, her maroon-and-black corset mostly covered by the iron-gray sweep of fabric over her shoulder. She had tucked golden hairpins in at the waist, pulling them out one at a time to tame Aniri's hair.

In the mirror, Priya's scowl of concentration made her creamy brown skin flush with effort, but her dark eyes were bright and shiny. By contrast, Aniri's eyes were the dull black of a raksaka's uniform, and her normally bronzed skin had turned an unhealthy pallor. The night had been filled with tumbled dreams of barbarian princes stabbing each other, then hoisting her head on a pike in a macabre and screeching dance. Even awake, her mind crowded with visions of balancing precariously on snowy mountain cliff, awaiting a thousand foot fall to her death.

"I'm going to have no hair left," Aniri said to Priya, "if you keep pulling at it."

Priya dragged a bristled brush upward through her hair. "My lady, if you look anything less than magnificent, I'll never live it down."

"It's just tea."

Priya paused to give a properly horrified look in the mirror. "Just tea? In the Queen's court?" She shook her head and returned to pinning Aniri's hair in place. "Is my lady feeling well?"

When Aniri didn't answer, Priya scowled more darkly, then laid Aniri's hair jewels in place and set to work pinning the elaborate gold filigree. It was studded with emeralds that accented Aniri's copper and sea-green dress. Her sleeves were richly embroidered, which meant they weighed her down like two daggers strapped to her arms. Aniri was short and slight to begin with, but the glittering green swirls must have been made of jewels because the entire outfit anchored her like it was made of stone.

Priya had selected the dress, saying it softened the angular muscle lines she had acquired through her fencing and climbing. The dress was no doubt perfect for the occasion. Plus Priya had a keen sense about fashion, which allowed Aniri to ignore it as much as possible.

"I've heard the adorable new diplomat and fencing instructor from Samir will be in attendance," Priya said, as if this was simply idle gossip.

"Did you?"

"Perhaps he can brighten my lady's spirits."

Aniri hoped so. She needed the comfort of Devesh's arms and lips to help her make the right decision about this arranged marriage. He would tell her she was right to follow her heart—she was sure of it. He might even have words to soothe the guilt that raged whenever she pictured herself refusing the one duty she had been born into.

Aniri peered at Priya's kind face. Priya must know about Devesh. Not much in the court got past her. In that moment, Aniri very nearly told her handmaiden everything, but she waited a beat too long to speak.

Priya gave her a sly glance in the mirror. "If my lady is not interested in the new Samirian diplomat, I know many ladies of the court who will be. I might even try a hand at him myself."

Aniri smiled. "Priya, you are wicked." She decided it was indulgent to burden Priya with her worries. She would have to figure this out herself. Priya stabbed in a final pin, making Aniri wince. "I also think you secretly train in the fencing room with those pins."

"Yes, my lady, I do." Priya pulled another pin from her waist and flourished it in the air. "Have you seen the fencing instructors? They are quite handsome, and strong, and very... sweaty in their earnest practice."

Aniri nearly laughed, but her sour mood returned when Priya stepped back, her primping complete. Aniri studied herself in the mirror. The girl who had run into the forest in her night clothes was completely erased, and a princess glowered back at her.

"Perhaps you could go to tea in my place, Priya."

"Oh no, my lady." Priya gave her a mocking half-curtsey. "My bravery is nowhere near equal to that task."

Aniri wasn't sure hers was either.

When they arrived, the Grand Chamber was already bustling with a hundred ladies and lords in their finest Dharian fashions, sprinkled with a few attendees in more austere Samirian attire. It was a garden of jewels and brass glinting amongst deep burgundies, lush greens, and purples the color of ripe plums and long sunsets. It even smelled like an orchard, with citrus teas and cut fruit perfuming the air.

The Queen arranged her high tea around a large U-shaped table set with broad cushions, elaborate silver tea services handcrafted in Samir, and bites to eat which were so tiny it took dozens to fill a platter. A few of the guests picked at the delicacies with dessert forks, but most were engaged in an intricate social dance, some sitting, others moving between the seated players, whispering and watching to see who was talking to whom and sitting where and for how long.

A quartet of strings played quietly in the music alcove. It wasn't a dirge, but Aniri moved through the room at a pace that would match one. Priya trailed behind her. Aniri searched the seated guests until she found Devesh. He sat to the left of the Samirian ambassador, wearing his diplomat uniform and smiling at something she said. His gaze met Aniri's for just a fraction of a second, long enough for her to know he noted her entry, but not long enough to be an unseemly glance that could spark rumors. Her heart squeezed. She wished she could could simply abandon her decision altogether. Let her mother realize her choice when she found her Third Daughter had run off with a Samirian diplomat to his country.

She beat back her fantasies and took a deep breath, keeping to the perimeter and walking slowly toward the head table. Priya fell behind, caught by one of the male courtesans who floated around the table and charmed the ladies of the court. Priya would watch for a sign from her in case Aniri needed something. Like an excuse to flee the Queen's tea after an obligatory amount of time in attendance.

Given she was late, her attendance time would probably have to be longer than usual.

The Queen was in her place at the head table, with Janak serving his ornamental purpose as royal guard behind her. His ever-keen eyes assessed everyone who came near the Queen, even the servants darting to refresh teacups. Aniri's sisters, Nahali and Seledri, had already taken their positions alongside the Queen, two bookends of perfect styling to accompany their mother. Long gone were the barefoot days of running across the palace grounds with nothing but catching butterflies and chasing servant children to worry their minds.

Even if Nahali wasn't First Daughter, she would still have been born to be Queen. More clever than the best professors of physiks, perfectly controlled in every action, and beautiful besides. Her future-king husband sat by her side, laughing and drinking in every word that fell from her lips. He was the son of a nobleman in the Queen's cabinet and ridiculously handsome—the Queen would have arranged a marriage for Nahali had she not found someone quite so suitable to love. Today, Nahali wore a loose fitting dress of emerald green silk that swamped the cushion where she sat, artfully concealing that her sister was with child. Married four years and already working on providing the Queendom with an heir: Nahali's life was perfectly planned and on schedule, as always.

Seledri's light laughter drew Aniri's gaze to her second sister, the one who had been forced into an

arranged marriage just two years earlier. Aniri had always thought Seledri was the most beautiful of the three of them. Her deep black hair had its own light, outshining her midnight-colored silk-on-silk brocade dress. Seledri's high cheeks seemed sculpted by an artist in love with his subject, too beautiful to be quite real. And her brown eyes were so deeply warm that looking into them was to feel instantly at ease, as if nothing in the world could go wrong when such kindness looked into your soul.

Aniri had no doubt her Samirian prince was madly in love with Seledri.

She lived in Samir now, and her severely corseted, high-collared dress, the height of Samirian fashion, just reminded Aniri that her sister no longer belonged to Dharia. One day, when the Samirian Queen-mother stepped aside, she would rule. Aniri wondered if she had yet found love in her arranged marriage—or if duty had exacted a horrible price from her beautiful, soft-hearted sister. But that thought faded as Aniri approached the head table: Seledri's beautiful face was closer to gray than her normal delicate brown.

"Are you all right?" her husband asked. His bronzed hand rested softly on hers, which had fallen palm up on her tightly fitting skirt. His gaze searched her face, but she stared at nothing across the expanse of the tearoom.

"I'm not entirely well." Her voice trembled.

Aniri's stomach clenched as she knelt by her sister's side. "Seledri, what's wrong?"

Seledri's eyes came into focus, and she smiled—a sickly look—then raised a fine-fingered hand to touch Aniri's cheek. "Aniri! You're here. I've been waiting for you to show."

Aniri glanced at the Queen, who was occupied with Janak whispering in her ear. "Well, I try to be fashionably late."

"You've never been fashionably anything in your life, little sister." Seledri laughed... only it also was sickly. Aniri took her sister's hand. It was clammy and shook slightly in hers.

"You're not well, Seledri." Alarm was starting to build in Aniri's chest.

"I think I'm just tired."

Aniri looked to Seledri's Samirian-Prince husband. "I'm going to take her to my room for a short while. So she can rest."

He nodded his approval and rose to help Seledri get up from her cushion. She wobbled and Aniri was afraid she might fall, but she righted herself.

Her rising drew the attention of the Queen, which quickly fell on them with a scowl. "Are you going somewhere, Aniri?"

"Seledri is unwell, Mother." Aniri dropped her voice because the chatter of the room had suddenly dimmed, every face drawn to the drama at the head table. "I'm taking her to my room to rest." Aniri tried to keep the bristle out of her voice.

"Seledri has her own room and her husband to attend her," the Queen said, and Aniri's bristle turned into a rising of the hairs at the back of her neck. "And you have an appointment with Prince Malik at the close of tea."

"I will take care not to be late, then." Aniri grasped her sister's cold hand between the two of hers. She turned her back on the Queen, fully aware of the held breaths that followed, and gently guided her sister from the table. Her husband trailed behind, then quickly caught Seledri's other arm.

When they had rounded the corner of the table,

Seledri whispered to her, "I see you haven't changed in my absence, little sister."

Aniri smiled. "I do my best."

Seledri smiled in return and let Aniri and her husband lead her from the Grand Chamber. Aniri didn't dare glance back to Devesh, to see his reaction to her little scene, but he surely heard the Queen's unsubtle announcement that she had an appointment with the barbarian prince. She only hoped he wouldn't leap to conclusions about a decision she hadn't even made herself.

Seledri's color was starting to come back.

Aniri had loosened the tightly-bound Samirian-style corset, wondering how her sister could breathe at all when so tightly wrapped, as if she were a package bound for rough passages over the sea from Samir. Aniri had fed Seledri some crackers Priya had brought, but now her sister lay with her eyes closed on Aniri's bed. Her beauty was more deathly than angelic, her skin having paled against the black embroidered silk, like it was funeral clothing. Aniri had banished Seledri's husband, mostly because she wanted to talk to her sister privately, although guilt wormed its way into her chest with the pained look on his face as she shoved him out the door.

"He's a good man, you know," Seledri said, her eyes still closed, a damp cloth resting on her forehead. "He'll worry about me. He's no doubt sitting outside the door right now."

"He'll survive." Aniri gently unbuckled her sister's silk slippers and worked them from her slender feet, one at a time. "I'm more concerned about you. Was the journey from Samir rough? Or is there more to it? Do I need to summon the doctor?"

"The doctor will only find out what I already know," Seledri said. "I'm with child, Aniri."

Aniri's fingers froze. "You're what?"

"You do understand how that works, don't you? First you get married, then—"

Aniri smacked her sister's arm with the feather-light slipper, and Seledri laughed in a way that lifted Aniri's heart. She swept her dress to the side so she could fold her legs underneath and sit closer to Seledri. They hadn't been alone like this, the two of them, since Seledri had married and left Dharia.

"I understood the mechanics before you," Aniri said with derision.

"Oh, I doubt that."

Aniri arched her eyebrow. "We clearly need to discuss *that* further." She laid her hand softly on her sister's arm. "But first I want to hear about this baby of yours." Somehow Seledri's pregnancy hit her more forcefully than Nahali's baby-to-be. "Are you... are you happy about it?"

Seledri pulled the cloth from her forehead and eased up to sitting. Suddenly Aniri could see it: the achiness with which she moved, the small bump where her sister's stomach had always been flat, the care she took to sit just right on Aniri's bed.

"I have a wonderful husband, an heir on the way, and a Queendom which will one day be mine." Seledri drew in a deep breath. "It is not a bad life."

Aniri let her shoulders relax. "Your husband must be beside himself with happiness."

"He does not know." At Aniri's questioning look, Seledri elaborated, "My handsome Samirian prince has

wished for a baby from the moment we were wed. I'll tell him soon. I'm waiting until I can be as filled with joy as he would want."

Aniri's heart clenched, and tears threatened to spring out. "Oh, Seledri."

"Hey, I'm the one who is supposed to be weepy, not you." Seledri's beautiful face drew into a frown. "Is it so bad to become Aunt Aniri? The sea between Dharia and Samir is not so broad. You will have to come visit. And bring food! The Samirians have no idea how to cook."

Aniri grinned through the tears that threatened to spill anew. That had been her plan all along. Run away with Devesh to Samir. Visit her beautiful sister. And now her new baby. "I would like nothing more than that. Tell me, what's it like living in Samir? Are all the men as ridiculously handsome as your husband?" *And Devesh*, she couldn't help thinking.

"The men are very fine to look at, the women are very stuffy, and the scenery is spectacular until the rains come. Then it's unbearably damp." Seledri paused, studying her. "What's wrong, Aniri? This isn't about the baby, is it?"

Aniri studied her hands. Seledri wouldn't want to hear that Aniri's heart was breaking for her. Again. That she dreaded being forced into the same loveless, arranged marriage. "It's nothing."

Seledri grabbed hold of Aniri's shoulders and plied her with those warm brown eyes. "Since when do you lie to me, Aniri? Am I suddenly First Daughter, Future Queen of Dharia?" She gave a small smile, and Aniri returned it. They had always kept things from Nahali because she would run off and tell their mother the instant she knew anything worth knowing.

"If you were First Daughter," Aniri said, "you would

probably be in on it."

"In on what?" Seledri frowned. "You know Mother never tells me anything anymore. I'm married to the enemy now."

"The *enemy*?" Aniri was genuinely shocked Seledri would use those words. The bonds between Dharia and Samir were long and deep, cemented by countless arranged marriages over time, even outside the royal family. Aniri was far from the only Dharian to fall in love with a Samirian. "Is that what you call your husband when you're in his bed?"

"Only if he's been very good."

Aniri laughed outright. It washed away some of her hesitation, and the tension in her shoulders calmed. Still, she dropped her gaze to her hands. "Mother wishes me to accept Prince Malik's offer of a peace-brokering marriage."

Seledri sucked in a breath. "Aniri..."

"I know."

"But he's Jungali..."

Aniri just nodded. It was as if the gods were playing a cruel joke on her.

Seledri paused and then said, "Has he already made the offer?"

"The formalities are after tea, but yes."

"But the decision isn't made? Maybe I can talk to Mother about this..."

Aniri looked up into Seledri's eyes and knew her sister would do anything for her. It swelled her heart. She took a breath and said, "Mother is giving me the choice."

Seledri's eyebrows flew up in surprise, then her brow wrinkled with a fierceness she hadn't seen since they were girls. "Well, then the answer is clear."

Aniri waited.

"You say no."

The strength of her sister's words stole Aniri's breath. They were exactly the words she wanted to hear, and yet they twisted her heart all the same. Aniri pulled her sister in for a hug, so she wouldn't have to see the look on Seledri's face.

The storm of anger that raged across it would only bring Aniri's tears back.

four

You say no.

Her sister's words seemed to echo in the spiral staircase even as Aniri's silk slippers made no noise on the sandstone steps. Her labored breathing was the only true sound, her chest heaving not from haste, but from the pain in her heart.

The Queen hadn't given her sister a choice, and Seledri knew her role from the moment she could understand such things. Aniri couldn't tell if her heart was breaking all over again for the plight of her sister, who deserved to love as much as be loved, or if it was breaking fresh from the fear of being trapped in the same cage. Seledri hadn't had a choice. Aniri owed it to her sister, as much as to herself, to live the life Seledri had never been offered.

She pushed open the heavy wooden doors to the

Queen's Grand Chamber. It was empty, vacant now that tea had finished. At the far end, the Queen stood with Janak, consulting in hushed tones. It irked Aniri more than normal, that her mother had such a close confidence with the raksaka who guarded Aniri. As if Janak were some kind of paternal force, a military substitute for the father her mother had abandoned. Meanwhile, she put Aniri through tests of worthiness as a daughter of Dharia.

It irritated her, like a loose hairpin scratching.

Aniri took her time crossing the long room, no longer hurrying. Before she left Seledri, she had washed every trace of tears from her face. She didn't want her mother to think she had been crying over this decision she had set before her.

"Aniri," the Queen said as she approached. "I'm glad you're here. I don't want to keep the young prince waiting any longer. He's already had a long journey from the north."

"I'm at your service, your majesty." The bitterness in her voice was unavoidable, but she stood as tall as her heavily embroidered dress, weighted with the obligations of royalty, would allow.

Her mother frowned, seemed tempted to say something, but held it back. Janak wore his usual impassive look—apparently his smiles were reserved for mocking her in private. The Queen nodded to Janak, and he motioned to a doorman at the anteroom where the Queen usually prepared for tea. The doorman disappeared, ostensibly in search of the prince. That her mother would allow the barbarian to use her private chambers disturbed Aniri.

"Have you already given him visiting privileges?" Aniri asked in a low voice.

"I'm simply treating him with the respect due a

sovereign of a potential ally."

"In your personal antechambers?" Aniri asked. "Are you certain the artwork is secure?"

"Aniri." Her mother's voice had gone cold, but Aniri already knew she had stepped over the limit of her mother's tolerance. "I expect you to—" She stopped when the door swung open, and the prince strode in. He was young, just as her mother had taken pains to note, as if that somehow would make a difference.

He crossed the floor with long purposeful strides. His finely tailored jacket and pants were current with the latest fashion befitting a nobleman in Dharian court: high-collared, deep navy silk, trimmed with twisted gold embroidery and reaching to his knees. Only he seemed awkward in the jacket, as if the silk chafed across his back. Or perhaps Aniri imagined his discomfort, the barbarian tales draped on him like an invisible cloak that he labored under. Then again, maybe he was trying to conceal a club.

She steeled herself against the urge to smile at his expense.

When the prince stepped from the shadowed back of the room and took in Aniri's face, he frowned and seemed momentarily disappointed in her. It stuck her as incredibly irritating. What did this barbarian have to be disappointed about? The question nearly leaped from her lips, but then the look was gone. Perhaps she had imagined it. In any event, he was now the picture of courtly dispassion, staring at her with strangely pale amber eyes. Did all that time in the harsh northern sun bleach the color from barbarian eyes?

The prince stopped at a respectable distance, in accordance with the most formal traditions. Only then did Aniri notice his servant, a massive man, stepping clear of the shadows. Janak, still in his royal uniform from his duties at tea, subtly angled his body between the prince's giant guard and the Queen.

The prince's servant merely stood taller and announced, "Prince Malik, of the Jungali Coalition of Provinces."

The prince pressed his hands together, held before his face in a position of high respect, then solemnly tipped his head forward to the Queen. "I bow to the great land of Dharia." Aniri hadn't heard the traditional greeting in a long time. She couldn't decide if he was quoting some kind of handbook on Dharian customs or if he had been coached to use the highest formality as a way to supplicate to the Queen.

Regardless, her mother seemed quite taken by it. She brought her hands together, touched them to her lips briefly, then spread her hands wide. "You are most welcome in our land," she said, the traditional response.

"Arama, your majesty," the prince said, bowing again and relaxing the formality. "You are most kind for receiving me with such unforgiveable shortness of notice. If it weren't for the urgency of my business with her majesty's royal court, I would have made proper entreaties for my arrival."

"We're honored to have you for our guest," the Queen said. "And your business is of great interest to the court." She smiled broadly. "May I present my daughter, Princess Aniri."

The prince turned to her, his amber eyes as cold as the frozen Jungali seas. He bowed, hands clasped, but did not repeat the greeting, not even the more informal *arama*, used by everyone, commoners and royalty alike. Aniri wasn't sure whether she should be insulted or not. She clasped her hands and bowed in return, although she may have done it too quickly. Her mother's keen look flashed disapproval.

"Well, I expect that you have much to discuss," her mother said to the prince. Aniri shot her a look, but she was focused on the barbarian. "Please inform Aniri's guard if you have need of anything, Prince Malik."

Aniri frowned. Was the Queen leaving? The prince had yet to make his formal request—what purpose could it serve for the Queen to leave before that happened? Before Aniri could form a question, her mother swept toward her antechamber, the jewels on her dress winking from the shadowed recesses. The prince, for his part, didn't seem surprised at all by the Queen's sudden departure.

Aniri glared at Janak, but she couldn't catch his attention. Instead, he coolly eyed the prince as he approached her.

"Princess Aniri," Prince Malik said, "is there somewhere we can speak in private?"

Aniri blinked. "In private?" According to custom, they wouldn't meet in private until *after* the arrangement had been negotiated. And she hadn't agreed to anything yet. She glanced at Janak, suddenly uneasy he might whisk away like her mother. "Whatever you have to say, Prince Malik, you can speak it in front of my personal guard." She hoped Janak understood her meaning—that he dare not leave her alone.

Malik stepped closer. A panicky feeling fluttered her heart, but he merely dropped his voice so Janak would have to strain to overhear. "Princess, it is your privacy, not mine, I wish to protect. Perhaps we could…" He glanced about the Queen's tea room. "…find a more open place to discuss our business." His gaze alit on the windows streaming the golden haze of summer into the

room. "Maybe the garden?"

The prince should not insist on speaking to her privately. Negotiations were always done with representatives of both courts present, given the arrangement was as much a joining of governments as a marriage. Was this a barbarian custom? It was odd and presumptuous.

And... intriguing. "The garden should afford a measure of privacy." Her silk skirts swished as she strode toward the side door to the garden. The prince was close at her heels, with his guard following at a distance. She glanced back to make sure Janak was following them. His impassive expression was holding back a scowl.

The Queen's garden was a maze of stepped reddish-pink sandstone, the same stone used to build most of the capital city. Sunlight draped heavy and bright on the plants and flowers in full bloom. The scent was pervasive, like a bath of flower petals had been crushed and thrown into a fine mist in the air. The garden held enough winding paths and tucked corners to hide a hundred feverish meetings of lovers. She had first kissed Devesh here, and it felt wrongly intimate to have Prince Malik by her side now. Janak continued to trail behind them, but he was holding close to the prince's overly large servant.

Aniri's silk slippers whispered next to the hard tempo of the prince's heeled boots. After a moment of pretending to inspect the garden as they walked, the prince spoke. "Your beauty truly outshines this astonishing garden, Princess. The rumors do not do you justice."

"Do you expect to flatter me into accepting your marriage proposal?" She kept her voice as cool as she could manage. "If you knew anything about Dharia," *or me*, she thought, "you would have known better."

He looked amused, but not insulted. "Is it bad manners in Dharia to tell a woman she is beautiful? If so, I'm a barbarian through and through."

She fought back a smile and ran a glance over him. "You don't look the barbarian part, Prince Malik."

"I try to keep up on Dharian fashion. It's a hobby of mine."

"Is it truly?" She turned to stare at him.

"No."

A laugh threatened to erupt out of her, but she managed to keep it in, amazed more at herself than the prince's attempts to charm her. "That's a good thing. I would hate to be the one to tell you how you've failed utterly to capture the latest nobleman's fashion sense at court." It wasn't true, but he certainly needed more practice filling out the clothes.

He fell quiet and studied the white granite pavers in front of their measured steps. "Princess Aniri..." He tilted his head towards her and lowered his voice. "You are a beautiful and powerful woman in the richest country in our world. I come from the poorest one, seeking your hand in an arranged marriage you surely do not desire. I understand this, and yet I'm here to personally entreat you to consider my proposal that we might have peace in our lands."

You say no. Her sister's words pressed on her, and every fiber of Aniri's being wanted to say just that. But her refusal might bring war. Which wouldn't be only a few barbarians with clubs if this new flying weapon was more than a rumor. "Of course, Dharia wishes for peace with Jungali," she said carefully.

"And Jungali wishes for peace as well," Prince Malik replied.

Aniri wasn't so sure. The prince stopped her with a

light touch on her elbow. He was tall and not unhandsome, except for the coldness of those eyes peering earnestly at her.

"I may not follow the fashions of your great country, but I have studied its customs. I know you are the Third Daughter and your birthday draws near. The Queen has informed me the decision rests in your hands. I would give my life to bring peace to Jungali, to end the fighting between our clans as well as the border skirmishes with Dharia. They take too many lives each year. My brother was lost in such a clash at a border station. It wasn't long after that our mother, the Queen, succumbed to a chill the warmth of summer couldn't banish. She was always most fond of him, being the youngest."

Aniri couldn't help but feel the pain that radiated from him. "I'm sorry for your loss. And I don't want to seem... unkind. But if you wish to stop the border skirmishes, you only have to stopping making incursions into Dharian territory. Dharia never would cross the border—"

"It's not that simple." The prince gave her a sad smile. "I don't know which province is behind the most recent incursion. I will make every effort to find out, but it was likely marauders acting alone, in which case... their clan will likely protect them. During my mother's reign, she won the loyalty of all the provinces—she brokered trade agreements, and with peace between the provinces, the raids lessened. When she died, that bond was shattered. I have enforced peace, for the moment, but the clans are restless and the raids have started again... I fear we're falling back into the ways of the past."

Aniri narrowed her eyes. "I don't understand. How would an arranged marriage with the Third Daughter of Dharia help keep your people from…" She didn't want to call him a barbarian to his face, especially when he seemed to be striving so nobly for peace.

"From falling back into barbarism and anarchy?" His smile was grim as he gestured to the palace walls surrounding them. "It must be hard to see, here in your beautiful palace and lush gardens, but you are fortunate to have a united people under a strong ruler like your mother. Jungali needs a Queen. A brand new alliance with the powerful country of Dharia would cement the tentative hold I have on the crown. This arrangement would bring peace to my country, and I wish for that even more than I wish for peace with Dharia."

"Surely there is another way to ensure peace between our countries." Aniri searched the pavers at her feet, as if she could find the proper words there. "A trade agreement or treaty, perhaps. This marriage would just be—"

"Princess Aniri." His lowered tone drew her gaze back up to him. "I am sure you have someone you would far prefer to marry. I had always hoped my Queen would be someone I loved as well. But I'm willing to forgo marrying for love in service to my country. I'm hoping you will be willing to make a similar sacrifice for yours. This arrangement will save lives and bring peace to both our countries."

Aniri looked away from his intense stare. "I fear that you may be more noble than I am, Prince Malik."

He took her hand, and she nearly jerked back, surprised he would touch her. But he had the desperate look of a man who believes he is about to lose everything.

"There will be no children," he whispered, his fingers warm and gentle. "Ours would not be that kind of marriage. I'm sure you already have a lover. You may keep him. I will even raise any children that come from your love union with all the rights of royalty in my land. All I ask is that you be discrete, that you help me maintain the fiction of our marriage, so it will bond our countries together and keep us from war."

Then he shocked her further by bending down on one knee, still holding her hand carefully in his. "I beg of you, Princess Aniri. Whatever demands you have, I will meet them. Please accept my proposal of marriage and help me to save lives in both our countries."

Heat rose in her face. "I…" She paused, desperately wanting to say no, but with the prince at her feet, clearly willing to do whatever it took to convince her, the shame of shirking her duty burned in her chest. "That is…" The words were choking her. "That's… the most noble thing I have heard in some time, Prince Malik. Please… please stand." She took his hand in her two and urged him up from the ground. "I will consider your proposal and give you my answer in the morning."

Prince Malik closed his eyes briefly, and Aniri could see the defeat on his face, as if she had already given her answer. But the truth was she had never been more uncertain. She hadn't expected him to move her. She hadn't expected him to be noble. It dragged on her even more than the embroidered silk that weighed her down like an iron casket meant to take her to the ocean floor.

He quickly opened his eyes, dropped her hand, pressed his two together. "I will await word from you then. Arama, Princess Aniri."

He bowed quickly, turned, and strode from the Queen's tea garden, leaving her alone with her uncertain heart and Janak's cool stare from the far side of the garden.

five

Aniri appraised her weapons, taking time to make her choice.

The table was spread with sabers, foils, and scimitars glittering in the cool yellow gaslamp light of the training room. Gleaming brass handguards and elaborate dark wood grips topped strong steel blades and curved bronzed tips. The Samirians were known for their metalwork, and these imported weapons were the finest examples of their handicraft.

Aniri pulled her leather fencing gloves up to her elbows, fastening the brass clasps in place, then selected the longest, most deadly scimitar. Its curved blade was perfectly balanced but still heavy. And definitely not for training. She unwrapped the scarf around her neck and let it pool on the floor—it would be sliced to ribbons if caught in the scimitar's sweeping path.

Her hair was bound in a braid behind her, and the rest of her fighting wear was suitably formfitting with no stray clothing that might be entangled in her swordplay. Rugged canvas breeches tucked into her leg wrappings at the knee, and she had strapped a woven brass chest protector over her high-necked fencing jacket. There was hardly an inch of her skin showing, yet the entire ensemble moved and breathed with her. She warmed up by twirling the scimitar on one side then the other. She crept across the stone pavers of the training room. Her thin, leather fighting boots made no sound as she snuck up on the motionless steam-powered automaton that would serve as her opponent.

She slowly moved the point of the sword closer to the large metallic figure. It had a can for a head and arms of metal tubing, but it could be surprisingly quick once activated. She gently touched the tip of her sword to the brass button that sat over its heart and danced back as it came to life with a steaming hiss. It already held a large steel blade, nearly as hefty as hers. She gripped the scimitar in both hands as the machine raised its blade into a ready position.

With a scream she reserved for the training room, Aniri whirled and slashed, bringing the full force of her blow to bear on the automaton. It quickly blocked, the ring of their blades piercing the air. She pulled back, took a balanced stance on the balls of her feet, and raised the blade over her head, striking again. The machine shifted quickly and met her blade with a blow she felt through to her bones. Twice more she jabbed and the machine parried. Slowly, the tension of the morning's garden meeting with Prince Malik eased from her shoulders. Every earnest word of that discussion kept replaying in her mind, despite her best attempts to disregard the barbarian's entreaties. Each stroke against her mechanical opponent beat back the words echoing in her head.

Fencing shoes shuffled softly on the stone floor behind her. The person—probably Devesh—was still safely out of reach of her blade. She swung it around for another hacking slash at the automaton. This time she connected with its metal shoulder, and her blade bounced off, making her stumble. She grimaced, not wanting her final blow to be so ungraceful.

"I hope that's Prince Malik's face you're imagining, and not mine," Devesh said.

Aniri's shoulders slumped, and she allowed the curved blade to sink slowly until the tip chinked on the floor. She wasn't imagining Prince Malik or even her mother. The automaton was the perfect metaphorical opponent for the villain she faced—nameless, faceless, implacable in forcing her into a life she didn't want.

Devesh moved quickly to stand close to her. He gently grasped her sword hand, holding the blade away, while he slipped his other hand around her waist. His warm fingers found the one unprotected spot at the small of her back. She drew in a breath at his boldness, but then his lips were on hers—a quick kiss which nevertheless pulsed through her body to the tips of her fingers. He pulled away again with lightning speed. A quick check of the servants at the far end of the room showed no reaction.

"You presume too much," Aniri said when she regained her voice.

Devesh grinned wickedly. "Only as much as you allow." With infinite gentleness, he tugged the scimitar from her grasp. "I would be foolish to presume any more when you are so heavily armed."

He lifted the blade and examined the jeweled hilt. "I

hope there's no hidden meaning in the fact that you chose to train today with a blade that was famously used against the Samirians in more than one ancient war. I do believe this particular weapon executed my great-great-grand-uncle, the Duke of Indira."

"That's a complete lie," Aniri said, her smile returning. "You were never related to royalty."

"Your majesty crushes me!" Devesh clutched his heart in mock pain, stepped back, and whirled the blade in a circle that traced behind one shoulder and then the other. "But if you wish to train today, I believe less dangerous weapons would better serve your purpose."

"My purpose?" Aniri's shoulders bent again, the full weight of duty dragging them down. "I'm not sure I'm disposed to training today." He had come fully dressed to be her instructor, wrapped in linen leggings, breeches, and a stiff, woven jacket under his ironwork chest protector. The many small touches involved in Devesh's careful instruction always lit a fire in her body. A painful reminder of what she had to lose in this decision between heart and duty.

Perhaps that was Devesh's intention.

"I judge the princess to be in need of a vigorous, yet more graceful sport at the moment." He returned the scimitar to the weapons table and hefted a foil blade instead. It was a gift from her father when she first took up the sport. It was far too heavy at first, especially the brass handguard, but she took it as a challenge, and it made her strong. Devesh held the sword flat across his palms and made a small bow with his head. "My lady's favorite weapon, as beautiful and deadly as she is."

Aniri bristled, the flattery needling her more than usual, given Prince Malik's earlier remarks. She lifted the blade with one finger at the balance point, tossed it in the

air, then grabbed the dark wood grip. The slashing arc of her blade just missed the floor and finished with the razor sharp tip screeching across the Samirian crest on Devesh's chest protector.

His eyes widened, but he didn't move. "Of course, I was hoping her majesty would be using the safety tip today, if I was to spar with her."

Aniri stepped back, and Devesh lunged for the sword table, coming away with a foil that matched hers except the hilt was ironwork instead of brass. He kept his distance while he added a rubber tip to the end of his sword. He tossed one to her, which she quickly caught and attached.

She smiled, saluted, and took an engarde position, feet positioned at ninety degrees to one another, knees bent. She was shorter than him, which meant his reach was longer, but skill and practice compensated for the difference. She jabbed forward, forcing him back, since he had barely assumed a fighting position. Then he lunged, striking at her heart. She parried, the sing of their blades bouncing off the smooth stone of the training room. She attacked again, compelling him two steps back.

"I was right," Devesh said with a grin.

Aniri approached, and Devesh retreated. She feinted again, and he shuffled a step out of her reach. "About what?" She looked for an opening, the split second between when he decided to attack and actually lunged with his blade.

"About my lady needing some vigorous sport to lighten her mood." He thrust forward, she blocked, but he advanced again and again, forcing her back several steps before he stopped.

"And I suppose a courtesan is well trained to provide the kind of sport I need?"

Devesh grinned, slightly dropping his fencing arm, which was exactly the minute distraction she hoped for. She struck for his chest and pinned him, her foil bending a graceful arc that landed in a point right above his heart.

"Touch." Devesh held his hands wide, not exactly looking displeased that she had landed a point. He didn't outmatch her, but she usually had to work much harder for the first point.

"You let me score." Suddenly, the fight went out of her, like steam fleeing the automaton, collapsing her into a similarly lifeless hulk. She released him from the touch, saluted, and swept her blade tip to the floor.

"Oh, Dev," she said quietly. "What am I going to do?"

He was instantly next to her, his hand gentle on her cheek. "Why are you so troubled? The Queen has left it to you to decide, hasn't she? You must simply refuse him, Aniri."

Aniri peered up into his deep brown eyes. How did he know her mother had given her the choice? "Yes, the Queen is graciously allowing me a full length of rope with which to hang myself."

Devesh frowned. "Your mother loves you, Aniri."

Aniri snorted very ungraciously. "She is the Queen first and mother second, Dev."

Devesh gently tucked a strand of hair that had worked loose behind her ear. "Of her three daughters, Aniri, she loves you most of all. Everyone at court can see it. And she's given you a choice in this matter. What greater proof do you need?"

"She is testing me, Dev. To see if I will step up to my duty."

His hand froze by her cheek. "But you will refuse him, right?"

Aniri placed her gloved hand against his chest to reassure him. "I want to, Dev."

But her face must have given away her worries. He dropped his hand and frowned. "It is a trap, Aniri. You have to know that."

She leaned away. "What do you mean?"

He gave her one of his slightly patronizing looks. "Sweet, naïve, rebellious Aniri. Someday you're going to need to pay attention to the intrigues of the palace."

"I thought that was your job." His tone irritated her.

"Indeed it is." Devesh smiled. "And as your secret advisor on all things political, I must warn you the Prince of Jungali is not a person you can trust in any way. Once he has you in his mountain palace, you will be his prisoner. And a very valuable hostage. Dharia will have to meet whatever demands the barbarians may propose."

Aniri frowned. "My mother wouldn't send me into an arranged marriage like that."

"The Queen…" He gritted his teeth. "Does not always see things for what they are. Not unlike her favorite daughter." His fingers gently traced her lips. "Aniri, my love, not all people have the best of intentions, and that goes double for the barbarians. They live a harsh life in the mountains. They are brutal to one another, and they are envious of their neighbors to the south. You would be a prized trophy for Prince Malik."

"I can't believe my mother would agree to this, if the danger were such as you describe."

"You are seriously considering his offer, then?" Devesh's mouth drew into a tight line.

"War is a serious matter, Dev." She held her hands wide, one still grasping her foil. "I have to consider it."

Devesh didn't respond, just gently took Aniri's foil and returned both their swords to the table. He paused

there a moment. "Can I tell you something in confidence, my love?" He glanced at the servants at the far end of the hall.

Aniri stepped closer. "Of course, Dev. You can tell me anything."

He smiled and drew her close, until she was flush against him. He kissed her lightly, but with a soft passion that spoke volumes. Then he pressed his cheek to hers, his lips near her ear. "I love you, Aniri," he whispered.

When he pulled back, she smiled. "I hate to tell you this, Dev, but I already knew that."

"If you go off with this Prince Malik, and anything happens to you, the Queen may dispense an army to come after you, but I will beat them there."

Aniri drew in a shaky breath. Prince Malik said he would allow her a lover, even though arranged marriages were expected to be true marriages, especially among royalty. But could she live that kind of life? A secret love on the side while performing the duties of Queen in a foreign land? The idea made her shudder. It pained her every day her love for Devesh was kept hidden. She couldn't imagine a lifetime of it. Nor could she picture Devesh, with his love of the court and all things political, banished to the frozen wastelands of the north simply to be her consort.

He must have seen the emotions warring across her face. "Tell him no, Aniri. Refuse him and come away with me. We could leave today."

"Dev—"

He cut her off with a kiss. "We could return to Samir," he whispered against her lips. "We won't be rich, but we could travel anywhere you wished, all the places your father would have taken you. We would have all the time in the world. To be together. To learn the truth about your father's killers. To make a family of our own."

It was precisely what they had planned. Now it all seemed like a hopeless fantasy. "Dev, I can't simply abandon my country. If I refuse Malik, and there is war to pay, I cannot just run away… Is this the confidence you wanted to tell me?"

Devesh looked torn, like there was something more he wanted to say but was holding it back. "I cannot offer you a Queendom, Aniri. My love is all I can promise. I hope it is enough to convince you to refuse Prince Malik's offer."

He stepped back, and with clasped hands and a short bow, he turned and strode away. Her heart tried to beat its way out of her chest to follow him. If she accepted Prince Malik's offer, she would lose the man she loved.

Unlike the Jungali prince, she wasn't sure that was a price she was willing to pay.

SIX

The night pulsed with dreams of flying machines, screams, and death.

She chased after a man who looked like Devesh only to find he was a specter, a black wisp of smoke that dissolved under her touch. The dreams left her in a cold sweat in the morning, and no more certain of what her choice should be, even as she stood in front of the Queen's chamber, hand on the brass doorknob, about to render her decision.

Her mother waited inside. The prince waited in the Queen's antechambers on the floor below. They both wanted a decision from her. She hesitated so long, fighting to calm the churning in her stomach, that the cool metal of the doorknob warmed in her hand. Finally, she turned it and pushed open the door.

The Queen sat at her desk, several papers spread

before her, but she wasn't tending to them. Instead she held the pencil sketch of her father, the one Aniri loved so much.

The Queen set it back down and rose as she approached. "Aniri."

"Your majesty." She pressed her hands together and made a small bow.

Her mother's bustled silks brushed the papers on her desk, setting them ajar as she came around. She looked into Aniri's eyes for a long moment. "Have you come to a decision?"

"No."

The Queen frowned, obviously not expecting that response. "The prince is awaiting a response. Should I send him away?"

"I…" Aniri covered her face with her hands, then swept them away. "Mother, are you certain this marriage will bring us peace with the Jungali?"

"No, I'm not certain of that at all."

Aniri gaped. "Then why are you proposing I accept his offer?"

"I only asked you to consider it, Aniri. I didn't tell you which choice I would prefer."

Aniri just stared at her mother. Slowly the realization dawned on her. This was another test. "You wanted to see if I would choose quickly or if I would struggle with the decision."

"No, Aniri." She sighed. "I don't torment you unnecessarily, as much as you might find that hard to believe." She walked back to her desk and picked up one of the papers. Curling paper strips were fixed to the sheet in her mother's hand. Aniri recognized them as notes from an aetheroceiver, the wireless device that transmitted secure communications over the aether from

Dharia's outposts in the northern reaches of the Queendom. "I've had several scouts working to infiltrate the Jungali provinces, going under cover as tradespeople."

"For what purpose?" Aniri hadn't told her about the internal warring between the Jungali factions, but she wasn't surprised the Queen already knew.

Her mother looked up. "To determine if Prince Malik is telling the truth about this Jungali flying machine."

Aniri nodded. "And what does he say?"

"The prince claims no such weapon exists. However, the young prince has a tentative hold on power, and even if he's telling the truth, I'm not sure I can trust him."

"Have your scouts found the flying machine?"

"No, but there are too many reports of workers moving to the far northern provinces for a short time, then returning south. Migrant work isn't the norm in the mountains, but my scouts are having a hard time getting the locals to talk about it." The Queen leveled a stare at her. "They are doing something up there, and I would like very much to know what it is."

"And if there is a flying weapon?" Aniri feared the answer: she would be all but obligated to marry the prince in order to broker peace.

"Then we need to destroy it," the Queen said. "It would be intolerable for the Jungali to have that kind of superior weaponry at their disposal."

"So you would go to war?" Aniri's eyes widened. Dharia hadn't been at war in a hundred years.

"I doubt our traditional weapons and armory would be effective in their mountainous terrain," the Queen said. "An open, armored assault on the mountains certainly wouldn't hold much element of surprise. But if we can discover the location of the weapon by stealth and then sabotage it before it can be deployed, we can avoid a costly war, in both people and expense."

"Can your spies in the Jungali provinces do this?" Aniri was still reeling that her mother was sharing this information with her, as if she had suddenly taken Nahali's place as First Daughter.

The Queen grimaced. "The Jungali clans are fiercely loyal and very tightknit, based on a kinship system not unlike our own. Their secrecy and security is impressive. And it is proving nearly impossible to determine if the weapon exists at all, much less where it might be hidden."

Her mother set the sheet of paper down and came around the desk again, taking Aniri's hands in hers. "You, on the other hand, would have access to the heart of their government."

Aniri's eyebrows hiked up. "You want me to spy on them?"

The Queen gave her a tight smile. "The marriage would be a pretext for you to get inside the prince's compound where our spies cannot currently reach. If you can find the weapon, you can send us information on how to destroy it. If you discover there is no weapon, that it's mere saber-rattling, then there is no threat at all. Either way, once you accomplish your mission, you could cancel the wedding and return home."

Aniri's heart pounded. There was normally a month-long courtship period before the actual ceremony. It would give her time. "What if I can't find it?"

"Then your intelligence will tell us whether a peace-brokering marriage is our only true way to secure the threat they pose."

It was risky. Aniri would be spying on an unstable enemy nation she knew nothing about. But if she could find this secret weapon, or prove it didn't exist, she

wouldn't have to go through with the marriage. She would be truly *free*. And she would have served her country in the process.

She found herself nodding vigorously, not wanting to put all those thoughts into words, lest her chance, her way out, evaporate like Devesh in her dream.

"It's dangerous, Aniri." The Queen gently touched Aniri's cheek, like she did when she was a child, stilling her frantic agreement. "I wouldn't even propose this if the potential threat weren't so grave to Dharia. A flying ship... it could tip the balance of power. I don't want to see it in any hand but Dharia's, much less the barbarians'."

"Because they're unstable—"

"They're fractious and war-loving. They kill their own as easily as you and I take a trip to market. If they could strike from the air..."

Aniri couldn't ever recall seeing her mother afraid. A chill ran over her, like a gust of northern air had just swept through the room.

"Even so," her mother said, "the idea of sending you into a den of barbarians keeps sleep from finding me at night."

"No, Mother, you're right." Aniri's heart skipped as she saw the plan become real. "If the threat is real, we must face it. If it's as much of a danger to Dharia as you say, it is worth the risk." Somehow the prospect of being caught as a spy in Jungali frightened her less than the prospect of marriage to a man she didn't love. At least then the pain would be over quickly.

The Queen smiled and brushed her hand along Aniri's hair. "My third daughter... I had a feeling you would say that."

"Why didn't you just tell me from the outset?"

Clouds crowded the pumping thrill of having found a way out of the marriage. "Your majesty can confide in me." Even as she said it, Aniri wondered how much the Queen had ever really confided in her. Even now.

"It is a lot to ask of you, Aniri." She dropped her hand. "The marriage may yet be required to stabilize the situation politically. I wanted you to seriously consider that option. If it wasn't something you would entertain, then—"

"You didn't think I would do my duty," Aniri said, her back straightening.

"I wanted you to give serious thought to whether you would sacrifice your future for Dharia," the Queen said stiffly, "before I asked you to possibly sacrifice your life."

She had expected Aniri to say no. *Expected* her to embarrass the Queen and shirk her duty. Never mind that Aniri would prefer almost anything to the arranged marriage, even if it meant risking her life. It was a test her mother had expected her to fail. She would no doubt find Prince Malik more noble than her own daughter, with his apparent willingness to sacrifice everything for his country.

Aniri wanted to say something, but words tangled in the hot burning on her cheeks. Her mother had returned to her desk, studying her communiques. Without looking up, the Queen added by way of dismissal, "The prince awaits your decision in my anteroom."

Finding nothing she could say without regret, Aniri turned to the door of the Queen's office.

"Aniri," her mother called, stopping her with her hand on the knob. "You understand the ruse must be complete. No one may suspect your true purpose, and you must communicate directly with me or Janak. He will

accompany you for your personal security. I will provide you with an aetheroceiver before you depart. You must not tell anyone else. You... you must not tell Devesh anything of your true mission."

Aniri's eyes narrowed. Her mother knew about that, too. For how long? Janak must have told her. A flash of anger heated Aniri's face further, and her heart pounded with the realization that of course she would have to lie to Devesh. If there was any hope of her mission succeeding, it would require the utmost secrecy.

She would have to lie. To the man she loved. And tell him she was marrying another.

"I'm at your Majesty's service." Aniri yanked open the Queen's door and left it wide as she practically raced down the hall. She choked back tears as the full force of what she was about to do hit her. Her anger was tamed only slightly by the knowledge that after the deception was done, she would be free—once and for all.

She only hoped Devesh would still want her.

She stalked down the stairs to the Queen's antechamber and flung open the door. When it banged against the stone wall, Prince Malik whirled to face her. He stood by the fireplace, looking off-balance by her sudden appearance. The deception had already begun, and from the outset, she was doing a poor job of it, storming in to accept his proposal.

"Prince Malik." She forced her voice to calm, and her steps to slow, as she approached.

"Arama, Princess Aniri." He pressed his hands together and bowed, but his eyes never left her, scanning up and down as if to discern some clue to her answer. As he straightened, his brows drew together. He seemed to steel himself for her refusal.

"I have given a great deal of thought to your

proposal." *A good lie is always laced with the truth.* Where did she hear that? Probably from one of her sisters, in a childhood caper where the consequences were no more important than stolen sweets from the kitchen.

Prince Malik nodded his head, defeat already on his face. He quickly approached her, covering the lush woven rugs with his long strides until he was at her side.

He dropped his voice. "Is there any possibility that I may yet convince you to accept this arrangement?"

"Yes."

The shock lifted his eyebrows, and he keenly examined her face once more. "I meant what I said about meeting any condition you demand. Name it, your highness, and if it's within my power, I will make it so."

Conditions? What made sense, if she were truly accepting his proposal? She floundered, this lie already drowning her. "I... I will need to bring my handmaiden with me." She scrambled to think of more convincing demands.

Prince Malik's cool amber eyes lit with hope. "But of course. I had assumed the princess would need an entourage."

An entourage? That might be too much to suit her needs for stealth. "That won't be necessary, but I would like to bring my guard, Janak."

"There cannot be too much security for my tastes when it comes to the future Queen of Jungali, so I am glad to hear it."

Aniri frowned. Apparently she wasn't the only one who thought this would be a dangerous undertaking. "I... I reserve the right to make further demands, as the occasion warrants."

"Granted," he said, his breaths starting to come quicker.

"And the conditions you stated previously would hold," she said in a rush, feeling like she had not demanded enough. "There will be no children. I will maintain the ruse, but I may have occasion to... to take a lover, from time to time."

"Understood." He seemed to be holding his breath, and there was no more putting it off.

"Then, Prince Malik," she said, pausing to swallow, "I accept your proposal of a peace-brokering marriage between Dharia and Jungali."

He let out a small huff of air. An uncertain smile crept on his face, but he seemed to fight it, trying to keep a proper respectful appearance. He surprised her by dropping to one knee and pressing the backs of her hands to his forehead. The fevered heat of his skin warmed them. "Thank you, your majesty."

Then he rose and regarded her as if she had transformed into mother-goddess Devkasera right before him. "Princess Aniri." He seemed to struggle for words. "I think perhaps you are more noble than you believe." He stepped back, formality thankfully returning to form an invisible wall between them. "I will make arrangements at once. At your leave, we can depart in the morning."

She nodded, but her heart sank under his words. Her mind insisted it was all subterfuge, that it would free her in the end, but her heart felt as though the trap were already sealed, and she was plummeting to the bottom of the frozen Jungali Sea.

seven

Great billows of steam rolled along the back of the train, huffing impatience into the sky as it awaited departure. A dozen passenger cars gleamed in the morning sun, the burnished red wood almost as bright as the brass. The train station bustled with passengers and their cargo. The two aft-most cars had been sectioned off, cleared for Prince Malik's return to Jungali. And Aniri's first trip beyond the borders of Dharia.

The daylong train ride would take them through Dharia's rolling farms and fertile fields, the ones that fed the world with their abundance. Aniri felt that excess more keenly as she surveyed the dozens of trunks being loaded into the baggage car by the Queen's servants. It was an embarrassment of riches compared to the prince and his tiny entourage, which consisted solely of the prince and his bulky attendant. They stood near his train car, consulting about something in earnest. Unlike earlier, his guard was now heavily armed with a wide-barreled flintlock pistol strapped to his leg and twin daggers sheathed at the small of his back.

The prince similarly carried both a sword and a bronze-handled dagger strapped to his waist. The Dharian finery he had worn at court had been replaced by rugged traveling attire more in keeping with her expectations of the Jungali—a linen shirt casually open at the neck but secured with leather bindings at the wrists and trim, woolen pants tucked into his black boots. His knee-length open coat, with its leather chest straps hanging loose, made him look like a Samirian pirate, the kind who raided Dharian vessels long ago, before peace had been brokered with arranged marriages and trade. Yet he still managed to look regal. Perhaps it was the way he stood: more confident in his barbarian clothing than when she'd first seen him in the Queen's Grand Chamber.

"He is rather handsome, in a coarse, barbarian kind of way," Priya said, standing at her side. As she spoke, the prince glanced their way, as if he could hear her over the chugging of the steam engine pulling at its brakes. Aniri quickly turned her attention to her handmaiden, avoiding the prince's gaze.

"I'm not marrying him for his looks, Priya," Aniri said quietly. Her handmaiden couldn't be trusted with the truth of Aniri's mission. Or even the contents of her daily diary, for that matter. "Or for his charm."

"Is he charming as well, my lady?" Priya's eyes lit. She must think this adventure grand, dangerous, and romantic, and Aniri couldn't entirely spoil her illusions without destroying her cover. The dangerous part was accurate at least. But Aniri's misery in this marriage would make little sense when she had chosen it herself.

"I suppose you will see for yourself, once we're in Jungali."

Priya smiled, unabashedly turning to linger a look on Prince Malik. "Do you suppose the other Jungali men are so handsome?"

"Priya," Aniri said, exasperated. "We're arranging my marriage, not yours."

"Of course, my lady." She leaned close to whisper. "And who said anything about marriage?"

Aniri rolled her eyes, tired of talking about romance that would not be hers. "Will you please check on our train car? Make sure there is nothing we will have need of, but somehow left behind. If that's possible." Their marriage had supposedly been arranged to bring peace and quell the incursions at the border. After the formal engagement party and courtship period in Jungali, the wedding would cement their new alliance. She was supposedly leaving Dharia for good, so it made sense to bring her every earthly possession. But she intended to be home again well before the month-long courtship period was up.

Priya scurried off in her silk-slippered feet to join Janak, who was supervising the servants loading Aniri's multitude of trunks. As soon as all her packages were loaded, she would board, but she wanted to stand on Dharian soil as long as possible.

She had made her goodbyes over an early morning meal taken with her mother and sisters. It had been a quiet affair. Aniri couldn't be sure if Nahali knew the truth, but she was sure Seledri had only been told the lie. The pain in her eyes had been nearly unbearable. Aniri couldn't face Devesh—she had taken the coward's way out by leaving him a note. Priya promised it had been delivered to his bedside, so he would see it upon waking.

The train station was just outside the gates of the capital city of Kartavya, whose sandstone walls caught the morning sun and appeared even more rosy. Aniri had spent nearly all of her life inside the city. For all the times she imagined breaking free, she hadn't ever pictured herself boarding a train for the mountains of Jungali in order to do it.

Aniri examined the couple dozen other passengers boarding the train: ladies in slim silk dresses with the kind of high collars fashionable in the Queen's court. The colors of their dresses blended in a bouquet of deep greens, burgundies, and golds. The men were slightly more muted with plum and black jackets over raw silk shirts. Only a few noticed her standing alone on the platform. They kept their stares respectfully short. It wasn't entirely unheard of for her to leave the palace grounds, but most of her travels had been limited to single carriage affairs to local climbing spots or on expeditions to a coastal town with the Queen and her court on holiday. On those occasions, they had the train to themselves, since the many members of the Queen's court filled every seat.

A figure caught her notice as he moved quickly through the crowd, skipping past the slower moving travelers and shouting apologies in his wake. Her breath caught in her throat.

Devesh.

Aniri looked to the train in a panic. All of a sudden, being so far from the car where she would board seemed foolish. Before she could think of a way to avoid him, it was all too clear she couldn't. He was upon her.

"Aniri!" Devesh called even before he reached her, and she was forced to turn back to him. His breaths heaved out of his chest when he arrived at her side, as if he'd run the entire way from the embassy. His hair was slightly damp, his linen nightshirt barely buttoned, and the laces of his boots pooled on the rough wood of the platform, clearly not having been tied in his haste. Dev set down the long traveling case he carried. In his other hand was clenched a piece of parchment. She recognized the royal stationary she had labored over last night, pouring her heart onto the page, hoping he could read between the lines and see that her actions didn't reflect her love for him.

But perhaps he had read too much, because here he stood. He grasped her shoulders, his hands warm and pulsing from the run, crushing the letter to her stiff silk traveling clothes.

"Devesh—" Aniri said, but then Dev broke all decorum and crushed his lips to hers. His arms wrapped around her, not holding back in the slightest in his passion. Aniri struggled to push him away, and suddenly she was free of him. Janak had hold of Devesh, literally yanking him off Aniri by the back of his half-buttoned shirt. Devesh swung at Janak, which pulled a gasped "No!" out of Aniri. Janak easily dodged Devesh's punch, landing one of his own in Devesh's stomach, which bent him over double.

Aniri found her voice, shouting an imperious, "Janak!" that caused him to pull a flat-handed chop that had been aimed at Dev's throat.

Janak roughly shoved Devesh away and turned to Aniri. "My lady, your train awaits." His normally impassive face was mottled, but with anger, not exertion. He could easily have killed Dev with that single well-placed strike, the kind that earned the raksaka their reputation as silent assassins as well as royal guards. But her anger matched his: it was not his place to come between her and Devesh. Not now, and not before, when he had betrayed their affair to her mother. Her anger reached a new height with that thought.

"The train will wait for me," she said to him, her voice harsh with anger. "And you may wait on board."

If he did not heed her command, she would banish him from the mission altogether, whether her mother approved or not. Janak hesitated so long Aniri nearly sent him packing... but either the fury in her face or his sense of obedience turned him sharply on the hard heel of his boot. He strode to the train, where Priya stood, hand to her face and horror in her eyes. Aniri ignored them both, as well as the crowd that had frozen all around them to watch. Devesh had straightened, recovered somewhat from Janak's blow.

"Devesh, you are a foolish boy." There were tears in Aniri's eyes, blurring her sight of him, even as she reached for his shoulders to see if he was all right.

"Foolish?" he said with a smirk. "I've been looking for an excuse to take a swing at Janak almost from the day I met him."

"He's *raksaka*. He could have killed you before you raised a hand to defend yourself. Are you *mad*?"

Devesh peered down into her eyes. "I'm mad about you, Aniri." He crumpled up the parchment still in his hand, threw it to the station platform, and took her hand in his. "You cannot do this. You know this marriage is a horrible mistake. I beg of you—come with me. It's not too late. We can leave right now. A cousin of mine is waiting with a carriage. He can secret us away in a cottage in the lowlands by the coast until we can find passage across the sea to Samir."

Aniri slowly pulled her hand from hers. "I... I can't,

Dev." She took a half step away and almost turned her back on his pain-filled eyes before her lips could betray her. Any declaration of love on the platform, with dozens of onlookers, would doom her chance of making the subterfuge work. He was her lover. She *had* to leave him behind. But her gaze fell to the trunk Devesh had brought, and she couldn't help hoping.

"Are you boarding the train, Dev?" Her voice was whispery and soft, her breath catching in her throat.

Would he leave everything behind for her? He frowned, then scooped up the case by the intricately carved handle. Only then did she recognize it. He held it up, flat, presenting it to her as he had her blade the day before.

"Jungali is no place for a Samirian diplomat, princess. But your majesty will want her favorite weapons for this trip." Then he clamped his lips into a tight line.

Aniri took hold of the handle and lifted it from his hands. It was heavier than she expected. "It was kind of you to remember."

Devesh stepped close to her, and Aniri was afraid he might try to kiss her again, but he held a respectful space between them.

"Be careful, my lady," he said softly. "These are dangerous people."

For a flash moment, Aniri thought he had guessed everything—her mission, the subterfuge, her true love for him—but the pain in his eyes told her differently.

"If anything happens to you, Aniri…"

She stepped back and gripped her trunk more firmly. She forced the words from her mouth. "Goodbye, Dev."

As she strode toward the train, every face on the station platform followed her. Priya awaited her at the door to the train car. Aniri climbed aboard and refused to look back. A part of her heart ripped from her chest and remained on the platform with Devesh.

eight

The sway of the train car and the heated, stale air within it made Aniri nauseous. Or possibly it was the fact that she was traveling to the frozen wastelands of the north, having abandoned the boy she loved in favor of a loveless marriage to a barbarian prince.

She breathed through her nose and let it out slowly between her teeth, calming the contents of her stomach and her nerves. It would only come to that if she failed in her true mission; yet it still felt like the train was barreling down its track toward a cage of her own making. Janak stewed in the corner, watching the waving stalks of grain fly past the window and studiously ignoring her. Their confrontation on the platform had left him in an ill-temper, and she wasn't any happier with him. Janak was fully aware that Devesh posed no threat to her, yet he had dared to lay hands on him. It was an insult under the guise of protection, and she knew it full well. Now that Janak knew the real nature of her mission, he was deprived of the chance to gloat over her impending marriage. It must eat at him like a burr buried under all those raksaka wrappings.

They had a long journey ahead in which he could stew. It was a small solace to her.

Priya floated the length of the train car, flitting from window to window and waving to the people whizzing past. If she hadn't already known Aniri and Devesh were lovers, she certainly did now. As did everyone on the train platform. Priya had wisely avoided the subject since they had boarded.

The car had been cleared of the normal rows of seats to provide a small receiving area, complete with large cushioned pillows for sitting, low tables, and tea service. Aniri sat on one of the few train car benches remaining, her gaze fixed on the subjects of her Queendom as the train hurtled past them. Word had traveled fast of her impending nuptials, and many citizens from the smaller villages had gathered at intersections to wave. Occasionally, a flower-laden wedding streamer had been hung, wishing her good luck.

It pulled at her, and not only because the marriage was a ruse.

The people of Dharia were gentle and loving to a fault, greeting her with nothing but well wishes on her departure. They were proud she was off to marry a barbarian prince to bring peace to borderlands and justice for those who had lost their loved ones. The nausea surged back, and Aniri stood, suddenly determined to combat it with more than sitting morosely in her seat. The train swayed under her, and the distant whistle of the engine called to her countrymen and women as it passed.

Aniri gripped the back of the seat and briefly contemplated returning to the tiny sleeping compartment in the back, near the privy. But her mission was to find what secrets Prince Malik was hiding, including his flying weapon, if it existed. Maybe pursuing that would keep the nauseous feeling that she was making the mistake of her life at bay. She marched to the front of the car and wrenched up the handle of the door to the brief passage between her car and the prince's.

The door was locked.

Her movement caught Janak's attention. "Where do you think you're going, your royal eminence?" Janak's usual lack of respect for her title arched a little higher. His insolence would wear thin, on this very train ride, she could tell already.

Aniri wrenched the door once more, but it wouldn't give. "I would pay my future husband a visit. The official courtship period has begun; I'm well within my rights to request an appointment. And I have several questions for the young prince." She dared Janak with her eyes. He could sulk all he liked, but if she were to be a spy, he couldn't be hovering over her every moment of the day.

Janak narrowed his eyes but didn't argue. "I hope your most royal highness will permit me to fulfill my duties as she fulfills hers."

If she were to have any hope of success in this mission, it would make sense to have Janak at her back. In Jungali, the threats would be more substantial than urgent kisses from a courtesan. Perhaps she should make peace with Janak now, before they reached the rugged mountain provinces. She tilted her head to him, very slightly. "Prudence was always your strength, Janak."

"And your weakness, Princess."

So much for peace overtures. "Will you request an

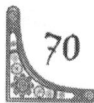

audience with the prince or must I do it myself?"

He nodded curtly and strode to a speaker box at the rear of the train car. While he navigated the niceties of arranging a meeting with the prince, Aniri studied the train door and its simple lock. Priya appeared by her side, a smile sly on her face. She pulled a pin from her hair and bent it until it snapped in two.

Aniri raised her eyebrows. "And what do you plan to do with that?"

"One should always make friends with whomever one can, my lady. One never knows what new skills one might learn." She bent to the door's small keyhole, slipping one-half of the pin in and holding it taut, while working the other inside. Two clicks occurred in quick succession, and the door cracked open.

Aniri shook her head and grinned. "And which friend of yours taught you to pick locks?"

Priya tucked the two half-pins back into her hair. "That, my lady, is a secret I am not at liberty to share."

She flashed a mischievous grin and slid open the door. It disappeared into a pocket, and the sound of train wheels biting into the tracks rushed in. A gush of air lifted Aniri's loose hair into a writhing mass around her head, bringing a whiff of earthen countryside mixed with the bitter coal smoke of the engine. The walkway between the cars swayed and bucked. Her traveling clothes—a full corset and jacket over her tight silk skirt—were ill-suited for traversing it, but she would manage. Priya was more sensibly dressed in a long jacket over trousers. At Aniri's hesitation, Priya quickly stepped ahead to repeat her lock-picking skills on the prince's door, and Aniri followed after, grasping the cool metal railings to keep her footing as her hair whipped more furiously about her. As the prince's door slid it open, Janak's curse and boot-pounding steps sounded from the car behind them. He appeared at Aniri's back, but he had no time to complain before Prince Malik's guard rushed the prince's door, blocking Priya's access with his massive size.

For her part, Priya seemed undaunted, looking up haughtily and saying loudly enough to be heard over the substantial train clacking, "The Princess Aniri of Dharia requests an audience with Prince Malik of the Jungali Provinces."

He frowned down at her, appearing unsure what to make of the spunky girl in the flapping silk jacket or the entourage behind her.

"Farid!" the prince's voice carried over the clattering. "Don't make the princess's handmaiden stand out between the cars. I'm sure she's not too much of a threat."

Farid kept his frown, but he didn't seem the kind of guard who was troubled by complicated thoughts, so he quickly stepped to one side. Even so, there wasn't room for even slender Priya to slip past him without brushing the barbarian's expansive chest, all the more imposing for his riveted leather chest straps and flintlock holstered at his side. Priya fluttered her hands at him, as if he were an enormous fly she could shoo away. He bumbled backward on unsteady clumping boots. Aniri struggled mightily not to laugh. The narrow entrance to the prince's train car was now clear, and the three of them shuffled inside. Janak glowered at her, then closed the door, dropping a curtain of silence around them.

The prince's train car had been modified much as Aniri's had, clearing space for the desk at which he sat. The car was less musty than hers, a fact she found annoying. Or perhaps the sweep of air from the open door had freshened it. A stray strand of her hair drifted in

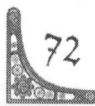

the residual breeze, and she hastened to smooth it down. The wind between the cars had probably left her less than royal-looking. The prince peered up from the papers he was studying and seemed startled to see Aniri.

He rose hastily to his feet. "Princess Aniri." He seemed indecisive for a moment as to what to do with the papers in his hands, then set them down on the desk and came around to greet her. "This is an unexpected surprise. I thought your handmaiden was simply requesting a visit."

"If this is an inconvenient time," Aniri said, "I can return later."

"No, not at all." He regained his composure with a small smile, pressing his hands together and giving a slight bow. "I will always have time for the future Queen of Jungali." He gathered a pair of plush, ruby-red embroidered chairs, arranging them to face one another. They appeared to have been scavenged from another car because they didn't match the blue-and-gold brocade of the rest of the room. As the prince gestured her to sit, he added, "I must say, I didn't expect to see you so soon."

Aniri frowned, afraid she had already misstepped. "I had assumed, with the marriage arranged, that our courtship would begin right away. At least, that is Dharian custom. Is it not the same in Jungali?"

"Our courtship?" the prince said, like he had forgotten that part of the arrangement. "Yes, of course. Although in Jungali, courtship is usually chaperoned by family members."

Aniri became suddenly aware of their audience in the tight confines of the train car. Janak and Prince Malik's personal guard, Farid, were in some kind of bluster standoff at the rear of the car. Farid rested his hand on his weapon, while Janak simply glared. Farid likely had no idea Janak's hands were at least as lethal as Farid's gun. Priya beamed, unabashedly listening in.

"I suppose we will have to make do with the chaperones we have," Aniri said stiffly.

The prince took the chair opposite her, his face alight with curiosity. "I imagine we will have to break more than one custom to make this arrangement work."

Aniri noticed he now had two small gold hoop earrings, one in each ear. He was wise not to have worn them in her mother's court, where the men did not wear jewelry—which only made her wonder what other things he had wisely kept hidden.

"I hope you are comfortable in your train car," the prince continued. "Is there anything I can request for you? The train staff seem quite happy to accommodate my needs so far, and I'm sure they would be doubly so for their beloved princess."

"I'm quite... comfortable, thank you." She was far from comfortable, but there wasn't anything the train staff could do about that.

Prince Malik had a small smile on his face. "Does the princess have any further demands she wishes to make?"

"No demands, simply a request." Aniri met the prince's slightly bemused expression with enough seriousness to make it fade from his face. "I'm afraid my education about the provinces of Jungali is woefully inadequate to the task of becoming Queen. I had hoped you might enlighten me on the important issues of the day, if you can spare the time." She glanced at the papers layered on his desk.

"Of course." His pale eyes measured her for a moment, not unfriendly but in an appraising sense, as if he wasn't quite sure if Aniri's stated purpose was her true one. Or maybe she was just squirming because her

subterfuges until now had been limited to sneaking out of the palace at night to meet Devesh. When Prince Malik spoke, his voice was softer, meant mostly for her, even if the others could be counted on to overhear. "You've made a great sacrifice for this peace-brokering arrangement, even more than I had suspected earlier. We will make sure it is a peace worthy of the price you have paid, Aniri."

Her face heated up. Of course the prince had witnessed Devesh's desperate display of affection at the train station and the ensuing drama. That incident would feed the gossips for weeks and would no doubt complicate their efforts to forge, or at least appear to forge, a peace between their nations. It was foolish of Devesh on many levels, but Aniri was quite sure he knew all of that before he did it. In spite of her words, she knew Devesh was no fool.

"Peace is my hope, Prince Malik," Aniri said, conviction ringing true in her voice. The only way through this would be to work as fervently for peace as the earnest prince seemed to want. "Which is why I need to know more about your homeland before we arrive."

Prince Malik settled back on the tightly cushioned chair. "Well, there are four provinces—"

"Bajir, Mahet, Rajan, and Sik." Aniri listed them rapidly. "My education is not so woeful as that."

He smiled. "My apologies."

The train car swayed, and her tight traveling clothes conspired against keeping her balance on the stiff chair. She gripped the plush arms to steady herself. "What I need to know, Prince Malik, is the temper of your people. What will they think of our arrangement? I can't help but wonder if they will accept a Dharian as their Queen." She imagined the barbarians were awed and impressed by

Dharian wealth, but she truly wondered what they would think of her, a Dharian princess, coming amongst them. She tried to banish images of her head on a pike being paraded amongst savage villagers.

Malik's smile fled, and the shadowed look he perpetually wore returned. "I worry about that myself. My home province of Bajir, especially, still mourns their Queen, my mother. While her rule was strong, the four generals who command the military in each of the provinces grow increasingly bold under my reign. You will notice that I am still a prince?"

Aniri frowned. "I had assumed you had not held an ascension ceremony out of respect for your late mother."

"That is partially true." Malik cast his gaze down to his hands, which had found each other and gripped in his lap. He seemed to force them to release, then looked up. "But the truth is I need the support of the generals to formally ascend to the throne. Or a wedding to a new Queen would make ascension automatic."

"I see," Aniri said. "Will the generals then have to support the marriage?"

"By our tradition, yes," he said. "In reality? Had I married any of the eligible ladies in one of the four provinces, it would have sown discord among the generals, thinking I was preferring one over the other with my rule. Even worse, if I had picked someone from my home province of Bajir."

"So the very fact that I am not Jungali," Aniri said, "is what makes this marriage possible."

"In a way, yes," he said with a smile. "The generals will see this for what it is—a strategic bond with a powerful ally. They cannot do anything but accept it at its face: something intended to unite all the Jungali provinces."

Aniri frowned. "And yet you're worried."

"It is the people I am most troubled about," Malik said. "Winning their hearts will be your most difficult task, Princess. One I hope you will be willing to take on."

"I will do everything in my power to do so, I assure you." Strangely, she felt the force of conviction behind that statement. She needed the facade of the impending marriage to hold, to give her time to find the weapon. And she would prefer not to have her head on a pike as well. "These generals, do they each command their own military? I hear the Jungali are fiercely loyal. Are you not concerned that they will incite their own people against me?" Aniri tipped her head toward the prince. "Against *us*, rather than taking the more obvious route of challenging you directly?"

Malik smiled broadly. "The princess is even more astute than I had assumed." Aniri wasn't quite sure whether that was a compliment or not. Devesh certainly never thought strategy, political or military, was ever her strength. "I am concerned," he continued, "which is why I've already scheduled an announcement of our engagement in front of the populace in my home province, quite literally as soon as we arrive. I wish to waste no time in introducing you to my people. A formal engagement party can follow in two weeks, the wedding in four, according to custom." He tipped his head to her. "According to Jungali custom."

"Dharian custom is the same," Aniri said. "Should we perhaps travel to the other provinces as well? A goodwill tour of sorts? That is, if your customs allow it." Traveling seemed like a better idea the more she thought of it. She might gain access to the prince's inner sanctum, if she was lucky, but she doubted he hid the flying weapon under his bed. Getting away from the capital could bring an opportunity for more investigation.

Malik raised his eyebrows. "We can certainly accommodate traveling the provinces, if your majesty wishes it. Although..." He frowned again.

"Yes?"

"I don't want to alarm you, princess, but..." He hesitated again. "I would just want to ensure your safety before planning trips around the frozen landscape of the provinces."

Aniri swallowed. Her safety wasn't from the landscape but the generals, she suspected. "Perhaps we should wait to see how things develop, then."

Malik took a breath. "I think that would be best."

Aniri rose from her chair. "I'll leave you to your planning then, Prince Malik." She made a small bow as he hastily arose from his own seat. "I apologize for the sudden intrusion."

"Anytime, princess, please. We are, after all, courting." He smiled, but the earnest look quickly took over. "And your counsel on these matters is greatly appreciated."

Aniri bowed again and turned to retreat from Prince Malik's car. She needed to think about how to win over a barbarian people she knew nothing about.

While at the same time betraying their prince.

nine

They arrived at the foothills of the northern border of Dharia where the land broke and transformed itself from a garden of rich soil and stable villages to a mountainous, forbidding land shrouded in mystery and gloom.

At least that's how it appeared to Aniri.

She stood on the train station platform, waiting for her parcels to be unloaded, and stared up at the fourteen-thousand-foot peaks disappearing into the clouds. Already the temperature had dropped from the balmy summer warmth of the central plain. Priya had unpacked a light wrapping coat, and Aniri cinched it tighter around her neck. The mountains were growing dark from more than simply the clouds that topped them. It would be nightfall soon.

"Are we traveling on tonight?" Aniri asked Priya

when she returned from consulting with the prince's bodyguard, Farid.

"Yes," Priya said, slightly breathless.

The train tracks ended where they stood, literally stopping at the foothills and the border between nations. It struck Aniri as strange there was no rail connection at all between Dharia and Jungali, just a weathered road of gravel that disappeared into the foothills. How could there be trade between their countries when they didn't even have a way to connect the goods?

"And by what means are we traveling?" Aniri asked.

Priya's smile was mischievous with adventure. "That." She pointed to the end of the train platform where a beast the size of a small cottage stood. It was draped in bright red embroidered cloth from the tip of its enormous, snuffling black nose to the blunt rear end. Its lumpy head and two giant horns were painted with elaborate swirls in shades of red and gold to match the embroidery, and its six legs the size of pillars were clad in shiny brass plating. The beast moved like a giant royal carpet and carried what looked like a miniature carriage on its back.

"You cannot be serious," Aniri said softly, mostly to herself. Of course she recognized the shashee—it was, after all, an incarnation of the mountain goddess Devpahar, embodying her supposed stately wisdom in its great, lumbering movements. In the traditional stories, Devpahar used her great horns to remove obstacles that might thwart the advancement of peace and learnedness. Aniri had seen drawings of the goddess's material form, but she had never seen one of the shaggy beasts in person. They were rare and confined to the mountains. And she certainly had never expected to *ride* one.

"The prince had to make arrangements for a half

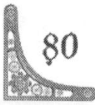

dozen extra beasts, just to carry your luggage, your majesty." Priya seemed delighted with this.

"But..." Aniri stalled out in her protest as the beast bent down one of its six legs, then another, slowly collapsing its shuddering hulk to the ground. When it had settled, like a massive, red landslide, the ornate carriage on top was nearly level with the train station platform. A servant whisked a step stool next to the beast and beckoned her with a fervent wave of his hand.

Priya leaned closer. "That's our ride, your highness!"

Aniri gaped but allowed Priya to guide her forward. A driver of sorts, or perhaps a beastmaster, sat atop the carriage, a slender pole in his hand that he tapped intermittently on the beast's carpeted head. Its wide head rolled at the intrusion, rocking back and forth, but its body didn't move.

Janak held the four-step stool as Aniri and Priya climbed up. He followed them into the carriage, which smelled of fresh hay and wood, and not the stench of raw animal that she expected. Once the door shut soundly behind them, the beast lurched, forcing Aniri to grip a rough wooden handle in the middle of the seat. They tipped sideways, then righted again, all in one rolling motion that made the endless rocking of the train seem like a paragon of steadiness.

When she dared to peer out the tiny portal windows, the train station had swung out of their view. They were high in the air, already lumbering away.

Priya gawked out her portal, chattering while Aniri tried to keep her lunch down. "The shashee are the royal animals of the Jungali. The driver told me they once were the main transportation for the Jungali people throughout the provinces. Now they are reserved for the borderlands and for Devpahar's festivals. This shashee is much more highly decorated than the one the prince is riding, my lady. I believe this must be his personal shashee, or at least a royal one of his court." Priya frowned when she looked to Aniri. "Are you feeling well, my lady?"

Aniri swallowed down the sourness at the back of her throat and kept her gaze out the window. It helped, slightly. Aniri breathed out her answer, "Yes, I'll be fine. Where on earth is this beast taking us, Priya?"

"Why to Jungali, I imagine, my lady." Priya went back to staring in wonder at the darkening mountains outside, as if Jungali were a magical place, so naturally they would ride a painted beast of the gods to get there.

As the rocking of the animal reduced to a gentle swaying motion, Aniri's stomach began to settle. She hazarded a glance around the interior, noting the plush red velvet of the walls, the thick glass of the windows, and the brass and wood trim at every corner. It certainly seemed lavish for a regular transport. Aniri poked the cushion and trailed her finger across the soft crush of fabric lining the walls, hoping for a hidden panel or compartment. Perhaps Prince Malik had stashed some of those communiques he had been so earnestly studying in his train car, but she found nothing.

Janak seemed satisfied that all was safe and secure in their tiny traveling cabinet, judging by the way he had tucked his chin down for a nap. The terrain outside quickly fell to darkness as they climbed the foothills. The path outside was lit only by the swinging spotlight of the oil lamps hanging from the corners of their carriage. It didn't seem wise to travel through the mountains at night, but on top of the giant beast, they felt untouchable by any threat.

She could see now why Dharia's steamer tanks wouldn't be able to penetrate the foothills. The canyons

were narrow, the rough road steep and narrower still, and there was little room for mechanized transport, especially the kind that relied on steady flat terrain. Surely their cavalry could climb the foothills as well as this shashee, but if the Jungali possessed war animals—armored not with ornamental brass and red carpet, but steel plating—they could prove formidable in the winding canyons.

The lights of the carriage danced around the darkness of the canyon, and they traveled some time in silence. Finally, a rapid series of taps from the front heralded an end to the swaying. Even though the beast was finally motionless, it was as if the ground still moved beneath her. It reminded her of the day her father had taken her out in a small skiff, sailing a peaceful, blue bay off the western coast. She had adapted to the gentle swells of the water, but when she returned to land, it was as if she had never walked before.

When the carriage door opened, Prince Malik himself appeared standing on a steel lattice outside. "Did you fare well with the travel, your highness?" Gaslamps hung from a large stone fortress behind him and put a halo of light around his face.

"I am fine. Are we arrived to Bajir already?"

She could just barely make out his smile in the dim light. "No, not yet. This is only a trading station, the first stop on our journey. But we will make rest here tonight and continue on in the morning." He held out a hand to her, and she tentatively took it. His grip was strong, which helped her unsteady legs as she joined him on the portable stairs. "I'm sorry for the steps, princess, but it is the best I could acquire on short notice. The stationmaster initially brought a ladder, but I ordered him away."

"I'm not a delicate flower, Prince Malik," Aniri said.

"I could negotiate a ladder."

"I have no doubt of that," Malik said, "but I don't think your gown would survive it."

She glanced down at the finely woven, tightly wrapped silk dress and nodded. "I'll make sure to wear more suitable clothing for the rest of our journey."

He didn't answer, focused on helping her down the steel stairs, each step creaking under their combined weight. He released her as soon as she was safely on the ground. His bodyguard loomed next to him.

"Farid will ensure you and your entourage make it safely to your rooms, princess," he said. "I have business to attend to, but I will meet you at the east cable station after your morning meal."

Janak and Priya had joined them on the cobblestones outside the trading station's massive wooden doors. Janak had resumed his glaring contest with Farid from earlier in the day, and Priya seemed wide-awake. She was already eagerly exploring their destination with her eyes.

Fatigue pulled at Aniri's eyelids. "Cable station?" she asked Prince Malik. "Do you send messages by cable?" The Queen used her aetheroceiver for secure transmissions, but most of the Dharian countryside still used wired transmission for their communiques.

"No, your highness." This time Aniri had no trouble seeing the prince's smile. "We are the ones who will be traveling by cable." He took a step back, bowing slightly with hands pressed, and left her with that mystery.

She followed Farid and Janak. Priya's arm hooked through hers in an entirely too familiar fashion, but she allowed it because it was quite possible she would fall over—either from fatigue or the residual unsteadiness from the shashee ride—without Priya's arm holding her steady.

Third Daughter

The morning brought blinding sunlight to the room where Aniri had quartered with Priya. Janak stayed in an adjoining room, having only agreed to leave her side because he still had easy access to them, and all the other doors were securely locked. He seemed to think barbarian assassins lurked in every corner of the small trading station.

Aniri choose traveling clothes more suited to the rigors of the mountains. Her rough canvas pants and leather corset, which laced over her linen blouse, were both suitably form-fitting, yet warm against the cold of the Jungali provinces. Her leather jacket met her laced boots at the knees and possessed a belt, in the event she needed to gird further against the cold. She wrapped her hair loosely in a brown scarf and let both trail down her back. Priya insisted Aniri wear a jeweled medallion, which peeked from the scarf and lay on her forehead, but that was the only ornamentation to mark her as royalty and not adventurer.

Their morning meal was delivered to the room. Afterward, Farid guided them through the winding stone hallways of the trading station. They met Prince Malik at a large receiving room with a balcony off one side.

Prince Malik's eyes were wide and approving as he took in her attire. "You never fail to surprise me, princess."

"I'm quite capable of dressing for travel, Prince Malik," Aniri said drily, and the prince was immediately contrite.

"Of course." He gestured toward the balcony. "Shall we be on our way, your majesty?" Without waiting for an answer, he pulled open the double doors, and the morning air swept in, brisk and scented with earth and the lush wide-leaved trees covering the mountains spread before them. A canyon dropped below the balcony, and its rocky sides lifted above them on either side. That was when Aniri saw the cables.

A twinned pair of them soared away from the trading station out into the sky, as if held up by the sun and air and nothingness. In the hazy mountain distance, a metalwork skeleton, like a giant man with pincher hands at the top, held the thick steel cable aloft, offering it to the heavens.

"But how are we going to..." Aniri gestured at the cable, her leather-gloved hand waving in the mountain air. Perhaps a flying machine was not beyond the capabilities of the barbarians if they already were traveling by flying wires. The prince's smile was wide, and for a moment he looked almost like a boy, ready for adventure in his rugged leather-strapped traveling tunic.

"Your cable carriage awaits, my lady." He led them toward a small shack at the end of the balcony where the cables came directly through the wall. As they approached, Aniri saw there was no wall at all, just an open space where the cables came in and out. The prince opened a door to the cottage, which let out a bellow of sound as if a shashee were raging inside. Janak held a hand up to stay them and stepped inside, forcing them all to wait while he checked the source of the noise.

"Do you think an assassin would make such noise?" Aniri called out over the racket. Janak scowled at her and waved them to follow. Not only did she doubt the dangers of the Jungalian mountains would be quite so obvious, but by the time Janak allowed them in, her curiosity had taken over completely. She eagerly stepped over the threshold.

Inside was a steel carriage, boxy like a small train car, only this one floated above the ground, swaying slightly as a porter brought a step stool for their party. Aniri wondered how it could hover like that, until she saw it was suspended, hanging from a muscular steel arm attached to the thick cable overhead, which in turn wrapped around a giant wheel fixed to the ceiling.

A man shoveled coal into a furnace in the corner, his brown overalls covered in black, tarry soot. Next to him was a large-bellied boiler, which drove the flywheel of the steam engine. Gears connected the flywheel to the larger wheel overhead, but while the engine loudly chugged its operation, the overhead wheel and cable carriage were motionless. The small shack reeked of both smoke and fresh mountain air, the way Aniri imagined a forest fire must smell.

Prince Malik leaned close so he could be heard over the hissing of the engine and clacking of gears. "They're waiting for us to board, your majesty."

Aniri nodded and hastened to the carriage. The rest of the party—Janak, Priya, Farid and the prince—climbed in behind her, and the footman carried away the stool. The prince and Farid took hold of the bronze handles, a dozen of which were interspersed between the glass windows around the perimeter of the carriage. Aniri hastened to do likewise, her ride on the shashee not forgotten. But there was only a slight tug this time as they started to move. The cable carriage floated through the cottage, circling slowly around, then gaining speed.

Only when it approached the missing wall did she remember there would soon be no floor below them. She gasped as they flew out of the cottage. She was embarrassed further when the ground fell away beneath them, and her squeak echoed in the sudden quiet outside the cable station and its steam-driven clatter.

The prince was grinning at her. Heat crept up her cheeks. She was dressed like an adventurer, but acting like a schoolgirl. She avoided his stare and gazed out the carriage window, trying to recover some dignity, but soon her jaw was dropping again. They soared over the ravine and quickly climbed higher in the air, as if they would fly straight to the black-dagger mountain peaks in the distance. An infinite palette of green spread below them, a lush forest garden like the Queen's, only it went on endlessly, broken only by a hidden stream peeking from the rocky bottom of the canyon. Past the receding trade station, Aniri glimpsed a sliver of golden fields: the plains of Dharia.

She was flying so high, she could see her home.

It was a wondrous feeling, and dizzying. Like she was a god—flying above the earth and surveying everything in it. What did the barbarians think, living here in the clouds and looking down on Dharia? She had pictured them brawling in dank caves and darkness, not here, perched in the blazing sun and blue sky, gazing at the fields below. Did they come down from their heights just to steal some of Dharia's riches? Or did their mountain living make them dizzy, and they sought the sensible solid ground of the plains?

Priya was similarly gape-mouthed and for once speechless. Even Janak seemed surprised, or perhaps alarmed, still gripping the carriage handles, even though their flight was as smooth as glass.

The prince's smile hadn't dimmed. He edged closer, daring to let go of his handle. "It is beautiful, is it not, princess?"

"It is astonishing," she said. "Do you always travel like this, in the sky? Does it not alarm you?" Aniri stole a

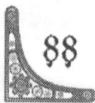

glance at Janak. He definitely was a shade paler than normal, and she took no small satisfaction in that.

"We are a mountain people, your highness." The prince leaned against the window next to her, quite close, their conversation clearly not private with nowhere for the others to go, but he acted as though they were alone. "We are used to high places and daring feats."

He was bragging now.

"Well, in Dharia, we have many wonders as well," Aniri said.

"I'm sure that you do." He smirked.

The giant steel man with his pinched grip on the cable was suddenly near, hurtling toward them. "Oh!" escaped her, and she grasped her handle again. They quickly glided past it. A small thump rocking the carriage was the only note that anything at all had happened.

She drew in a breath and frowned at the smirk that had grown even stronger on the prince's face. "You must think I'm very pampered and naive, Prince Malik."

He looked contrite again. "Not at all, princess. But I do find pleasure in sharing the wonders of my country with someone who hasn't seen them before. And it is soon to be *your* country as well. I hope you find it pleasing."

"I'm still working on wonderment and exhilaration. I'm sure pleasing will come eventually."

He smiled, and she managed to relax her grip on the handle, although she noted Janak still had hold of his. "Will this cable carriage take us to another trading station?"

"Yes. And another one after that. But the trip will be short. We will be in Bajir before lunch. Which is good, because they are waiting for us."

"They?"

"My people. Soon to be yours." His eyes traveled the length of her outfit. "As much as I approve of your traveling clothes, you may want to change once we arrive. I've arranged for us to make an appearance."

"To announce our engagement." The words, spoken aloud, made her stomach feel like a small flock of birds had taken up residence. Somehow flying through the clouds seemed less daring than publicly proclaiming her intent to marry the Prince of Jungali.

"Yes," he said softly, then peered down at the ground far beneath them, whisking by in a blur of leaves and sparkling gray granite boulders. He looked back to her. "Are you ready to meet your new subjects, future Queen of Jungali?"

"I supposed I shall have to be." She smiled to take the edge off her words, cringing at how easy her thoughts came out in her voice. She would have to play her part better than that, if the ruse were to hold long enough to complete her mission. In spite of the unexpected beauty and lightness of their means of transport, the Jungali remained barbarians, ones who would likely slit her throat if they knew her purpose. She might mock Janak for his overcautiousness, but she was also concerned about the dangers that could be found in the mountains of Jungali.

Not least that their young prince might discover she was a spy.

ten

People choked the streets, spilling from doorways and leaning out of windows to catch a glimpse of the prince bringing his bride-to-be home to Bajir. The prince told Aniri the capital city was named Bhakti, which meant devotion or loyalty. It wasn't as large as Kartavya, Dharia's capital, but it seemed to hold just as many citizens, as if the entire population of her capital were squeezed into a quarter its size. Bhakti perched at the edge of a mountainous plain that overlooked a thousand foot abyss. Aniri imagined the white granite walls surrounding the city kept out the cold winter winds as well as other Jungali clans. In between drafts of fresh mountain air, the city was squalid with the smell of coal smoke and too many bodies.

And the colors!

They were an assault on the senses as well.

Buildings were stacked one on top of another, every surface painted green or yellow or blue—especially blue, as if the Jungali had pulled down the vibrant clear sky above them and splashed it on the walls. Lines of wash were strung between the buildings, across streets and to lampposts, tying the entire city together with sheets and cloaks and bloomers that fluttered like brightly colored flags. The rooftops were so close together they formed a maze where one could run from house to house and never touch the ground. In fact, a small flock of children was doing just this as the royal entourage paraded through the streets. Aniri gasped and thought one of them might fall, but they clung to the edges and waved to the prince as he passed. He smiled, waved, and shouted something to them in a language she could not understand.

When they reached the prince's palace, the white granite was a relief to her eyes. The glittering rock rose and fell in graceful, pointed arches and domes that were reassuringly strong and clean. During their passage through the city, she thought perhaps the panic had finally caught up to her because it had become increasingly difficult to breathe. But the prince calmly assured her the air was thinner so high in the mountains, and she just needed breathe more deeply and perhaps limit her movements for a while to acclimate to the change.

Her panic eased. When they arrived at their appointed room, Priya helped her dress and ministered to her hair. Eventually, Aniri calmed enough to feel presentable for the engagement announcement to the prince's people. She couldn't think of them as her people—that wasn't her mission and hopefully never would be. She needed to test out her mother's aetheroceiver, but that would have to wait. The prince expected her in his receiving room in advance of the announcement.

She had brought several outfits worthy of a Queen, but was frankly confused as to which would be best. Priya selected the least ornate among them for this first appearance, and Aniri trusted her judgment. The Jungali wouldn't approve of a preened peacock from the rich Dharian countryside below, but the dress was still undeniably Dharian: silk skirts draped in lace, a formal corset, and a sweep of silk clinging to Aniri's shoulder. She had thought the plum-and-cream fabric colorful before, but now it seemed dull compared to the riot of color outside the palace. She wore no veil, not wanting to appear already the bride, so Priya pinned her hair into a simple crown of curls with a single pearl hanging to her forehead.

She hoped her attire would meet the approval of the prince's subjects.

When they left for the prince's receiving room, Priya and Aniri took care to move slowly and keep their breath. Janak hovered close behind them, silent as always. Aniri couldn't tell if he labored to breathe like they did, even with him constantly at her side, ever vigilant for attacks. The welcome to the capital had been so warm, Aniri couldn't imagine one of the prince's people leaping out to plunge a dagger through her heart.

Then again, Malik had posted several guards outside her room, as if he expected barbarians—*different* barbarians—to storm the gates of his estate at any moment. Janak seemed none too reassured by their presence either. He pulled open the door to the prince's receiving room, and Aniri restrained herself from making an awkward sound of surprise when she saw the prince.

His royal Jungali clothes bore no resemblance to the Dharian ones he had worn at court, nor to his rugged traveling attire. He was encased almost entirely in black, his trim jacket clasped at his neck with a small, bronze crest. As she stepped closer, the fabric of his jacket seemed to come alive with glints of black diamond, but it was merely brocade with a silver-black thread that caught the light. The coat fell to his knees, revealing black trousers below. The only true color on him was in his clear amber eyes, which stared at her with the same amazement and disbelief as when she first accepted his proposal. A trill of worry swept through her. Had she made the wrong choice with her dress?

The prince stepped toward her, but an older man slid between them, reaching Aniri first. His movement was smooth, like a panther moving through the dark, and the midnight-black, knee-length leather coat, slicked-back hair, and dark, tightly-trimmed beard added to the illusion. His thin copper-wire spectacles gave a hint of learnedness, but beneath them, his dark eyes were still predatory. They raked over Aniri and her outfit in a way she would have found insulting if she wasn't concerned she had dressed badly for the occasion.

She felt Janak's presence at her shoulder. The look hadn't escaped his notice either. Then the older man smiled, a thing that more resembled a leer and caused creases to race across his face. He pressed his hands together, the black gloves covering them squeaking slightly as he did so, and gave a very small bow.

"Arama, Princess Aniri. Welcome to Jungali."

She bowed in return but wasn't quite sure what to say.

The prince sent a barely concealed glare toward the older man, which was clearly ignored, then said, "Princess

Aniri of Dharia, please meet General Garesh of Sik Province."

"Arama, General Garesh," Aniri said, bowing again. "It's my pleasure to be here."

"Indeed. I would imagine so. It's not often we have Dharian royalty grace us with their esteemed presence." The general could give Janak instructions in how to insult a royal while appearing to show respect. "I'm sure our country must seem a poor, bedraggled cousin compared to the riches of Dharia."

"I… I find your country quite beautiful, actually." Aniri inwardly cursed her stumbling, even more certain she had violated some Jungali dress code with her Dharian fashions. "The views are stunning."

"That is true," the general conceded, but the sly look didn't leave his face. "But make no mistake. The beauty masks a bitter coldness that must be shocking for a refined lady such as yourself. Our mountain weather can be quite brutal. And unexpected."

Aniri's lips pressed tight. She knew a threat when she heard it.

"Speaking of which," the general continued, "I trust our reparations have arrived safely to enrich Dharia's coffers? Jungali has so little to spare, I would hate to think any of it was lost in transport."

Now Aniri was truly speechless, and the prince's glare was plain on his face. He inclined his head to Aniri. "Can I have a word with you in private, princess?" He took a half step back and gestured for her to follow.

"Of course," she said, relieved the prince was extricating her from the general's hostility.

Janak gave her a wary glance, but she stayed him with a nod, and he turned his attention back to General Garesh. The two of them were a matched set: Garesh's spectacles a thin disguise over his simmering looks of malice, and Janak's formal Dharian uniform riding lightly over his restrained raksaka strength. Priya retreated to the door to flirt with one of the prince's uniformed guards, and the prince took Aniri's elbow and steered her towards the far end of the expansive and richly appointed receiving room. They passed a fireplace crackling in the center of the room, adding heat to the already too stuffy air, and the prince stopped near the balcony where they were apparently to address his people. She could see the flashes of color from the throngs outside, and their murmur floated in through the flung-open crystal doors. The guards, General Garesh, Janak, and Priya lingered by the entrance, and the size of the room and the noise of the crowd allowed some measure of privacy.

Tension gathered in Aniri's stomach. "Is there something wrong, Prince Malik? Have I caused some offense?" Her face grew even warmer than the room. "Is it the way I've dressed? Have I missed some protocol?"

"What?" He seemed befuddled by her question for a moment, then smiled. "No, no. You are the very picture of a Queen today, Aniri. Please ignore General Garesh's ill temper. He has no love for Dharians. Or royalty of any kind." Then the prince's gaze fell to steadily examine his shiny, black boots.

"Then what troubles you?" Aniri glanced at the balcony. "Has something gone wrong with the plans for the announcement?"

He looked up again. "Can I—" He stopped. "Would you be willing to—" He was flustered. In a matter of seconds, she saw more emotions pass across his face than she had seen in the entire time she had known him.

"Prince Malik, I've agreed to become your Queen. Is there truly something more difficult you wish to ask of

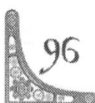

me?"

"May I kiss you, princess?" He let it out in a rush.

She drew back from him. "What?"

"On the balcony. For the announcement. Just this once, I promise you." The words were tumbling out of his mouth.

"But..." Now it was her turn to have a loss for words. "But I thought we agreed. No children. No... no... I thought it was understood it wouldn't be that kind of... arrangement." Her face flamed with a heat that put the fireplace to shame. She fought the impulse to flee. What had she gotten herself into?

"No, Aniri, I swear to the gods," Prince Malik said. "I'm not going back on our agreement. It's just that... well, word had traveled about the incident at the train station."

"With Devesh?" Aniri asked, horrified. But of course, gossip like that would travel faster than shashees and flying cable carriages.

"Who is Devesh?" Prince Malik asked, looking lost again. "Oh, yes, the young man on the platform. Your lover."

Aniri swallowed. She had never heard him called that before, but of course he was, even if their trysts were limited to fevered kisses and clutched embraces in the Queen's tea garden and under dark bridges.

"Word has traveled, and my people were already suspicious that you were not here for your stated purpose." He glanced at General Garesh, who watched them steadily from across the room. "And General Garesh is certain of it."

Janak appeared coiled tighter than a clockwork spring, his attention flipping between the general and Aniri. She was afraid he might become unsprung at any moment. Had her mission already been found out?

"I want my people to love you as their Queen, but you have to understand how mistrustful the Jungali are of anyone from the plains. I've been trying to counter the rumors since we arrived earlier, but it is proving difficult, and General Garesh's presence isn't helping. The only way to truly quash the rumors, I believe, is to perhaps convince them this marriage is not simply arranged."

"What do you mean?" Aniri dragged her gaze away from the menace in General Garesh's face.

"My people cannot conceive that you would be so noble as to resign yourself to our *barbarian* lands simply to procure peace. I thought maybe they would, once you were here... but then the incident on the platform..."

"What do they think I'm here for?" She searched his amber eyes. Did he suspect the truth?

"To spy on us. To secretly start a war." He gave her a tight grin. "To assassinate me perhaps."

He said these possibilities as if they were absurd. She couldn't stop the short release of breath in relief. Of course, she *was* there to spy, but in hopes of averting a war, not starting one. And she was genuinely shocked his people would think her capable of assassinating anyone.

It wasn't a struggle to affect a wounded reaction to that possibility. "Do they really hate Dharians so much?"

"Yes, Aniri, I'm afraid they do. There's only one thing they might believe would overcome your, uh, natural tendency toward such violence and deception."

"And what would that be?"

"Love."

Aniri was speechless again, a lump in her throat rising from nowhere. "Love."

Prince Malik sighed. "The Jungali people are fiercely loyal, just as you said before. We believe family is a tighter

bond than almost anything. But we are also a very romantic people, and fiercely passionate in other ways. If my people believed we were truly in love, that the marriage was more than simply politics, they would have to change their thinking. It could be the foundation of a true and lasting alliance, building on the support of the people behind it."

The tightness in Aniri's throat eased. "Won't they be suspicious if we announce we are madly in love?" she asked with raised eyebrows. "After all, I just arrived. And we only met a few days ago, when you already had come to ask for my hand. And there's the matter of the incident at the train station... it begs for disbelief."

"Yes, but we could say we've been secretly meeting for months," he said breathlessly. "I've made several trips to Dharia in the past few months—"

"You have?"

"Yes," he said patiently, "for trading partnerships, working on arrangements to strengthen the bonds between our peoples, hoping that might help solidify my reign—"

"Did the Queen know about this?" Aniri cut him off again. Would her mother have told her? Did she even know?

"I'm sure she did. That's not important. What *is* important is it's plausible I have been having secret rendezvous with the Third Daughter of Dharia during that time."

"I see." And it almost did seem plausible, the way he said it. A tightness drew across her chest, and she wasn't sure if it was the mountain air or that she had no good reason not to agree with the prince's suggestion.

"I've also made trips to the western coast of Dharia, in the sea town of Timbar, where perhaps we could have met without onlookers noticing either one of us."

Aniri breathed through the constriction in her lungs. "You've given this some thought."

He looked helplessly at her.

"Well," Aniri said, trying to play her part. "I suppose Timbar does have excellent food."

He lost the panicked look and smiled. "And the black sand beaches on the eastern shores near Chira are very mysterious and romantic."

"Have you been to the lava flows?" For a moment, she forgot she was pretending. That was where her father found the black sand he'd brought back to her mother. She had always planned to go there, someday.

"I could have." The prince's smile grew. "In fact, I'm certain I snuck away to Chira during a trade meeting last fall. I can find other times when we could have met as well. The rumors could start immediately." His smile faded, replaced by the earnest look he usually wore. "What do you say, princess?"

"Definitely the shores of Chira," Aniri said with a smile. "I've always wanted to see the black sand shores there."

He hesitated. "I meant the kiss."

"Oh." Aniri's smile dimmed. Did the rumors travel as quickly from Jungali to Dharia as they did in the reverse? Would Devesh be soon hearing about her supposed secret love affair with the Jungali prince? Even as she thought it, she knew the answer. It was far too good of a story to keep quiet—it would run like brushfire down the mountains and burn down any chance of Devesh waiting for her to return. But she wouldn't be able to stay long enough to find out about the Jungali's flying weapon if she were sent packing just after she arrived. And now that she had seen the cable carriages, it didn't seem so impossibly strange that the Jungali might have advanced technology secreted away in their many mountain ravines.

She took a deep breath. "If we are in love, then I suppose we must kiss."

Prince Malik took her hands in his, like he had in her mother's chamber. "Thank you, princess. I promise, this isn't something we will need to do often. Only whatever is necessary for the rumors to take hold."

"I can't imagine it will take much," Aniri said, forcing a smile to her face. "It's too good a story not to believe."

He returned her smile, shyly. "I am sorry. For the pain this must be causing you. I wish... there was a better way."

She nodded. "As do I, Prince Malik."

He gave her a curt nod, then dropped one of her hands, leading her with the other toward the balcony. "Are you ready, your highness?"

With her assent, he led her through the doorway to the balcony outside. The bright mountain sun seemed to steal what was left of her breath. Or perhaps it was the colorful crowd of people thronged below them. The balcony was pure white mountain granite and gleamed from a million tiny points of reflection. A steel transmitter sat propped on the edge, its silver orb surrounded by a halo of sound sensing instrumentation. The prince had told her the balcony was wired for transmission throughout Bhakti, but much of the overcrowded city would be able to see them from their rooftops and windows. The colors of the city dazzled her eyes, blending in a way that made it difficult for her see properly.

The prince spoke into the transmitter, greeting his people. A snapping sound rose up, the crowd quickly drowning him out with their applause. Their hands and fingers rippled like wind-tossed grain. The prince waved to his people, and squeezed Aniri's hand, prompting her to wave as well. The snapping went on for some time, and there was no ability or sense to speak above it. Gradually, it faded, and the prince spoke into the transmitter again.

"It gives me great pleasure to introduce to my fellow Jungali, to my beloved Bajirans, the future Queen of all our mountain provinces." His voice rang out clear and calm, and if Aniri didn't know better, she would have thought she heard a genuine affection in his voice, not only for his people, but for her. He was playing his part very well. She would have to do the same.

He turned to her, pulling her close with their clasped hands and gently touching her cheek with the tips of his fingers. "Are you ready to be Queen Aniri?" he asked, although she understood he was really asking permission, again, for the kiss. She nodded, and he dipped his head to press his lips to hers.

Aniri didn't know what to expect. Five minutes ago, kissing the Prince of Jungali on his balcony certainly didn't reside anywhere within the universe of her thoughts. But a quick peck on the lips wasn't what the prince had in mind. His hand slipped to the back of her neck, his kiss soft but urgent, as if he wanted to make sure his people saw his passion for her. She tried to picture Devesh, but that only ripped pain through her chest. Instead, she closed her eyes and pressed deeper into the kiss, lifting up on her toes to return the urgency and make it appear as genuine as possible. A roar filled her ears, and when the prince pulled away, she realized it was the crowd below, snapping and calling their approval. Aniri teetered on her toes, then sank back to the stone floor of the balcony.

She blinked and looked to Malik for some indication of what to do next. He had already turned back to his people, smiling and waving. She did the same, a strange pounding in her head seeming to match the tempo of the crowd. The kaleidoscope of color blurred before her, and she suddenly remembered to breathe again.

Only she couldn't seem to get enough air.

She kept trying to pull deeper and deeper gasps, but it wasn't enough. Why did people live so high in the sky that there wasn't air left to breathe? She jerkily squeezed Prince Malik's hand. He needed to get her off the balcony before she passed out in front of his people. He glanced at her and seemed to realize the problem at once. Slipping his arm around her waist to brace her, he gave a final wave to the crowd and pulled her toward the door.

eleven

Prince Malik's arm around Aniri's waist was the only thing holding her up.

She grasped the slippery fabric at the back of the prince's jacket, trying to keep the dizziness from sending her to the floor. He tightened his one-armed embrace and practically carried her over the threshold and back into his overly warm receiving room. She still couldn't get enough air, and the fine draperies on the walls blurred into a colorful stream as the room spun.

Janak appeared out of nowhere. "What did you do to her?" There was low-pitched danger in his voice, and his iron-strong arms yanked her from the prince's relatively gentle embrace.

"No—" Aniri gasped, but the effort to speak was too much to manage. Instead, she raised her hand to stop Janak from hurting the prince, but it only wavered in the air and landed on Janak's face. He brushed her hand away and bent to lift her completely off the ground. She was just as glad—having his hands full with her kept him from attacking Prince Malik.

"Not," Aniri wheezed between gasps for breath, "the prince's,"—gasp—"fault." Janak only scowled. She closed her eyes and willed the world to stop spinning, but her head only lolled against the rough fabric of his uniform. A pounding started on her temples, and a pressing headache welled up behind her eyes.

"My lady!" Aniri heard Priya arrive at her side. "What is wrong with her?"

"It's the thin air," Prince Malik said. "We came up the mountain so quickly... I shouldn't have asked her to do the announcement so soon. She needs rest and plenty of water."

The iron bands of Janak's arms tightened around her, and she sensed they were moving for real now, not the surreal motion inside her head. She kept her eyes tightly shut, pressing the heel of her hand to them and trying to shove the pain away from her skull. Janak didn't say a word. His movements were smooth but gained speed. She was thankful for once to have his strength at her disposal, to whisk her away from the embarrassment of nearly fainting in front of the prince and his people.

Her people.

Soon they were back in her room. Janak carefully laid her down on a bed with silken covers that felt cool against her skin. All she wanted was to crawl under the heaped cushions and feather-down blankets and wait for the headache to pass, but Priya pried her hands from her head and forced a glass of water into them. Aniri drank as much as she could, then lay back and watched the draped sheer fabric that flounced the top of her four-poster bed spin in a dance without music or actual motion. She couldn't decide if it was better or worse with her eyes open, but she shut them anyway.

It took nearly two hours, and several glasses of water tended to her by Priya, before the room stopped moving. When she finally opened her eyes again, she found Priya had shut out the bright afternoon light with heavy drapes drawn across the windows.

"Are you feeling better, my lady?" Priya sat at the end of Aniri's bed, far enough not to disturb her, but close enough to be on hand. Aniri gingerly sat up, afraid the headache would rush back.

Priya edged closer, but Aniri waved her off. "I can't believe the thinness of the air could render me so... insensible."

Priya leaned toward her on the bed and said with a soft smile, "Perhaps it was the prince's kiss that stole your breath."

Aniri grimaced. "I didn't swoon because of the prince, Priya. The kiss was simply... necessary."

"Oh yes." Priya's eyes were wide and her nod fervent. "Completely necessary. I agree."

Aniri shook her head, but that only brought back a sense that the room was about to spin, so she stopped.

"Prince Malik says the air sickness is common." Janak's voice came from a desk in the corner of the room where his black boots were propped. "Visitors from the plains experience shortened breath and sometimes dizziness in the first few days after arrival."

"How well are you faring, Janak?" Aniri asked.

"Fortunately, this mountain sickness has only afflicted you and your delicate disposition, your most royal highness." He was back to insulting her, which Aniri took to mean he thought she would survive. "While

you've been recovering your health, I've received a message from your mother."

"Have you?" Aniri blinked. Her eyes were still having difficulty seeing properly. She eased her bare feet—Priya must have removed her shoes—to the cool stones of the floor and shuffled toward Janak's carved wooden desk. She held on to the posts of the bed as she went, still unsteady. Priya fluttered around her. When Aniri reached the desk, Janak waved Priya off, a motion she ignored. Laid out next to Janak was a contraption so complex, Aniri's blurry eyes had difficulty deciphering it.

Janak frowned. "Please send your handmaiden away so we may conduct our business."

"We are the only Dharians deep inside enemy territory," Aniri said. "Do you not think that perhaps we should trust each other? Priya already knows most of our secrets, anyway, Janak. Probably more than you."

Janak narrowed his eyes at Priya, who gave him a haughty look that only soured his temper more. "As you wish, your supreme eminence," he said to Aniri. "Perhaps we should call in the prince's guard outside the door as well? He'll know as soon as your handmaiden goes whispering favors from him."

It was Priya's turn to glare, which Aniri interrupted with a hand on her shoulder. "This requires the utmost secrecy, Priya. Please tell me we can count on you to keep it."

"Of course, your majesty." Priya did a small curtsey that made Aniri smile.

"It will disappoint you to know we are not here for marriage or swoon-worthy kisses or romance of any kind," Aniri said. "Our mission is espionage. And I imagine we will need your skills if we are to find the Jungali's secret flying machine for the Queen."

"Oh." Priya's mouth still formed the circle of that word long after sound stopped coming out.

Aniri grinned, then turned to Janak and gestured to the box splayed before him. "What is this device?" The mechanism had concentric wheels, a small crank, gears throughout, and a series of keys with odd shaped symbols. She couldn't discern the function of any part of it.

"This is your mother's aetheroceiver."

Aniri nodded. She knew of the devices, of course, but she had never seen one. There were only a few, and the Queen restricted their use to those who had need of them. Janak proceeded to fold up various flaps and hinged parts, tucking them neatly inside one another like nested boxes, until the entire thing collapsed into a rectangular box no bigger than her feet put together. There seemed no obvious way to make it come back apart again.

"In the event that something happens to me, princess, I want you to know how to open and operate it yourself."

Aniri nodded gravely, not missing Janak's dark undertone. He always believed the world was one breath away from catastrophe, but in this case, the danger they faced if the prince discovered their true intentions was probably high enough to warrant it.

Janak placed three fingers on three symbols along the ornately carved brass surface of the box: a clutch of wheat, the Queen's crown, and a feather. When all three were pressed simultaneously, a clicking sounded deep within the device, and the box loosened itself, slowly unfolding before her eyes. When it came to rest, it had returned to its original position.

"They are crafted in pairs, and this one is matched

with the aetheroceiver in your mother's office," Janak said. "They are actually Samirian in design, replicated by our Dharian tinkers. The Samir think themselves very clever with their mechanical devices, but the technology is not so difficult to copy."

Janak showed her how to fold it up again, and then he pointed to the three symbols.

"Can you remember them?" He wasn't mocking her, and for a change, he appeared deadly earnest. She matched his serious tone with a sharp nod. The symbols were obvious, at least to a member of the royal family. The clutch of wheat was straight from the Dharian royal crest, symbolic of Dharia's breadbasket plains, which fed the world. Several crowns adorned the box, in various sizes and orientations, but the one belonging to the Queen was clear to someone who had grown up knowing she would never wear it: a tiny pearl drop in the center gave it away amongst its many cousins. And the feather—it was her mother's nickname for her father. A personal thing. Would the Queen have shared the significance of it with Janak? Aniri had a hard time imagining that conversation, and it brought a queasy feeling to her stomach.

She brushed that aside with a deep breath and quickly pressed all three symbols.

The device unfolded itself before her.

"While the aetheroceivers speak to each other," Janak said, turning his dark gaze up to her, the seriousness making it sharp as well, "it's still possible another aetheroceiver could intercept the signal. Especially when the device itself was originally designed by one's enemies."

Aniri didn't think of the Samir as their enemies, but technically Janak was right, so she didn't correct him. He pointed to two concentric spinner wheels lying flat on one side. One wheel was etched with the strange symbols of the keys, while the other contained letters.

"It's a code," Aniri guessed.

Janak turned the outer wheel, one click for each letter-symbol combination. "The code provides encryption. An additional level of security for the transmission. Your mother and I agreed on the key before we left." He clicked the wheel to a stop. "Align the triangle with the letter A. Then the wheels act as a decoder. Here is the message I received earlier from the Queen."

Janak pulled a long, curled tape from a cubby within the machine. It was punched with the symbols on the keys, and below each one, in Janak's meticulous print, were letters that spelled out a message.

KISS WELL RECEIVED IN DHARIA WELL DONE SEND INTEL

Aniri braced herself on the desk. The rumors were even faster than brushfire, it seemed. Hours later, her mother no doubt expected Aniri would have a full report on her true mission. Instead she had spent the last couple of hours in a swoon in her bed. It was rather monstrously embarrassing. Aniri straightened from the desk.

"Please send a reply," Aniri said. "Ask my mother if the prince has previously traveled to Dharia."

Janak frowned, but didn't question it. He took out a small notebook tucked into a pocket at the back of the aetheroceiver. He jotted a message in it:

DID PRINCE TRAVEL PREVIOUS TO DHARIA

He carefully consulted his encryption wheel, assigning the appropriate symbols to each number. Then he wound the side crank of the aetheroceiver several dozen times, setting in motion a whir of clicks inside the

device. When it was thrumming, he carefully tapped each key in sequence, sending the message.

Then he turned to Aniri. "You seem to have made some strides in gaining the prince's good graces, your most royal highness," Janak said drily. Aniri glared at him. "Perhaps you can put that advantage to work."

The aetheroceiver began to spit out more of the curling tape, a return message. He pulled it out, quickly consulting his decrypter and making careful marks on the tape.

YES WHY

Janak looked to her.

"Just checking one of the prince's stories," Aniri said. "I'm not sure how truthful he is being. But I think you are right, Janak. I need to have a more intimate conversation with the prince if we hope to make any progress on finding this flying machine." She gestured to the aetheroceiver. "Please tell my mother we will report back soon."

While Janak scribbled and transcribed the message, Aniri searched the desk for parchment and found a quill pen as well, but no ink. The pen had a large crystal barrel with some apparent clockwork inside. It seemed designed to twist, and when she did, it hissed. A tiny drop of ink appeared at the nib, so she hastened to write her note. When she was done, she untwisted the pen to stop whatever pressure was pushing out the ink. She folded the paper and gave it to Priya, who had been reading over her shoulder the entire time.

"Please deliver this to the prince."

While Priya scurried off with her note, Aniri turned to Janak. "The prince spoke about the four generals in charge of the military in the different provinces. He seems to think they are key to solidifying his hold on the

crown."

"The military is always the key to holding power." That, of course, was how Janak would see things. But the Queen's court was driven far more by political intrigue than a jostling of military might.

"A good Queen rules by the consent of her governed." Aniri was surprised to find herself quoting her mother. "However, maybe Jungali is so riven by internal strife that military power reigns stronger than love of Queen and country." Although the prince certainly seemed as concerned with the temper of his people as her mother often was. "If the flying machine exists, it seems logical it would fall under the purview of one of the generals to maintain and operate."

"Indeed," Janak said. "Which means that general would have the most knowledge of its inner workings as well as how it could best be used in an attack on Dharia."

"I'm not entirely convinced the Jungali mean to go to war with us," Aniri said. "Perhaps the generals are infighting to gain control of the provinces for themselves. General Garesh seems to pose a particular threat, and he apparently has little love for royalty. Maybe he means to put Jungali under military rule. We need to learn more about him."

"I don't care for the idea of you having any more contact with General Garesh," Janak said. "He is certain to be more dangerous than our young prince. And more likely to want to kill you than kiss you."

"Perhaps I should bring a dagger. For any unwanted advances," Aniri said coolly. Not that she cared to be alone with General Garesh any more than Janak wanted.

Janak pushed back the aetheroceiver and laced his fingers. "Your supremely royal highness may not recognize it, but my job here is simple: I am to return you

alive to her majesty's court. It is my first, and only, duty as raksaka. One I imagine will be challenging enough, given your suitability—or should I say lack of suitability—for this mission, either in training or temper."

Heat rose fast in her cheeks. Aniri opened her mouth to object, but Janak raised a hand to cut her off.

"The Queen did not consult me on the wisdom of sending you here. And if you fail in your mission, that is… not of tremendous concern to me. However, I will not fail in mine. The Queen has tasked me with keeping you alive, a direct order from the crown that I will follow or die trying. Therefore, I will not allow you to take unnecessary risks with your life, no matter the outcome otherwise."

Janak's words stoked the heat in her face to near combustion. She said nothing for a moment, trying to find words that would not prove her to be exactly as Janak accused: reckless. Childish. Ill tempered. Finally, she managed, "You can think what you wish of me, Janak, but I'm in no hurry to put myself in needless danger."

"Your supreme eminence and I have a difference of opinion on the meaning of the word *needless*."

Aniri felt her temperature drop a little. At least he was taking her seriously. She folded her arms. "My mother must have also instructed you to help with my mission."

Janak leaned back in his chair and folded his arms as well. "The Queen only instructed me to protect your life."

"Well, *I* am instructing you to help me in my mission."

They stared at each other.

She knew Janak well enough to realize a battle of wills was lost before she started. She had to strike where he lived, the one thing he cared about above life itself: the crown. Her mother. Aniri took a deep breath. "This isn't just about me, Janak, and whether I fail in my duty or not. If this flying weapon exists, the Queendom is in danger. The *Queen* will be in danger. You need to assist me where you can, for her safety as well."

His dark eyes flashed but the rest of his face was impassive.

Aniri gritted her teeth. A compromise, then. "Perhaps I don't need to meet with the generals." She gestured to the aetheroceiver. "If the flying machine exists, someone must be communicating with the prince about it. An undertaking such as building a flying warship cannot take place in complete secrecy—it must leave a trace of itself, if only in the prince's most personal sanctum. The answer may be hidden in a communique or a secretly held file. What I need is access to such a place, somewhere he would allow in only his most trusted advisors."

"And you think he counts you as one of those?" Janak's eyebrows rose. "Because of one kiss?"

"Yes," Aniri said stiffly. "Because he needed it, and I allowed it. I've gained some measure of trust from him already. But if I'm to glean anything more from him, I will need to spend time alone with him. Without a raksaka shadowing my every move."

Janak narrowed his eyes. "I suppose the young prince is not the type to murder you by his own hand in his private sanctum."

"Janak," Aniri said, throwing her hands out in frustration. "The prince is the least likely Jungali to want me dead. He believes I am the key to his holding the crown."

Janak hesitated, studying her, then tilted his head in

silent agreement. Which was all the approval she supposed she would get. Hopefully, when she survived a private audience with the prince, Janak wouldn't think of her as quite such a foolish girl anymore.

As to whether she could actually fulfill her mission here, gaining the prince's trust enough to discover his closest held military secrets… unfortunately, Janak's words rang far too close to the truth about that. She was trained in fencing, climbing, and avoiding the court as much as could be allowed the Third Daughter of the Queen. She was possibly the least likely person to succeed in a mission of espionage that required navigating the politics of a country she barely knew.

But she had no choice. Her future depended on it.

twelve

"Thank you for agreeing to meet with me, Prince Malik."

Aniri had worn one of her more bedazzling dresses, in case that might lull the prince into thinking she was making an entirely social call. While a servant laid out tea service, Aniri cast a casual glance around Malik's private office. It was adorned with personal items. Perhaps they had stories behind them, like her mother's relics. Discussing them might prompt the prince to lay down his guard while she looked for evidence of the flying machine. Malik dismissed the servant with a flick of his finger, and the door close quickly behind him.

They were alone.

"I'm simply relieved you are feeling better, Aniri," Prince Malik said. "The guilt of rushing you in front of the crowd right after your arrival was weighing heavy on me."

"I'm sure the thin air would have affected me either way. But I am glad that it's passed."

"And please…" He came around the edge of his desk, then leaned back against it, his long legs stretching near where she sat in an ornate stuffed chair. "You needn't call me Prince Malik, especially when we're in private."

"Malik, then, if that's your preference." She smiled her most winning smile up at him.

He returned it, then shook his head. "I forgot about your custom. Malik is my family name. My given name is Ashoka."

"Oh," Aniri said, put off balance for a moment. "Forgive me, Prince, um, Ashoka."

"Well that does sound awkward, doesn't it? How about just Ash? That's what my friends call me."

"Are we friends?"

"No." His face fell into a mock severity. "We are secret lovers, mad for each other. Haven't you heard?" Then he grinned again.

"So the rumors are working, then?"

"Splendidly."

She adjusted her seating and leaned back to gamely inspect the prince. He was out of his formal all-black attire and back into clothing similar to his travel wear. His linen shirt was open at the neck, and his pants billowed slightly before tucking into his boots. He wore the golden loop earrings again, and she tried hard not to stare, still unused to the sight of jewelry on men. She noticed for the first time a woven leather bracelet on his wrist, and it reminded her of the braided one her father had given her, only of more sturdy construction. She'd left hers in her room. It was the kind of thing she wore for good luck when climbing down walls to see Devesh, not meeting with foreign princes in order to spy on them. Although spying seemed the more dangerous of the two activities at the moment. She pushed aside thoughts of Dev before they leaked out onto her face.

"Do you think General Garesh is more convinced of the genuineness of our marriage now?" Aniri asked. "Or is he still suspicious of me?"

Prince Malik—no *Ash*, Aniri reminded herself—folded his arms. She should endeavor to use the familiarity now that the prince had offered it.

"I'm sure he sees through it," the prince said, "but it doesn't matter. He will bend to the people's will, along with the other generals, just as I must. Our communities, our families, are too tightly woven, filling the walls of our mountain capitals too snugly for an autocratic approach to governing. But surely your Queen understands this as well. I hear the people of Dharia are very content under her rule."

It irked Aniri to talk about her mother; plus she needed to steer the conversation back to the general. "Most of the people love my mother, it's true. But while everyone at court pretends to adore her, there are many who would just as soon slip a dagger in her back." Aniri had left her dagger in her room, even when Janak pressed her to take it. Coming armed to a social call was hardly the way to win the prince's confidence. "But surely it's the same here. Are the generals all equal in their attempts to dislodge you from the throne?"

"No," Prince Malik said. "Of them all, General Garesh would most especially like to see my head on a pike."

The image from her dream, with her head on a pike, surged forward and caused her to shudder involuntarily.

She shifted in her seat to mask it, uncrossing and crossing her legs under her layers of silk skirt. Finally, when she recovered, she said, "Does General Garesh strive to take your place as king?"

"He would prefer there were no monarchy at all."

"He prefers a military rule?"

"Yes. Or at least one based on merit, not bloodlines. It doesn't help that the monarchy sprang from Bajir, and there are a hundred years of bad blood between Bajir and Sik provinces. Sik is the poorest of the regions—it is truly a harsh existence there, and they have the weakest attachment to the crown. I'm sure he wishes I had passed on with my mother." Prince Malik sighed. "Our past is sometimes a weight around our necks, dragging us back into the dark times of anarchy. I would like to take us forward with trade and peace agreements, but Garesh sees no advantage to that. He's a fiercely proud Jungali. He believes our provinces deserve a greater standing in the world and the only way forward is through military strength. The tribal ways still appeal to many Jungali. Garesh is not alone in believing military might is the solution to every problem. "

"Maybe Garesh is the one behind the rumors of the flying machine."

The prince's eyes turned cold, and he pushed up from the desk. "There is no flying machine, Aniri."

She winced, cursing herself inwardly for approaching the subject so directly. "Of course. My mother reassured me of that before I left." Artful spying was obviously not her strength.

The prince had turned his back on her, retreating behind his desk again. She rose up from her seat, holding her hands wide. "It's simply that everyone in Bajir now believes we are in love, a rumor that didn't take much prompting. I was only saying perhaps Garesh could just as easily spread rumors of a flying machine, if that would serve to destroy your attempts for peace."

The prince picked up a frame on his desk, which Aniri couldn't see the face of, sighed and replaced it. "You are probably right. Garesh is certainly doing everything he can to bring a quick end to my reign."

Aniri trailed her fingers along the prince's heavy, dark wood desk as she came around the end, taking time to examine his personal effects. There was a tiny shashee carved from obsidian and clad in brass armor, with even its horns tipped in metal. A royal symbol of the Jungali provinces? Or homage to the mountain goddess Devpahar? The beast looked more ready for war than the contemplation of peaceful wisdom.

Next to the beast lay a dagger. The sheath was highly ornamental, but the grip looked plain and well worn. She touched the weapon gently. The jewels encrusted on it sparkled, then went dim as she passed. She glanced over her shoulder. What she had thought was merely a window at the far end of the room was in fact a door to a stone balcony with an expansive view. The prince's office must be on the side of the estate with the sheer cliff she had seen coming in. Which made it highly inaccessible, no doubt on purpose.

Turning back to Prince Malik, she said, "This is a beautiful weapon. Is there some significance to it?"

The prince glanced at the knife. "It was my brother, Toshan's." He met her halfway and stopped her from coming completely around the desk. He unsheathed the dagger. It gleamed at the edge, recently sharpened, but the blade itself was aged. "Tosh had it when he fell from a third story window. There was blood on the knife, and I don't believe it was his. I think he was using it to defend himself from a Sik marauder. I had asked him to accompany a trade mission to Dharia, but they only made it as far as the trading station at the border when the Sik gang attacked. They ransacked the station and disappeared into the hills. The murderers were never caught." The prince sheathed the blade and set it in its place again.

The familiar wrenching of justice denied squeezed her heart. It was a pain Aniri knew well, even if the Sik barbarians weren't the same as the Samirian thieves who murdered her father. "I am so sorry, Ash. I know what it means to lose family like that." She laid a hand on his, which was still resting on the sheathed dagger. "Do you think the Sik were targeting your brother?"

Prince Malik took a breath and let it out slowly. "I'm certain they were. Everyone knew Tosh was the Queen's favorite. It was a strike to her heart." Then he held up his hand, the one with the bracelet, and made a fist. "This was also his. Just some handicraft he picked up from his travels in the provinces, but he liked it. Said it reminded him to keep the old Jungali ways close, even as we brought our provinces forward into the future."

A strange awkwardness made her hold her breath. "You must have been very close," she said softly.

"We were brothers," he said simply, and Aniri felt something stir inside her. Like the time in the garden, when they first met: the prince had *moved* her. With his words and the passion in them. Before it had been his nobility, and now his pure love for his dead brother. It pulled at her, and at the same time, somehow shamed her that she was standing before him in subterfuge.

When she didn't reply, he continued, "My brother, Tosh, is the reason I fight so hard to keep my reign, Aniri. He has two small girls who do not understand why their father didn't come home from the trade mission I sent him on. Not that I could have held him back if I tried. Tosh was working for peace, always. I promised his wife I wouldn't let his death tear our provinces apart. That would have been the opposite of everything he worked for, everything he dreamed of. When my mother passed… well, now it falls to me to ensure my brother's death brings peace, not war."

Looking into the prince's pale eyes, Aniri forgot her purpose. Where they were so cold before, now they held a pain she understood. The moment was suddenly too intense, and she cast her eyes down to the desk, scouring it for a change in subject. "It is clear you have the love of your people in Bajir, in any event."

"With your help." His voice was soft. He hadn't moved away.

She gave him a bright smile. "And hopefully the rest of Jungali will approve of me as well."

"I can't imagine it any other way."

Desperate to avoid the intensity of the prince's gaze, she glanced over his shoulder. A glint on the high shelf behind him caught her eye: a familiar metallic box was bracing the end of a row of leather-bound books. She stepped around the prince, pretending to examine the contents of the shelf. As she got closer, she realized exactly what the box was: an aetheroceiver. Like her mother's, only this one was iron with flared tips at the corners and different etchings. The question was: who had its twin? Obviously she could do nothing about it now, but just knowing the aetheroceiver sat so near made her heart pound. She picked a book at random off the shelf.

"Do you mind?" She cast a glance at the prince, who was watching her every move. "I love to read." Which

wasn't exactly true. She loved to fence and climb walls and chase after Samirian courtesans she shouldn't love; but she tolerated reading well enough, and occasionally there was something useful to be found in ancient texts like these.

He grinned. "Please, your majesty. Take it with you. It's a collection of ancient Bajiran love sonnets."

She paused in her unwinding of the rough leather cord that bound the volume. "Poetry, Prince Malik?" She smiled. "You surprise me."

"I told you, we're a romantic people." His grin grew sly, the sadness fleeing away. He leaned against the corner of the desk once more. Over his shoulder, she noticed a second balcony, beyond the prince's and one floor up. She wouldn't have recognized it necessarily, but for a brief moment, Priya shook out a blanket over the balcony's edge, then retreated back inside.

Aniri tore her gaze away before her face could betray her surprise and delight. A plan had sprung up in her mind.

"If you don't mind parting with it, I think I will borrow this." Aniri wrapped the poetry tome back in its cord again. "Maybe it will help me to better understand your people." She drifted past him to the door of the balcony. "You have a beautiful view, Prince Malik."

"Would you like to go outside? I believe it's still warm."

When he opened the door, it didn't appear to be locked. Once they stepped outside, it was clear there was no need. The only place to go was straight up to the top of the stone fortress or plummet a thousand feet down to the ravine below.

"You Jungali certainly like your high perches." She strode out to the edge, only glancing to the balcony where she had seen Priya, so as not to give herself away. She judged the distance. It wasn't far. It might be possible.

"It lends a certain perspective." Prince Malik rested his elbows on the tall, white-granite wall surrounding the balcony edge.

"It reminds me of my aetherscope observatory back home. Not because of the rather extreme height, but because it's a place where I can have my solitude." And her skills in escaping it might come in handy to spy here as well.

"I do come out here to think sometimes."

She turned to face him. "Do you read your love poetry aloud to the birds as they race by?" she asked with a mischievous grin. She pretended to look for birds, but was actually checking the wall between their balconies for grips and toeholds.

He chuckled softly. "No. But I do think sometimes how much simpler love would be if I hadn't been born to the crown. If I had the luxury of finding someone who would be only for me and not for my country as well."

She stopped the grin. There was definitely a melancholy side to the prince. "What would this woman be like, the one you would choose if you had the luxury of being a commoner?"

He stared at her with mock seriousness. "She would be beautiful and brilliant, of course."

"Naturally. She would probably need to read up on her poetry as well."

He grinned again. "She would have a wicked sense of humor."

"Wicked as in evil, or wicked as in indulging in the soft arts of love?"

"Oh, definitely the latter."

She couldn't help smiling at that. "And what else? An

eye for art? A love of nature? A strange predilection for picking fruit at its most ripe?"

He grew thoughtful for a moment. "I've always had this image of her with a sword in her hand."

Aniri's eyebrows flew up. "A sword? As in a dagger?"

"No, more of a foil or saber. Somehow I pictured her as a fencer."

Aniri's mouth opened and closed. Did he know she fenced? Was he teasing her? She covered her awkwardness by peering at the dizzying expanse below them. It wasn't unheard of for royalty to fence, but it was an ancient art, leftover from a time when the cavalry carried swords rather than long rifles. Her country hadn't seen war for a hundred years, but if drawn into one, it would rely on steam tanks and warships, not the fencing skills of the Queen's court. Although the Queen's armory might as well be daggers if the Jungali truly possessed a flying weapon.

When she looked back to the prince, he had grown quiet, gazing at some point on the distant mountain peaks. This intimate conversation was meant to pry loose information from the prince about his affairs of war, not the heart. And she didn't expect it to leave her so unsettled.

Aniri pretended to shiver. "I believe it's colder than my attire is meant to withstand after all."

The prince snapped out of his thousand-mile gaze and smiled. "Of course. Let's get you back inside."

On their way in, Aniri was careful to note whether the prince locked the balcony door behind them.

He did not.

thirteen

That evening, it was difficult for Aniri to evict Priya from her room for the night. Both Janak and Priya objected to the propriety of sharing the anteroom next to Aniri's guestroom, but she couldn't convince either one to take a guest room still farther from hers. And Aniri needed her room to herself to carry out her plan—if either of them knew what she intended, they would be violently opposed to it.

Finally, she claimed ill health from the thinness of the air and banished them both, much to Priya's dismay. Even so, Aniri waited until well after dark, when the flickering gaslight under the anteroom door had finally gone out. Janak surely slept with one eye open, so she kept her movements quiet. She stripped her enormous bed of its sheets and carefully twisted them into knots, tied one to the other, mixed with a few of her coats, chosen for the sturdiness of their construction. She intended to keep her promise to Janak about not dying during his watch.

The trick would be finding a good place to attach her handmade rope: there weren't any lion's head parapets conveniently nearby. She could tie it around the desk leg, but she was afraid even its bulk might not be heavy enough to hold her. The bed was farther, but it was the most sturdy thing in her room. Even with all her strength, pressing a shoulder into one of the four posters, she couldn't move it even a hair's breadth. She lashed the rope securely to it, then turned down the last of her gaslamps and gathered up her armful of cobbled-together rope. On the bed, she constructed a lumpy facsimile of herself comprised of pillows under the heavy bedcover. She hoped the dimness would prevent anyone from checking too closely.

She nudged open the balcony door with her foot and pulled up short when she noticed the lights were still on in the prince's study below. She ducked behind the white granite rim of the balcony, her heart pounding before she realized it was unlikely the prince could see her. The twin moons had faded to half-moons, casting only a pale light. The darkened glass of the prince's office would act more as a mirror than a window, given the strength of the gaslamps within.

She eased to sitting and leaned against the cool wall of the balcony, testing her knots and biding her time. Eventually, the prince's lamplights went out. She waited several extra minutes to be sure he had truly left and wasn't planning to return, then tied the rope around her waist.

Aniri carefully climbed on top of the white marble ledge around her balcony, giving thanks that her climbing shoes had been buried in the dozens of trunks that came with her. Priya must have packed them before she knew their travels were not permanent, and Aniri was glad now for such over-zealousness. Her lightweight silk pajamas provided minimal weight and maximum mobility for the climb, and her father's bracelet circled her wrist for good luck.

She was as ready as she would be.

Aniri slowly fed the rope over the edge of the balcony until her end was taut and the rest swung freely in a loop that ended at her waist. A cool draft rose up the side of the fortress, and she peered at the moonlit rocks a thousand feet below. The glittering silver thread of a river snaked between them. She reminded herself that falling a thousand feet was no different than the drop from her observatory back home. Dead would be dead. The only difference would be the size of the pieces left.

Drawing in a breath, she focused instead on her objective: the prince's balcony. One story below and a dozen feet between them. She should be able to use footholds on the wall to walk over, while hopefully not losing her grip. Even if the rope stopped her from plummeting to her death, the jerk might snap her spine.

Janak's heart would probably stop dead if he saw her now.

She held tight to the rope and slowly walked her way down the outside of her balcony, staying as close to the main estate wall as she could. Her breath started to come in gasps, and she whispered a curse. She had forgotten about the effects of the thin air.

Best to make this a quick journey then.

Once she reached the bottom of her balcony, she twisted her feet to gain purchase on the estate wall. Slowly letting out the rope, she wall-walked toward the

prince's balcony, making her way, toehold by toehold, along the gleaming granite. She forgot to breathe until her lungs screamed for air, then gulped in heavy draughts and paused when black stars darted in front of her eyes. She was level with the prince's balcony now, but still a few feet away. Her angle wasn't quite enough. If she let out the rope more, she would be too low. And she couldn't go higher: her feet were already losing traction. If she released her toehold and swung back to her balcony, assuming the bed-anchor held and she let out a little more line, she might get to the prince's balcony on the rebound—or she might crash into it.

Or she could reach for it now. But that would leave only one hand on the rope, and her grip was already weakening.

Her breathing became even more erratic.

She let go of the rope with one hand and reached toward the prince's balcony, adjusting her feet, her grip on the rope sliding slowly down, her hand reaching… reaching… Finally she gripped the edge. She let go of the rope, grasping at the granite with both hands and heaving her body onto the ledge. The rough stone cut into her stomach as she hauled the rest of her body over and dropped to the smooth stone pavers of the balcony.

Her gasping breaths were so loud, she was shocked they didn't wake Janak and Priya, two rooms and an abyss away. She rested a moment, letting the stars clear from her vision, before daring to stand. At least the trip back should be easier. Although she might want to make sure she had caught her breath.

Aniri untied the rope from her waist. The weight of the rope wanted to drag it right off the balcony again. There was no railing, nothing to affix it to, so she was left with carefully winding the remaining length and tucking it into a corner, hoping the friction against the balcony edge would hold it until she returned. If she lost the rope at this point, there would be no getting back to her room undetected. If she was lucky, they wouldn't put her head on a pike, just send her back to Dharia as a spy.

She had better find some information in the prince's office to make it worthwhile.

A quick peek showed nothing inside but shadows and strikes of moonlight across the desk. Her breaths still rushed in the cold summer's night as she slowly turned the doorknob. The door eased open and she was quickly inside.

Aniri went straight for the box and pulled it down to a moonlit spot on the desk. The light also fell across a picture frame, the one the prince had picked up before. She hadn't asked, but looking at it now, she didn't have to. It was Prince Malik's brother dressed in royal garments. The resemblance was striking, down to the dark, straight hair and the light amber eyes. Even in the silver moonlight, Aniri could see he was handsome, but in a boyish way, whereas the prince had the strong jaw and build of a man. A melancholy man, who loved his younger brother so much he would go to any length to preserve the peace in his name.

She glanced at the box in her hands, for a moment tempted to let it keep its secrets. The prince's noble efforts for peace seemed so genuine. His sorrow so real. Unless he was a masterful liar, she couldn't reconcile it with anything but a real desire for peace. Yet... he had turned cold when she asked him directly about the flying machine.

The box would have to give up its secrets.

It was covered with the same closely packed array of symbols as her mother's aetheroceiver. She pressed three

fingers to random choices on the box, all to no avail. There were dozens of the tiny, etched images. She would be there half the night if she had to guess. Perhaps there was some logic behind the code.

She studied the symbols more closely and quickly found one of a cable carriage. Did that represent the Jungali people, like the wheat did for Dharia? Or was it the miner whose shovel loaded coal into the cart by his side? The etching with two men engaged in a swordfight seemed more likely. She thought of the Jungali as club-wielding barbarians, reclusive in their high mountain hideaways, coming down only for raiding parties and war. But that was the Dharian view. How would the Jungali see themselves?

The Jungali were a mountain people—they built cable carriages in the sky and palaces on the sides of cliffs. One of the tiny symbols was a trio of jagged triangles disappearing into a puff of cloud. Aniri placed her finger on that one. The others had to be within a hand's distance. The second symbol had been a crown for Dharia, and there were similarly a half dozen crowns on the box. Aniri had no idea which was the right one, but with only six, she could try them all.

What was the final symbol? If it was personal, like the nickname her mother had for her father, she would have to try every symbol on the box. Maybe it wasn't the nickname, but what it meant: something that captured the heart of her sovereign. Just under her thumb, on the side of the box, was a heart. Would it be so literal? *We are a romantic people*, the prince had said. Did the box belong to the Queen or the prince? Was the mother as sentimental as the son?

Aniri pressed the mountains, the heart, and then each of the crowns in succession. On the fifth crown, the box whirred and clicked. She nearly jumped out of her pajamas with the sound of it racketing around the room. Aniri glanced at the door, afraid a guard would come barreling through at any moment.

But the box unfolded itself on the desk and lay still, waiting for her, and still no guard. She searched and quickly found a scrap of wound tape with messages still decoded on it. There was no small notebook, like Janak had stored in her mother's aetheroceiver, and the message tape was short, as if the last user of the box had forgotten to clear it away before packing the box again. She held the slip under the light so she could read the string of words.

PEOPLE PLEASED WITH KISS GARESH DOUBLED MINING NAVIA

The first part was clear enough, but what was *navia*, and why was Prince Malik's arch-rival General Garesh doubling the mining of it? There were all kinds of rare minerals that were mined in the mountains of Jungali, although mostly they were the source of coal for Dharia. Metalwork came from the mountainous regions of Samir. But navia? She had never heard of it, but that didn't mean much.

Her education in the commerce of Jungali was apparently woeful indeed.

She had hoped for more. There was nothing to support, or deny, the idea of the flying machine, but the prince clearly had a spy in General Garesh's province. He was monitoring the Sik people's response to the announcement of their marriage. He hoped to win their hearts to peace.

What would happen when her mission was complete, and she abandoned the pretense of the marriage? Would it destroy the young prince's attempts to build peace? She tried not to think on that while she quickly folded up the aetheroceiver and placed it exactly where it had been on the high shelf, erasing any evidence of her intrusion into the prince's inner sanctum.

She crept to the balcony door, then froze, hand on the doorknob, looking through the glass toward her guest room

Great billows of gray smoke spilled from her balcony into the mountain air.

fourteen

An orange flame licked the wall above Aniri's balcony. Clouds of black and gray smoke churned and crawled up the estate's granite wall.

Her guest room was on fire.

Even if she was willing to dare another climb across the abyss, there was no returning to her room now. Then she realized Priya and Janak were in the anteroom, with only one door: into her room. They were *trapped*. She spun away from the prince's balcony and flung open the door to his office, bolting through the receiving room and spilling out into the fine-tiled hallway of the prince's estate.

Where were the stairs that led up to her room?

It took a moment to gain her bearings, then she sprinted down one hall, turned a corner, and found a familiar-looking set of stairs. As she took the steps two at a time, she heard shouts coming from the floor above. She ran faster. When she arrived at the top, she choked on the smoke-fogged air. The space was crowded with people: chambermaids and guards, some dressed, some in their pajamas, some running from the fire, others toward it, many with buckets that sloshed precious fire-eating water on the floor. Aniri clung to the wall, pushing toward the fire and scanning every face through the thickening smoke, searching for Priya and Janak among them. Her eyes stung and watered, making it even more difficult to tell one face from another.

Finally, she reached the door to her room, which was blocked with people coming and going, disappearing and reappearing out of the thick billows of smoke that roiled inside. The heat was intense, scorching her face as she blinked away tears and looked for an opening to lurch inside. Prince Malik emerged from the wall of gray and stumbled toward the door. He carried Priya in his arms, and she clung to him, coughing so hard her entire body shook. Aniri leapt back to give the prince room, and he brushed past her, hurrying Priya out into the less toxic air of the hallway. Janak followed close behind, coughing and stumbling and pushing away a guard who tried to help him. That he was well enough to be surly gave her a surge of warmth that surprised her. She wiped her face and followed them a few steps down the hall, where Prince Malik was gently setting Priya on the floor.

Aniri's heart squeezed as Priya coughed and struggled for breath. She reached out to touch her handmaiden's cheek. "Priya! Are you all right?" Her voice trembled as much as Priya's thin frame.

Priya didn't answer as the coughing took her again, but Janak looked up sharply when Aniri spoke. His face went through a fleeting flurry of emotion: shock that she was standing before him; a rapid scan of her person to ensure she was untouched by the fire; and slack relief that made Aniri's throat close up. Priya bent over, still coughing, and Janak gently took hold of her shoulders, keeping her upright. He nodded to Aniri, and she pulled back, crossing her arms tightly over her chest. She was glad for Janak's strength; her shaking arms wouldn't have been much comfort to her handmaiden.

Only then did the prince seem to recognize her. "Aniri! By the gods—" He seized her shoulders like he couldn't quite believe she was real. His face was blackened with soot and the arm of his night tunic was pockmarked with burns. He threw his arms around her, hugging her fiercely to him. "We thought you were—" He stopped to cough, the force of it shaking her. He pulled back and scanned her pajamas, which of course were unmarred even by smoke. "Are you all right?" There was amazement in his eyes when his gaze traveled back to hers. "We thought sure you had perished in the fire. I tried to... I couldn't find you anywhere in your room, but the heat was so intense, I thought there was no possible way that..." He was rambling. And stunned.

"I'm all right. I was never in the room."

He frowned in confusion. Priya had stopped coughing, and Janak still held her, but Aniri could tell he was paying attention to her words. Prince Malik must have felt the heat of Janak's stare because he quickly dropped his hands from Aniri and took a half step back.

She needed a cover story, but floundered for something plausible. The smoke made breathing even more difficult than the thin air, but her cough was more to buy time than clear her lungs.

Finally, she said, "I wasn't able to sleep, so I went for a walk. I had no idea what had happened until I returned." Aniri glanced at the chaos still reigning around her room. The guard always present at her door would quickly counter her story, but she didn't see him. And her handmade rope would certainly give her away once the fire was tamed. Unless she was lucky enough to have the flames send the evidence of her espionage plummeting to the depths of the ravine.

Janak's face was alive with suspicion, but he held his tongue. The prince's frown grew into a darker look. Her heart seized. Did he suspect her?

"It is tremendously fortunate you took your stroll when you did, princess," Prince Malik said. "I don't know who threw this fire bomb, or how it was possible for them to get past my guard, but I assure you I will find out."

She hoped he wouldn't search too hard.

But her alarm eased, and she coughed out more smoke, for real this time. The prince's face softened. He gently took her shoulders again, this time steering her down the hall and away from the fire.

"Thank the gods you are safe," he said quietly. "And your handmaiden and guard, too. That is the most important thing." Priya and Janak followed them closely down the hall.

Aniri gave the prince a grateful smile. He had saved them. From the looks of his tunic, he had risked his life to save her, too. Not his guard. Not his personal servants. He himself had plunged into the smoke and fire-filled room to save her.

While she was busy spying in his office.

A turmoil of feelings rumbled through her chest as the prince gently escorted her, Janak, and Priya to a new room. It was far from the fire, literally on the opposite side of the palace from her damaged room. The prince seemed to take comfort from having his arm around her as they walked, as if he didn't want to release her lest an assassin leap from the drapes to plunge a dagger into her heart. She wasn't entirely sure his fears were overstated, so she allowed it.

Even inside the room, Prince Malik stayed by her side, sitting with her on a small couch near the window. His arm left her shoulder, but only traveled as far as the back of the couch behind her. Janak gave them room, attending to Priya by another window, thrown open so she could obtain fresh air. Aniri couldn't see the side of the palace where the fire had raged, but they had carried the smell of smoke with them. It still clogged her lungs, and her labored breathing filled the silence around them.

The prince seemed deep in thought, clenching and unclenching his fist on his knee. Aniri didn't want him to ask any probing questions about her "walk," so she didn't disturb him.

Finally, a small battalion of guards arrived at the room along with a servant—six in total, looking like they had been roused from bed and hastily put on their starched uniforms. They were armed with pistols and daggers and ferociously serious looks. Prince Malik arose and went to speak in hushed tones with the servant at the door, who was then promptly sent away.

The prince returned to her, his face grave. "These men will ensure your safety. Please, do not go anywhere without them, or your private guard. I don't want you to feel like a prisoner in your own palace, but there's an assassin who just tried to take your life, and I'm not inclined to give him another chance."

Aniri nodded, not missing the way he referred to his palace as her own. A flinch of guilt clenched her stomach even tighter. The prince acted as if they were already married, giving her the benefit of full privilege in his home. And he had just tried to save her life. He kept moving her with his words and actions in a way that left her off balance and dizzied like the thin mountain air in which he lived.

"We found a rope dangling from your balcony," he continued, "although I can't imagine how the assassin thought that might lead to an escape. It will be lucky for him if the bottom of the ravine finds him before I do." The dark look was back, and it made Aniri shudder. "However, I doubt very much the assassin turned into a bird and flew away. He is likely still here in the estate, or possibly trying to flee Bajir. He may also return to make another attempt on your life. Or others may follow where he has failed. Regardless, for now, I would greatly prefer it if you stayed in your room."

"Of course," Aniri said, surprised how shaky her voice sounded.

The prince must have heard it, too, because he shifted closer, kneeling on one knee in front of her. He took her hands in his still soot-covered ones. "I am so sorry, Aniri. If I had known the risk would be this severe..." He stared at her hands, then met her eyes again. "Perhaps we should reconsider our arrangement."

"No!" Aniri said, too quickly. She reflexively glanced at her father's bracelet and the prince's soot-covered fingers gently holding her hand near it. She wasn't entirely sure why her reaction was so strong. But she couldn't leave, not yet. There was too much at stake in the success of her mission. And she knew the dangers when she agreed. Even more, she didn't want to prove Janak right about her unsuitability to fulfill her duty. She calmed herself and sat straighter, patting the prince's hand to reassure him. "I am fine, Prince Malik. And I refuse to be frightened off by a clumsy assassin who can't even firebomb my bed when I'm actually in it."

The prince's face broke into a smile that he tried to contain but failed. "As your majesty wishes." He looked like he wanted to say something more… but thought better of it and rose up to standing instead. "Please let me know if there is anything I can get for you."

"Just my things—" She cut herself off, realizing that included her mother's aetheroceiver. It should be packed away, but who knew how many of the dozens of suitcases would be damaged by the fire, their contents exposed. "That is… whatever remains from the fire. Please bring the cases here, and I will take the trouble of sorting through them to see what can be salvaged." Her mission could be cut very short if the prince's servants went through her things.

"I will have everything brought immediately, along with anything else your majesty needs. Please, do not hesitate to ask. I wish to erase your memory of this night as quickly as possible." Prince Malik templed his hands and bowed a quick *arama* before striding purposefully from the room. She noticed his hands were clenched again before he reached the door, full of anger and purpose.

She was glad his dark looks were directed at the assassin, not her.

fifteen

Two days since the fire, and Aniri was indeed feeling like a prisoner in a velvet cage.

They were confined by the prince's fears of another attack and hadn't left her guest room for any purpose other than using the attached privy. All their meals had been brought to their room. Twice she had to request cutlery be included—it was obviously true the Jungali ate with their fingers, just as she had always heard. The prince himself had stayed away, apparently too busy with actual royal duties to pay a visit. He did send a note, saying the engagement party had been moved forward due to the nature of the attempt on her life. He wanted to send a clear message that he was in no way deterred by their act of violence, even though the assassin—whoever he was—had escaped. The guard who had been posted outside her original room was a likely candidate, since he was nowhere to be found. Plus it had been discovered that his family was originally from Sik province, migrating before he was born to Bajir. The prince suspected he had been recruited by General Garesh.

Aniri returned the prince's note, saying he was right to proceed, even though it sent tremors through her. Moving up the party meant shortening her time until the wedding, leaving her even less room to discover the truth about the skyship. The prince had sent back details about preparations for the party. She was disappointed he had not come in person to deliver that information, even though there was no reason for him to do so.

Priya spent her time rotating their entire wardrobe—the ones saved from the fire at least—giving each a thorough airing by draping them across the balcony. A couple of her dresses had been lost to the wind, fluttering into tiny colorful specks in the ravine. It was the only event which broke the monotony, and Aniri had nearly cried she laughed so hard.

She was clearly not made for confinement. Immediately after the fire, Janak had helped her send a message to her mother, but since then, she had nothing to report. Indeed, Aniri had gained very little knowledge over what she had when she came to Jungali. That, more than anything, was eating at her every thought. What little time she had to complete her mission was ticking away.

Aniri stilled her pacing across the length of the room, coming to rest by Janak in the sitting area, which was comprised of two chairs and a small couch. Priya was out on the balcony tending their clothes, and the prince's guards had taken a station outside their door to give them privacy.

"Are you certain," she asked Janak, "you've never heard of this navia General Garesh is mining?"

He didn't look up, busy sharpening his dagger. His thin-leather raksaka boots were propped on the prince's wooden-edged table inlaid with marble. "You've asked me about navia seven times now, your most royal highness. I'm sorry my education in rare earth elements is inadequate for your purposes."

"But it must be more than that!" Aniri resumed her pacing. Her fencing outfit was overly warm, which just added to her agitation, but it was the only thing that wasn't either airing on the balcony or forbidden by Priya to be worn until they left the room again. "The prince's spy wouldn't message him about the navia unless it was important."

"It ranked after your kiss, so I'm not sure where that leaves us in our hypotheses."

Aniri scowled. Janak seemed to take endless pleasure in needling her about any part of their mission she might find unpleasant—a small consolation to him, no doubt, for the arranged marriage being only a ruse. Yet, in the wake of the fire, he had hovered over her, barely allowing her a visit to the privy without him.

It must be the natural reaction of raksaka for their charges. Even the ones they despised. It certainly didn't stop him from showing contempt for her at every turn.

She stopped her pacing at his side again, drawing his attention up with her urgent stare. "Both the navia and the kiss must be important in some way to the prince's plans for peace," she insisted.

"Or his plans for war."

Aniri examined Janak's face for signs of humanity. Or at least a limit to his cynicism. "Do you truly believe he would risk his life to save me from a fire if all he intends is war with Dharia? He could have accomplished that by letting the fire do its work."

"That would only bring the war to him sooner, and not on his terms," Janak said coolly. "If he has this flying machine, he will want to surprise us with it."

"It's not much of a surprise if we're already looking for it."

"Looking for what, precisely?" Janak asked, rising and planting his knife in the fine wood of the table with a swift flick of his wrist. "We don't know its size or capabilities or threat it might pose. All we know is the thing may fly like a bird. Or perhaps like a stone. Or that it is no threat at all, just barbarians with fanciful notions from spending too much time in this thin air." He waved his weathered hand around for emphasis.

Aniri clenched her fists. She wasn't quite sure why Janak's speech angered her. He hadn't seen the impassioned look on Prince Malik's face when he spoke of peace. Or of his brother's death. The prince would have sent her home rather than risk her life further with an assassin on the loose. It simply didn't reconcile with also secretly planning to launch a surprise attack on her nation.

Maybe her judgment was being clouded.

Maybe she had simply been cooped in this room too long.

Aniri flung her hands open with a small sound of frustration. "Where are my swords?" she demanded of Janak.

"My lady?" he asked, leaning back, thrown by the change in topic.

"The small trunk that carries my weapons. Where is it?"

His disgust came swerving back. "We're confined to this room, in case your most royal eminence hasn't noticed." Janak had taken to sleeping on the couch, and

Priya made a small bed on the floor near Aniri's. He gestured to the four-poster bed where Aniri slept. "Are you planning to fence the bed for practice? Because your royalness would not fare well in a sparring match with me, I assure you." The scowl Janak always wore grew into a darker look.

Aniri didn't trust herself not to stab him either.

"I need a break from this room!" She threw her hands up, as if imploring Devkasera herself to slash her sword through the roof of the palace and free her. And now that the words were spoken aloud, Aniri was even more certain she must do *something* or go mad.

She stalked over to the piles of traveling trunks, all stamped with the royal Dharian crest, and searched for the long, slender one Devesh had brought to the train platform. She had to dig through a dozen, making uncertain piles while Priya fluttered around her and tried to right them, but at last she found it. Janak had returned to his spot in the sitting area and didn't look inclined to remove his boots from the table, so she brought the case over to her bed instead.

As she undid the latches and lifted the lid, she had half a mind to see how fast Janak was on his feet should she come at him with the foil. But her hands stayed on the propped open lid, staring at the contents of the case. Inside wasn't only her normal training foil, but her saber as well. Or more accurately, her father's saber. The one Janak had brought back from Samir instead of bringing her father home safely. It was the only time a raksaka had failed to keep alive the royalty on his watch. If anyone had asked her, that alone seemed grounds for early retirement, but her mother had kept Janak even closer to her side than before. Just one more way the Queen didn't give her father the honor he was due in death.

Aniri lifted the saber from the case, balancing it in her hand. She remembered claiming it for her own when her father's body returned from Samir. Her mother had allowed it, even though Aniri was barely strong enough to lift it at the time. The bracelet she wore had been a gift from her father's heart, from the time when he was still alive, but this... this was more. Aniri pictured him fighting off the robbers who stole his life. She imagined their blood on his blade before he succumbed to the vermin. When the day came, she planned to use her father's saber to finally deliver the justice they deserved.

It made her throat tight, knowing Devesh had sent it to her. He was reminding her of what she would lose by marrying the Prince of Jungali. She blinked away the tears that summoned. Then she noticed there was a small metallic box inside tucked at the end of the case.

An aetheroceiver.

Smaller than her mother's or Prince Malik's and more crudely crafted, it had less ornamentation and was made from a dull metal. But there was no mistaking the tiny swirls of symbols all over the box. She lifted it up. Devesh had given her a way to communicate. A way out of the mountains, if she had been taken hostage. It made her heart pound that he had held out hope for her.

She missed him terribly.

"Where did that come from?" Janak's voice came from behind her, startling her. "Is it from your courtesan?"

"He *is* from Samir," she said, keeping her back to Janak. "You said they are very clever with their devices." But how did Devesh expect her to open it? Then she spied a tiny parchment note where the box had lain. It had her name in Devesh's sweeping print. She unfolded it, revealing three, hand-drawn symbols: a tinker working on a tiny clockwork invention, a crown, and a sleek bowed ship, probably emblematic of Samir's navy, of which they were very proud.

"Is this a royal Samirian aetheroceiver?" Aniri asked, partly to Janak, but mostly of herself.

"I doubt it," Janak said. "Your courtesan certainly isn't of the royal house."

"No, he's a diplomat with the Samirian ambassador." Who, of course, worked for the Samirian royal family, of which her sister was now part. But Aniri wouldn't have expected Devesh, a low-level courtesan, to have access to royal aetheroceivers.

"I was under the impression he mostly fenced and drank tea," Janak said drily.

Aniri spared him a quick glare, then pushed the three symbols on the box. It unfolded before her, revealing a decryption wheel just like her mother's, only on a smaller scale. She pumped the tiny crank, and once the aetheroceiver was humming and clicking, she quickly scanned the dial and typed in DEVESH one symbol at a time. It clacked as it sent off the message, and continued to hum afterward, but no response came spitting out immediately from the machine.

Well, she had taken nearly a week to open the case.

Still, her heart sank. Maybe he had despaired, having heard of the kiss, and locked his twinned version of the aetheroceiver away. Certainly he couldn't be counted on to sit by it day and night, waiting for her to pick it up and respond. And yet, before the crank could wind completely back down, a response slip unfurled one keystroke at a time from the machine.

"I have need of a pen, Janak!" She excitedly smacked his chest with the back of her hand, and he lumbered to the other side of the room, returning with the pressurized quill pen they had scavenged from the previous guest room.

She quickly transcribed the message.

IS THIS THE THIRD DAUGHTER

She let out a small girlish squeak.

Janak stayed her hand before she could compose a response on the keys. "How do we know, my lady, who is on the other end of this aetheroceiver?"

"Devesh hid it in my sword case," Aniri said with a frown. "Who do you think it is?"

"I think your young suitor is one of our enemies, the Samirians, and works for the Samirian Ambassador. And I think this device may well be in the ambassador's hands."

That gave Aniri pause. It was quite possible. How would Devesh get hold of such a device without the approval of the Ambassador? And it appeared to have royal symbols as well, although that could simply be the standard way the boxes were encrypted.

"I will be circumspect about my communications," Aniri said. "But Devesh doesn't want to hear my secrets, Janak. His concerns are only for me. The Ambassador is probably just loaning the device to him out of sympathy for our situation."

"Yes, ambassadors are known for their generous and sympathetic hearts," Janak said with derision.

Aniri ignored him and punched the code YES to Devesh's query.

SO WORRIED ARE YOU OKAY came the response after a short pause. Devesh must be an excellent decoder. It took Aniri longer to respond.

AM FINE PLEASE IGNORE RUMORS

It took too long for a response this time. Aniri had to walk away from the bed several times and pace the

room. She cranked the aetheroceiver again, just in case it might wind down in the middle of the message when it came. Janak retired back to his table.

GOOD TO HEAR HAVE YOU FOUND THE FLYING MACHINE

Aniri froze in her translations, her hand shaking a little when she copied over the last few letters.

"What?" said Janak, looking up from his spot across the room where he had resumed his relaxed pose with his boots on the table. "Does he have a new lady love already?"

"Janak, you best take a look at this."

He grumpily got up and crossed the room to peer at her small writing on the thin white strip. He didn't say anything for moment, but when he did, his voice was harsh, barely holding back his anger. "Did you tell him?"

"I swear to you, I did not," Aniri said, her mind whirling. "The Queen forbade it."

"Then how does he know of our mission?"

"Maybe you are right." She crumpled to sitting on the bed. "Maybe this isn't Devesh. Perhaps it was planted in my case and he simply delivered it, not knowing what was within."

Janak snatched up Devesh's note, crumpled it, and threw it to the floor. "He knows exactly what he is doing."

"But how would he know about the mission?"

"I don't know." He stabbed a finger at the small aetheroceiver next to her. "But you cannot communicate any further with him."

"Just let me tell him—"

"Princess! We are here on a highly sensitive mission to find a secret weapon of war. And we *do not know* who you are talking to!" His face was turning red with anger, and she knew he was right.

"I will… only reply that I miss… fencing with him. He will understand, and no one can take it wrongly."

Janak shook his head and stomped back to his seat, taking up his knife and throwing it back into the table again.

MISS FENCING WITH YOU

Aniri's response felt forced and awkward, like unknown eyes were peering into her heart. But if Devesh was somehow involved he would at least get part of her message. It didn't take long for the message to come back. When the machine started to whir and click the message out, Janak came back to her side. He watched over her shoulder while she decoded.

THE FLYING MACHINE DOES NOT EXIST IT IS A RUSE DANGER LEAVE NOW

"Your Samirian friend is far more than a courtesan, Princess," Janak said.

"I think he's just trying to convince me to come home again."

The machine clacked and whirred again. This time Aniri was almost afraid to see what the message would be.

IF YOU MARRY WILL TRIGGER A WAR LEAVE NOW

Janak took the box, ripped the paper slip from it, and hastily folded it up again. The gears ground as it was forced into its smaller shape before having fully wound down.

"Janak!"

"Princess, whoever is on the other end of this device is not your friend." The anger had flown, leaving a cold hardness to his face. "You need to message the Queen immediately and tell her she has spies in her estate."

Aniri's mouth fell open. "Devesh is not a spy!"

"All diplomats are spies," Janak said. "You will message her or I will do it myself, Aniri."

He never called her by name, and his quiet anger would have sounded like fear if she hadn't known raksaka didn't experience such things. Aniri swallowed and nodded. Whoever was in possession of the aetheroceiver knew far more than they should about the mission and perhaps even more about the flying machine itself.

"I will message my mother right away."

sixteen

Aniri feared what would happen to Devesh. She took great pains to tell the Queen she didn't know who had sent the message on Devesh's aetheroceiver, that she couldn't be sure it was him, and at any rate, she couldn't believe he was a spy. But the Queen's return message was cryptic, chilling, and final.

UNDERSTOOD

The aetheroceiver was a cold device, spitting out its encrypted symbols one at a time. Aniri wanted to shake it and shout at her mother across the aether. She wanted assurance that her entreaties had taken hold. Or some sign of what would happen to Devesh. If he was involved, he had to know something had gone wrong when her messages abruptly stopped coming. Maybe he would flee the grounds before her mother's guards could find him. Maybe the ambassador would protect him.

He shouldn't have tried so hard to keep her. For all she knew, the messages were simply his lies made up to convince her to come home. And now they had triggered so much more.

The two days until the engagement party with Prince Malik dragged in a torment of imagined scenarios of Devesh in her mother's jail cells. Her mother wouldn't torture information out of Devesh—such things were the province of barbarians, not the Queendom of Dharia— but summary execution of spies wasn't unheard of. Or the Queen could simply hold him prisoner. Or send him packing back to Samir.

One thing seemed certain: Devesh would no longer be there when Aniri returned home. She daydreamed of fleeing to Samir and finding him in a small village surrounded by his extensive family. She would stay there, becoming a wife and mother, with many delightful Samirian children filling her days and her heart. But she had a hard time fully picturing it, like it was a gauzy wish she once had, but now it was simply a childish fantasy filled with holes, not the solidity of truth. A dream that had slipped through her fingers.

Devesh's lies had cost them both.

And what if they weren't lies at all?

Janak refused to discuss the transmission, saying it wasn't information they could trust, much less act upon. But it nagged at her. How could marrying the Jungali Prince possibly trigger a war? She wasn't going through with the marriage, but Devesh didn't know that. Was there some danger in marrying the prince that she had missed?

She was certain she didn't have anything to fear from Prince Malik himself—he had already offered to release her from their arrangement when he thought her at risk.

But General Garesh and the prince's enemies... the danger there was clear. Someone had already tried to stop the marriage by ending her life. But how could the marriage itself bring war? The entire love-story ruse was premised on winning the hearts of the people and bringing the peace the prince sought, not an internecine war.

Ruse. The word sent a small shiver down Aniri's spine as she watched Priya pin her hair in the mirror. There were so many layers of ruse now. Aniri longed for when her most bold lie was that she was stargazing when in fact she was kissing her lover under a bridge.

Priya's preparations had gone on half the morning; the engagement party was to finally commence at noon. Priya and Janak would represent the Dharian contingent, something Priya was beside herself with joy about, endlessly fiddling with and arranging outfits for herself. Janak seemed to think it was tolerable. He had brought his formal royal uniform for just such an event.

Priya tugged Aniri's hair into one more tuft, held aloft by a jeweled pin.

"Are you sure this is the fashion for Bajiran brides?" Aniri asked her, pulling slightly away from Priya's deft hands. "I think I resemble an exotic bird more than a Queen-to-be." Priya had segmented her hair, pulling it back all around her face and fixing it with jewels that looked like a crown, but in fact were merely adornments.

"I am quite certain," Priya said, with a frown. "Now hold still."

Aniri did as she was told and gazed in the mirror. On her forehead hung a large blue crystal, intricately set in gold with a flower of clear stones circling it. A gift the prince had sent in advance, with a note saying it had been his mother's, along with a request that Aniri wear it. That

part she didn't mind. In fact, she was touched, even as she understood the political significance. The people would recognize it and think it a treasured gift from a boy prince madly in love with his new Queen.

It was a lovely story. Too bad it was only a ruse as well.

Aniri took a deep breath and tried to hold still as Priya fussed. Her engagement gown was royal blue, the color of the united Jungali provinces. Yards and yards of fabric billowed below the tightly fitted corset and short sleeves. Priya had inked the backs of Aniri's hands—one with the Dharian crest, the other with the four crests of the Jungali Provinces. She was laden with jewels she had brought from home: a heavy blanket of interlocked gold weave and crystals circled her neck and more hung from her ears. She normally eschewed the royal jewels, but they were required for occasions like this.

And there was the ring. Both she and the prince would be wearing the finely filigreed rings that encased nearly the entire length of the third finger on their left hands. They were customary engagement rings, Priya had told her. It wasn't the thin marriage band that would bind them in the eyes of the gods for the entirety of their lives, but the engagement ring still felt heavy and restricting. A cage of gold so stiff her finger couldn't move. If she failed in her mission, this was her future: a prop for the politics of a nation that wasn't even her own. She was heavy with symbols all up and down her person, but the meaning—the truth of who she was—was invisible, buried under all of it.

All of a sudden, the thin air caught up with her again, and her chest started to heave. The stifling warmth of the room threatened to overtake her as well.

"My lady?" Priya asked. "Are you all right?

Aniri stood and gripped the edge of the dressing table to stay upright. "Yes, I... I just think I need to take a walk."

Janak looked up from a book on military strategy he had acquired to pass the time. "A walk, your most royal highness?" His voice arched with disbelief.

"My lady," Priya said. "The party is beginning within the half hour. We are expected in the main hall shortly."

"I know. I just need a bit of time alone."

Janak set down his book. "You don't have the luxury of being alone, Princess, not anymore." He seemed to take some pleasure in that.

"I will take one of the prince's guards with me," Aniri said coldly, sweeping her skirts away from her chair and striding towards the door to their room.

Janak jumped to his feet. "Your highness—"

"Do not follow me, Janak," Aniri said harshly. If he refused her order, she was not above sending him home. Or messaging her mother that his services were inadequate. Or some such thing. She could make his life more difficult if she wished, and with the days and burdens wearing on her nerves, she *wished* it very much.

He must have seen the determination in her face because he didn't follow her to the door. She pulled it open and startled the guard outside by staring up into his face. There was a full complement of guards on duty, but she would only need one.

"I will be taking a walk before the engagement party," she said to him. "I have need of a guard to accompany me."

"Yes... uh, yes, my lady." He glanced at the other guards, who had quickly come to their feet, leaving some kind of game with stones scattered on the floor. "How many guards would you like?"

"Just you." Aniri strode past him, heading down the hall. His boots scuffed the floor, hastening to follow her, but she didn't look back. She had no idea where she was going, only that she had a need to walk, to breathe some fresh air for a moment before committing herself to performing this role at the engagement party. Before putting on another ruse, another show, for everyone but herself.

The guard kept pace behind her, careful to avoid the train of fabric which floated above the granite floor in her wake. She didn't know her way around the estate at all, but she had to be near a balcony where she could find fresh air. She might resort to throwing open one of the windows lining the wide empty hall and letting in the brilliant sunshine and brisk mountain air. But as she rounded yet another corner, she nearly tripped over her slippered feet in coming to a halt.

At the far end of the hall was the prince. And he wasn't alone.

Once more in his all-black royal garb, the prince's arms were wrapped around a beautiful woman in a hug which was anything but formal. The richly-colored blue silks of her dress hung off her shoulders, which were nearly bare, and pooled on the floor. The woman was clearly dressed for the engagement party. The prince's face was buried in her long waves of black hair, as silky and lush as her dress. The couple hadn't noticed Aniri. Her guard managed not to run into her when she suddenly stopped.

The prince pulled back from their embrace then cupped the woman's cheeks and spoke softly, his face near hers. The words were obviously meant to be intimate, but Aniri couldn't help straining to hear.

She couldn't discern them, and then the heat of

embarrassment crawled up her neck. She was spying on the prince—not on his plans for peace or war, but on his love life. One she hadn't given a thought to. Aniri turned away, no doubt befuddling the guard who was looking rapidly back and forth between Aniri and the prince with wide eyes, saying nothing.

Aniri marched back to her room, her chest growing more tight with each step. What did she expect? They had agreed they would have lovers—the prince explicitly brought it up as a condition, saying he knew well what she was giving up. *She* had a lover, even if she might never see Devesh again. It shouldn't bother her in the slightest if the prince had one as well. She had no intention of even going through with the wedding, so what consequence could it have for her?

Yet, she still was fighting a vise clamping down on her chest.

He hadn't lied to her—at least not directly. And really, for what purpose would the prince have told her he had a lover? He was seeking out her hand in marriage for explicit political purposes.

By the time she approached her room, Aniri convinced herself the tightness was merely nerves about the formal engagement, nothing any more complicated or emotional. Or perhaps a twinge of jealousy that her own lover might be on his way to prison if he hadn't already fled her country.

When she stepped into the room, Priya seemed frantic, imploring Janak to send out a search party for her. Janak, for his part, was a strange bundle of agitation and seemed nearly willing to do so. One of the prince's personal attendants had arrived to escort them—he stood off to the side at a proper distance of respect, but he had a look of panic as well.

"My lady!" Priya seized Aniri's hands. "Thank the gods you have returned! We are due at the party. We must leave at once."

Priya flew around her, making minute adjustments to her hair and bringing a veil to drape over her head. Aniri pulled it off, causing small cries of alarm from Priya as the veil pulled at the jewels she had carefully placed in Aniri's hair. "I'm not wearing a bridal veil, Priya."

"But it's tradition—"

"We are making some of our own traditions today," she said impatiently. "A Dharian has never wed a Jungali before, anyway. I think there is some leeway to make adjustments."

Then she turned her back on her handmaiden and gestured for their escort to lead the way.

seventeen

Aniri took deep breaths as she slowly followed the prince's attendant. She ignored the sideways looks from Priya, determined to affect a calm demeanor by the time they reached the engagement party. The prince's six guards, plus Janak, formed a ring of starched, uniformed protection around them. Aniri couldn't imagine any assassin foolish enough to attack her in the hallway in broad daylight, but she held her tongue and focused on playing her part.

When they arrived at a pair of large, ornate doors, the prince and another assistant were waiting for them. The doors were still closed—apparently they would make their entrance together. Garlands of white and yellow flowers framed the door and draped along the walls and windows in great sweeping lines that left trails of fallen petals on the floor. Their fragrance infused the air with a joyful feeling that matched the prince's broad smile. He stood tall in his formal black clothes. She came to stand by his side, her dress trailing behind and stirring the flower petals into the air.

"Don't tell my mother, gods rest her soul, but I believe you may be the most beautiful Queen that Jungali has ever had." The prince took her hand and wrapped it around his arm. He faced the door, awaiting their entrance, but slipped a sideways smile to her.

"You're flattering me again, Prince Malik."

"I am a barbarian, after all," he said with a grin. "It's not as if I can help it."

Aniri squeezed his arm lightly, tugging him closer. "Could I have a word in private with you, before we go in?"

He frowned. "Is everything all right?"

"Yes, I just..." She wasn't quite sure what to say without the dozen people standing around them all overhearing.

"Of course we can take a moment to ourselves. I think the party will wait for us."

He led her down the hall, waiving off several guards who seemed unsure as to whether they should follow or not. He pulled her into an alcove, just far enough that they couldn't be easily overheard or fully seen. The window backlit his broad shouldered frame as he leaned against it.

"What is it, Aniri?" He still held her hand, running his finger over her ring and taking in the Jungali crests inked on the back of her hand. "Or are you trying to feed the rumors with an obvious tryst in the hallway?"

Heat ran up her face. "No, I just wanted to..." She swallowed, not quite sure how to admit to spying on him with his lover without embarrassing them both. Her gaze dropped to his chest, avoiding the humor in his pale amber eyes. Today he wore crown jewels as well, in the form of a glittering cascade of black crystals that ringed the neck of his embroidered jacket. They blended with the black and silver brocade until it was difficult to distinguish one from the other.

He touched her chin, bringing her gaze up to meet his. "What's wrong?"

She forced the words out in a rush. "Do you think we'll need to kiss during the engagement party?"

"Is that what you're worried about?" He seemed puzzled and slightly amused.

She sighed and pulled her hand from where he still held it, putting a small distance between them, but keeping tucked in the alcove, shielded somewhat from their onlookers.

"I don't think it will be necessary," he said gently. "The rumors have been quite effective, all on their own."

"I simply wanted you to know I would understand. If you would prefer not to. Given that your lover is here for the party." There, she had said it. Somehow it felt better not to have that secret within her, along with all the rest.

"My lover?" The prince's eyebrows had flown up to the top of his forehead, and he seemed truly surprised.

"Yes, I..." Why was this so difficult to admit? It had been an innocent mistake. "I happened upon you in the hallway. She's quite lovely. I'm sure this is difficult enough for you, the sacrifice of not marrying her, without having a public display as well—"

"You happened upon me? In the hallway? With my lover?" The prince's frown and puzzlement grew deeper with each word.

"Well, yes, just a few moments ago... I didn't mean to intrude, but your guard was with me, and he saw you as well. I thought you might want to say something to him

before a rumor started—"

"Ah!" The puzzlement disappeared, and the mirth was back on his face. He let out a small laugh. "Yes, I will definitely have to speak to my guard. Although he probably recognizes the princess." A smirk was growing on his face.

"Princess?" Aniri asked, feeling like she had suddenly lost her footing.

"My brother's wife? She became a princess once he married her." Prince Malik's grin grew. "And no, she is not my lover. Although that would be quite the gossip, so you are quite right I should make that clear to my guard. In case there was any misunderstanding."

Aniri's face flamed again, and she couldn't meet his eyes. "I'm sorry for... making assumptions."

His voice grew gentle. "No, Aniri, I'm sorry." His finger touched her chin again, the warmth of it lifting her gaze as much as his touch. "This all has to be very difficult for you. First, leaving home. Then the fire. Then being locked away all week like a crown jewel hidden in a vault."

"It *has* been driving me mad," Aniri said with a sigh. Finally, some of the tension drained from her shoulders. "I'm not sure how much more I'll be able to stand."

"Then we shall have to make sure you are safe wherever you wish to go. It's not fair to lock you up, like a criminal, when the ones who attacked you have their freedom."

"It seems there's never much in the way of freedom for royal members of the court." It felt good to say it aloud, and the tightness in her chest eased as well.

He gave her a small, sad smile. "Or privacy, I'm afraid. I was telling Nisha, my brother's wife," he said with a small tip of his head, "that the rumors were true."

"That we're madly in love?" Aniri said, looking askance at him.

"No. That you are brave and noble, in spite of being a princess from the plains. That you're undaunted by assassins and fire, still determined to marry to broker the peace I promised when my brother died. The people are quite taken with you, Aniri."

"You were telling all this to your brother's wife?"

"Actually she was informing me about the people's feelings. They've always had a special place in their heart for her, and when my brother died... well, let's just say, if the lineage were a little more direct, she would be Queen, and I could comfortably retire."

"Would that be your wish?" Aniri asked, her discomfort completely vanishing under the prince's words. "Would you leave the crown behind, if you could?"

He leaned back against the window, crossing his arms. "There are days I am tempted. I won't lie. But as long as my duty calls, I'll heed that."

"I understand." And she did, maybe more than he knew.

His voice softened. "Once the engagement is formal, there should be a brief respite from all the scrutiny. It's normally the time for courtship, and with the wedding only two weeks away, the people will expect us to spend time together. Perhaps that would be a good time for us to travel the provinces? I can't think of a better use of the future Queen's time than getting to know her country and her people."

Travel. In a new exotic land. It was just what Aniri had wanted all her life: to get out of the capital and the courtly life in Dharia. And traveling would give her a chance to find out more about the flying weapon—if it

even existed at all.

"I would like that very much."

"It is settled, then." He reached to the garland of flowers tracing the edge of the window behind him and plucked one white bloom from the string. He tucked it behind her ear, and for some reason that simple motion stirred something inside her again. The prince had a way of doing that when she least expected it.

"I can't wait to show you the beauty of my kingdom. But first, I'm afraid we must receive all the well-wishers who want to meet their future Queen. Do you think you can manage?"

"Of course. And I think we've been here long enough to ignite quite a few new rumors." The blush that was creeping up her cheeks would surely feed it even more.

He grinned. She stuck a royal smile on her face and took his arm, pulling him with mock urgency from the alcove. His eyes danced as he feigned a protest, then joined her in returning to the entourage awaiting them.

eighteen

The engagement party was a spectacle.

A sweeping curved banquet table embraced the ballroom. Instead of cushions, like at the Queen's tea, immense chairs crowded the table with seatbacks two times taller than the dignitaries and diplomats seated in them. Attendees filed by, and Prince Malik introduced them to Aniri. General Garesh had packed away his menacing looks in the presence of the court—he paid his respects, then was lost in the crowd. There were many other representatives from each of the four Jungali provinces, but also dignitaries from Samir, which surprised her. She didn't have long to think on it as the steady stream of guests required their introductions.

Once everyone returned to their seats, the prince introduced her to his brother's wife, the same woman she saw in his arms in the hallway. Her heart-shaped face and sparkling black eyes were even more beautiful up close. Not all of the royal Jungali had the pale amber eyes Aniri had quickly become accustomed to on Prince Malik.

"Princess Aniri of Dharia, it's my pleasure to introduce Princess Malik of Jungali. Also known as Nisha to her friends… and sometimes detractors." His voice was formal, but there was a laugh underneath it, and a barely disguised smile on his face.

Aniri extended her hand, but Nisha enveloped her in a hug that rustled the silks on both their dresses. She held Aniri for several seconds, and Aniri struggled to return the unexpected affection.

Finally, Nisha pulled back. "I'm so very glad you're joining our family, Aniri." Her warm manner left Aniri stumbling for words.

"Thank you," she managed, then felt a twist her in stomach, knowing the ruse would eventually wither any affection Nisha had for her now.

"You've already had such a positive effect on our Ash." She patted his arm.

He gave her a subtle shake of his head, as if to warn her off whatever story she was about to tell. Nisha's eyes managed to smile even more than her lovely face in response. He studied his feet and sighed. Aniri couldn't help smiling at the whole unspoken conversation bouncing between them.

"Oh?" Aniri asked, encouraging Nisha and enjoying the grim look on the prince's face. "And what effect do I have on Jungali's future king?"

"Well…" Nisha dropped her voice so the drifting noble from the Bajiran court wouldn't overhear. "Those dreadful melancholy walks around the perimeter of the estate have stopped. And I hear he has given up reading poetry altogether."

"That's a complete fabrication," the prince objected.

Aniri kept her voice conspiratorial as well. "In

fairness, I did take one of his poetry tomes. I believe it was the one with the ancient Jungali love poems."

She had read it through twice in the time she had been sequestered in her room. It had a soulful beauty that was entirely unexpected, and she flushed with the memory of how wrong her preconceptions had been about the Jungali people. Her uncharitable thoughts were proven even more wrong by Nisha's embrace, not to mention the prince himself and his noble acts.

"Have you now?" Nisha's almond-shaped eyes went round, and Aniri was sure she mistook the heat in her face for something else entirely. Then Nisha gave the prince a look that was both teasing and gleeful with this new information.

"Tell me," she said, returning her gaze to Aniri, "did he show you his favorites?"

Nisha could give Priya serious competition in her fascination with all things romantic.

"I think we're quite done discussing poetry," the prince cut in, taking Aniri by the elbow and steering her toward the head table. "And I believe the party awaits us."

Nisha grinned her goodbye and swept her skirts to take her place at the head table. It was slightly elevated from the others and arranged at one end of the hall. The prince and Aniri sat in the middle, side by side, with Nisha on his left and Janak already settled on her right. Priya bounced slightly, barely able to contain her joy at filling out the remaining head table seat, while to Nisha's left was another woman who could easily be her sister, with the same stunning Jungali beauty.

Once they were seated, the prince leaned over to whisper, "I'm sorry about Nisha."

"Sorry about what?" Aniri asked, grinning. "I

thought she was quite charming. Although I am now extremely curious as to your favorite poems, Prince Malik."

He shook his head and returned his attention to the table and gathered guests. The head table was arranged with more platters of food than needed to feed all the people in attendance twice over, but there was a complete absence of forks or spoons and only the occasional knife for cutting meat. Aniri hoped she could negotiate it. The small dishes of some kind of sauce did not look promising. Perhaps she would forgo eating.

The wide center of the ballroom was left clear, with tables lining the sides. Music swelled up from the alcoves behind the guest tables. It was lively and fresh, and the spirits of the room seemed to lift right out of the heavy chairs. Aniri had never heard Jungali music before, and maybe this was only reserved for celebrations like royal engagements, but it was so full of life that she couldn't help but tap her feet under the brocade blanketed table. Voices joined the strings and horns and made a sensual sound that made her almost embarrassed by the grin it brought to her face. Then she turned to Prince Malik, and he wore a grin so broad, she felt instantly at ease, as if nothing could make her uncomfortable when the earnestness he normally wore could be wiped away by this lively celebration.

Then the dancers came out.

They flooded the floor with whirling blue dresses, flowing the Jungali colors like an ocean coming in for tide. Bare arms and feet flashed and pounded the air and floor tiles, floating and beating with the tempo of the music. A dizzying flurry of voices seemed to come from every crevice of the room. The dancers moved with sinuous, rhythmic motions, synchronized with the singers so that each movement felt like a reverberation of the music now pumping through Aniri's entire body. Then their voices rose with the music, the flicking of their hands serving as punctuation for words that slipped one past the other. The language was beautiful, but she couldn't make sense of it.

She leaned over to the prince and asked, "What are they saying?"

He tucked his head to the side, so his lips were near her ear. "It's an ancient Jungali tongue. They are saying the wind sings of our love, the flowers bursting with joy."

She smiled and pulled back, struck by the loveliness of it all. One of the dancers swept forward, carrying two tiny white blossoms, one in each hand. She wove a story in the air with them, then presented them to Aniri and Ash, arms outstretched across the head table, her head bent until her blue-black hair cascaded in front and obscured her face. Ash reached out to take his, so Aniri did the same. He turned to her, flower in hand, a sly smile on his face. While looking deep in her eyes, he gently cupped her hand with the flower and brought it to his face. Before she realized what he intended, he had snatched the delicate flower from her palm with his lips and drawn it into his mouth. Aniri gaped.

He was eating a *flower*.

A smirk grew while he chewed. She felt the heat of every pair of eyes in the room as he raised his flower to her lips. She struggled to keep her face neutral, afraid the blossom would be horrid, but she opened her mouth and let him feed it to her. It was delicate and sweet, slightly waxy but reminding her of spicy tea and honey. She managed to chew with some small amount of dignity, and when she swallowed, the prince, whose eyes had never left hers, gave her a wide smile that made her blush.

Meanwhile, the rhythm of the music picked up, beating faster and faster and drawing her back. The colors and arms and bejeweled feet whirled quicker, the singers' words taking on new urgency, whatever their meaning. Just when she thought she might be compelled to sweep out of her seat to join them, the music shifted to a more base, almost guttural, pounding of drums and deeper stamping of feet. The female dancers parted and a tumble of male dancers stomped their way to the center. Their flowing pants legs and tight bronze-buttoned vests, with bared arms and naked feet, virtually screamed masculinity, as if the music and muscular beat didn't pulse it loud enough.

Aniri's mouth hung open as they leaped and clapped and generally made her forget to breathe. Their shoulders slinked up and down, undulating with the music. They touched their chests, then threw out their hands as if casting their hearts to the head table, then jumped one after another, hands in the air, their moves showing every muscle straining with their acrobatics. Aniri closed her gaping mouth and stole a look at Prince Malik. He was watching her with no small amount of mirth on his face, but she found it impossible to be embarrassed, so she grinned right back, and he laughed, a sound that was lost in the music still climbing to the highest corners of the ceiling.

She was captivated by the dancers right up to the moment they finished with a flurry and a held pose that seemed to defy gravity.

A thunderous snapping of fingers filled the air, the guests showing their appreciation, and Aniri joined right in, following the prince's move. As the dancers bowed and slowly backed out, taking their leave, the snapping of fingers faded into a tinkling sound of a thousand glasses clinking. Confused, Aniri looked to the guests to find them all facing the head table, tapping small sticks against their cups. Aniri looked to Prince Malik—his eyes had gone wide, and he wasn't smiling anymore. For a moment, she was afraid something had gone wrong. The prince turned to her, looked at her for a brief moment, then leaned over to speak into her ear.

"I forgot about this part. They expect the engaged couple to kiss after the nuptial dance. We don't have to, if you don't—"

Aniri cut off his words by pulling back, then brought her hand to the prince's smooth-shaven cheek. Before he could say anything more, she leaned forward and kissed him.

Maybe it was the thrum of the music still echoing through her body, or the demands of their audience, or simply that she wanted to maintain the ruse which allowed her to stay in Jungali a while longer, but she didn't find it anywhere near as difficult to kiss the prince this time. Her lips pressed urgently to his, and a half heartbeat later he responded just as strongly, his hand finding the back of her head to pull her closer. He tasted of honey flower. His thumb trailed across her cheek. A warmth surged through her that could have been wine… if she had been drinking any. It rushed through her body and settled to her toes, making them buzz.

The clinking of glasses turned to a snapping of fingers, and the prince pulled away, hesitating for a brief second to look her in the eyes. Then he ducked his head away, releasing her completely to face the expectant guests. A smile was back on his face, and he waved to them. She tried to catch his eye, but he refused to look at her, so she turned to smile at the crowd as well, with a small uncertain wave.

Her hand still tingled from its brief encounter with the prince's cheek. That kiss didn't make her lose her breath entirely, the way the first had in a thin-air induced panic on the balcony, but it left her... more affected than it should. She blinked and tried to catch the prince's eye again, but he was busy having a whispered conversation with Nisha over the still fading noise of snapping fingers and calls of good-natured appreciation.

Aniri swallowed and scanned the faces around the expanse of the curved table, wondering once again what she had gotten herself into. Then she froze. A familiar form leaned against a pillar behind the farthest table, cool dark eyes staring at her and capturing her gaze even from across the room.

Devesh.

nineteen

Aniri nearly bolted up from her seat, but shock kept her muscles from responding to her body's alarm. What was Devesh doing in Jungali? At the prince's engagement party, no less. The room was suddenly too hot, and the bustle of dresses and conversation faded from her mind, leaving only Devesh's silent gaze locked with hers. His arms were crossed, his face frozen, but it was clear: he had seen everything. He held her with a heart-stabbing look, then unfolded his arms and slipped around the column he had been leaning against, disappearing from view. Aniri had an urgent need to run: chase after him, explain that it was all a ruse, that it meant nothing. She stopped half way out of her chair. She needed some kind of excuse. She couldn't simply flee the party.

Prince Malik turned to her. A frown appeared on his face once he saw the panic in hers. Had she already given it away?

"Is there something you need, Princess?" His voice was flat, and she couldn't imagine what he was thinking.

She floundered for a reason to leave. "I just need a visit to the privy."

His face relaxed, still unsmiling, but calmed. He signaled a guard from the small battalion stationed around the perimeter of the room. When he arrived, imposingly tall in his royal uniform, Prince Malik said to him, "Please escort the princess." The prince turned away as Aniri finished rising out of her seat, but Priya popped up from hers, and Janak's eyes were narrowed, already taking in the scene.

She tipped her head to Janak. "Just tending to a lady's business." She hoped that excuse, plus Prince Malik's guard, would keep him from insisting on coming. His eyebrows rose in suspicion, but he didn't object.

"My lady?" Priya asked. "Do you need me to accompany you?"

Aniri motioned her to stay. "I can manage on my own." Which was, of course, ridiculous—navigating her dress would take two at least—but Aniri shook her head slightly in warning. Priya frowned, and before she could object further, Aniri quickly lifted her skirts free of the chair and worked her way toward the door to the chamber. How would she find Devesh, much less meet with him privately, with Prince Malik's guard in tow?

Out in the hallway, the bulky guard kept to her side, marching so close he narrowly missed stepping on her skirts. For such a large man, he had a skittish look about him, like he thought she might disappear into smoke if he took his eyes off her. When they arrived at the privy, he reached for the door, as if he would come inside with her. Aniri gave him a withering glare, and he snapped to attention, hands tucked behind his back. She pushed through the heavy door alone.

Once inside, she leaned against the cool, tiled wall next to the door. The privy was spacious, an entire room with a washbin, sitting area, and a toilet. Aniri ignored all of it and tapped her head gently against the wall. How was she going to meet with Devesh? And how on earth did he get here? Clearly, he had escaped Dharia without capture. But why was he *here*?

Voices sounded outside the door, one deep and serious, the other friendly and light-hearted. She tensed as she recognized Devesh's smooth voice, the one he used to court her, only now he had added a manly undertone in his banter with the guard. What was he thinking? That he would talk his way into the privy? No, he was waiting for her to come out. But they could hardly talk in front of the guard. Maybe she could insist he give them some privacy, as long as she was still within eyesight.

She took a breath and pulled open the door.

The guard turned toward her, and in that moment of distraction, Devesh hit him hard on the chin, snapping the guard's head to the side. The large man slumped into the wall, and Devesh hit him again, landing a blow behind his ear with a flat hand chop. The guard never made a sound, and his eyes glazed as he slowly slid down the wall.

Aniri's mouth hung open. "Dev!"

Devesh ignored her outcry. He hooked his arms underneath the guard's, then dragged him backward over the threshold of the privy. Aniri had to jump out of the way, grasping the doorframe to keep from falling as her feet tangled in her skirts. She righted herself and followed Devesh, closing the door as he leaned the guard up against the wall.

"It will take longer for them to notice he's missing in here." Devesh's voice was flat and cold.

Aniri just stared as he dusted off his hands in an entirely unnecessary flourish. Then he planted them on his hips and returned her stare.

"What are you doing?" Her voice was weak.

"Rescuing you, of course." His voice was still flat, but now she could hear the anger underneath it.

"Dev!" She threw up her hands and looked fretfully at the unconscious guard. How would she ever explain this? "I'm not in need of rescuing."

Devesh folded his arms and leaned against the nearby washbasin. "Yes, I see you and the prince are getting along quite well."

"It's not like that."

"No?" he asked, a small rueful smile on his face. "You two were pretty convincing." He took the flower the prince had placed in her hair and tossed it into the washbin.

She balled up her fists. "It's a ruse, Dev. Just a story, a rumor to help build peace with Jungali. I'm doing my duty."

"And a fine job of it, too."

"Dev." She refused to cry, but the tears were close, so she got angry instead. "If I needed your help, I would have messaged you on the aetheroceiver. But then I couldn't be sure if it wasn't some trick. Was it really you on the other end?"

His anger surged up and colored his face. "Of course it was me, Aniri! Didn't you see my note?"

"Yes, but... how did you know? About my true mission here?" Aniri felt like a small tugboat being tossed in a sea of emotion. "Has it always been just about the politics for you? Did it... did all of it, *all of us,* mean nothing to you? Have you always simply been a spy in the Queen's court?"

His anger fell off him like a shrugged winter coat. When he came to her, his hands on her shoulders were warm, his deep brown eyes soft. She swallowed, uncertain if she could trust the man she loved, which left a hollow pit in the depths of her stomach.

He touched her cheek with his fingertips. "My feelings for you have always been real, Aniri." Warmth flooded her heart with his touch and his words, but she didn't miss his evasion.

"So you are. Always have been. A spy." The warmth clashed with a cold front that started in her head and worked its way down.

He closed his eyes for a moment, then gave her one of his patronizing looks. "Aniri, my love, you never have paid enough attention to the workings of the court. I am a *courtesan*."

"I'm not a fool, Dev!" She pushed away from him, but he held fast to her shoulders. She didn't have the heart to stop him from pulling her back.

"No, you're not," he said softly. "But you don't always see what is right in front of you. What do you think courtesans do, Aniri?"

"Play with the hearts of gullible women at court?"

"Aniri..."

"Pretend at love when you're only fishing for secret information?" Her anger flared back. "What a noble cause you serve, Devesh, lavishing your soft attentions to deceive."

He tipped his head back, eyes closed for a moment again, then stared deep into Aniri's eyes. "Aniri, *all* courtesans are spies. You must know this." His voice dropped. "It doesn't mean that we don't also fall in love."

She shook her head—it was telling her to flee, but her heart wouldn't let her rip herself from Devesh's grasp.

"I don't know what to believe anymore."

"I know." He softly touched her cheek again. "But all those times I told you I loved you—it was the truth. I need you to believe that much, if nothing else. And I need you to trust me now. I'm here because I'm afraid for your life."

"If you want anything from me, you'll need to explain yourself much better than that. What did you mean by your aether message? How can you be certain the Jungali's flying weapon doesn't exist? And how can the marriage possibly trigger a war? That doesn't even make sense, Dev."

"I know the flying weapon is a ruse," he said solemnly, "because I know why the rumors are being circulated. It's a distraction, a way to keep the eyes of Dharia all focused on the north, on a threat that is as thin as the air up here."

"A distraction from what?" she asked, but there was some truth to what Devesh was saying, she could feel it. Her mother's court was tied in knots, chasing vapors of rumors, trying to discern whether the flying weapon even existed. It was something so potentially devastating it could not be ignored, but so ephemeral it threatened like a ghost moaning from the high, dark mountains. It so thoroughly distracted her mother that she sent her Third Daughter on a dangerous mission to find the truth.

Devesh wasn't answering her question.

"What is the rumor distracting us from?" Aniri asked again, fear forming a cold pool in her stomach.

Devesh looked into her eyes. "Can I trust *you*, Aniri?"

"What do you mean?"

"If I tell you something, I need you not to tell your mother, the Queen."

"You can't ask that of me!" Aniri said, pulling back.

"No. You are probably right." Devesh released her and rubbed the stubble on his face with one hand. He studied her, obviously debating whether he could tell her.

"You said you feared for my life," she said. It was a challenge.

"You are in grave danger here, Aniri."

"And you claim to love me."

He just gave her a hopeless look.

"Then tell me, Dev."

He turned away from her, pressing a fist to his mouth and staring out the far window of the privy. The afternoon sun shone brightly on a clear blue sky. It seemed to be made darker by the lack of air—the skies were bluer in the mountains than anywhere she had seen before.

So much was different here, a change of perspective, as Prince Malik rightly pointed out. She had never been more uncertain of what was true and who she could trust—even the man she loved, who was staring out the window, contemplating whether *he* could trust *her* enough to tell her the truth.

Her gown and the crown jewels around her neck weighed heavy on her as she waited, wondering whether she should trust anything he might choose to tell her.

When he turned back, Devesh's face was resolute. "The Samir are planning war, Aniri."

She leaned away from him, giving him a skeptical look. "On the Jungali?" That didn't make much sense. She'd seen the Samirian dignitaries at the engagement party. They seemed very comfortable here in the wilds of the Jungalian mountains, very amiably partaking in the festivities.

"No," he said. "On Dharia."

twenty

"How can Samir be planning war with Dharia?" Aniri's voice was climbing, but her heart was sinking. Devesh wasn't telling her the truth after all. "We have been allies for a century. We have bonded through countless marriages. My *sister* is married to the prince heir apparent. This cannot be so, Dev."

"I didn't say going to war with Dharia was a grand idea," Devesh said sarcastically. He folded his arms again and leaned against the washbasin of the privy. "And I'm not the only Samirian who thinks the plans are foolish. Nevertheless, they are real."

"That makes no sense," she said, throwing her hands out in exasperation. "We are the breadbasket to the world. We feed Samir—"

"And we provide you with the latest technology." The sarcasm was still heavy in his voice. "How do you think that feels, Aniri? To be more advanced, more proficient in metalwork and clockwork and all manner of steam-driven wonders, but beholden to a backward-looking Queen because she happens to control the food supply?"

Aniri swallowed. Devesh had never talked like this before. As if Samir and Dharia were truly enemies, not allies.

"The Queen would never threaten Samir—"

"She doesn't *have* to," Devesh cut her off again. "Short of a full military assault and occupation of Dharia, Samir is at the mercy of whatever terms the Queen would like to set. Do you ever wonder why the Queen is so enamored with tradition? Why she clings to gods like Devkasera as if she's given your mother a divine right to rule?"

"My mother just… likes the traditional ways." A tremble started in Aniri's stomach. She never had given it much thought, and she feared what Devesh would tell her next. His words were taking on more weight of truth the more he spoke.

"Your mother clings to the past because she knows Samir is the future."

"What do you mean?" But that trickle of fear was turning into a gush.

"Steam-driven technology is the way of the future, Aniri. It is unstoppable. It is only a matter of time before our technology is strong enough to outmatch Dharia's greater numbers and resources."

It was true that Dharia had greater size, both in land and army. Most of the world was ocean, and most of the land belonged to Dharia. The Jungali claimed the frozen mountains and seas in the north, and Samir was a small, mountainous country, less than half the size of Dharia, and separated from it by a hundred miles of water. There was a saying about good water making good neighbors, but the Samirian strength had always been its trade boats, the ability to bring manufactured metal goods from the Samirian mountains to Dharia in exchange for the food that kept Samirians well fed.

Devesh was watching her carefully as she thought on his words.

"Just because you have superior technology does not mean we need to be enemies," she said at last.

"I agree," Devesh said calmly. "But the Queen has grown lazy with the abundance of her land and the riches that allow her to buy whatever trinkets she wishes from Samir. She doesn't see the changes roiling through my country, the dissatisfaction with always being second-class citizens in the world. The Jungali understand this better than your Queen. They know what it's like to be impoverished. And thought of as barbarians. Your mother doesn't see the real changes coming. She would rather have her teas and play at court in her traditional costumes than see what is right before her."

Aniri cringed, because at least that part had the ring of truth. And hearing General Garesh's sneering taunts come from Devesh's mouth unsettled her even more.

"There are factions within Samir," Devesh continued, "who believe our technology will finally bring us the stature in the world that we rightfully deserve."

"The flying machine?"

"No! I told you... that is just a rumor. The Jungali are happy to join us in the deception for a small slice of the future spoils. The threat of a flying machine in the north is there to deflect attention, so the Queen doesn't notice Samir is bolstering her fleet."

"But a strengthened trade fleet is no threat," Aniri argued, hoping he was still wrong about some part of this, even though the sinking feeling in her stomach felt like a

Dharian warship on its way to the depths. "Stronger trade strengthens our bonds—"

"They're not building a *trade* fleet, Aniri." His voice was patronizing again. "Those trade vessels are very well armed. The Samirian government has quietly been building its reserves, buying time with rumors of flying machines in the north to keep Dharia focused on a common enemy."

He took hold of her shoulders again, speaking softly. "I am betraying my country by telling you this, Aniri. I wouldn't do so if it weren't so dire a situation. If you go through with this marriage, the prince's reign will be solidified. There will be no threat any longer, whether the Queen believes the ruse of the flying machine or not. With that threat removed, with the distraction gone, the Samirians will move up their plans for attack. And no matter what the prince says, the Jungali are not your friends, my love. They despise the plains people. They have never been allies with Dharia, and they never will."

"You don't know that!" All she had been working for with the prince—even if it was half ruse on her part—all of it was to bring peace between Dharia and Jungali. And it was a peace Prince Malik wished for as well. He wanted to honor his dead brother with it, to keep his country from falling into chaos—all of that couldn't be lies. She'd seen the passion for peace on his face, heard it in his words. And peace was what she was risking everything for. Hearing it was impossible made her want to cover her ears and run from the room. But she knew that was a child's reaction to something she didn't want to believe.

"I know much more than you can possibly realize, Aniri." Devesh's voice was low and soft now, dangerous. "These rumors did not start on their own. The Jungali hope to get their rewards once the war is finished, once Samir controls all the land and goods of Dharia. If you go through with the marriage, you will be in a literal trap—a prisoner of war. You need to believe me, Aniri, and you need to leave Jungali at once without raising suspicion that you have knowledge of the truth."

"But if the flying weapon is just a ruse, I can simply tell the Queen—"

"Aniri, think!" Devesh cried out, his grip on her shoulders pinching tight. "If the Samirian government knows you are on to their ruse, they will be forced to move up their plans. You need to be safely back in Dharia before anyone knows. I can take you with me, now. I can get you out of Jungali, but you need to leave with me. Right now. Please."

Her mind still spun with it, but she couldn't miss the panic in Devesh's eyes, the fear she might say no. "But I can't leave Priya and Janak behind! They will be in danger, too."

"Not as much as you, my love. The people who want you dead have already tried once."

Aniri's breath caught. She had thought it was General Garesh behind the attempt on her life. Was the Samirian government trying to kill her, too?

"I... I can't leave them." She wrung her hands, her mind clouding, then clearing as she pictured what would happen to Janak and Priya in her absence. "If I am gone, they will be held prisoner. Hostages, if nothing else. Or worse... they will have no value at all." Her heart squeezed at that thought, but her mind was still in torment. She couldn't imagine the prince would actually harm them; but *someone* had reached straight into his palace to attempt to assassinate her—if it were the Samirians, Janak and Priya would be just as vulnerable as she had been. Aniri balled up her fists again, frustrated, indecisive. She had to trust her heart, because her mind was a muddled mush.

"I'll go back and let Priya and Janak know we must leave immediately," she said.

"The prince will not let you go so easily," Devesh warned.

But that didn't sit right with her. "He has already offered to allow us to return to Dharia," she said, more confident now. "I will tell him we wish to make a quick trip back home, now that the engagement party is complete."

Devesh ran both his hands through his hair, frowning deeply. "He won't allow it."

Aniri didn't believe that, but it *would* be a suspicious move. And the forces who were trying to kill her might find a way before she secured passage for the three of them. "Then we must sneak out without his knowledge. Tell me where to meet you. I will bring Janak and Priya with me, and you can take us all out of country."

Devesh scrubbed his face with his hands. "All right. But it must be soon. I will make arrangements to spirit all three of you out tonight. Meet me at the Samirian consulate, at midnight. Ask for an audience with the ambassador. You can trust her. Do you know where the embassy is?"

"Is it here in Bhakti?"

"Yes."

"I can find it." She put a hand to his cheek. "Thank you, Dev."

He looked uncertainly at her.

"You took a tremendous risk coming here, telling me all this. Helping us." She couldn't ask for a more complete assurance of his love, that he was willing to

betray his country to save her.

He cupped her cheek with his hand. "Aniri." His voice was a breathless whisper. Then he kissed her, crushing his lips to hers, pulling her body into his. It was brief and fierce and protective. It settled her heart even more than his words and his actions. When he released her and stepped back, he said, "Midnight. Do not be late, my love."

She nodded.

"Go back to the party." He nodded to the body of the guard. "I will take care of this. Let no one suspect you are planning to make your escape."

She picked up her skirts, so they wouldn't drag over the guard, and quickly left the privy.

Her heart quivered all the way back to the party.

twenty-one

The guard at the entrance to the engagement party frowned when she returned without her escort, but he held the door open for her anyway. Whenever the guard Devesh had attacked recovered, she hoped it would be after she was long gone. At least for the moment, no one seemed inclined to question her. It helped that the formal part of the celebration had passed, the meal already half consumed. Guests were coming and going freely from their seats, visiting and politicking with their neighbors and allies long-separated by the miles between provinces. She slipped into her chair between the prince and Janak, hiding her shaking hands under the richly embroidered tablecloth that covered the table. Her plate was full of roasted meat and some unidentifiable delicacy, but she couldn't stand the thought of food. She was desperate to lean over to Janak and tell him everything, but that was impossible. She would have to wait until they were safely back in their room.

She nudged the delicacy with her finger, moving it around so no one would notice she hadn't actually eaten. Perhaps she could leave the party early, given it was already winding down, except she had no idea of the protocol. The prince was turned away from her in his seat, busy talking to two Jungali dressed in military finery, their cloaks long and black and buttoned with wide bronze-festooned ornaments along one side.

Aniri leaned toward Janak. "How soon do you think we'll be returning to our rooms?"

Janak raised an eyebrow. "You are eager to return to our confinement, Princess? You seemed to be enjoying the change of pace." Priya grinned at her from the next seat over. Of course, they would have no understanding of how dramatically things had changed in just a few short minutes.

The military men left the prince's side. Before anyone else could command his attention, she lightly touched his arm. He immediately turned to her, his look uncertain, as if wary of what she might ask.

"I'm sorry to disturb you, Prince Malik," she said, "but what is the protocol for the rest of the celebration?"

He frowned, and she cursed herself internally for how awkward and forced she sounded. She needed to continue the ruse, at least until they were away. She added a smile, but that only made her feel more off balance.

He leaned toward her, concern in his eyes. "Are you well, Princess?"

That would make a fine excuse. "I'm not quite myself, I'm afraid. I was thinking of returning to my room."

The prince eased up from his chair and held out his hand to her. She looked at it, hesitating a moment too long, before taking it and rising herself.

"I will accompany you back to your room, your majesty." He pulled her closer as she cleared her skirts off the chair. His voice dropped, and he whispered in her ear, so only she could hear. "I quickly grow tired of these formalities myself. You've given me the perfect excuse to escape."

She looked wide-eyed at him, which thankfully he took as some kind of mock-reproach, because he grinned and placed his hand at the small of her back to guide her through the guests still circulating around the head table. Aniri glanced back to see Janak frowning, but he made no move to follow. She would have to meet him back at the room. For once, she hoped he wouldn't delay.

Prince Malik stopped for a brief moment at Nisha's side. "Will you make apologies for me, Nisha? Princess Aniri needs a rest from the press of the court."

Nisha smiled wide, her gaze at Aniri full of warmth. "I know well the fatigue of these functions, Aniri. Take all the time to you need to become accustomed. There will always be more parties to attend. The public can wait." Then she turned a knowing smile to Prince Malik, who frowned some kind of annoyance at her. Nisha quickly stood to intercept a Samirian diplomat headed for the prince with an expectant look. "I will hold off the diplomats for you, Ashoka." She waved them away.

The prince's hand remained at the small of Aniri's back while they navigated the crowds, leaving by the same door she'd just come through. As they crossed the threshold, she had a quick moment of panic, imagining Devesh dragging the body of her unconscious escort down the hallway, but of course it was clear. The prince nodded to the guard at the door and waited until the rise and fall of the banquet room chatter had faded, and they were alone in the hallway, before speaking.

"I hope you're not truly ill." He gave her a sly smile, like he saw right through her excuse.

Her chest grew tight. "I'm sure I simply need a rest."

He nodded, but didn't say anything more, seemingly lost in his thoughts. Which suited Aniri because she was suddenly unsure about speaking to him, afraid all the fears Devesh had aroused might come spilling out of her. Had Prince Malik planned from the start to make a prisoner of her? Trap her in his mountain palace while the Samirians attacked her homeland? Even as those thoughts tumbled through her mind, they evaporated like mist. They were so tenuous compared to the gentle hand at her back and the sweet concern for her well-being that radiated from him.

When they arrived at her door, she placed a hand on the knob—an anchor to steady her as she said her goodbyes. "Well..." This would be the last time she saw him, and suddenly that made her hesitate. She smiled. "Thank you for the escort. Assassins wouldn't dare make an attempt on my life when I'm so well guarded."

His smile flashed and was gone. "Oh, I suspect whoever wants you dead, princess, would want to see me likewise."

Aniri swallowed. This conversation had quickly gone the one place she wanted to avoid. The prince suddenly seemed uncomfortable as well, examining his shiny black boots and then the doorknob with great interest before meeting her gaze again.

"Would you mind—" He stopped. "May I come in for a brief visit, your highness?"

Aniri's heart skipped a beat. "A visit?"

"If this is a bad time..." He took a half step back, as if he might run away down the hall. He stopped himself, then nodded. "Right. You probably want to rest." She

frowned. Why was he so nervous? Did he sense a change in her demeanor? He obviously didn't believe her feigned illness.

"But…" He hesitated again. "As your guard of the moment, I should probably check your rooms to make sure they are free of fire-bomb wielding assassins."

She smiled at his humor, but her chest was tight. Maybe a few moments for a visit would put him at ease, make him believe she was just escaping the party. She couldn't afford to have him checking in on her later, when she was attempting to flee for real.

"I would appreciate that, Prince Malik." She tilted her head toward him, cringing at the mistake of formality again. "*Ash*. And I'm fine, truly. But a visit is more than welcome."

He smiled and turned the knob for her, passing through the threshold and making a show of scanning the room while holding the door open for her. She swept in, waited while he closed the door again, and then strode over to the sitting area.

She gestured to the small couch, planning on taking a seat in one of the chairs Janak habitually occupied. "Please have a seat. I'm afraid I don't have tea. I'm not exactly prepared for entertaining."

"That's hardly necessary. I *did* invite myself in." He gestured for her to sit first… on the couch. When she did so, he took a seat next to her, closer than she was expecting. His arm draped across the red velveteen and dark wood of the back. His earnest look said he had something in particular to discuss. She tried to draw in a calming breath without looking like she was doing so. Hopefully she could put him at ease quickly and send him on his way.

"Ash," she said, trying for a teasing smile, "if I didn't

know better, I would think you were truly courting me." She hoped a little humor would short circuit the niceties and get him straight to the point. Instead, he looked shocked and dropped his gaze to his hand, which was white-knuckle clenching the back of the couch.

"Oh," she said, suddenly off balance again. "I didn't mean to offend. I—"

"Aniri," he cut her off, looking back at her with those earnest amber eyes. "When I asked you to accept this arrangement, I knew it would be hard on you. Hard on me." He smiled a little. "Honestly, I never really expected you to accept. And when I first saw you... I have to admit the prejudice of my people had its grip on me as well. I didn't think a princess from the plains could ever do something so noble as give up marrying for love to serve her country. Not when she had a choice."

She raised her eyebrows, stunned out of her concerns for the moment. "What do you mean, when you first saw me?"

"That day, outside the Queen's anteroom, you were the picture of what I expected from a Dharian princess: beautiful, dressed in the finest silks imaginable, with an air of..."

"Regality?" she asked, desperately trying to lighten the mood. "Nobility?"

"Arrogance."

Her mouth hung open in mock shock, and his smile tipped up on one side. She smacked him playfully on the shoulder, but he caught her hand and quickly brought it to his lips. His kiss touched the crest of Dharia inked on the back of her hand. Before she could recover from the shock, it was over.

Although he still held her hand in his.

"I quickly found you surprised me." All humor had

fled from his face. "And you have been constantly surprising me ever since, Aniri."

She should pull her hand away. She knew this. Yet she couldn't quite bring herself to do it, not while he was looking at her that way. "Why did you propose to arrange the marriage, if you thought there was no chance of me accepting?"

He let out a laugh and a small shake of his head. "I was desperate. Trying to hold my kingdom together, with no way out of the box of politics I had found myself in. I had tried everything, every alliance or ploy to cement my hold on the throne. You were my last hope." His voice dropped on the last word, and his eyes dropped to the Dharian crest on her hand. He passed his thumb over the deep burgundy tattoo, sending that same flush through her as during their kiss.

She blinked, not expecting that thought, and feeling even further off balance.

Somber again, he continued, "I know you have a lover at home. I knew as we left Dharia that this would be hard for you, and yet you've done nothing but help make this peace arrangement work. I thought it would be hardest on you, this arrangement. But I was wrong. I think it's going to be much harder on me."

Aniri's eyebrows lifted. "Is marrying me such a difficult thing?" She tried to make it light, but her chest was pained with not remembering to breathe, and her voice sounded breathless instead.

He grinned. "Horribly difficult, actually. At least, as long as you are only marrying me to bring peace."

Her mouth opened, but no words had formed in her head. "What are you saying?"

He inched closer on the couch, holding the tips of her fingers near, but not quite touching, his chest. "I'm

saying I wish I had not so readily agreed to allow you to have other lovers."

She sucked in a breath that probably sounded like a gasp. "Prince Malik." Was he saying he was in love with her? How could that be? The ghost of their kiss brushed her lips. That had been… something more than a feigned affection. "I… I don't know what to say…"

"No, Aniri, stop." He brought her hand to his lips again, effectively freezing her words in her throat. When he released her, it felt strange to have her hand back. "I am true to my word, if nothing else. I just… I simply wanted you to know. And, in the future, perhaps it would be best if we avoided any more kisses."

He gave her a sad smile, and it broke something loose inside her. The circumstances he thought he was in… to be trapped in a loveless marriage when you actually loved the person you were bound to… she shuddered with the thought. It compelled her to speak.

"I'm not deserving of any feelings you may have for me, Ash."

He frowned. "What do you mean?"

Her heart beat hard against her ribs. There was no reason for him to say he cared for her, unless it was actually true. And if he cared, she couldn't believe he would hurt her. "You… you don't need to worry. I'm not going to trap you in a loveless marriage." She knew he would let her return safely to Dharia; he had offered as much before.

"You've changed your mind." His face fell. "You're not going through with the wedding."

That look tore into her, and suddenly she couldn't bear the idea of him holding more pain inside than he already had. If she was going to desert him—and his attempts at peace—he at least deserved to know why. She couldn't believe she was going to say this, in spite of all Devesh's words and warnings, but she knew in her heart that Ash would never hurt her.

"I know the truth."

He looked confused. "The truth about what?"

"About the flying machine." She swallowed. "I know it doesn't exist."

He narrowed his eyes. "As I've been telling you from the beginning—"

"Yes, but now I know for sure. And so my mission here is done. I'm going to return to Dharia."

His face grew cold. "Your mission."

The pounding of her heart grew, like a small beast was tearing her up from the inside out. "I'm sorry, Ash. I never meant for you to..." Words had deserted her.

Realization dawned on his face. "You were only here to find out if the rumors were true."

His disgust made her throat close up. Of course she had lied to him. And now it was worse: he had feelings she not only wasn't going to return, but she would ruin all hope for the peace he had worked so hard for. Whatever nobility he thought she might have, clearly he was mistaken.

"Ash, I'm sorry," she said again. "When I agreed to this, I didn't know about your brother and how you were trying to hold the provinces together. I wish I could help, but I can't—"

"But you can't give up your future for something as simple as peace among the barbarians." His voice was so cold it made her shudder.

"I want peace as much as you do!" She hated the look he was giving her, like his first impression had been right all along. "I've been here, all this time, because I thought if I could just learn the truth about the flying

machine, I could avoid this,"—she motioned to him, their marriage, the whole arrangement—"this thing neither of us wants, not if it's not necessary. I was trying to find peace by finding the truth about the flying machine."

He scowled. "And what makes you so sure the flying machine doesn't exist?"

She opened her mouth, then closed it again; she couldn't endanger Devesh as well. "I know the truth. You can't lie to me now." She dropped her gaze because she couldn't stand to look him in the eye. "I told you from the beginning, Prince Malik. I'm afraid you're much more noble than I am." She forced herself to look up. "In fact, I'm counting on it with my life. If I believed you were merely orchestrating this to hold me hostage, a prisoner to be used against Dharia—"

"*That* is what you think?" He was truly horrified, and Aniri felt another stab for even entertaining the thought.

"No, I don't. Everything I've seen shows you're nothing but a man of honor. Someone Dharia should be proud to be allied with. But I understand you've made this... this *alliance*... with Samir."

He grimaced.

"And now that Dharia knows the flying machine is a ruse, maybe we will be at war soon enough. But for now, I want you to know the truth. I truly was trying to find a way for peace between our nations. And I trust you are a good and decent man who won't make me pay for that with my life. That you'll let me return home now, because that is my wish, Prince Malik. Please."

His face softened, wounded, and she felt doubly awful. This was a mistake. Even if he didn't mean any harm to her—which she still couldn't imagine—she could have snuck out in the dead of night and at least avoided seeing the disappointment in his face.

"The flying machine exists, Aniri."

"Ash, please—"

"I can prove it to you."

She looked up from her twisting hands. "What?" Her heart seized. Was this some kind of trick? But there was no need for that. She had truly thrown herself on his mercy, trusting his noble heart not to kill her for it. If he wanted to lock her in a cell, he could. Or he could keep her in velvet chains in this room, sequestered, cut off from anyone in Dharia as long as he wished. So he had no reason to lie to her now.

"I can take you to see it." His voice was cool, his eyes measuring her.

Her mouth didn't seem to function for a moment, and then she said, "Why would you do that?"

"Because, Aniri, I think you are much more noble than you believe. And I think, once you know all of the truth, that you might be willing to help me."

She swallowed. There was no way she could refuse. As soon as he offered the chance to see the machine, she knew she would take it. Because if it were actually true—if the flying machine actually *did* exist—then it would mean one simple thing: everything Devesh had told her was a lie.

And that was something she had to know.

twenty-two

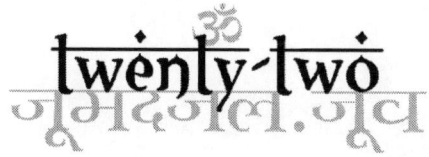

Within an hour, Aniri and the prince were leaving Bajir, traveling north by cable carriage. The outside air grew colder as they flew toward the frozen peaks, but that wasn't why Aniri wore a long black cloak, buttoned tight, with a voluminous hood that covered her hair and shadowed her face.

The prince insisted they travel incognito as much as possible.

No one would mistake her for a princess, that much was certain. A female mercenary, perhaps, or a well-armed trader. Her rough canvas pants were tucked into black boots, and the cuffs of her coat were coarse leather, clamped around her forearms. She possessed a dagger strapped at her hip and her father's saber hidden in the long drape of her cloak.

The prince was similarly dressed, only he carried a small pistol in full view over his jacket. Their carriage sailed over trees frosted with cold, but it was still warm inside the carriage from its time in the stationhouse. They had already passed through two trading stations, each less populated than the last. These cable routes seemed less traveled than the main arteries into Bajir, but even so, the prince was still recognized.

However, the station attendants only raised an eyebrow at his female companion before waving them through. Although the rumors were rampant about the love affair raging between the Prince of Jungali and the Princess of Dharia, apparently her face was much less well known.

The two of them didn't speak when other travelers were present. Their carriage was now headed for the province of Mahet. The sun had started to dip, and she didn't know if they would be staying in Mahet or traveling farther on. But she certainly wouldn't be in Bajir at midnight, meeting Devesh at the Samirian embassy.

Her heart twisted, but her mission was still in play—to gain the truth about the flying machine—and Prince Malik seemed determined to take her straight to it. Unless this was some elaborate deception she couldn't quite parse. If the prince wanted her dead, he could have accomplished that without dragging her to a distant Jungali province. Devesh said not to trust the prince, but she had already trusted him with her life. And she was still alive.

Would Devesh even be in Bajir when she returned? He may have decided she didn't love him and left Jungali altogether. He could return to his Samirian homeland and wait out the war with Dharia he said was coming. Or maybe he would be found out. Certainly, the ambassador would not be pleased he had leaked the Samirian's top-secret war plans to her.

Or everything he told her could be a lie. Aniri had

brought her mother's aetheroceiver in her small traveling case. In the event they ran into trouble, she could send one more message home before her demise. Janak would be furious about her taking off to find the skyship with the prince, which was why she hadn't told him where she was going. Plus he would have insisted on coming along or done everything in his power to stop her. Neither of which served her purpose.

She and the prince were the only passengers in the carriage now. The coal-smoke of the station washed away as they sailed higher into the air. The waning light turned the broad-leafed trees below them a darkish red. The prince seemed to relax a little compared to the brusque efficiency of before, transferring them from station to station and keeping silent in between.

He turned away from the landscape and finally spoke. "I asked Nisha to spread the tale that we've gone off for a lover's retreat, just the two of us. It's contrary to our custom, but the people already believe we have been meeting in secret before. We're supposedly in the Rajan province, taking in the high plateau wildflowers in a mountain retreat away from prying eyes."

Aniri nodded. "Does Nisha believe the rumor?"

"She didn't ask if it was true," he said cryptically. He leaned against a bronze railing that ran the perimeter of the carriage and returned to staring at the forests below.

Not wanting to lose her chance at more information, Aniri pressed on. "Can you tell me something about this mysterious flying machine? I have to say, I'm impressed already with your cable carriages. No offense, but before I arrived, I didn't think the Jungali were so advanced in technology."

He didn't look at her. "We carefully cultivate a reputation of inferiority."

"I didn't mean—"

He smirked and slid her a glance. "I am making a joke, Aniri."

"Oh."

He took a deep breath and let it out slow. "Much of our technology comes in our trade relations with Samir. Their metalworking knowledge is superior to ours, but we have trace minerals that are essential to giving the processed metal ore from the Samirian mountains the kind of strength necessary to hold up our cable carriages." He pointed to the giant ironwork man holding the cables aloft as it approached their carriage. "There are many ways in which the partnership is beneficial. But it was one of our own Jungali miners who discovered the navia."

"Navia?" Aniri's heart took a leap. That was the term in Prince Malik's aetheroceiver message, the one he still didn't know she had read.

"Navia is the lighter than air gas that makes it possible to build the flying machine in the first place. The gas is used to inflate a giant bag, which then allows the ship to float."

"Like a child's fire light?" Sometimes, especially at traditional festivals, children in Dharia would stretch thin tissues over a lightweight cage of folded paper. A small paper bowl would dangle below it, filled with kindling. As long as the kindling burned and heated the air, the paper cage would rise. Eventually the entire ensemble would flame out in a puff of smoke that would drift on the winds.

"It's not unlike a fire light in basic construction," the prince said. "Except the gas within the bag is not heated air, but lighter-than-air navia instead."

"You said you mine this navia out of the ground?" Aniri asked. "So it is a rock?"

"Actually it is a gas trapped within the rock. When it is crushed or heated, the navia is released. We capture it, then fill the skyship with it."

"Skyship." Aniri rolled the term around on her tongue. It was fitting. "A ship that sails through the sky. Does it look like a trade ship?" Her curiosity piqued now, and she forgot for a moment that she should be skeptical of the skyship's very existence. But the way the prince spoke of it, so concretely, with such assurance, she couldn't help but think of it as real.

"You'll see when we get to Sik."

"I wondered where you would have hidden the flying machine—the skyship—but I would never have guessed Sik province. Isn't that General Garesh's province?"

"Yes."

"And that's where we're going?"

"I didn't say it would be a safe voyage, princess." He gave her shrewd look. "Only that I could show you the machine."

"Does he know we're coming?"

Prince Malik gestured to their hoods and weapons.

Aniri guessed not. "But you're still the Prince of Jungali. Surely you can visit your own skyship if you choose. Is it just because I am along to see it as well?"

Prince Malik shook his head and sighed. "My brother was the spearhead for the initial design of the skyship. He was the first to see the potential, as soon as the navia was discovered. It was his dream—he wanted to see Jungali an equal among the nations of our world, not just a group of warring provinces and backwater barbarians. He saw it as our ticket into equal status, a power to be respected, but above all, he saw it as a way to bring even more trade deep into the mountains. He liked to say it would make our world smaller."

"I… never thought of it that way." And she hadn't. She had only conceived of the flying ship as a weapon, a threat to Dharia, even when it was only a bare rumor she hadn't paid much attention to. Which a skyship certainly could be, if it existed. Would be, in anyone else's hands. She had that peculiar shame again, like the prince and his thoughts were instinctively more noble than hers. She hadn't even imagined the Jungali could want something more than war for their own nation. And she had taken for granted the status of her country, not realizing that others—the Samirians as well as the Jungali—might want also want the respect Dharia commanded.

"Tosh had wonderful plans," the prince continued. "From the beginning, he fought with Garesh, who saw only the military potential. When my brother died, and the Queen soon after… I'm not just trying to honor the peace he was working toward, Aniri. I'm doing everything I can to make his dreams come true with the skyship he built. The last thing I want is to destroy the ship, but I need to gain the crown before I can make it bend to the purpose my brother originally intended. For now, the last person the general wants to see at the airharbor is me. In fact, I'm fairly certain he's looking for a reason to have me arrested, no matter how thin the charge. If I were to bring a Dharian, before we are officially wed, to see our most secret military weapon… well, that would surely qualify."

She stared at him. "You're taking a risk in showing this to me."

He looked out over the forest to the distant horizon, which included several peaks shrouded in clouds. Although the farther north they traveled, those peaks seemed less high. "In more ways than one, Princess."

She crossed the small stretch of carriage between

them and touched the sleeve of his jacket. "Tell me."

He gritted his teeth, then turned to her. "For one, I think the general is behind the attempt on your life. For another, you may decide to simply take this information back to Dharia, rendering the skyship less effective in a military sense. Although, honestly, I would welcome that at this point. At least it would reduce the skyship's usefulness as a weapon of surprise. Does that make me a traitor, Aniri?"

"No," she said, and meant it. "It makes you someone committed to peace." And she believed that, too. Devesh's words were still in her mind, but they had slunk into a dark corner to fester amongst themselves. Whatever the truth of the skyship—whether it existed or was merely some deranged figment of the prince's imagination—he truly believed in peace and was trying to pursue it. She didn't doubt that in the slightest.

The prince looked back at the horizon. "Sometimes I wonder." Strangely, as convinced as she was of his intent, the prince seemed to doubt it himself. "General Garesh may be right. Perhaps I'm too soft to be a leader for a mountainous people whose only strategic advantage is that of a quilled rodent you can't get hold of. Maybe I should seize the one offensive advantage we would finally have in this weapon."

"I don't believe you truly mean that," Aniri said softly.

He took a breath and turned back to her, a small smile on his face. "Which is why I'm taking the risk of bringing you with me, Aniri."

She shook her head and leaned slightly away. "I still don't understand why you trust me. I lied to you." She shrugged, hands out. "About practically everything."

"You did." He smirked. "And rather convincingly,

too."

Aniri flinched, his remark far too close to Devesh's accusation in the privy about her performance in kissing the prince. That she was skilled in lying was not a tremendous shock—she had been raised in the Queen's court after all—but it bothered her that the prince would know this about her. Which struck her as strange in itself.

"Maybe I am too soft-hearted, just as General Garesh believes." The prince's smirk softened into a shy smile. "But I still believe the woman who left her home on the plains in search of peace for her country is worth taking a risk for."

Aniri felt heat creep up her neck. "I think you need to read less poetry, Prince Malik."

He laughed and returned his sight to the horizon. "You're probably right."

She left him to his thoughts for the rest of the trip into Mahet, not wanting to push that line of reasoning too far. She was simply thankful he trusted her enough to take her to see the skyship, whatever his reasons.

twenty-three

Aniri kept her hood up, face nearly obscured, even though she and the prince were inside a shadowy inn of very dubious patronage, and the dim gaslamps barely gave off enough light to see the rough floor beneath her boots. They had arrived in Mahet, and it appeared they were staying the night. The prince insisted it wasn't safe for her to room separately, and the innkeeper only spared her a glance or two while the prince made arrangements. Rooming together would invite extra scrutiny for the prince's mysterious female companion, but she was beyond arguing with the prince about things which weren't absolutely necessary.

The tiny establishment was inside the Mahet capital, but just barely, wedged against the perimeter granite walls and sandwiched between a stable and a butcher where animal carcasses competed with the raw manure from the stable for the most offensive smell. The fact that the innkeeper appeared to know the prince and asked few questions told her the prince made a habit of traveling along unconventional routes. He offered to carry her parcel, but she insisted on keeping it, afraid he would detect the heavy weight of the aetheroceiver inside the small trunk.

The prince marched ahead of her, with the innkeeper ahead of him, slipping surreptitious looks back at her, in spite of the extra bills she saw the prince slip to him, no doubt to keep his silence. What must he think? That the prince was having a secret affair on top of his recently revealed secret affair with her, the Princess of Dharia? What must the people think of their young sovereign? Or did his people indulge their young prince, recently bereft of his mother and brother both? She couldn't tell, because the innkeeper kept his thoughts to himself as he unlocked a room on the highest floor, three levels up and with a view of the dark cobbled road below. There weren't even gaslamps to light the way, only dim flickerings in the few cottages down the street, probably out of range of the stench. There was no one to see her standing at the window of their room, but just in case, Aniri pulled the curtains tight.

The prince was busy lighting a fire in the fireplace, but she kept her cloak in place. The outside chill pervaded the room, and a fine layer of grit lay on the neatly made bed dominating the center of the room, as if no one had occupied it in a very long time. She eyed it warily, wondering about the prince's intentions only for a moment. Surely he would offer to take the floor. Or the heavy chair by the fireplace, but that didn't look to offer any more comfort. By all rights, she should be the one sleeping on the floor, but she was sure he wouldn't allow it. The privy was down the hall, but she wasn't much inclined to use it, either to change or to use the facilities.

She was cold enough that sleeping in her traveling clothes, cloak and all, might be the best option.

A small flame flickered in the fireplace, adding a bit of light if not yet warmth. The weak shadows it cast competed with the single gaslamp by the bed, somehow increasing the gloom by making the shadows move. The prince stood, clearly proud of his accomplishment.

He turned to her. "Are you ready for bed, Princess?" His face was cloaked in shadows, but she heard implications in his question that she chose to ignore.

"I may need to warm myself first." She rubbed her arms over her coat and drifted to where he stood by the fireplace. "Is there any hope for heat from this tonight?"

He glanced at the bed. Now that she was closer, she could tell he was holding back a smile. "Whatever wicked thoughts you're having, Prince Malik, be out with them already."

"My honor, your majesty!" He threw a hand over his heart. "You tarnish it with your implications."

"Please." But she couldn't help a small smile. "Your honor was tarnished as soon as we walked into this inn together."

He grinned widely. "Perhaps that was my intention all along."

"How many pretend lovers do you wish to have, Prince Malik?"

His grin tempered. "I *am* getting quite a reputation, the more time I spend with you, Princess Aniri. Apparently I'm the kind of sovereign who sneaks off for secret trysts with all manner of women in all kinds of exotic locales, even the rather smelly side of Mahet." She turned away from his devilish grin and held her still-gloved hands out to the fire. There was still no discernible heat from it.

The bed let out an ominous creak as the prince bounded onto it. Aniri gave him a startled look, at once amazed that the ancient bed, which was probably stuffed with straw rather than a proper feather mattress, held up to his abuse at all, and doubly amazed he was in it. He patted the tattered bed covering next to him and arched his eyebrows, his grin still demonic.

"I suppose I'm sleeping on the floor, then," Aniri said coldly, turning back to the fireplace and wondering how close she could sleep to it without running the danger of catching on fire. She cast about for at least a blanket to keep her warm, but there was only the bedding on the decrepit mattress behind her, which creaked again as the prince rose from it. Aniri grabbed hold of the heavy wooden chair and dragged it toward the fireplace, but only succeeded in moving it an inch or two before the prince arrived to help. The thing was ancient, with carved wooden arms and a straw-filled cushion, which probably weighed as much as the wood. It smelled of dewy must and horses.

The prince smiled softly when she finally met his gaze, the firelight dancing orange flickers across his face. "I can see you're not much for humor right now, Aniri. Please excuse my sad attempts at it."

She stood straight and tried to relax her shoulders, not sure why they were so tense. Then she gestured to the chair. "I'll be fine here. It looks comfortable enough."

The prince looked askance at it. "It looks like it's fit for the stable, but I'll manage what sleep I can with it." He slipped between the narrow spot between the chair and the fire, taking a seat and stretching his boots out so they nearly touched the growing flames of the log he had set.

Aniri just stared at him. He was honorable through

and through, and gentle with her as well, even when she mostly deserved his scorn for deceiving him. By all rights, he should have thrown her in the dungeon or whatever cell he kept for traitors and spies. Instead, he was taking a tremendous risk to show her his top military secrets and allowing her to sleep unmolested on the only bed in their chamber in the process. She felt... unworthy. Like it shamed her to be near someone with such a keen moral compass. In all her time at her mother's court, filled with intrigue and pandering courtesans, she wasn't quite sure if she had ever met someone so thoroughly *good*.

She unstrapped the dagger belted to her waist and set it on a small table by the fireplace. "I don't deserve the bed, Prince Malik."

"True," he said with a straight face, examining the fire, then tilted a grin up to her. "But someone must sleep in it, or the rumors won't be nearly as convincing."

She shook her head and leaned against the stone facing of the fireplace. A small drift of heat snuck past the toes of her boots and crawled up her leggings underneath the cloak. "Will we reach Sik province on the morrow?" she asked.

"Yes. The skyship is hidden in a ravine to the north in the farthest reach of the province, not far from the navia mines. We will have to travel by shashee for the last leg of our trip. If we're lucky, we'll arrive before General Garesh can travel back from the engagement party."

"If he finds you, it will go badly for you." This concern weighed heavier on her than she expected.

"Then we'd best take care not to be found." The prince stretched his arms, then laced his hands behind his head. He was still wrapped in his long, dark jacket with the bronze clasps along the top, but he had left his dagger by the bed, and his hood was thrown back. Flickers of firelight streaked his hair with orange, and his amber eyes shone in the dim light as he stared at the fire.

"I could go alone," Aniri said.

The prince turned to her, his gaze slicing through the dark. His eyebrows lifted subtly. "I forgot. You're a spy." A hint of smile came out. "But I doubt you have experience navigating Sik security in secret retrenchments in the frozen mountains of the north."

The heat from the fire was wafting stronger under her coat now. She unbuckled it, letting it hang loose. "Even if General Garesh has not returned," she reasoned, "surely the people will recognize you."

He touched his hood. "I will be as unobtrusive as possible."

"You will be recognized. Word will return to General Garesh. You said he has been looking for a way to arrest you. If you accompany me, it will be even more obvious that you have been the one to secret me to the skyship's hiding place. Perhaps we can observe it from a safe distance."

"They've built a special encasement that spans the ravine," he said. "It's an engineering marvel, truly, and wouldn't be possible without the Samirian engineers. But you cannot see anything until you get inside."

Aniri held her jacket open. The fire had finally blazed up, and it quickly had become almost too hot to bear. "Then take me close, and let me go the remainder of the way. I only need to see the skyship to know for certain you are telling the truth, no more."

He shook his head. "I can hardly let you go alone, Princess. You will need someone to ensure you are safe. The last thing we can afford at this point is for you to be caught infiltrating the skyship hideaway."

Aniri sighed in frustration, putting her hands on her

hips. Realizing she was still armed with her saber—her father's sword—she decided to make her point that way. She quickly reached inside and drew her sword. With a quick arc overhead, she brought it down to point at the prince's heart. He jerked at her sudden movement, his hands becoming unlaced from behind his head. The razor sharp tip was a good foot away from his body, putting him in no danger.

"I am capable of defending myself."

"I see," he said with a small smile and a luxurious look along the length of her blade. "I shall have to reconsider my plans to steal into your bed later this eve."

She arched an eyebrow at him and slowly withdrew her weapon, steadying its blade in the air between them, before sheathing it again.

He relaxed but didn't fold his hands behind his head, instead running a hand across his face. "If you are caught, I will be forced to come after you."

"Then I will be certain to not get caught," she countered with a smirk.

He shook his head but didn't argue. Suddenly he leaped up and lunged for her, catching her around the waist and pulling her to him. She instinctively pushed against him, but he held her firmly, then beat at her legs. Only after a moment, did she realize what he was doing. Part of her cloak had caught fire, and he was beating it with his bare hands. She froze, rigid against him, letting him put the last of the embers out by striking her leg, none too softly.

When he stood, his face was flushed, and she could see a roil of emotions playing across it. He still held her close around the waist.

"Thank you," Aniri said, breathless, her face close to his. There was a warm flush through her body which had nothing to do with the heat of the fire, and she was glad for the dark that covered her blush at having him hold her so intimately.

"Trying to save you from fire is becoming a habit of mine." His face relaxed, and a small smile returned as he released her. Aniri tried to ignore the feeling that she didn't want him to let her go. Then he shook his head. "This seems like a very bad idea, you going alone, Aniri. I don't like the odds on it."

She straightened, trying to banish the still-traveling flush that warmed her body. "If you're lying to me and hauling me out to the frozen north to see nothing at all, then I'm in trouble regardless. But if you're telling me the truth, and this skyship really exists, then we need you to stay out of General Garesh's cells. And we both need to return to Bajir to find a way to ensure peace. That won't be possible if you are caught. If I'm caught, well, the Princess of Dharia will have turned out to be untrustworthy after all. You'll need every bit of help you can get to defeat your own general, and that is where Dharia might actually be able to help."

"Not if their princess is being held prisoner by General Garesh."

"Especially if the Third Daughter of the Queen is being held by a general in the mountains of Jungali," Aniri said. "I promise you, Prince Malik, my mother will not stand for that. And I will let her know who her true allies are." She tried to muster the confidence she should have in those words, but she wasn't at all sure the Queen would come after her. She hadn't gone after her father's killers, and he hadn't disappointed her the way Aniri had.

The prince smiled. "Well, if she's anything like her daughter, I certainly would not want to cross her."

Aniri resisted smiling in return. Her mother was not

like her. If it served Dharia, the Queen would abandon her to the barbarians in the freezing mountains. Aniri had brought the Queen's aetheroceiver, but any messages at this point might work their way back to Janak, who would surely come after her and ruin any chance she had at discovering the skyship—and whether or not Devesh had told her the truth about the Samirians.

She might be caught by General Garesh and hung for treason, but that was a risk she knew going into this. With a distasteful glance at her singed black coat—it was fortunate the burnt portion did not stand out—Aniri turned to claim the bed for the night, ignoring thoughts of Prince Malik just recently in it.

She would need her rest for a day that might be her last.

twenty-four

The shashee stable housed at least twenty of the beasts, all snuffling out mist in the crisp morning air. The mountains loomed over their stable, like Devpahar herself accepting their vaporous offerings in return for safe travels. Aniri was thankful the cold contained the stench of the stable—which was more than she could say for the stable owner. He was as wide as he was tall, covered in a vast furry wrap that smelled like damp shashee. He lumbered like his beasts, but his disposition was nowhere near as gentle or calm as the creatures he tended.

"Twenty yakles," he said to Aniri. It was as much grunt as words.

Prince Malik was doing his best to hide under his hood by pretending to examine a selection of tapping canes hanging on the wall. They both had acquired new coats over their hooded cloaks—a tan hide of some kind, trimmed in fur at the hood and sleeves. According to the prince, the overcoats would disguise them as Sik traders, and they were definitely suited to the frigid mountain weather, if less so for stealth. Although she supposed camouflage was a relative thing.

Aniri had no idea if twenty yakles was excessive for a day's shashee rental. "Twenty?" she said, aghast. "Is there no law against robbery here in Sik province?"

The stable owner huffed and crossed his arms across the expanse of his chest. He only managed to reach far enough to tuck his hands under his armpits. "Nineteen."

"Sixteen." She cast a look over the beasts as they shifted in their pens, the thin rails too frail to keep them quartered if they had any mind to leave. But they seemed content to stay, huddled together no doubt for warmth. "And don't give me the sickly one in the middle." She gestured with her chin. She had no idea if there were any sick shashee, but with the size of the herd, there must be one lesser among them. Her hair blew slightly in a gust of air from the open door of the stable shop. She had bound it in a braid, but the double hoods of her cloak and the overcoat had worked it loose. She probably looked as bedraggled as the shaggy beasts.

"Seventeen," the stable owner said, "and no lower. And you will have to use ring saddle. No carriages today."

"Deal." Aniri had no idea what a ring saddle was, but it would have to do. The prince said they weren't going far. The round man shuffled off to find their mount, and Prince Malik drifted her way once he was out the door.

"Princess, spy, *and* experienced tradeswoman," he said from under his hood, still up. "Is there no end to your talents?" The sarcasm was heavy in his voice.

"I'm fairly certain we were robbed."

The prince paused a beat. "Actually, I think you got quite the deal. I think he was intimidated by your beauty."

Aniri just shook her head. "Please tell me a ring saddle isn't going to present a problem."

"We only have about an hour journey. I think I can tolerate sharing a shashee with you for that long." He grinned, then ducked his head as the stable owner's heavy footfalls sounded outside. The prince slipped a few paper bills into her hand. Keeping his back to the owner, the prince shuffled into the sunshine outside. A young stableboy clad in heavy coats brought the animal to him for inspection.

The stable owner beckoned her to come outside as well. The weathered, grayish beast he had selected for them had clumps of fur that hung below its massive chin. The "saddle" was barely more than a brilliant red blanket draped across the animal's back and looked more to protect it from the cold than to hold them securely to its back. In fact, it looked as though a good wind could lift it clean free. A shape under the blanket formed a ring of sorts, and sat between the hump at the rear and the massive shoulders in front.

The stableboy tapped his cane on the animal's nose, bringing it to a stop, then fetched a stepladder that reached halfway up the beast's side. It didn't seem nearly enough, but the prince quickly climbed the steps and grabbed hold of something hidden under the blanket. Then he miraculously flung himself up onto the animal's back, landing perfectly in the saddle.

Aniri just stared.

She could see the grin under his hood, so she strode forward, determined to at least appear she knew what she was doing. She shoved the bills into the fat hand of the stable owner and gamely climbed the steps, but when she reached the top, she couldn't tell what she was supposed to do next. The prince reached down and grasped her arm, so she grabbed onto his rough hide sleeve and tried to leap up on the beast. She only made it halfway, but the prince managed to haul her up the rest. The saddle was smaller than it looked, forcing her forward into the dip at the center. She couldn't help but sit pressed against the prince's back. Their bulky Sik overcoats provided plenty of padding between them, and her thin leather gloves gave her some sense of propriety, but it still felt strangely intimate.

She wished she had bargained harder for a carriage.

The stableboy handed up the tapping cane, and the prince gave two light taps to the beast's forehead. It swayed forward in a great motion that felt like it would fling Aniri from the saddle. She clutched at the prince's overcoat to keep from falling off. A low chuckle came from him, barely rising over the shuffle of woolly feet on the frost-crusted ground. The swaying grew more rhythmic once the beast got going, but Aniri still was forced to hold fast, synchronizing their bodies in order not to bang against one another.

An hour suddenly seemed like a very long time.

They lurched away from the outskirts of the trading village and into a steep canyon carved from granite. It was dark, the sun not yet cresting the mountains. Tiny shrubs clung to crevices in the shadowed walls, their gnarled branches permanently bent in a perpetual battle against the wind. They pointed back to the village like a thousand fingers of warning against their slow progress deeper and deeper into the canyon.

Aniri knew this would be dangerous. Her boasts of the Queen coming after her were simply that. But even if her mother chose to rescue her from the barbarians in the frozen north, Aniri wasn't sure how the Queen's infantry would fare against the harsh climate and difficult terrain.

Lives would certainly be lost in the process. The Queen could well be right to forsake her.

Aniri and Prince Malik didn't speak. The sound of the shashee's grunts and the scraping of its feet on the graveled road mixed with the hollowness of the wind, making speech seem a lost effort. Eventually, Aniri tucked her head behind the prince's back, sheltering her face from the cold.

The road narrowed as it hugged the craggy mountainside, winding higher and higher. How could any kind of flying weapon have been built in such a remote area? Then she spied a thin rail line at the bottom of the canyon. Supplies and materials must run by rail, because only a shashee or a drawn wagon could navigate their increasingly narrow foot trail.

The air grew even thinner as they climbed. The cold turned Aniri's breath into a steaming cloud. It left her warm spot behind the prince and trailed behind them. The rhythm of the beast lulled her, and time passed quicker than Aniri thought possible. Soon the prince tapped the beast to a stop, and she lurched against him, clutching again. The shashee slowly knelt to the ground, one giant tree-trunk of a leg at a time. When it folded down, the prince slid off, then held a hand up to help her.

"Are we taking a rest?" she asked once she was on the graveled dirt beside him.

The prince pointed farther up the road. It disappeared around a bend in the canyon. "This is the last turn before the airharbor."

"Airharbor? As in a harbor for the skyship?"

"It's rather more like a small city than a place to dock the ship, but yes." The prince turned to her. "I'm still not enamored of this plan where you try this alone."

They had already discussed how she would slip in as

one of the workers. Aniri patted her gloved hand on her hip, where the prince knew she carried her father's saber buried under the thick overcoat. At the small of her back was her dagger as well.

"Just tell me how to find the entrance."

Getting in wouldn't be the challenge; it was getting out again, once she had seen the skyship itself, that would prove the most difficult. And where her weapons might come in handy.

The prince sighed and pointed down the footpath again. "Keep following the road to the north end of the airharbor. The workers live outside the harbor in a small camp during the week. At week's end, they generally return to their families in the trading town we just left. You're too late for the morning shift, so if anyone asks, say you're late returning from the festival in town."

He examined her a moment, and she thought he might put up further objections to her mission, but he only reached up to pull a tendril of her hair free from her double layered hoods. "If you look a little more disheveled, they might actually believe the story. Garesh has workers on round-the-clock shifts now, so there should be a lot of people coming and going."

"So perhaps it will not be so difficult to leave?"

"Or you may be stuck breaking navia ore for a shift, princess," he said with a small smile.

She grimaced. It would be tough to pretend to be a manual labor worker for long. Her climbing and fencing kept her strong, but she was not used to labor of that kind. "Is there another way out, perhaps?"

The prince frowned, then glanced at the thin railroad track. The morning sun, which was just now climbing over the ridges of the canyon, glinted off the rails as though they were made of silver, not steel. "You might be able to slip out through the rail entrance. But I'm not sure that's any less hazardous than braving security to leave before the end of your shift."

He handed Aniri what looked like a small coin with wings. It was rimmed in copper, and the center was inlaid with intricate clockwork, tiny gears interlocked with delicate metal levers. The layout of the gears and wings made the device resemble a mechanical bird. The wings, indeed the whole mechanism, had a distinctly Samirian flavor.

"What is this?" Aniri turned it over. The other side was stamped with a sleek boat, which had a multitude of folding sails. It was definitely a Samirian skiff in design.

"This is your key to a day's wages at the airharbor. Back in Mahet, while you were sleeping, I met with my spy in Garesh's employ."

Aniri raised her eyebrows, but he went on without missing a beat.

"He gave me this token. The workers use these to gain access to the airharbor. You can't get in without one. The workers turn one token in each day and are issued a new one for the next shift."

Aniri frowned. "Won't Garesh know the coin came from your spy if I'm caught?"

Prince Malik gave a small smile. "No, he'll be fine. It's not uncommon for the tradespeople in town to trade tokens. They're like currency. And besides, my spy is a long-time member of Garesh's household. He worked for my brother when he was first developing the skyship design. He'll be above suspicion." The prince paused, then looked into her eyes. "The skyship isn't something I want to destroy, Aniri. Most of Jungali is remote and isolated. If Dharia and Jungali were allies, the skyship could be the beginning of a new transport system, something that could connect our two countries for trade in a way we've never been able to accomplish before. If we can keep Garesh from using it as a weapon, we can make it an instrument of peace instead. With your help—with Dharia's help—we can make that happen. Together."

"I know you're working for peace, Ash," Aniri said softly. "But I still need to see the skyship for myself." She slid the small, weighty token into her overcoat pocket. "Are you sure this coin will get me in?"

"It should. There are plenty of new workers with the extra shifts. A new face shouldn't raise any alarms. Just try not to be..."

"What?" Aniri countered his disapproving tone.

"Try not to be quite so... *regal*."

"You mean arrogant."

"Even as a tradeswoman, you weren't exactly humble, Princess." But he was smiling now, and Aniri wasn't sure if he was serious or not.

"I'll do my best to be demure."

He laughed at that, but then sobered quickly and placed his hands on Aniri's shoulders. "Do your best to not get caught. It would be quite challenging to get you out again."

"If I'm caught, you should head back to your palace immediately. If you want to keep hold of your reign, you have to disavow all knowledge of my spying activities. You can't work for peace if you're in Garesh's prison." She swallowed. That was almost certainly the right thing for him to do, but she wasn't at all sure about being left to fend for herself. She had snuck a message to her mother while in the privy in Mahet, telling her the prince was a worthy ally. It was a message that wouldn't bring her mother's infantry, or Janak for that matter, storming the mountains to find her before she had a chance to see the skyship. But if she were caught, it would serve as a cryptic, but hopefully instructive, final note. The Queen might even heed it.

The prince was studying her with those odd amber eyes, like he wasn't quite sure he should let her go after all. Then he released her and said, "Just don't get caught."

"I'll meet you here in an hour," she said. "If I'm not back by then, I may have to wait out the shift."

His face was pinched with concern, as if he was still undecided. She turned her back on him, before he could change his mind, and edged around the shashee, who took up most of the narrow dirt path chiseled out of the mountainside. When she rounded the bend in the road, she saw what the prince meant by the airharbor being a port city in the mountains rather than a simple hidden dock for a skyship.

The harbor was *massive*.

Giant beams of lumber spanned the canyon, like an enormous V-shaped box had been wedged down between the sides. At the bottom, it nearly reached the rail line. As it went up, the harbor widened with the canyon. The flat top spanned from one rocky edge to the other, soaring a hundred feet above Aniri, at least halfway up the canyon. She stared up the full height, its tremendous size making her dizzy. Or perhaps it was the thin air again, working against her. She braced her hand against the cool rock wall bordering the path and breathed deeply a few times. Exerting herself as an ore worker would make it difficult to keep up the pretense of being a native Jungali.

Once the dizziness faded, she continued down the path, stealing occasional peeks at the airharbor structure. It was as large as a small village, encased in wood, and suspended in the middle of the canyon. No wonder the

rumors had been swirling for months—this kind of undertaking would have required that amount of time just to build the structure, no matter what was housed inside. Aniri nearly stopped in her tracks, almost convinced of the prince's truth simply by the presence of the harbor. What else could it be but something that housed a skyship?

Yet, her mission wasn't simply to verify its existence, but to discover its exact nature and capabilities. If Dharia was to defend herself against such a weapon, the Queen would need to know exactly what she was facing. And, not for the first time, Aniri wondered if she might have a chance to sabotage the skyship as well. Dharia might never have a better chance than right now to strike at the heart of the weapon. Aniri could destroy it, take it out of the equation that would force her into an arranged marriage with the Prince of Jungali. But the prince himself had brought her here, with full knowledge that she had come to spy on him. Because he believed she would help him work for peace. The prince could have killed her or had her imprisoned many times. Instead, he brought her into his deepest confidence. To betray that trust now felt... wrong. But could Aniri pass up the chance to destroy the weapon, if she had it?

She would see what opportunities presented themselves once she was inside.

twenty-five

The rocky path passed under the airharbor, creating a tunnel with three solid sides: the rock wall of the canyon, the narrow dirt path, and the wooden structure heavy above Aniri's head. The fourth side was a sheer drop to the rail line below. She hesitated only a moment before striding into the darkness of the tunnel. At the far end, a lone security guard leaned against the wall of the canyon, warming his hands with misty breaths. She had to give credit to Garesh's military foresight: the mountain provided such restricted access as to be practically unassailable. The harbor itself was a fortress. Even if Dharia knew the location of this mountain hideaway, the possibility of launching any kind of successful assault was practically nonexistent.

This one guard was almost laughable in the face of such natural defenses.

Yet, she still had to get past him.

The crunch of her boots on the ground drew his

attention. He pushed away from the edge and shifted his rifle so it was held loosely in front of him, its strap looped over his shoulder. The steel barrel glinted in the morning sun, blinding her. He waited until she was close to speak.

"What's this, now?" he asked.

"I'm... I'm here to work," Aniri said, suddenly unsure of how to appear sufficiently *demure* to get past the guard.

"Shift's already started."

Aniri stepped into the sun, and it took a moment for her eyes to adjust. The guard was young, not much older than her, dressed much like she was in a hide coat rimmed with fur. His eyes were dark, and not unfriendly, especially once she was in the light. His gaze seemed drawn to her lips, dancing between them and her eyes. Perhaps demure was the right approach.

She dropped her gaze and dug the token out of her pocket, holding it out in the palm of her gloved hand. "I have a token, and I've walked all this way." She gestured to the empty stretch of road behind her.

His gaze held hers for a moment, dropped to the token, then bounced back. "That's last week's token." His voice was filled with sympathy, even though he was slowly shaking his head.

Aniri feigned shock, which wasn't hard with the sharp churn in her stomach. She turned the token end over end. "But... but he told me it was good." She looked up at him. "He *promised*. Please... I really need the wages. It's for my family. We just had a new baby arrive, and we need coal for heat…"

The boy's face softened even more. He bit his lip and glanced over his shoulder. At a distant gate, a line of workers waited to gain entry to the harbor. They were all clad in tan leather and fur trimmed jackets, like her and the guard. Then he slung his rifle to the back of his shoulder and fished a token out of his pocket. It was the same as hers, only rimmed in iron instead of copper.

"Here." He held out his hand. "Trade me. I'll tell them they gave me the wrong one last time."

She quickly placed her token in his hand and tucked his into her palm. She gave him a sincerely surprised and grateful look. "Thank you."

He smiled. "Maybe, when you're done with your shift, you can meet me? I get off at the end of second shift. I'm staying at the number two barracks." He pointed a thumb over his shoulder. Past the line of workers was a row of wooden shacks that must be weekday housing. Aniri returned his smile, feeling slightly queasy with this deception. "I'd like that."

His smile brightened, and she gave him another promising look but strode past him as quickly as she could.

As she approached the two guards stationed at the door of the airharbor entrance, she pulled her hood tighter around her face. Their jackets were ink black, with thin, twisted ropes across the center span, like sinister railroad tracks running up their chests. The only fur they wore adorned their squarish box-like hats, sitting low on their brows and making them all the more menacing. They struck Aniri as more Samirian than Jungali, with deep brown eyes and angular cheeks rivaling Devesh's. For all the severity of their looks, they only spared her a cursory glance.

The person ahead of her slipped the token into a slot. After a small whirring and clicking, the token was swallowed inside and the door clicked. The worker rushed to open it. Maybe the lock was timed? Once the girl ahead of her was through, Aniri stepped up and did the same, trying to not let the trembling in her hands show, but the Samirian guards weren't paying her any attention. The token spun and whirred and disappeared. When the door clicked, she rushed ahead to push it open, then stepped into the relative dark inside.

The door shushed closed behind her. Aniri sensed the movement inside the airharbor even before her eyes adjusted. Workers crisscrossed in front of her, hurrying down a passageway in front of a low wall. The woman in line before her was already gone. Aniri blinked, and the rest of the harbor came into focus, soaring high above her. It was like a dark cavern, lit only by tiny, round windows in the murky heights. Their light speared the dusty air like sunbeams after a thunderstorm. Something in the high reaches of the harbor caught one of the beams, glinted, then moved back into the darkness. Aniri squinted, trying to discern it, but the door behind her clicked. She barely skittered out of the way before it was flung open by another worker.

"Ay!" the young man said as he nearly collided with Aniri on his way in. "Whatcha doing, standing there?"

"I... this is my first day," Aniri said.

"Aye, and you're late, too." The man loomed over her. He was either very muscular or his winter jacket was extra padded. Either way, he seemed a better candidate for ore breaking than her. He looked askance at her relatively slimmer build. "You're not headin' to the slurry mech, are ye? Ye won't last long there."

"Is there a better shift to be on?" Aniri asked, looking hopefully up into his eyes.

"Don't be batting those eyes at me, love." He smirked. "I'll not be working your shift for ye, no matter what yer offering."

"Oh!" Aniri's eyes went wide. "No, I didn't mean—"

He laughed, and the wrinkles around his eyes said he

was older than Aniri had first thought in the dim light. "You really are fresh, aren't ye?" He studied her for a moment. "All right, then, I'm late already. Let me check in, and I'll see about gettin' the shift cap to move you to shiners. You're not afraid of heights are you, freshness?"

She shook her head rapidly, not sure what was happening.

"Good." He turned and strode down the hall, throwing a look back to her. "Well, are ye comin' or not? Don't have all day."

Aniri unlocked her legs and followed him, unsure exactly what she had agreed to.

The hulking worker weaved through a maze of low walls that separated one work area from the next. Aniri was just tall enough to peek over. They passed one compartment filled with metalworkers banging out enormous copper and iron fabrications over coal-fired ovens. Another housed a legion of seamstresses bent over vast skeins of blue fabric. It pooled on the floor, making them look like sea creatures afloat on an ocean of silk. They dipped their large needles below the surface only to pop them up again a moment later.

Aniri and her escort wound their way deep into the center of the airharbor. Eventually they came to an enormous version of the automaton she had sparred against back at home, only this one chugged and shuddered with a sound that seemed to shake the floor under Aniri's boots. Workers gathered at the machine's feet, breaking large, glistening pieces of black rock into smaller chunks and feeding them into the belly of the beast. A belt ran continuously into it, dumping bits of ore into the machine, looping around and coming back for more. Giant pipes took the place of arms, hissing and leaking small wisps of steam. At the top, the head sprouted another giant tube that disappeared into the tall darkness of the airharbor.

"That's the slurry mech," the man said loudly, to be heard over the hiss of steam and guttural sounds of the machine. "Where they take that blasted ore and turn it into their special gas."

"Gas for the skyship?" She coughed on the soot-choked air. The workers all had masks that covered their noses and mouths, as well as shiny, black goggles that made them appear to possess giant, automaton eyes. The workers who weren't feeding ore to the slurry mech were at the controls—giant wheels they clutched with both hands.

"Aye, you'll see the ship for yourself, if you're lucky." He leaned away from her and waved over a skinny man who was yelling into the face of one of the workers. The man noticed them and raised his goggles to his forehead, leaving brown moons around his eyes amid a face black with ore dust. He strode quickly over to them, scowling the whole way. His dark eyes seemed like they had been carved from the dull, unglittering parts of the ore itself.

Her escort gestured to Aniri. "This is my sister's friend's cousin," he said to the man. "Her first day at harbor. What say you pretend like you have a heart today, Flinch, and give her a boost up to shiners?"

Flinch was an odd name, and Aniri wasn't sure if it was his real name or not.

"I don't care who she is, Karan," Flinch said. "Everyone starts on ore."

"Aye, and ye still working it, aren't ye?"

Flinch narrowed his eyes. "Just while we're working double shifts. Then I'll be back on engines."

"Keep tellin' yerself that, Flinch. 'Course I could put a word in for ye with the captain. Might smooth things along a bit."

Flinch raised an eyebrow, then glanced at Aniri. "In exchange for what?"

"The girl's going to be no use to ye here," Karan said. "Might as well have her on shiners, where she can do some good."

"And you'll get me back on engines?"

"Can't guarantee." Karan shrugged. "But I'll be up there next shift. Might have a chance to drop a word about yer wasted talents down here on slurry."

Flinch lifted his chin. "All right, take her. But then get back here to finish the rest of the shift. You're already late." Flinch slid his goggles back down and returned to harassing one of the other workers.

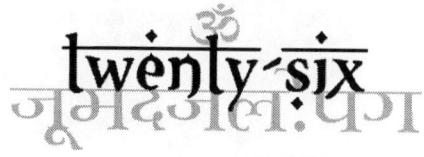

twenty-six

The sound of the slurry mech faded as Karan led Aniri away. They passed an enormous steam-crane, belching smoke and steam as it reached through a hole in the floor and pulled out a cargo container the size of a shashee. With a slow shuddering movement that reminded her of the beast, the crane settled the wooden container onto the dock. A worker in coveralls dashed in to unhook the crane before it drifted back to the hole for another load. A metallic screech rose up from the opening, along with a whiff of steam and shouts from more crew. Aniri suspected it was the rail entrance to the harbor, but Karan whisked her back into the maze of compartments before she could get a better look.

They soon reached a metal cage set against a wall that rose up into the darkness. He unlocked the door to the cage with a mechanical key that was pocketed again before she could see how it worked. He held the door open for her to go first.

In the bustle, she hadn't said anything about his assistance in avoiding slurry mech duty. "Thank you," she said belatedly. "You... didn't have to help me that way. I... really appreciate it." Somehow her gratitude sounded false, knowing she was here to spy and might end up getting Karan in trouble for his efforts.

He shrugged and followed her into the cage. After he pulled the door shut, he punched a red button on a metal strip on the side. They lurched into the air, and Aniri had to claw her fingers through the wire mesh of the cage to keep her footing. The floor fell away, and as they rose, Aniri could see the full layout of the airharbor. It was a crazy quilt of compartments, each colorful and busy in its operations to support the skyship. As the cage rattled higher, she spied a train car beneath the hole by the crane. As another load settled onto the harbor floor, a second crane, even larger, hooked onto the cargo container and lifted it up into the dark reaches above.

"Ye weren't going to be much use on slurry anyway, fresh," Karan said, drawing her attention back to him.

"But you didn't have to trade favors for me. You don't even know me."

He half-smiled down at her. "No worries. I've no intention of saying anything to the Captain. The last thing I want is Flinch up in engines with me."

"You work on the engines, too?"

"Yeah, that's my normal shift." He leaned against the wire mesh of the cage and examined the steadily retreating floor. "I'm just pulling extra shifts in slurry because the captain's in an all-fired hurry these days to get aloft."

"Why is that?"

Karan didn't say anything, simply peered at her with

his deep brown eyes. They weren't unkind, just curious. If one could overlook the size of the man, his face was actually alight with intelligence. He smiled, and Aniri decided he was younger after all, merely weathered with work. And not bad looking as well.

"What did you say your name was, fresh? I don't think I've seen you in town before."

"Um, I didn't say..." She stumbled for a moment. "My name's Priya." She turned away, hoping her lie wouldn't show on her face. The lift passed a floor, and the view opened to a giant wooden platform that stretched across half the harbor. Aniri could see now why the harbor below was so dark. The flooring must have blocked much of the modest light from reaching the lower level... then she saw it: *the skyship*. Her mouth fell open.

Karan followed her gaze. "She's a beauty, isn't she?"

The ship was docked on a lattice of iron beams. An enormous bag billowed above it. The boat wasn't like any sea vessel she had seen, Dharian or Samirian, but it reminded her of the skiff stamped on her token—only instead of a dozen folding sails to capture the wind, the masts were turned sideways. It was like a beautiful fish with a dozen delicate fins all caressing the air with tiny, fluttering movements. In the balloon above, small waves running along the surface turned the sky-blue fabric shades darker and lighter with each ruffling pulse. The balloon offered little resistance to the waves, as if there wasn't quite enough gas inside to stretch the brilliant fabric taut. Even if the ship had enough gas to lift itself, a cascade of rope ladders strapped to the sides held it firmly to the dock. But it wasn't until Aniri looked up the full height of the skyship that she saw the most breathtaking part. Perched on top of the balloon was a giant golden butterfly… if a butterfly could have a multitude of wings each pivoting in different directions.

Aniri blinked. "What is it?"

Karan grinned and handed her out of the cage lift. "That's your new job, freshness."

She frowned, then squinted at the device. Short figures climbed up and around the golden wings, like tiny insects flitting back and forth. The wings were the color of brass, and the workers seemed to be scrubbing them.

Shiners. They were polishing the wings until they shone. And when the burnished metal caught a stray beam of light from the windows ringing the top of the airharbor, the wings gleamed with a brightness that hurt Aniri's eyes.

She blinked to clear them, then rubbed the spots away.

Karan nodded. "Best not to look straight at the shiners while they work."

Aniri had to agree with that. There was more light on the skyship deck than down below, but it was still relatively dim—no doubt to keep everyone from going blind from the reflections. Not far above the skyship was the harbor's ceiling. It was comprised of giant wooden beams that let in only cracks of light where the bright blue sky peeked between. Another strip of blue ran the length of the harbor. It took her a moment to realize that the seam marked the place where doors—enormous doors large enough for the skyship to exit through—met in the middle.

Karan's boots clanged on the girded metal walk as they neared the ship. The boarding plank was well guarded by two Samirians dressed in black and armed with polished steel blunderbusses. A slender man with a tall build and a trim, military-style jacket stood at the entrance as well, watching with a stern look as workers unloaded a large copper tube from the crane. They carried it across the gangplank, a bit unsteady in spite of their muscular arms. Aniri was afraid they might drop their cargo over the rail and down the hundred-foot drop to the harbor floor below. Their overseer must have thought the same thing because he only turned to face Aniri and Karan once the workers had reached the ship.

"Morning, Captain," Karan said, in the most polite and respectful voice Aniri had yet heard him use. "Have a new shiner for you. Flinch sent her straight up, said she would be of use to you up top."

The captain's eyes were black as midnight and glistened with an unspoken danger that made her think of birds of prey. He looked down his long, sharp nose at her, his gaze lingering on her hands poking out from her overcoat. It made her shiver.

"Take off your coat," he said.

"What?" Her heart seized, as much from his tone as his words.

Karan turned to face her, his back to the captain. "It's all right, fresh," he said quietly. "He just wants to see if yer light enough for the job."

Aniri frowned, but quickly unbuttoned her overcoat and shrugged it off. Underneath, she still wore her hooded cloak. She hesitated. Her dagger was tucked safely at the small of her back, under her shirt, but her saber would be apparent as soon as she took off her cloak. The captain threw an impatient look at Karan, so she slipped out of her cloak as well. Karan took them both from her, his gaze not missing the large weapon strapped to her side. She kept her gloves and stood straight under the captain's unnerving examination.

Karan's eyebrows were raised, looking back and

forth between her and the captain. He spoke first. "Always come armed to work, do ye?"

"I walked here this morning," Aniri said. "Alone. It's just for protection." She had no idea if the villagers casually wore blades, but they were mountain people. It had to be reasonable to be armed. She hoped.

"She will do." The captain turned his attention to Karan. "Tinker, they're having trouble installing the new boiler in the port engine. I'd like you to oversee it."

"Aye, sir," Karan said. "Although Flinch is expecting me back."

The captain's face twisted into a look of disgust. "He can spare you."

"Aye, sir," Karan said again. Aniri was relieved when Karan took hold of her elbow and steered her away from the captain, past the gangplank, to one of the ropes that lashed the skyship to the metal girders that surrounded it. The ropes formed a taut ladder between the railing and the ship.

"You're a tinker?" Aniri asked quietly. "You said you worked the engines, not that you *designed* them."

Karan gave her a sly grin, then grabbed a pair of goggles from a hook by the ropes. "You'll be needing these up top. And leave the sword here. Don't want you slicing anything inadvertently up there."

"Maybe I could come work the engines with you instead?" Getting inside the ship seemed a much better way to see its capabilities, and she loathed the idea of leaving her father's sword behind. "I've been known to do some tinkering myself," she lied, hoping she could pull that role off convincingly.

"Just make yerself useful on shiners, and you'll get to come back. Maybe next shift we'll see what you can do on engines." He gave her a kind smile, but of course there

wouldn't be any next shift for her. She would be lucky to get out of this one without being caught. She hesitated, then unbuckled her saber and propped it against the rail. "I'll leave it here until my shift is over."

Karan gave her a short nod and draped her jackets over the blade. "Now, up you go."

Aniri stared at the ladder—it was really just a series of ropes twisted together—and reminded herself that a fall from that height was no different from any other. She put the goggles on, but they were far too dark to see, so she pushed them up on her forehead.

With a hand on the ropes, she stopped. "I wish I had some way to thank you for helping me." And she meant it. She only hoped she could get through the shift and escape again without getting Karan in trouble.

His smile was half-laugh. "Ye need to stop saying things like that, fresh." He gestured to the crew working the skyship. "These are mostly sailors, ye see. They'd be happy to take you up on that offer."

Heat crawled up her neck, but it eased a little with his grin.

"Up you go," he said again with a nod to the ropes.

She hoisted herself up on the rail and got a foot on the rope rungs of the ladder. It swayed and dipped under her weight, but mostly held taut between the skyship and the deck. Hand-over-hand she scaled the ladder, trying to ignore the drop below and telling herself she was lucky to be here and not on slurry mech duty.

She was already halfway up when she heard Karan shout behind her. "You're a right monkey, ye are!" But his voice faded against the whisperings of the fins and the breeze and the thrum of a distant pump.

She had found the skyship; it was time to figure out what exactly it could do.

twenty-seven

Aniri took her time climbing up the rope ladder of the skyship, absorbing as many details of the ship as she could and trying to commit them to memory.

The bow was encased in glass, and from the sailors' movements inside, it appeared to be the bridge. The captain was there now, giving stern-looking orders she couldn't hear from her perch on the ropes outside. A giant pipe rose from the gloomy depths, ran past the bow, and fed into the nose of the balloon. A steel cable ran from where the pipe joined the balloon, to the tip of the wooden platform above, to the dock below, and back to the nose again: it formed a triangle that held the pipe steady as it pumped navia gas from the slurry mech at the base of the harbor. Aniri was so fixated on the pipe, rippling the bag as it filled with gas, that she nearly missed her next handhold.

She focused on the rope for the rest of the climb,

finally alighting on the thin wooden platform at the top of the balloon. It covered half of the giant gasbag and supported the massive butterfly on top. She slipped her goggles over her eyes to keep the glints off the wings from blinding her. Through the darkened glass, she could see the other shiners moving amongst the wings. They all had dull gray cloths in their hands and rubbed furiously at any specks that dared touch the beautiful brass insect.

The device was absolutely stunning. She had no idea what its purpose could possibly be, but she understood why the last thing Prince Malik wanted was to destroy it. Or any part of the skyship, for that matter.

She shuffled closer to the workers—they were all slender and short, like her, some barely larger than children. A dozen boots lined the edge of the platform, and the workers' bare feet balanced on the slender rods that held up the wings. The way the mechanical linkages were arranged, the butterfly must open and close like a flower, or perhaps each wing could rotate on its own. One young girl handed her a polishing cloth. Her dark hair was trapped beneath the strap of her goggles, but the long strands floated behind her in the constant breeze. She returned to her wing, climbing the linkages on the underside, careful not to touch the shining brass surface.

Aniri kept her boots on—she needed to be ready for a quick exit. She pretended to polish an unattended wing while inspecting the device. The wings were turned in every direction for polishing, but their linkages clearly showed they were intended to all focus inward. She leaned over the wing, pretending to reach a spot on the far side. An enormous crystal, the size of her head, sat in the center where the butterfly's body would be. The crystal had a thousand facets shaping it into a cone, only inverted—the flat part at the base of the wings and the point diving below the thin wooden platform. It seemed foolish to have something so sharp near the billowing fabric of the balloon, but as Aniri craned her neck to peer at it, she could see the crystal pointed down a darkened tube. She carefully stepped between the linkages, leaning over for a better look—

"Hey!" a soft voice came close to her, making her jump. "You have the wrong cloth for polishing the crystal."

"I wasn't..." Aniri stole a final glance at the tube: it went deep into the balloon, but that was all she could see. "I was just curious," she finished, turning to find the same girl who had given her the cloth.

A frown crinkled above her goggles. "If you touch it, we'll all get in trouble. They won't let us back on shiner duty."

Aniri ducked her head and worked her cloth in her hands. "I'm sorry."

The girl smiled. "Don't let it worry ye. Everyone wants a peek. I bet the Queen, gods rest her soul, never seen a jewel so big." She made a small bow, hands pressed together, as she said the Queen's title.

"No, probably not." Aniri nearly tripped in her haste to return to her wing. She lightly ran her rag over the shimmering brass surface and studied its construction. The brass was just a thin coating over a wooden panel underneath. The linkages were the same light-colored wood with metal hinges and articulators that disappeared under the platform.

It all looked so delicate, but she doubted its purpose was peaceful. Garesh wanted to bring Jungali to prominence through military might. The butterfly had to be some kind of weapon. Aniri pretended to adjust her goggles while eyeing the rest of the mechanism. Thoughts of sabotage tumbled through her mind. Could she do it? Maybe undo one of the hinges or take her dagger to the center crystal? Everything seemed to depend on a perfect state of polish. Maybe she could wreck Garesh's plans by cracking the crystal or dragging the tip of her blade across the wings. Although she couldn't be sure either of those would actually damage the weapon substantially.

And she would surely be caught.

Garesh would parade her across Jungali as a Dharian spy, the prince's plans to claim the throne would be ruined, and she wouldn't be able to message her mother about the skyship, to warn her the threat was no rumor, but very real.

Still, despite the risk, the temptation was great to do some kind of damage while she had the chance. Garesh had put his workers on extra shifts. He was rushing to get his skyship fully functional. Perhaps she could perform some sabotage without detection. Or possibly damage something on her way out. She might not stop Garesh, but she could at least slow him down.

She set back to polishing, looking surreptitiously for escape routes. A stray beam of sun glinted off the steel line that anchored the navia pipe and crisscrossed the air between the ship and the dock. Past that, the crane caught her eye. Its dark cable and massive steel hook swung another cargo load from the depths of the rail depot to the lofty lattice of the skyship dock.

The rail.

All at once, she saw it in her head. But she would have to move fast.

She ducked under the wing she was working on and crept away from the workers, edging along the platform to the corner by the steel cable. The shiners didn't seem to notice, and no one was close enough to stop her, if they had a mind to. She pushed her goggles up on her forehead, so she could see better, then reached under the back of her shirt and drew out her dagger. She held it close to her body, hidden from the workers below. The crane had nearly reached the dock. It was now or wait—who knew how long—for another lift.

With a quick movement, she knelt at the edge of the platform and plunged her dagger into the bright blue fabric of the balloon, dragging it in a foot-long gash. Navia gas blasted out, gusting against her face and forcing her to narrow her eyes against it. She raised the dagger and slashed again, cutting cross-wise to form a t-shaped vent in the surface of the balloon. This time, the gas surged even faster and suddenly the platform tipped underneath her. She gripped the edge with one hand and sheathed her dagger at her back. Cries rose up from the shiners as they were caught off balance as well. Aniri swallowed, praying to the gods the shiners all had purchase somewhere and wouldn't tumble off, but she had no time for looking back. She looped her shiner cloth around the cable, wrapping each end around her hands as well, and leapt off the balloon platform.

The slide down the cable wasn't nearly as smooth as she expected. The jarring worked her goggles loose, and they tumbled past her dangling feet, disappearing into the hundred foot drop. Just as she was worried the steel of the cable might eat through her shiner cloth, her thoughts shifted to the dock rushing up at her. She managed to swing her feet in front of her to absorb the impact, but it took a long, twisting, pawing moment to get her foothold on the railing. She was gasping by the time she managed to grapple her way over and land on the dock itself.

She lunged for her coats and her father's sword. Shouts sounded from the direction of the gangplank.

Most of the workers were pointing at the shiners and the bleating hole atop the skyship, but some had noticed her, including an overly tall, muscular tinker standing on the gangplank and staring at her.

Karan.

Aniri pivoted away, hiding her face, and sprinted for the crane. She wrestled on her hooded cloak, still grasping her shiner cloth and her sword, but the fur-lined overcoat slipped from her fingers. She had no time to stop. Clutching her saber and the shiner's cloth in one hand, she scrambled up the side of the cargo container. The workman on top had just unhooked the crane. Aniri shoved him from behind and he toppled over, stunned. She leapt up to grab the thick cable of the crane line, bracing her feet on the bulbous metal hook at the bottom, and her momentum swung her out over the edge of the dock, into the free space above the harbor busily working below.

The crane arm quickly lowered her down, returning for another load. Just before she dropped below the dock, she caught Karan's brown-eyed gaze locking with hers.

His frown felt like a dagger aimed at her.

Aniri glanced at the rail station below. If they knew she was coming... if he alerted the workers... this plan might not work as well as she had hoped.

She hooked her arm around the cable, careful to keep her footing on the slippery hook. Ignoring the twirling steamworks below her, she strapped her saber on and drew it out. She stuffed the shiner's cloth in the pocket of her flapping cloak and breathed through the clench in her stomach as she neared the rail station. Several workers were dashing to and from a small wooden enclosure, and a smaller crane was still pulling up cargo from the rail. Aniri, and the hook she was riding, were rapidly approaching a line of containers that stretched in front of her like a very solid-looking wall.

The station workers had definitely noticed her. Several stared wide-eyed even as the crane lowered her close enough to the floor to jump. She landed, saber ready, and ran straight for them, praying to the gods that none had a blunderbuss tucked in their grimy overalls. They scattered. She managed to reach the edge of the hole that led down to the rail tracks, only to hover there, uncertain how to get down.

The train below had been relieved of cargo, all the half-dozen cars just empty frames where the containers had been. The whistle from the engine was drowned out by the screeching of metal on metal as the wheels started to turn. The drop was too far. She would break a leg at the least, with a high likelihood of not surviving at all. There was a ladder around the far side of the hole that she could use to climb down, but it was a dozen yards away. The line from the smaller crane—the one used to unload the train cars—dangled to the ground below, but it hung in the air, a yard out of her reach.

A pounding of feet and shaking of floorboards behind her meant she had no time to decide. She sheathed her sword and leapt for the crane line.

She grasped her gloved hands hard around the two-inch cable, trying to keep herself from tumbling to her death. After a heart-stopping drop of several feet, she wrapped her boots around it as well, slowing the plummet, but her hands burned as the cable slid between them, shredding her thin gloves and racing pain across her palms. Fortunately the cable was heavy enough to keep from swinging back to the platform. She loosened her grip, gritting her teeth through the pain, and hand over hand, she shimmied down the cable, quickly reaching the gravel next to the rail line. The train had already picked up speed, and she had to sprint to match it.

She barely caught hold of the final car, clutching the iron skeleton and hauling herself up onto the wooden floorboards. She rolled on her back, lying low on the floor as it shook and bounced underneath her, barely daring to lift her head and see the harbor workers tumble out into the bright morning sun.

They stood, watching her go. But they didn't come after her. She thunked her head back down on the floorboards and tried to calm her pounding heart.

twenty-eight

Aniri was a half-minute out of the rail station, eyes shut tight against the burning in her palms and the beating sun, before she remembered the prince. She raised her head and scanned the rocky wall of the ravine for the narrow pathway, then glanced back along the rail line, afraid the workers had decided to follow her after all. They might find the prince if he tried to meet her on the train. But the harbor had slid from view around a corner.

Shading her eyes—the sun was all light but no heat—she looked ahead for the prince. He was half tumbling, half scrambling down the steep, rock-strewn embankment alongside the rail. She tried to get to her feet, but the rocking of the train brought her flat to the floor again. The biting cold whipped through her clothes and numbed her body, making it even more difficult to think of standing. She managed to push up to sitting, then tried to button her cloak. On top of the shaking cold, her hands were burned, a white heat against the frozen wind. She couldn't get them to work properly.

The prince was running now, trying to match speed with the train even as it chugged ahead faster and faster. She gave up on the cloak and crawled across the floor on fisted hands toward one of the skeletal girders that framed the car. Her hands screamed in pain. Once she reached the steel post, she pulled herself to standing, steadying against the swaying by wrapping an arm around the girder. The prince raced alongside. She wanted to help him, but her hands were useless. He caught hold of the edge of the floor and hauled himself aboard. He stood, flinging his arms out against the rocking of the train, and stumbled to where she stood.

His first words were harsh against the wind. "Queen's breath, Aniri, what are you doing?"

"Es… escaping." Her teeth chattered, breaking her words.

He looked her over. "What happened to your overcoat?"

"N… no time."

He looked frustrated. "Well, at least button up your cloak. You'll catch your death with it open like that."

She held out her gloved hands, the burns even uglier than they felt. Brown stains seeped at the edges, which were torn and ratty from their encounter with the steel cable. Was she bleeding? Her head suddenly felt woozy. She clutched her arm tighter around the girder to keep from losing her fight to stand.

The prince spoke harshly in a language she didn't understand, maybe the ancient Jungali tongue he spoke of before. Probably a curse, by the way the anger rolled off him in puffs of steamy breath. He roughly pulled the hood tight around her face and started buttoning her coat.

"Why didn't you wait out your shift? You could have been hurt—" He stopped, biting his lip as he worked her buttons. The cold still rippled in waves through her, but not quite as bad.

"Too busy… sabotaging the ship." The prince froze in his progress down her coat, then resumed even more quickly than before, finally rising to look her in the eye.

His face was impassive. "You sabotaged the ship?" The wind whipped the fur of his hood and the loose strands of his dark hair. It brought a chill into the close space between them, but his amber eyes were even colder.

She shuddered. "Just a small hole, Ash." She focused hard on not stuttering with the cold. "They'll repair it. I was in need of a distraction."

He nodded, and the corners of his eyes crinkled. It took her a moment to realize he was smiling. She wanted to smile back, but the cold sank deeper, suddenly reaching her bones, and a tremendous shudder took hold of her. It shook loose a scattering of thoughts. The skyship was real. She had seen it. It was an undeniable threat to Dharia. Devesh had lied to her. Her brain picked at the thoughts like a bird trying to snatch seeds from the dirt, but she couldn't get hold of them. As if the wind had frozen her mind along with her body.

She tucked her hands under her arms and blinked to attempt to focus her thoughts.

The prince's face drew serious. "You're too cold." He worked open the buttons of his own fur lined coat. "You need to stay warm or you will succumb to it." He wrapped his arms and the coat around her, holding her in an attempt to shelter her from the wind and lend his body's heat to hers. She tucked into the warm harbor that

was his body. Her arms rattled uncontrollably against his chest, and he clamped her tighter.

She remembered what he'd said, so long ago, about his mother succumbing to a chill. Was this what he meant? They never had this kind of cold in the plains of Dharia. She tried to think of the warm fireplace of her room, the bright sun of summer, the cozy blankets of her bed... anything to keep the chill from working its way farther into her body.

After many, long minutes in silence, the shaking of her body quieted. The prince whispered to her. Even his breath brought puffs of warmth to her ear. "They will no doubt be looking for us at the train stop ahead in town."

Aniri just nodded.

"Once we break from the foothills, we'll need to jump from the train. Are you warm enough to attempt it?"

She nodded again.

It was painful, and she was clumsy, needing his help on several occasions, but they managed to get off the train, back to the village, and aboard the cable car. None of Garesh's men spotted them. Aniri and the prince didn't speak of the airharbor or the ship the whole way, but as her body and thoughts thawed, she worked through the implications of what she had seen.

Her heart sank further and further.

The skyship was real. Garesh was in control of it and would use it against Dharia unless the prince secured the throne and control of his kingdom. The prince was right: now that she knew, there was nothing she could do but help him with his plans. An empty ache in her stomach felt the truth of it, but she was having a hard time facing what that would demand. What it meant. Devesh had lied to her—had probably been lying all along. That thought was bitter in the back of her throat. It didn't start with the skyship. It had started from the first moment in the fencing hall, when he challenged her with those deep brown eyes to a dance of not just swords, but hearts.

Eventually, Aniri and the prince arrived at his hideaway in Mahet. They had to discuss what came next, but she was loathe to do it, like poking at a wound that was still fresh. That she knew would hurt like nothing else before. The prince seemed to notice her dark mood. The room was cold just like the first time they arrived, the day before, and he busied himself with building a fire. She unbuckled her father's saber and laid it on the bed. She sat next to it, huddling under thin blankets draped across her shoulders, pretending the chill was deep in her body, not her soul.

The prince brought a bowl of water, a small copper tin, and some strips of cloth to the bed. Wordlessly, he took her hands from under the blankets and gently pulled the gloves from them, careful to keep her bracelet around her wrist. He dabbed at her palms. They were still raw and red, but no longer bleeding. He dipped his finger into the tin and put some kind of salve on her wounds. The coolness alone eased some of the fire; she didn't know what medicine might be in it as well. He carefully wrapped the white strips around her palms, tucking the ends in a practiced way.

"This should help with the pain," he said. "But if it's still a torment for you, I can send for a healer."

Aniri didn't know what more a mountain healer could do, but the salve already made it tolerable. "No, I'm fine." She let her hands fall limp in her lap. Her shoulders drooped, the heaviness of the blankets feeling like all her future burdens had come to rest there.

"Are you certain? You seem... unsettled."

The worry in his voice forced her to look up. His amber eyes seemed warmed by the firelight—not the iciness of before, when he thought she had sabotaged the ship, but ringed with concern instead.

"You've been very quiet since we left the airharbor," he said. "I expected you to be angry, perhaps, that the skyship was real. Or maybe afraid of the threat it poses to Dharia. I thought you might even intentionally get caught, maybe spark a war, so your mother would come to rescue you."

Aniri just shook her head and dropped her eyes back to her hands. "My mother, the Queen, would do what is best for Dharia. Which may include leaving me in a foreign top secret military facility, if I was foolish enough to be caught there."

"I can't imagine that is true."

"It's what happened with my father."

He frowned. "Your father... I thought he was set upon by robbers in Samir?"

She nodded. Of course Ash would keep informed of the deaths and changes in power in the royalty of other countries. "That much is true. My mother says she couldn't keep him caged, that he loved to travel, and she had to allow it because she loved him. But when he was lost, she never held the Samirians to account. She never even looked for the murderers. She simply asked for his body to be shipped back to Dharia." She touched the blade by her side, but her hands protested, so she left it alone. "Janak brought my father's saber back with his casket a week later."

"I'm sure there was an investigation—"

"I was only ten, Ash," she cut him off. "But I wasn't a fool. The Queen never sent so much as a guard over to Samir. She chose peace with Samir over justice for my father. I am sure she deemed it in the best interest of relations between the nations at the time." Aniri couldn't keep the bitterness out of her voice. "Believe me when I say it is quite possible the Queen would leave me to rot in a Jungali mountain prison if it served the best interests of Dharia."

The prince frowned and said nothing for a moment. "Is that why you're... sad?"

Aniri sighed and spoke to her hands. "I think I will have to marry you after all, Prince Malik." Then she raised her gaze to the prince's concerned eyes.

He winced. "And *that* is what makes you sad."

"No." She studied the tattered drapery, so she didn't have to see the look in his eyes. "I understand what you're doing now. I see how Garesh has built this weapon—this beautiful weapon—and you see it only as an instrument for peace. I'm not sure what the butterfly does, but—"

"The butterfly?" the prince asked, eyebrows raised.

"The device on top," Aniri said. "I'm not sure what to call it. Where the shiners work."

"The shiners?" The prince looked even more confused.

"You *have* seen the ship, haven't you, Prince Malik?" Aniri said, a little annoyed. Had he lied about that, too?

He gestured with his hands to show his exasperation. "Yes, but the last time I saw it was before the Queen died. Garesh has been far too suspicious for me to chance a visit. When I last inspected the skyship, they were striving to mine enough gas to fill the balloon. I worked with my brother on the original plans for the ship. I know the tinkers who designed it. There was never any... *device* on top."

"Oh." Aniri's annoyance evaporated, taking what

little strength she had with it. "Well, I think they've nearly finished with the gas, although perhaps less so now that I've let some of it loose. And now there's a giant mechanical butterfly on top, with shiny brass wings and a crystal at the center. I don't know its purpose."

The prince frowned. "I doubt it is peaceful."

"I know," Aniri said. "The skyship alone is a threat to Dharia. With the skyship sailing high above the reach of any Dharian weapons, conventional bombs could be dropped with impunity. But with this butterfly... I don't know what it's capable of, but I am certain the only way to keep it from being a weapon of war is to have it safely in your hands, Ash. For that, you need the crown. And to gain the crown, you need me to marry you. The only alternative is for Dharia to immediately go to war with Jungali, and even then, even knowing the capabilities of the weapon, even if we could strike before the skyship is ready to launch, I cannot be sure we would win. The airharbor is so remote... the mountains are virtually impregnable... the losses on both sides would be extreme. I can forestall all of that by forging a bond between our people. By becoming your Queen. I understand that now. It's what's best for both our nations."

The prince's face brightened while she spoke. "Then why—"

"Because the skyship is *real*. And that means Devesh lied to me. He's been lying all along."

The prince's face fell again. "Your lover."

Aniri nodded, her gaze falling back to her hands. Her fingers lightly turned the thin, braided bracelet her father had given her. "Devesh promised to help me find my father's murderers. He promised we would marry and run away, leave the court behind and seek the things that mattered to my heart." She glanced at her father's saber. "I was going to have my vengeance on the vermin who killed my father. I would have found them and killed them with his own sword."

The prince held very still.

"Devesh promised to help me," she said, her chest sinking in on itself. "It was all a lie."

The prince hesitated, and when he spoke, it was very softly. "I don't understand—how could he have actually known one way or the other about the skyship? Maybe he was just mistaken."

"He knows because he's a Samirian diplomat!" Aniri said, her voice rising. "And apparently a spy. And your airharbor is crawling with Samirians—guards, workers, even the tinkers seem to be Samirian!"

"It's true the alliance with Samir is what's allowed the skyship to go forward," the prince said with a grimace. "Their tinkers and technology combined with our access to the navia gas mined out of the far northern mountains is what makes it possible."

"There's no way Devesh didn't know all of that." Aniri's shoulders slumped again. "He wanted me to leave, Ash. He said Samir was using the rumors of the skyship to distract Dharia, all while they were preparing to invade." She gave him a grim smile. "All this time, I thought he was in love with me. I thought he was simply looking out for me, afraid for my life, worried about me. But it turns out he understood the politics much better than I did. He always did. He knew marrying you would stop whatever plans the Samirian's had for the skyship once it was complete. I just thought... I thought he was..." She took a deep breath. "I was a fool."

This time her chest caved completely, and her head hung down with the weight of it. *Sweet, naïve Aniri.* She

could hear Devesh's voice softly mocking her. It ripped her heart, carving a wound so deep it felt like it split her in two.

The prince was silent. She hoped he would leave her to the wounds in her heart and burning quietly on her hands. She wanted to curl up under the covers and wait for them to scab over. Then she would be ready to carry forward with the duty she knew she needed to perform. Instead, the tip of the prince's finger brushed the underside of her chin. She pulled away, then thought better of it. He was only trying to help. She looked back to his clear amber eyes.

"Perhaps," Prince Malik said, "it's not as you think. Maybe your lover was speaking from his heart and not his head. It wouldn't be the first time a man lied to a woman in order to keep her."

Aniri peered at him. "You think he knew the truth but lied about the skyship out of love?" She couldn't quite piece it together.

He gave a small shrug that seemed to pain him. "It's something I would do." He coughed. "I mean, if I was a Samirian diplomat in love with the Third Daughter of Dharia." He dropped his voice. "There are worse things he could do, Aniri, if he simply wanted to hurt you."

It never crossed her mind that Devesh would intentionally want to hurt her. Lie to her in service of his country, yes. Use her for access to her mother's court, definitely. But hurt her just out of spite? That wasn't the Devesh she knew. And if he knew the truth about the skyship, maybe he had lied because he truly wanted her to run away with him to Samir—even if it allowed a war to go forward. Maybe he loved her more than either of their countries.

That sounded more like the Devesh she had fallen in

love with.

Aniri gave a shaky nod, sitting taller under the blankets. "I'll come back to Bajir with you, Ash. And it's imperative we go through with the marriage, as soon as possible, so you can take the throne and claim control over the skyship. And we must warn my mother as well. But when we return to Bajir—"

"I know," the prince said, wincing again. "You need to pay your lover a visit."

She gave him a grim smile, but hope bloomed in her heart. Even if duty required her to marry Prince Malik, he wouldn't make her give up Devesh. She knew enough about Ashoka, the young prince of Jungali, to know that was true. With Prince Malik crowned King, he could protect her—protect both of them—from the Samirians who would lay claim to Devesh. Jungali was already allied with the Samir; they had an embassy here. How hard would it be for Devesh to be stationed there if it was a request straight from the King and Queen of Jungali?

All her plans to search for her father would have to be put on hold. Her dreams of a free life with Devesh would be gone; they could be lovers in secret only. The thought tore at her, but it was far better than nothing. And someday, when there was a lasting peace in her country, she would set out to find the truth about her father. Perhaps she would even be able to bring Dev with her, under the guise of a faithful companion and guide in his home country of Samir.

Maybe there was a way out of this with her heart in one piece after all.

twenty-nine

Aniri hovered outside the door to her room at the prince's estate in Bajir.

It was late and the palace was dark. The prince had insisted on accompanying her all the way to her door. Their cover story about sneaking off for a lover's courtship retreat must have been believable, given the guards weren't surprised by their late-night return. Or the prince's arm draped protectively over her shoulder. She and the prince had abandoned their cloaks and simply wore their adventuring clothes now that they had returned to the warmer southern province. The household rumors must be afire with their secretive comings and goings.

"Are you sure you're all right?" the prince asked for the tenth time since they had left Sik province.

"I will be... until Janak realizes I've returned." Slipping away had been a frontal assault on Janak's duty to keep her safe. It wouldn't help when she told him he was right about Devesh being a spy.

"And you're still planning on visiting your lover?" the prince asked with a frown.

"Yes." She wasn't sure what the outcome would be, but she had to know if Devesh ever really cared for her. "I'll go this eve to the Samirian embassy. I'll wait until it's dark, with less eyes to see and mouths to chatter. If he's still in Jungali, that's where he'll be."

"Do you want me to go with you?" the prince asked softly, ducking his head.

"I can handle my lover, Prince Malik."

He smirked, eyes still averted, and made a short nod. "Of that I have no doubt." Then seriousness returned to his face. "Just be sure to take an escort." His gaze lingered on her face for a moment, and Aniri thought he might say something else. Instead, he turned and strode away, his boots making hard sounds on the tiled floor.

Aniri took a deep breath and opened the door to her room. She expected Janak to be angry, but she wasn't prepared for Priya's disheveled state, curled upon the sofa, head in her hands apparently crying.

"Queen's breath!" Priya yelped and leaped off the couch. "You're alive!" She flew across the span of their apartment and nearly tackled Aniri with a hug. Priya recovered her senses quickly, though, alternately brushing at her tear-streaked face and reaching out to smooth Aniri's travel-worn clothes as if a stray wrinkle caused by her hug might be the worst of what could be found there. It took a moment for Janak to stalk across the room, the anger a dark cloud gathering on his face. Aniri took that time to set down her valise, the one heavy with her aetheroceiver, making note she needed to message her mother soon. She unbuckled her saber and was setting it with the luggage just as Janak arrived at their side. That was when Priya noticed the bandages around Aniri's hands.

"My lady! What has happened to you?" she cried, gently cupping one of Aniri's hands in her two and staring at it in horror.

"It's only a small burn," Aniri said. "It's healing already. The prince had a salve—"

"The prince?" Janak's face was downright murderous, and Aniri was sure it was directed at her. "So he actually did steal you away, without a guard, without a note. Gods, Aniri!" He balled up a fist, flexed it, then ran it through his hair, turning away from her in frustration. He paced only two steps before turning back. "How foolish can you be? What if he discovered you? What if he found out your mission? How can you run off on… on…" His face turned red as he chewed on the words before spitting them out. "…some *childish* trip across the countryside without so much as a guard to keep you safe?"

"The prince knows about my mission, Janak."

"What?" he cried. "He *knows*? And then you ran off with him, *alone*? It's a wonder you only burnt your hand, with the way you play with fire, Aniri! How stupid and arrogant can you be? You're a child dressed in royal clothes." He threw his hands out in frustration and turned his back on her, as if he could barely stand to look upon her.

"You are not my father, Janak," she said through gritted teeth. "You are—"

"No!" he cut her off, swinging back to her and striding up to stare down at her. "I am *not* your father." Then he straightened his jacket and regained the military bearing he carried like a weapon. "Your father was a coward."

Rage clouded her vision and before she thought about what she was doing, Aniri slapped him. A surge of pain ripped through her palm, but that wasn't what caused tears to jump to her eyes. "How dare you…" Her words strangled on her anger.

He slowly turned back from her slap. "It is the truth. Your father was an embarrassment. He was never good enough for her. *Never.*" His fists clenched and unclenched at his side. "I tried to warn her. I implored her to… to pick someone else… someone who would give his life for her…" He faltered, then looked away, jaw working. "She was too swept away. She wouldn't listen. Wouldn't see him for what he really was."

The pain in his voice sliced through Aniri's anger and opened her mind. She could suddenly see it in the tension coiled in his body, in the passion always in his eyes, veiled, kept at a proper distance… because it was impossible for the Queen's guard to be her lover. Impossible for a raksaka to marry a royal. But Janak loved her, and not simply because he had sworn to honor and defend her. Not simply because she was the Queen.

Then a terrible thought seeped into Aniri's mind.

"You… you *let him die.*" It was such a shock, her mind almost couldn't grasp it. Her anger was frozen in horror. "My father is dead because of *you.*"

"Dead because of me?" His face contorted into a new level of disbelief and anger.

"You were his bodyguard! You are *raksaka!* You were supposed to keep him safe!" Aniri vented her rage in angry stabs of her finger at his face. "What? Were you drunk at the time? Sleeping? Are you such a pathetic raksaka that common thieves can sneak under your nose without your notice? Or did you *let them in*? Did you simply want him dead so you could win the Queen's favor for yourself?"

The horror of it unlocked her frozen body, and she moved to strike him again. He caught her hand by the wrist in a lightning move that immobilized her but caused no pain. Except the one in her heart.

Janak's voice dropped low and dangerous. "I did *not* fail in my duty." Anger was a hot ember in his eyes. "Your father is *not* dead."

Aniri blinked. Time seemed to stop. Breath halted in her chest. "What?" she whispered, then stronger, "What did you say?"

The murderous look returned to Janak's face, but he released her hand and eased back from her. "Your father did not die in that gods-forsaken Samirian province, your most royal highness. He *left*. He was a coward who couldn't face his royal responsibilities, so he simply walked away from them."

"But… you said… my mother said…" Aniri's heart shattered into pieces, shredding the words before they could form in her mind.

"Your mother let it appear he had been taken by robbers. She let it appear he had died because that was what was best for Dharia. Your mother is a true sovereign, one who has always known how to put her country first. Unlike her husband. Or her third daughter."

Aniri gasped as the weight of Janak's truth sank into her.

Priya made a small squeak next to her, but beyond that, the room was deathly quiet. Priya placed a hand on Aniri's arm, but Aniri pushed her away, taking a step back. The pieces, the fragments of recollection that had never made sense before, all fell into place.

"My mother never went looking for him, never chased after the robbers…" Aniri's voice faded off.

Because her father wasn't dead at all. He had left his wife, the Queen, and the court, and everything that came with it.

He had *run away*.

The very thing she had dreamed so many nights of doing.

"He left a note, warning us not to look for him," Janak said stiffly. "I searched anyway, because there is no force in this world which could make me let that coward bring embarrassment to our Queen."

Tears chased each other down Aniri's cheeks, but she had no doubt whatsoever Janak was telling the truth. She could see him, frantically searching the Samirian streets for the runaway king before he could embarrass the Queen who Janak loved.

"You couldn't find my father," Aniri whispered. "Because he didn't want to be found." Her father had left his Queen. He had left his three daughters. He had left *her*. He had allowed her to believe he was dead, all because he wanted to run away. Aniri sucked in a breath. The shards of her heart crashed to the ground.

Devesh would have searched all of Samir with her until they found her father's killers, would have helped her to unlock the secrets of her past, but Janak had thrown the vault wide open, and it was empty.

Her father had left her.

"I…" Aniri faltered, the images of Janak and Priya swimming in front of her. "I am going to… take a walk." She backed toward the door she had just come through, nearly tripping before slowly pivoting around to walk forward.

"Yes, run away," Janak said softly. "Who are we to stop you?"

His words would have sliced pain through her—if

she had been capable of feeling anything at all.

"My lady, wait!" Priya said, her silk dress whispering behind Aniri. "I'll accompany you."

"No!" Aniri flung out her arm to stop her handmaiden without looking back. Devesh knew her heart better than anyone; he would understand. He would hold her while she put the pieces of it back together again. Aniri turned her head to the side and softened her voice. "No, Priya, stay here. I need to be alone for a while."

Aniri forced her feet to move, her boots scuffing heel marks on the tiled floor. Pain laced through her palm as she gripped the doorknob and wrenched it open, but she welcomed it.

Anything to distract from the cavern of agony in her chest.

thirty

Aniri wandered the hallways of the palace in a daze, her steps pulsing in her hands, keeping time with the beat of her heart. It pounded in her head as well, making her thoughts fuzzy.

All this time, she had thought her mother had abandoned her father's body, but in truth, her father had left her mother. Everything Aniri knew about the world had somehow gone false. She could hardly trust the steps in front of her to remain solid as her boots silently stepped down them.

She was outside, with no recollection of how she got there.

But she knew where she wanted to go: the Samirian embassy.

The granite outer walls of the Bajiran capital towered above the colorful tumble of houses, marketplaces, and stables that filled it. During the day, the walls were white, but in the twilight, they flickered with gaslamp, the warm amber dancing along the polished rock. Even now, past the dinner hour, people filled the streets. Some spilled out of taverns, clearly gone with drink. Some tucked into darkened crevices, lovers who thought they couldn't be seen, only the flash of bronze-trimmed buttons gave them away. Everywhere, the city thrummed with heartbeats.

Even at night, Jungali made her dizzy with too much brightness, too much life.

Merchants were still closing up their shops. Aniri pulled her hood forward, shadowing her face. She approached a clockwork tinker, her wares silent except for one tiny automaton lumbering across the table she had set up outside. The shop was a cubby in the lowest level of a three-story stacked apartment, which was crammed between four-story structures on either side. Each ramshackle dwelling seemed to hold the other up, as well as the next one and the next. Aniri pictured one small timber out of place, one decrepit wall falling, and the entire city would crumble after it. It was like Ash said before: the Jungali were all dependent upon one another, too tightly packed together to exist any other way.

"I'm closed for the day!" the tinker shouted from inside. The shopkeeper fussed with something, her dress a flurry of blue as bright as the Jungali sky and woven with a white thread that ran in jagged lines like mountain peaks. She was bent with age, but she moved fast, scurrying out of her shop to face Aniri. She snatched a tiny automaton from Aniri's bandaged hand—it was a child's toy Aniri hadn't even realized she had picked up. The woman twirled away, waving her off with a wrinkled hand, then stopped, turned back, and peered at Aniri again. Aniri shrank back from the light of the shop, tucking herself farther under her hood, but the woman was upon her again before she could flee.

The tinker examined Aniri's bandaged hands, then her face in the darkness under her hood. "Do you need some clockwork, child?" Her voice was rough with age, or maybe a cough that came with it, but it was also kind. The woman gestured to her table of clockwork toys. There were all manner of beasts and birds, including a shashee that glinted in the gaslamp.

"No, thank you," Aniri said. "But I do have need of directions to the Samirian embassy."

"The embassy?" The shopkeeper swept the gray straggles of her hair off her shoulders. "Are you in some kind of trouble, child?" Her voice was so soft, Aniri could barely hear her over the boisterousness of the street, and she was forced to lean closer.

"No, I..." she stumbled, not expecting to have to explain herself. "I have a message to deliver to the ambassador. I've news from Sik province." She hoped that lie would be sufficient for the shopkeeper. What she really needed was to find Devesh, to have him settle her heart, heal her wounds... but once she gained an audience with the ambassador, finding Devesh should be straightforward.

The shopkeeper hesitated, cocking her head right and left, frowning. "Is it the fashion in Sik, now, to hide your face from your mountain kin?" Her words had some warning in them, but Aniri wasn't quite sure what it was. She pursed her lips together and stepped back, ready to flee. She would have to find the embassy on her own.

The tinker's eyebrows lifted, and she raised her hands to stop Aniri. "Do not worry, child. Whatever trouble you are in, I will not speak of it."

Aniri's shoulders relaxed. She wasn't quite sure what trouble the tinker thought she was involved in, but that

would suffice as a cover story.

The old woman held up one gnarled finger. "Wait here. I have just the thing for you."

She shuffled away and disappeared into the shop. Aniri pulled in a slow breath, unsure if she should stay for the woman to return. Before she could decide, the tinker returned. She carried a small basket of cloths, brushes, and tiny bottles with a rainbow of colored liquids. She set the basket on the table with the clockwork, then surprised Aniri by taking her hand.

Aniri nearly pulled out of the old woman's light grasp, but then she saw the Dharian crest from the engagement party was still inked on the back. The ink had started to fade, and it was half-covered by bandages, but it was clear as day to anyone who cared to look.

And the shopkeeper was staring right at it. "If you are from Sik province, I believe some new ink is in order." She dropped Aniri's hand and fished in her basket, coming up with a rough cloth and a bottle of clear liquid that smelled of lemon and oil when she uncorked it.

Aniri simply stared as she wetted the cloth and rubbed it over the exposed crest on Aniri's hand, wiping away the ink as easily as if it were dirt. This woman was helping her. She had no idea why. Seeing the Dharian crest... the tinker had to know who Aniri was. And yet, without a single question, she was helping Aniri keep her pretense of being from Sik province.

She swallowed back the tears gumming up her throat.

The tinker wiped the last of the ink from the back of her hand and blew on it, bringing a slight chill to Aniri's wetted skin. Then she retrieved another bottle, this one dark with ink, and a quill with a tiny tip. Not looking up, the tinker asked, "Northern Sik or Southern?"

Aniri cleared her throat before trusting herself to speak. "Northern."

The woman carefully swiped a curling set of swirls and dots. A bird's wing appeared; the tinker labored over it with an artist's love. When it was done, Aniri had half of a Sik crest peeking from her bandage. The shopkeeper gestured that Aniri should blow on it, which she did. The ink quickly dried in the cool mountain air.

She didn't know what to say. "Thank you," was all she could manage. The tinker ducked her head, a nod of sorts, as she tucked the bottles back into her basket. She shuffled back inside her shop, and Aniri waited for her return, wishing desperately for some way to thank the woman for her help. She reached into her cloak pocket, hoping she might have a spare yakle from the shashee trader in Sik, but there was nothing. She looked again at the Sik crest—it was on the same hand as her father's bracelet.

It was difficult with her bandages and only one hand, but she worked the tiny leather clasp free. Just then, the tinker returned. She stood tall now, her slender frame no longer bent. Her hands were cradled, palm up, in front of her, and in the center sat a tiny mechanical shashee—like the one on the table, only more beautiful. Small brass plates covered the skin of the clockwork beast, like toy armor, and it was speckled in minute crystals that caught the gaslamp and sparkled.

"A souvenir for you." The woman gave her a quick wink. "When you return to Sik province, you can tell them Bajiran clockwork is finer than any Samirian design."

"I… I don't have any money," Aniri stumbled.

The woman frowned deeply, wrinkles appearing to

chastise Aniri.

"But I have something for you as well," she said hastily. She held out her father's bracelet, laying it next to the shashee before gently retrieving the tiny mechanical wonder from the woman's palm.

Aniri marveled at the device. Jewels outlined a tiny ring saddle on its back, and the horns were sharpened like blades. "It's beautiful. We have nothing so lovely in… Sik province."

The woman's face lit up, wrinkles banished, and Aniri felt a flush of warmth run through her.

"There is a small key in the belly of the beast," the tinker said, pointing one delicate finger at it. "With winding, it moves. Like Devpahar has come to life in your hand. She is wise and steady and will calm all your troubles if you but ask."

Aniri looked at the tiny beast and could see the goddess paintings on it now. Tears pooled in her eyes. Aniri slipped her arms around the tiny, old woman and embraced her. Then awkwardness overcame her, and she pulled back, wiping her face and tucking the shashee into her cloak pocket.

The woman smiled broadly. "The embassy is at the gate to the city. You would have passed right by it on the way in." She pointed down the cobbled street. "Look for the big, ugly guards with the blunderbusses, and you'll know you've found it."

"Thank you," Aniri repeated. Before she could tear up again, she whirled around, her cloak fanning out and sweeping the street around her. She pulled her hood tight and skirted the raucous men and laughing women who lounged in the darkening streets.

Somehow they no longer seemed too bright or too many.

thirty-one

Aniri made quick time through the narrow streets. The teetering apartments and taverns still bustled around her, but the shops were closing, and the streets grew more quiet and dark as she approached the edge of the city. When she finally came to a massive gate in the outer walls, she knew the Samirian embassy must be close. The enormous metal-strapped, wooden doors looked like they could withstand a battalion of armored shashee. Nearby, thick chains on wheels would open the gate, but it was shut tight for the eve. To the right sat a large, red stone building. Two men armed with blunderbusses guarded the wrought-iron gate of the entrance. Their black coats and midnight-dark squarish fur hats were similar to the Samirian guards at the airharbor.

They were quite ugly, just as the tinker had said.

Aniri took a steadying breath and approached them. She held her hood close around her face, careful to keep her newly-inked Sik province crest visible. "I have an appointment to meet with the ambassador. I have news from Sik province."

The guards frowned, then looked at each other. Some silent understanding passed between them.

The ugliest one said, "It's late. The embassy is closed for the eve."

She squared her shoulders and tried to look intimidating without baring too much of her face. "Surely the ambassador hasn't already taken to her bed. Even if you have to wake her, she'll want to hear my news." When they hesitated, she added in a lowered voice, "What are your names? I'll be sure to tell her who turned me away while she awaited my report."

The less ugly guard shifted from foot to foot, then gave the other a meaningful look.

His partner sighed and grunted out, "Follow me." He pressed a heavy ring made from tiny clockwork to a mechanism in the gate. The lock hummed and clicked, and he withdrew his hand again. She followed him through a short courtyard of neatly-trimmed prickly bushes, the kind that could survive a winter in the mountains of Jungali. Then he held the door to the embassy entrance open for her.

She stepped into the relative light and warmth. Finely woven tapestries depicting rural Samir covered the walls and stone flooring, feeling at once warmer and more stifling than the open corridors of the prince's palace. The warmth drew out the pulsing in her hands, now more a dull ache than actual pain. The air scented of dinner recently past, making Aniri's stomach clench. She couldn't remember the last time she'd eaten.

The guard led her to a desk where a woman sat tensed on her chair. Her black uniform was similar to the guard's, only more tightly wrapped, and her thin nose and dour expression were even more severe.

"A visitor," the guard said, introducing her to the receptionist. "Claims an appointment with the ambassador. Says she has news from Sik province."

The woman's coal black eyes sparkled in the flickering low light of the lamps. Aniri feared her penetrating gaze would see right through her shadows and deception.

"I see," she said, making Aniri twitch. Then the woman's face transformed into a smile that seemed as practiced as her intense look before. She arose and pressed her hands together. "Arama. Welcome to the Samirian embassy. I'm sure the ambassador is eagerly awaiting your news. Please follow me." She flicked her hand to dismiss the guard, who automatically took a step or two back as if the tiny motion had been a powerful physical force. He straightened and turned on his heel, retreating back to the entrance.

Aniri followed the woman down a hall, passing painted scenes of tinkers and Queens of Samirian past. Each Queen held a clockwork ship, the ocean-going kind, and a ceremonial sword—the twin symbols of Samirian power. The secretary led her deeper into the embassy, each turn more poorly lit than the last. Finally, she unlocked a carved wooden door with an elaborate key she pulled from deep within the bosom of her tightly-fitted jacket. The key had tiny wings at the tip that clicked and flared out as she pressed it into the keyhole. A mechanism whirred before she withdrew the key and pushed open the door.

Inside was a small waiting room with another door on the far side. Aniri stepped in, while the receptionist lingered by the threshold. When Aniri turned to her with a questioning look, the woman's friendly demeanor vanished.

Aniri took a step toward her. "The ambassador—"

"Will let you know when she is ready to receive you." Before Aniri could respond, the woman slipped out the doorway and pulled it closed. A mechanical whirring assured Aniri it was locked once more.

She pressed her lips together, hoping she hadn't just made a tremendous mistake. She was here under false pretenses, without a guard. Once she explained to the ambassador that she only wanted to speak to Devesh...

Aniri swallowed. Devesh said she could trust the ambassador, but she didn't know the beginning or end of his lies. What she really needed was to find Devesh *before* the ambassador discovered she had the Third Daughter of Dharia sitting in her waiting room.

The way into the room was locked for certain, but maybe there was another way out. Aniri approached the far door—there was no light coming from underneath, and when she tried the knob, it was locked. She knocked lightly, but there was no response. On closer examination, the lock was a simple one, not the elaborate clockwork that had just trapped her, but a regular keyhole... like the one Priya had so expertly picked on the train.

If only Aniri had a hairpin.

She searched her pockets, coming up with only the mechanical shashee the tinker had given her. However, its horns were quite sharp. She slid one into the keyhole and could feel some motion in there, but all her jiggling came to nothing. Priya had broken her pin in half, using two pieces to work the mechanism loose. *The clockwork key.*

Just as the tinker promised, a key was tucked in the belly of the beast. It was slender and fit in the keyhole but left room for the blade of the tusk. It took a minute of working the lock mechanism by feel, but to her surprise, she was able to nudge the pins inside and the knob finally turned.

She slowly eased open the door and slipped the shashee and its key back into her pocket.

The room beyond must be the ambassador's office with its rich appointment of shelves, books, and mechanical trinkets. An enormous desk in the center held a couple of communiques, and closer examination showed them to have embassy letterhead. Another door stood off to one side, probably the ambassador's private chamber. A quick check revealed its lock to be clockwork. She couldn't begin to know how to pick that.

Aniri sighed, loosened her cloak, and threw back her hood, the warmth of the embassy starting to make her uncomfortably warm. She resigned herself to waiting, and prayed to her tiny shashee manifestation of Devpahar that meeting the ambassador first wouldn't spell any more trouble. Aniri was about to retrace her steps, so as not to be found prying in the ambassador's office, when a glint shined from the bookcase and froze her in place.

On the shelf sat a dull metal box which was unmistakably familiar: an aetheroceiver.

She paused and listened for anyone approaching. Hearing nothing, she hurried over and pulled the aetheroceiver from the shelf. It was crusted with coal dust, identical to the one Devesh had sent her. Was this its mate? It made sense, since Devesh had been working with the ambassador all along. Aniri searched for the three symbols Devesh had given her for a key: a tinker at work, the Samirian crown, and a ship from the Samirian navy. She pressed them and the box unfolded, revealing the same inner workings: a decryption wheel, a tiny crank to power it, and a dial to type the symbols for the

message. There were no residual curls of paper lying inside, but a tiny notebook peeked from the back.

Aniri quickly plucked it out. A large sheet of parchment had been folded to precisely fit inside the confines of the notebook, and it sprung out once open. She spread it flat on the desk. Even in the dim light, it was obvious what it was.

A schematic of the skyship.

Complete with fin-like rudders protruding from the sides. The pencil drawing laid bare the inner workings that powered the ship, including engines in the aft section and the linkages to the steamworks. The butterfly was perched on top of the gasbag, just as she had seen in the airharbor. The wisps of charcoal lines didn't do justice to the beauty of the actual device. Notes overlaid the wings, calling out the precise angles to which they were to be aligned. Lines focused on the crystal in the center, and a tube ran from there, deep through the ship, all the way to the bottom. The drawing didn't state the butterfly's purpose—the tinker who designed it surely knew and had no need for spelling it out in a mechanical sketch.

Below the ship was a map—at least Aniri thought it was a map. It had lines like mountain ridges, but instead of trees, it was covered with tiny arrows. She couldn't make sense of it, so she peered closer at the notes, trying to decipher the miniscule print.

A door clicked.

Aniri's heart stuttered. The sound came not from the entrance door, but from the ambassador's private quarters. Before she could move, the door swung open, and her heart nearly leapt from her chest. She was caught, hunched over the ambassador's private aetheroceiver device.

But that concern slipped away when she saw who

walked through the door.

The ambassador strode in, her silk coat not quite buttoned up the full way, and Devesh stumbled in behind her, straightening the high collar of his jacket and hastening to button the top button. Aniri might have expected the ambassador to be half-dressed, given Aniri had roused her from bed. She didn't expect Devesh to be in it as well.

An ice-cold chill burst from her heart and drenched the rest of her body. "Dev." The word was soft on her lips, mostly a gasp spoken to herself.

Devesh looked up from fussing with his clothing and saw her. His mouth dropped open. "Aniri!" He threw a panicked look to the ambassador. "What... what are you doing here?"

The ambassador stumbled to a stop, just now seeing Aniri in the dim light. "Do not speak, Devesh!" she hissed at him. He cowed under her admonishment.

The cold seeped into Aniri's bones. She didn't want to see what was plain before her, but it was unavoidable. He had never loved her. Even when he was professing it in fevered kisses, he had always been a servant of the Samirian crown. And apparently in service in more ways than one to the ambassador as well.

The heat came back to her body and face all in a rush. She should have known better than to love a courtesan. Everyone knew they broke hearts. They were good only for dalliances and affairs. She had been foolish to think the Third Daughter of the Queen would somehow be different.

Devesh winced at the look on Aniri's face, then hurried toward her. "It's not what it seems, Aniri—"

She came around the desk and hit him with her bandaged hand, palm open. She was sure it hurt her more

than him, but he cringed under it. She hit him again and again, slapping his face and shoulders, each sting in her hands beating back the tears in her eyes. Devesh finally caught her hands, holding them away from his face.

Aniri twisted out of his grasp and stumbled back. "Never touch me again." Her voice was raspy with the tears choking her throat.

A gaslamp on the desk flicked on. "Princess Aniri," the ambassador said coolly. She stood over the splayed-open aetheroceiver. "If you're done assaulting my diplomat, perhaps you can tell me exactly what you know about our skyship."

Aniri's heart surged again, this time beating wild with fear. Devesh had deceived her. The ambassador knew about the skyship. Aniri had been caught spying in her office.

How on earth would she get out of this with her head still attached to her body?

"I know you're no friend of Dharia," Aniri said, summoning as much royal presence to her voice as she could. "I know you're planning war, and this weapon will be used against the Dharian state. I've informed the Queen. She knows everything and is already on high alert. She will be waiting for you. And she knows I am here, so if any harm comes to me, she will consider that an act of war."

She hadn't had time to message her mother about the skyship. She hadn't even told Janak about it in her fight with him. She had simply fled, feeling sorry for herself and seeking out her lover.

She was the worst kind of fool.

The ambassador studied her. "I think not, Princess Aniri. I think you came here hoping to meet your lover." She glanced at Devesh, and the coldness of her look angered Aniri. Even if Devesh had clearly used Aniri, even if he never loved her, it was obvious the ambassador held nothing but contempt for him. She had used him with more cruel intent than Devesh was ever capable of having. His face flushed, turning darker in the dim light.

The ambassador drew her attention back by speaking again. "Maybe you were even considering taking Devesh up on his offer of running away to Samir." She glanced at the schematic. "How unfortunate you stumbled upon the truth first."

The door to the outside waiting room flung open, and Garesh marched in, trailed by four guards clad in black Samirian military uniforms. He exchanged a quick look with the ambassador as he entered her office. Devesh stepped hastily back from Aniri, as if she had suddenly burst into flame.

Panic ramped up through Aniri's body. She struggled to remain still, not giving in to the impulse to attempt to flee, even though it would be useless. Garesh stopped a few feet in front of her and appraised her.

"Princess Aniri of Dharia," he said. "So nice of you pay us a visit."

The ambassador tapped twice on her desk, rustling the schematic as she did so. "She knows, Garesh."

"Oh yes, I'm quite aware of that," Garesh said, not looking at the ambassador, but boring a look into Aniri instead. "She knows quite a lot. Tell us, Princess Aniri, what did you think of Sik province? Did you enjoy the weather? I can't imagine a pampered royal from the plains would last long in the cold embrace of our mountains, but tell me: did you find the view stunning?"

Aniri curled her fists, mostly to keep herself from slapping Garesh. Her mind whirled. He knew she'd broken into the airharbor. How? Not that it mattered. She

would be lucky if Garesh would only take her prisoner as a traitor. More likely, her body would be found at the bottom of the ravine, the victim of an unknown assassin. She mentally cursed that she had left her saber back at the palace. But she still had her dagger. If they were going to kill her, she would take at least one of them with her. She quickly pulled it from its sheath at the small of her back and held it in front of her.

Garesh looked unimpressed. He drew a pistol from within his dark coat and cocked it back. It contained a single shot, but it was aimed for Aniri's head. She glanced at Devesh, but he wasn't looking at her, his horrified gaze fixed on the gleaming barrel of Garesh's gun.

She looked back to Garesh. "You won't get away with this. You can't simply kill a royal from Dharia and expect no repercussions." Of course, that wasn't true either. At most, her mother would go to war with Samir or Jungali or both. But they had the skyship; her mother wouldn't know what had happened to her until long after it mattered.

"And why not?" Garesh said with a smirk. "I've done it before."

Aniri frowned, her hand with the dagger wavering in front of her. What was he talking about? Did he mean her father? Was he truly dead after all, and Garesh was somehow involved? He made a motion with his head, and before Aniri knew what it meant, Devesh had grabbed her knife hand. She struggled, but she was no match for his strength. And he was being none too gentle.

His voice whispered in her ear. "I'm sorry, Aniri. It wasn't supposed to end like this." He wrenched her wrist, painfully making her drop the dagger, which thumped weakly on the tapestry that carpeted the floor. He moved behind her and held her securely with his arms wrapped around her, trapping her arms at her sides.

Garesh returned his pistol to its holster under his jacket and leisurely strolled until he was just out of her arm's reach. Had hers been free, she would have lunged for his throat. It would have been worth choking him for a moment, even if it had no chance of success. He kicked her dagger, and it tumbled away from her. His entourage of guards must not consider her a threat because they remained by the door.

"I did try to warn you the harsh mountains were no place for a royal from the plains." Garesh gave her a patronizing look. "But you royals only listen to each other and the courtesans who pander to your vanity in your courts. And while I would take pleasure in removing one more monarch from the world, I'm not going to kill you, Princess Aniri." His smile grew. "At least, not yet. It will be convenient for me to have someone officially surrender Dharia to the Jungali-Samirian coalition. Then, when I have no need for you any longer, I will happily toss you out the nearest window."

Aniri felt the blood drain out of her face. Ash's brother had fallen from a window... "You killed the prince's brother," she guessed, eyes widening as it sank in.

Garesh gave an elaborate sigh. "Jungali is poised on the brink of having the respect it deserves, and the royal family would like nothing more than to trade it for a little more wheat. They would keep our country imprisoned as a backwater nation. So, yes, princess, I have no compunction about removing a few royals when they stand in the way of Jungali's future."

The ambassador came to Garesh's side and handed him a white cloth folded into a square the size of his hand. He gestured to Devesh to bring Aniri closer.

"You won't get away with this," she said, hating the

way her voice squeaked. She tried to kick Garesh when his legs came within striking distance. He growled, lunging to smother her with the white cloth in his hand. She whipped her head back and forth and held her breath, but he grabbed hold of her hair and held her still.

The sickly sweet vapors from the cloth seeped through her nose and finally her body couldn't help but breathe it in.

It took a long time, perhaps a minute.

Through the whole struggle, as the darkness crowded in, all Aniri could think was how Devesh's arms held her still for her enemies to drug and eventually kill her. The pain gripping her chest came not from the drug, but from the last vestiges of her heart breaking into a thousand irretrievable pieces.

thirty-two

Aniri awoke with a start when someone hit her in the face.

She fought through the sickly sweet haze that clouded her mind. Her body was numb. Something rough was pressed against her cheek. Whoever had hit her must have knocked her to the floor. She tried to open her eyes, but her eyelids were impossibly heavy. When she finally managed to crack them open, everything was blurred, and she couldn't see her attacker. Colorful strands of floor tapestry tickled her nose, and her throat felt stuffed with cotton.

She coughed and twisted onto her back—at least she could face whoever had hit her—but she saw nothing but ceiling. Her arms wouldn't obey her commands. It took a lurching struggle to prop herself up from the floor. Once up, she slit her eyes against the sun, which was streaming through a window above a desk that cramped the small room. She swept a look around.

She was alone.

Next to her was a cushioned bench that looked like a bunk, and tangled around her feet was a thin blanket. As the haze in her head cleared, she realized no one had hit her: she had simply fallen off the bench.

The floor lurched, making her fingers dig into the tapestry to keep upright. Her stomach threatened to climb into her throat. It was no wonder she had fallen off the thin bunk. Eyes now wide and fully awake, she fought her way free of the blanket and braced herself on the bunk so she could stand.

What manner of floor moves like that?

Aniri stumbled to the window, holding onto the bookshelves along the way, in case the floor decided to come to life again. When she reached the window, she had to blink several times to make sense of what she saw.

She was flying. Higher than the precipice outside the prince's estate. Higher than the cable carriage. So high her eyes could barely make sense of it. The clouds weren't above her but at the same level. The mountains of Jungali were spread below her, their frosted tips transformed into an expanse of snow-covered fields. She was so high the mountains seemed flat, like crumpled fabric below her.

She was aboard the skyship.

There was no other explanation, and as she gripped the edge of the window, the thrum of the engines tickled her fingers. Her limbs were still awkward—the vapors Garesh had used made them heavy and numb—but the vibration hummed through them. Then she heard the beating of the blades: the propellers must be nearby. She peered out the corners of the window, craning to see the ship around her, but there was only a trail of steam and smoke behind and an expanse of earth thousands of feet below. As she watched, the mountains turned flat and golden. Smooth, brushed fields replaced the rough texture of the forest.

They were over the flatlands: Dharian territory.

She leaned away from the window and against the edge of the desk, her bandaged hands braced against it. The skyship was headed to Dharia, where her mother, the Queen, would have no warning, no defenses against the bombs the skyship must be carrying. No one knew where she was. Devesh had abandoned her, leaving her to die in Garesh's grasp.

She had been a fool of the highest order, just as Janak had thought all along.

She could see now why Janak despised guarding her. She was the daughter of the man who stole—and then abandoned—the woman Janak loved. He could have resigned his commission as raksaka and left the court. Or stepped down and tried to win the Queen's heart. But he did neither of those things. Faced with the worst, he remained true to his calling to serve the Queen, in whatever task she set before him. Even when it meant guarding her Third Daughter: a younger, more reckless version of a man he loathed. Janak had performed his duty under the worst of circumstances, whereas the king had fled the court when it suited him.

And she had proved to be just like her father.

Janak must think she had truly run away. The prince would surely decide she had run off with Devesh rather than keep her promise to marry. Whatever Garesh's true purpose for her, she had no doubt it would end in her death. And who knew how many others would die because of her foolishness?

Her face ran hot with the shame of it. She pressed her wounded palms to her eyes, trying to keep the tears from coming. If Janak were in her place, he wouldn't sit crying like a child. He would do his duty. He would find a way to foil Garesh's plans and protect the Queen, no matter the cost.

Aniri dropped her hands.

The tiny cabin was richly appointed, possibly the captain's keep, but it had been stripped bare of anything that might resemble a weapon, leaving only the desk she was leaned against, a few trinkets and books on the shelves, and the bunk. A door stood opposite her. She was certain it was locked, but she hurried across the floor anyway, stumbling once as the ship swayed again. The air tossed the skyship far more than she would have expected. She tried the knob, but it rattled without effect. A loud pounding on the door startled a gasp out of her and forced her to step back.

"Settle down in there," a rough voice said through the wood. "You're not going anywhere."

They had posted a guard outside her door.

Aniri stepped back farther, running her bandaged hands across her face. She had to think. Escape seemed unlikely, but eventually Garesh would come for her. She had to be prepared. What was he planning for her, and how could she ruin it? He was keeping her alive and bringing her along for some reason. Maybe it was as he claimed—so she could officially surrender Dharia to him. She had no intention of doing that: her life would end shortly after anyway, and by the Queen's breath, her final act would not be surrendering her country to her enemies. Or maybe he would use her as a hostage, threaten the Queen with bombs from the sky and the death of her Third Daughter? She could deny Garesh that possibility, spare her mother that choice, if she was no longer alive when they arrived at the capital.

She looked to the window and slowly crept toward it.

It might be possible to break. Her dagger was gone, but they'd left her cloak. She dug in the pocket and pulled out the tiny clockwork shashee with its strong armored legs. It fit easily in her hand. She held it with the legs protruded, ready to pound on the window. Her stomach churned. How long would it take to fall thousands of feet? Would she die of fright before striking the earth?

She swallowed and pounded the tiny shashee against the window. It made a small scratch and the window rattled. She struck again and again, trying to hammer the same spot to force a crack, but it just lanced pain through her bandaged hands. On the fifth or sixth strike, the shashee shattered into a thousand clockwork pieces and littered the thin rug on the captain's floor.

Tears filled her eyes at the destruction lying around her boots. All the prince's plans for peace were similarly in ruins. All her efforts to keep her country from war had likewise failed. All her attempts to avoid the peace-brokering marriage were for nothing. The boy she loved was merely a spy who had betrayed her and her country. Her father was a coward who had abandoned her long ago. Everything she thought she loved was pieces on the floor, destroyed by her foolishness and wishful thinking.

She beat at the window with her fists, pounding it with her anger and shame. Her hands were as useless as she was, only causing her pain and having no effect on the scratched window. Air slowly leaked out of her, her assault slowed, and eventually her shoulders caved forward into stillness.

She failed even at this.

The expanse of bright blue sky outside the window burned her eyes. The clouds were blurred by her tears. The glass had stopped her, but the truth was, jumping to her death was the coward's way out. She would rather die by Garesh's sword.

And she was done being a fool.

She angrily wiped her cheeks, and as her vision cleared, she could see a trail of smoke billowing up from the fields below. A dark line had been drawn on the earth, and orange flames danced around it, igniting a wildfire on either side that was quickly spreading through the dry grasses. The line followed the skyship, traveling in their wake as they flew deeper into Dharia.

The butterfly.

Aniri sucked in a breath. The skyship was thousands of feet up in the air. That line on the earth... it had to be a dozen feet across. Somehow the butterfly was gathering the brilliant sun which shone all around them and focusing it down into that enormous crystal, producing a single, flaming beam of fire and destruction. It was consuming even the earth and igniting walls of fire on either side.

And they were heading for the capital. Aniri shrank back from the window. Garesh wasn't simply going to drop bombs on the capital city or hold her hostage. He was going to turn the city, the capital of Dharia, her *home*, into cinders.

Aniri searched the desk with renewed urgency, looking for something, anything that could serve as a weapon or a way out of her prison in the captain's quarters. There was nothing but a few scraps of cable communique and a map of the kind she had seen before in the ambassador's office. The capital of Dharia was clearly marked. Aniri's chest tightened. Her mother was there. Her sister, Nahali, and her unborn child. The heart of her country beat in that city.

Aniri rifled through the drawers, but they were similarly empty. She hurried past the bookshelves, her hands skimming them as if she could conjure something that would help by touch, but there were only a few heavy books and a tiny clockwork bird.

Then a shuffling sound came from the door, and a loud thump as something hit it. The door rattled, but held. And a moment later, a grinding sound, like a Samirian's mechanical key. Aniri grabbed the heaviest book from the shelf, a tome with gilded wings titled *Aerophysiks*, and rushed the door, poised to bludgeon whoever was coming through. She had no idea what she would do from there.

The doorknob twisted. Aniri held the book high and back, ready to swing. As the door opened, she swung with all her might, aiming for the head of the person coming through.

The person ducked back, and the book slammed into the door, knocking it open farther and throwing Aniri off balance. She stumbled away from the door, but managed to bring the book around for another swing.

She jerked back when she saw who it was.

"Ash?" Her voice was hoarse, still raspy from the vapors. "What are you...? How...?"

His hands were up, but he was smiling. She let her hands drop, so she wasn't threatening him with the book anymore, but words still tangled in her mind as she tried to make sense of him being on board the ship.

His rugged work pants were tucked into leather-laced boots. He had a double belt hung with tinker tools, their weight held up by suspenders over his rough brown shirt. His overcoat seemed like he was hiding something under it. Goggles were pushed up on his forehead and fingerless gloves encased his hands.

He had come undercover, not as a prince, but as a tinker.

She stepped closer and whispered, "You came for me." There was wonder in her voice and in her mind.

He glanced at the book dangling from her hand and smiled. "I was certain you had the situation well in hand, but Priya insisted you might need help."

She shook her head. "But... you didn't have to..." Somehow he'd found out where she was. But why would he risk everything to come after her? He could have let Garesh have her. He could have embraced the inevitable war with Dharia and still retained the throne. He didn't have to risk the crown to rescue her. "Why are you here?" she finally asked.

The merriment left his face. "Aniri." He stepped closer. "I couldn't let you pay for my mistakes."

"Mistakes?" she asked, even more confused.

"Soon after you went missing, Garesh brought the skyship to Bajir, along with half his military, preaching about a new day for Jungali. It was impossible to make a move against him. I searched for you, hoping we might marry and stop him. When I couldn't find you, I thought... I thought you had changed your mind. When I found he had taken you prisoner, I was maddeningly trapped. If I demanded your release, Garesh would trumpet you as a spy and use it to justify attacking Dharia. And probably kill you as well... Aniri, you're only here because I didn't force Garesh to relinquish the ship when I had the chance."

"Forcing the issue would have just pitched the provinces against each other, with your brother's skyship in the middle." She almost told him Garesh had murdered his brother, but she stopped herself: it would only pull open the wound further, and now was not the time. "You were working for peace. We both were."

"I had no right to drag you into this." His voice was

pained. "I knew Garesh was bent on war. I should have fought to destroy the skyship before he turned it into this..." He gestured to the window where wisps of smoke filtered through the air around the ship. "...this abomination that's going to kill who knows how many people. I wanted so badly to honor my brother's death, to use his skyship for peace, that I was blinded to the true threat Garesh posed. I should have stopped him, or at least tried. Even if I lost the crown, I could have destroyed the ship. Now... I've only endangered you and your people and given Garesh exactly what he wants: to turn Jungali into a military power that can wage a horrific war on its enemies. I'm the one who should pay the price for that mistake, not you, Aniri."

A flush of warmth filled her. He had come for her, risking everything to save her, to save her people, and to stop one of his own. He hadn't abandoned her for what was easy; he hadn't left her to fight this alone. She dropped the book to the floor and slid her bandaged hands to his cheeks, pulling him down to crash her lips to his. They were warm and soft, and his cheeks were hot against her fingertips. Craving welled up in her, a desire to run her hands through his hair, across his shoulders... she pulled back quickly, shocked by its intensity. His eyes were wide and questioning, and she cringed, suddenly unsure if he had even wanted her kiss.

"I'm sorry. I shouldn't have presumed. I just—"

He stopped her with a leather-gloved hand soft on her cheek. His bare thumb ran lightly across her lips. It felt like a kiss had been painted there, igniting something deep inside her. She leaned into his hand.

He teetered on the edge of moving closer. "We haven't time for..." He stared at her lips, as if contemplating replacing his feather touch with something

stronger. Then he pulled his gaze up to meet hers. "We're expected in the engine room."

She gave him a tentative smile and pulled back slightly. "I'll have to thank you later, then."

A smile lit his face. His hand left her cheek, slowly, in a caress full of meaning.

Then he pushed back the hanging edge of his trenchcoat—underneath were two swords, both sheathed and buckled over his tinker tools. He worked one loose and handed it to her. "Garesh's Samirian sailors may yet kill us all. You'll have need of this, I imagine."

Only when it was in her hand did she recognize the jeweled hilt of her father's saber. She held it for a moment, staring at it, then looked up at him.

"Ash..."

"Priya told me." His soft smile said he knew about her father. "You're not him, Aniri. You're better than that. You always have been, though I don't think you've ever seen it. And just because he ran away doesn't mean there aren't still things left worth fighting for."

He smiled, then glanced down at the threshold of the door. Only then did Aniri notice the guard lying on the floor right outside. Ash hooked his hands under the inert guard's arms. As he dragged the guard into the captain's quarters, Aniri pulled herself together and buckled on her sword. She didn't know how much Ash knew about... everything. Priya had obviously told him something. Perhaps many somethings. Aniri would have to query her handmaiden at length when this was done.

When Ash stood, she looked up steadily into his eyes. "I'm going to stop Garesh from burning down my home or die trying."

He smirked. "That wouldn't make for much of a rescue, my lady."

She grimaced. She didn't know what his plan was, but being rescued was not her top priority. "I believe you said something about the engine room?"

He tilted his head toward the door, and she followed him out of the captain's cabin, determined to stop Garesh. Even if it meant taking her father's sword to the gasbag, slicing it open, going down with the ship.

thirty-three

The corridor outside the captain's room was narrow, with tubing that brought the ceiling low, and handrails that crowded the walls. Aniri kept one hand on the cool brass rail—her legs were still a bit unsteady, and the bumps in the air continued to make the ship sway unexpectedly. The captain bunked near his sailors if the string of narrow doors along the hall were any indication. The doors had drifted open, but there were no occupants.

"Where are all the sailors?" Aniri asked.

"In the engine room or on the bridge," Ash said. "The skyship is flying light on crew." He threw a smirk back to her as they crept down the corridor. "Capturing you forced Garesh to move up his plans, and that gash you made left them low on navia. The only way he could get the skyship in the air was with minimal crew. That's one reason I delayed coming for you until we'd gone aloft."

"Because there would be less sailors?"

"Less armed guards. Garesh had to leave most of his military forces in Bajir." Prince Malik pressed a finger to his lips as they stepped over the threshold of a bulkhead door. The layout of the ship reminded Aniri of a Samirian submarine she had once toured: she was ten and her father had brought her on the tour in one of his many official duties. It was only a few weeks before he died. *Ran away*, she reminded herself.

She gripped the railing of a metal-grated staircase and followed Ash down. He was well camouflaged as a tinker, including black swipes of soot across his face—the Samirian sailors might not recognize him, but they had to know she was a prisoner on the ship. Or did they? How long had she been out?

"How did you know Garesh captured me?" Aniri asked in a whisper. The thrumming of the engines grew louder as they descended, vibrating her hand through the metal railing.

Ash didn't answer, just darted looks around and beckoned her down another flight of stairs. When they reached the bottom, he pulled her close enough to be heard over the engine noise emanating from down the corridor. She could count the inches between their faces. His nearness made the air thick.

"Priya insisted you wouldn't run off without telling her," he said quietly. "I knew something was wrong. The Samirian embassy had no record of you visiting, but someone must have seen you because word got back to one of our tinkers that the captain was keeping the Princess of Dharia captive in his quarters. It seems you've won over the hearts of more than just my people."

"Well, Garesh certainly isn't counted among them," she said ruefully. "How long have I been under the

vapors he used on me? It was nighttime when he knocked me out at the embassy."

"You were missing for a day when Garesh arrived with the skyship." Ash tucked a strand of her hair behind her ear, lingering his hand there. "It was another day before we discovered what had happened. Our tinker couldn't get you off the ship without the contingent of Garesh's guards stopping him, so he arranged to get us onboard as tinkers instead. We had to wait until we set sail to come for you." He gestured down the empty corridor with his chin. "We need to hurry, Aniri. They won't wait much longer for us."

"Who?"

"Our spies in the engine room." Ash took her hand. "I'll fill you in as we go. Just follow my lead." He tugged her through another bulkhead door, and the sound of the engines grew. This corridor had only a single door in the middle. The prince dropped her hand when he reached it. He pushed it open, and she followed close behind.

The two-story room hummed with energy, sound, and activity. Two great brass engines hissed with steam fed from twin massive boilers, one on each side of the room. Soot choked the air, and the sulphurous smell of burning coal singed her nose. Two crewmen, one at each boiler, fed shovels full of broken coal bits into the furnace, sweat drenching their tinker outfits and soot smearing their faces. Light filtered through the dusty air, streaming from the windows above the grinding engines. Just outside, a blur of propeller blades drove the skyship through the heavens.

Perhaps a dozen engine room workers were stationed at the control panels, reading needle gauges or scribbling notes on tiny pads or attending to the machines with wrenches. They all wore the same uniform as Ash:

laced boots and suspendered work shirts. A large man with an instrumented leather armband was directing them in their duties. She could see some of the worker's faces, but others were turned away, focused on their work. Which were the spies? And what was Ash's plan?

He stood by her side, just inside the door, and motioned to a couple of workers to their right. Then the large man in charge caught notice of them. In a few long strides, he closed the distance between them. Aniri's heart skipped a beat as she recognized his overly broad chest, meaty hands, and quick, intelligent eyes.

"Karan," she said, a half gasp sucking in air. She darted a look to Ash, but he didn't seem alarmed in the slightest.

"This is the tinker I spoke of," Ash said over the engine noise, choosing his words with some apparent care for the ears around them.

"Hello, fresh," Karan said with an inscrutable look, as if amused and deadly serious at the same time.

Ash gave her a quizzical look.

"I... um..." Was Karan on their side? She bent her head close to Ash and whispered, "This would be a good time to fill me in on the details."

"Not planning to put another hole in my ship, are ye?" Karan asked, folding his arms.

Aniri coughed uncomfortably. "It was just a small hole."

Ash's eyes went wide in recognition, and he reached for his sword, still hidden under his coat. Karan's shoulders began to shake, and a booming laugh emanated from his barrel chest. The sound carried over the hiss of boilers and thrum of engines, attracting the attention of a couple of workers, but they quickly went back to their business.

Ash stayed his hand, keeping the sword hidden.

"I knew you weren't from around here," Karan said, the smile now wide across his face. He dropped his voice and leaned forward so the low timbre of it wouldn't carry. "But I didn't figure ye for a Dharian Princess. Or a spy. Are you a tinker too?" He smirked at her expense.

"No," she said, her face hot. "I'm much better at tearing things apart than putting them back together."

"There's use in that as well," Karan said solemnly, standing straight again. He nodded to the two workers who had arrived at their side. Aniri was shocked to see Janak and Priya, dressed as engine crew. Janak's face was angry, but for once she didn't think it was directed at her. His arms were folded tight across his chest as if to hold himself back from exploding.

In spite of everything, he was *here*: ready to save Queen and country, loyal to the end. He surveyed her sword strapped to her side and gave her a quick nod. It flushed warmth through her, his silent acknowledgment: he knew she hadn't run away after all. She was *here*, just as he was, ready to do whatever was necessary for Dharia. She returned his nod, and it bridged everything else that had gone before.

Janak's hands were marred with grease, his face smeared with soot, but Priya somehow had managed to remain spotless in her neatly tucked work shirt and pants. Her hair had been plaited and fell behind her back, and she wore a broad smile that encompassed all four of them.

"Glad to see you again, my lady," Priya said. "Mr. Karan has been very helpful in designing a rescue plan for you." She beamed at him, and Aniri was dumbfounded to see red creep into the giant man's cheeks. A lot had indeed happened while she had been knocked out. But she couldn't exactly ask Priya about it in the present company and circumstances.

Instead, she turned to Ash. "What exactly is the plan here?"

"To take the engine room," he said quietly. "And hold it long enough to disable the weapon, turn the ship around, and return to Jungali. At which point, I plan to put Garesh under arrest for unauthorized acts of war against the Dharian people."

"And you're on board with this?" Aniri asked Karan. Ash said the tinker had helped smuggle them on board to rescue her, but a mutiny on the ship? She was still trying to figure how this odd alliance came to be.

"I didn't design this beauty to be a merchant of death," Karan said. "I didn't know all the captain's plans for her, but war was never a part of the prince's plan, gods rest his soul." He meant Ash's brother, Tosh, and Aniri suddenly realized he must have known the younger prince. Worked with him on the skyship. No wonder Ash trusted Karan with their lives.

She gave a short nod. "Then we'll have to stop that from happening."

"Exactly so, fresh," he said with a smile.

"We're wasting time," Janak growled. The energy coiled inside him seemed to have settled into a dangerous calm.

"Right, then," Karan said. "Now that we're all in attendance, perhaps we can stop this ship from raining fire from the sky."

Priya moved quickly to the door behind them, closing it quietly and putting a Samirian key in the keyhole. The whirring and clicking hopefully meant that it was locked. Janak took a station next to Karan.

The tinker fisted his large hands on his hips and

bellowed out to the room to be heard above all the racket of the machinery. "All stations, report."

One by one, starting on the left and moving clockwise, the engine workers called out their status, loudly, like Karan, in practiced, formal voices.

"Forward vent, closed."

"Aft vent, closed."

"Rudder, carrying six degrees."

"Starboard throttle, full."

On through the stations they went, ending with, "Stern fins, twenty degrees rise, trim."

Karan met each with a short nod, which could only be meant for himself, since the sailor's gazes were fixed on their levers and needle gauges.

When they were done cycling through, Karan called out, "Forward vent, how is your ballast?"

"Control, forward vent, ballast full."

"Bow fins, make ready for trim," he called out.

"Control, bow fins, ready for trim," a worker in the back answered.

"Stern fins, make ready for trim."

"Control, stern fins, ready for trim," came the reply.

"Starboard throttle, set your power to half." Karan waited for the call back before saying, "Port throttle, set your power to half." The immediate whining down of the engines made the thrum both less loud and deeper. It shook the floorboards of the engine room through Aniri's boots.

"Rudder, set your angle to zero one zero," Karan said, "and hold until our bearing is one eight zero."

There was a pause. "Control, repeat?" came the answer from a worker standing in front of a panel filled with needle gauges, instruments, and one large lever that his hand rested upon.

"Rudder, bring us to bearing one eight zero," Karan repeated.

"One eight zero, sir?" The sailor at the rudder station looked to the sailor next to him, doubt wrinkling his brow. "That will return us to Bajir, sir."

"That's an order, sailor," Karan said.

The sailor hesitated. Every head in the room swung between the rudder station and Karan. Janak stood by his side, all tension at the ready, but Aniri didn't know if the sailors could see that in the smoky light of the engine room.

"Captain's orders," Karan said carefully. "We're coming about and heading back to Jungali."

A muttering chatter rose up.

One man stepped away from his spot by the boiler, his shovel still in hand, and his face slick with sweat. "What about the mission, sir?" he called out.

"It's been aborted," Karan responded, then pointed to the rudder station. "Rudder, make your angle zero one zero, or I'll come there and do it myself, sailor."

The sailor's eyes went wide, then he slowly eased the lever to the left and shouted, "Control, rudder, angle set to zero one zero."

Aniri could feel the slow tilt as the ship heeled over into the turn.

"Belay that order," a voice barked. It was the man who had spoken before. He swung his shovel onto his shoulder and called out, "I didn't hear any order come down from the bridge."

"Aye," said a second man, closer, standing near a large brass tube that flared into a horn shape. "There was no order on the tube."

"Well, that's that, then," Karan said quietly and nodded to Janak, who looked like he was ready to burst.

He moved so fast, Aniri could hardly track him. He leapt from Karan's side and landed at the rudder station. His hands blurred, connecting with the sailor in at least two spots. Aniri wasn't quite sure what he did, but the man crumpled to the floor at Janak's feet. The nearby engine workers shrank away, fear flashing across their faces.

Then everything went to madness.

"Bridge!" the man at the large brass tube shouted into the horn. "Mutiny on the engine deck—" Janak was on him, stopping his breath with a quick strike to the throat, and soon he lay in a heap on the floor as well. The man from the back surged forward, readying his shovel to swing, and several more workers lunged for Janak.

He whirled, his hands flat planes and his boots swiping high then low, a spinning figure in the middle of the melee. She didn't see him actually touch any of the sailors attacking him, but they flew backward, one by one, landing motionless on the floor or slumped against an instrument panel. The man with the shovel lay flat on his back, splayed out, unmoving. His shovel skittered to a stop against another worker's feet. Janak stood in the middle of the bodies, back straight as an arrow, feet wide and hands splayed, ready for more.

No one moved.

"Now, then," Karan said, commanding the attention of the remaining workers. "The rest of ye want to question my orders?" There were still eight engine workers left at their stations, but no one so much as twitched an eyebrow.

"Right." Karan strode to the rudder station, checked quickly on the status, and seeming satisfied there, moved two stations forward, closer to the door, where an array of tiny levers bristled from the instrumentation panel. It also had a larger handled lever like the rudder station, and Karan clacked it down with a heavy mechanical thunk. But when he examined the needle gauge, his face pulled into a scowl.

"Ashoka," he called out, and the prince, who had stood by Aniri's side during the entire brief showdown hurried to the control station. Karan pointed to a gauge where the needle was well into a red zone that Aniri could see even from her spot by the door. "The burning glass is still operational. I've thrown the main switch; it should have laid all the wings flat, cutting off the rays to the central crystal, but the tube is still hot." He tapped it. "Could be it will take a moment to cool, but it should at least have dipped." His face was solemn when he turned to Ash. "There's a manual override control on the bridge. They could have cut us off before I was able to shut it down."

Ash ran a hand across his face. "There's no way to turn it off from here?"

"From here… no. Not if they're controlling it from the bridge now." Karan glared at the sailor at the station next to them. "We could try to take the bridge, but…"

Ash gave a small shake to his head, and Karan nodded. They didn't seem to think that was a viable option. Aniri glanced at Priya: her face was scrunched with worry. This obviously wasn't part of the plan. Janak appeared by Karan's side, startling the large man out of his frown for a moment.

"We can turn back to Jungali," Janak said.

"We can't return to Bajir like this," Ash said. "With the burning glass still operational, we'll just destroy whatever's in our path."

"Continuing on to the capital is not an option." The menace in Janak's voice made clear he wouldn't

countenance that. "No," Ash agreed. "We can't do that either."

"We could vent some navia and bring 'er down," Karan offered, carefully. "Of course we'll be landing in our own flaming pit of fire, so I'm not keen on those odds, Ashoka."

The prince glanced at Aniri. She gave him a weak smile and a nod. She knew it might come down to destroying the ship, which would likely mean themselves as well, in order to stop it.

He turned back to Karan. "If that's what it takes to stop the destruction of the capital, I want you to do it. But I would like to hear any other options you have first."

"Aye." Karan leaned a hand against the panel, the other one working the goggles on his brow, as if that motion was helping him think. "If there was some way to get directly to the burning glass…" He studied the small forest of switches on the panel. "It wouldn't take much, only a few of the panels out of alignment might reduce the power enough… or we could disable it entirely by—"

A loud rattling came from the door behind Aniri and Priya. Aniri had just enough time to shoot an alarmed look to Ash, Karan, and Janak, all of whom had swung to look their way, when a tremendous crack sounded from the door. A split second later the door flew open, catching Priya in the back and sending her crashing into Aniri. They both tumbled to the floor as several sailors armed with blunderbusses stormed into the engine room.

Janak ran toward her, but before he could reach the cluster of armed sailors, a shot rang out, and he flew backward. Aniri stared in horror as he fell to the floor and didn't get up. She scrambled to her feet, ready to join the fight, when Karan's voice bellowed out.

"Stop!" Surprisingly, the command brought everyone

to a halt. "Garesh, you fool, you can't fire that thing in here! You'll burst a boiler or worse. With your aim, you'll probably put a hole in the bag."

Garesh stepped to the front of his sailors, blunderbuss extended, a grin on his face. "Then I'll be careful to aim well, tinker." But his gun wasn't pointed at Karan, it was leveled at Ash's head. "The Jungali people will have to mourn the loss of yet another royal. How appropriate for him to die at the hands of mutineers on board the country's finest war vessel. But no one will be surprised that the Dharian princess he wanted to marry turned traitor. Such is the bad luck of the Malik royal household."

Ash bore his taunts with a cold look of disdain, as if Garesh were beneath his contempt. Garesh cocked the hammer back on his gun, and Aniri didn't hesitate. She whipped her sword from its sheath and lunged at Garesh's arm. The tip of her blade barely reached him, but it smacked against Garesh's gun just as it fired.

Garesh swore and whirled on her. Aniri backed away and looked to see if Ash had been hit, but a cloud of steam billowed out to swallow half the room. Garesh and his men were distracted by the sudden hiss that came with it. Karan bellowed and appeared out of the cloud, tackling Garesh. They went down, wrestling on the floor, with Karan's massive hand around Garesh's throat. With his free hand, Karan snagged the goggles off his forehead and tossed them to Aniri. She clumsily caught them.

"Go, fresh," he wheezed, then pulled his arm back to punch Garesh in the face. Two sailors fell on him, trying to wrest him away. Aniri stared for a split second at the goggles in one hand and her sword in the other, then hooked her arm around Priya's and dragged her through the blasted-open door.

thirty-four

Aniri didn't look back, just ran through the corridor, retracing her steps up the stairs to the captain's quarters where Ash had rescued her.

Ash.

Tears blurred her eyes. She kept her father's sword in front for any of Garesh's sailors along the way. Janak was shot for certain—she couldn't tell where or how badly he was hurt.

Or if he was dead.

The tears made it impossible to see, so she swiped at them. Her boots pounded the metal steps. Ash could be dead as well. She told herself the bullet must have gone wide—otherwise steam wouldn't have filled the engine room. Or was that Karan's doing? Priya followed behind, face drawn. They reached the captain's quarters, and Aniri paused, making sure they hadn't been followed. At least not yet.

"Did you see the prince, Priya?" she couldn't stop

herself from asking.

"No, my lady." Her delicate face was taut with worry. "But I'm sure Karan will protect him, if he can."

Aniri's heart squeezed. Priya was as worried about the tinker as Aniri was about Ash. But she had no time for that now.

She held up Karan's goggles. "Why did he give me these?" She was asking herself as much as Priya. "He said *go*, but go where? I don't know if there are escape boats, but I've no intention of leaving. Do you know what he meant?"

"No, my lady. But Mr. Karan, he's..."

Aniri's heart wrenched further as tears glistened in Priya's eyes.

"He's a brilliant tinker," Priya said. "I'm sure he meant for you to do something important with the goggles."

Of course. "The butterfly!"

"My lady?"

"The burning glass, or whatever its proper name." Aniri sheathed her sword and pulled on the darkened goggles, securing the strap and propping them on her forehead, so she could still see. "Karan mentioned something about getting to it and disabling it."

"Do you know how to do that, my lady?" Priya's eyes were wide.

Aniri grimaced. "Not exactly. But I know where it is, and there must be a way up top to reach it." She glanced down the end of the hall. "Priya, how do I get to the upper decks of the ship?"

"This way, my lady." Priya scurried with light steps down the hall, past the captain's quarters, to another set of stairs at the end. At the top, the brilliant summer sun shone through a window in the door. Pounding steps

sounded somewhere in the ship—Aniri hurried up the stairs and threw open the door.

It flew back and smacked hard against the wall, carried by the wind that buffeted Aniri's face as soon as she stepped over the threshold. The edge of the ship was near, a bare wooden railing waist high. It was the only thing standing between her and thousands of feet of empty air. Near the door, a rope ladder was lashed to a cleat on the railing. It was just like the one Aniri had climbed at the airharbor.

Priya lingered at the threshold, giving the railing a wide-eyed look.

"Priya!" Aniri shouted to be heard over the wind. "Do you still have that key? Will it work on this door?"

Priya gingerly stepped onto the wooden deck and wrestled the wind for the door, bringing it around to bang shut again. The key was on a ring, which she pressed into the keyhole. The whirring just carried over the sound of air whipping around them.

"Stay here!" Aniri said.

Priya flattened herself against the wall of the ship. Aniri grabbed hold of the rope ladder, took a deep breath and a final glance at her handmaiden, then climbed up on the railing.

One wrong placement of a foot, and she might get a chance to fall to her death after all. She tried not to look down. Once she had both hands on the rope ladder and both feet on the railing, she felt more secure.

The gasbag of the skyship billowed above her. She couldn't see the top, but the ladder hugged the balloon all the way out of sight. Downwind, clouds of thick gray smoke stacked on top of one another like great pillows, burgeoning up into the skies. She didn't know how close they were to the capital, but she didn't want that fire anywhere near it.

She climbed hand over hand, her saber banging against her leg, her cloak flapping like a winged beast strapped to her back. She should have discarded it before the climb. Scaling the ladder seemed a much longer trek this time, now that she was climbing the skin of the gasbag itself. The wind surged against her in uneven gusts, and the blue fabric of the gasbag smacked underneath her handhold, as if the sky itself were fighting to dislodge her.

She finally saw the tips of the butterfly wings overhead. They focused inward in a perfectly spaced formation; tiny flashes escaped at the corners where the reflective surfaces weren't completely focused on the burning glass. She slid the goggles down with one hand, the other tight on the rope. The goggles turned the brilliant sunshine dark, but she would be quickly blinded without them.

She reached the top and climbed onto the platform, hunching into the wind. It wasn't strong enough to blow her off, but it was uneven, gusty, and there wasn't much to hold on to for steadying. She pushed through the wind to the butterfly itself and drew her sword.

The wooden linkages that supported the big brass plates were only a few inches thick, but they were solid. Her repeated strikes with the saber only reminded her that her hands were still healing. The miniscule cuts she made were going to accomplish nothing. She tried kicking at the linkage, venting all her frustration into every boot pounding, but the wood held steady against her onslaught. Then the platform beneath her heaved, and she fell to the wooden deck, grasping for a handhold between the planks in case the ship decided to simply toss her off for daring to assault it.

What had Karan said? That it wouldn't take much change in the alignment to stop it? She carefully climbed to her feet. The linkages were wooden beams connected by metal pins and a gear at the base. The control mechanisms must be below, inside the ship. Aniri stabbed her saber into the base gear and tried to leverage movement with that. She pushed to the limits of her blade without breaking it. The gear didn't budge.

If she couldn't move the wings out of alignment, maybe she could do something to the crystal. She carefully peered between the wings, afraid that looking directly at the burning glass might be too much, but very little light came from the crystal. Tiny pinpoints inside winked at her, but it seemed all the light channeled down into the fiery inferno below. Waves of heat pulsed from the plates, then were swept away by the wind.

Scuffling sounded behind her.

She turned, saber in hand, in time to see Garesh pull himself to his full height at the top of the rope ladder.

She was tempted to charge him, saber first, maybe push him off, but she would go right over with him. Garesh drew his sword and stalked toward her. His goggles masked his face, but she didn't have to see it to know what he intended. The platform was barely five feet wide next to the butterfly, not much room for a saber fight, and a painful death on either side: plummeting to her death or falling into the burning plates of the butterfly.

She retreated to where the platform opened up—still only about twenty feet square.

Garesh charged her. Aniri parried and lunged back to strike at his chest, but he had already danced out of her reach. She edged toward him—maybe she could force him off the platform—but he slashed and cut his way forward again, pushing her back. She had to glance at the platform behind her to gauge the distance to the edge. His sword caught her cloak, and the wind snarled it, giving her a split-second to cut up with her blade. She barely missed his angular face with the tip.

He stumbled back.

The ship swayed under them, nearly sending both to their knees. Aniri widened her stance for balance. "Forget to bring your blunderbuss, Garesh?"

He steadied himself on the platform. "I don't need a gun to kill a royal." Which Aniri took to mean he had lost it in his battle with Karan. Or maybe realized it would be foolish to bring a gun on top of a gasbag.

She tried not to think of Karan. Or Ash or Janak. But while she and Garesh circled each other, the ship was flying closer to her home, bringing an inferno with it. That thought caused her to involuntarily glance toward the bow of the ship. Clearly visible in the distance was a familiar square perimeter with faint red coloring and a tall building in the center.

The palace. Her home.

Garesh seized on her distraction, and she barely dodged his blade as it thrust past her ear. She shoved into him, knocking him backward, then brought her sword around in a slashing arc, but he blocked. She tried to whip over the top of his handguard, at least draw some blood with the tip, but the blade whispered past his cheek, and he managed to slip out of reach again.

This time he shuffled back, looking shaken.

Aniri was desperate for some end to this that would actually stop the ship. It was just as likely, if not more so, that Garesh would kill her than the other way around. Meanwhile, the burning glass was still decimating the landscape of her homeland. Even if she defeated him,

how would she disable the butterfly? All she had was her sword, her cloak, and... *her sword.*

It was heavily jeweled and the finest steel Samirian smiths could forge. Perhaps it would hold up to the heat within the butterfly and block the light that was finely focused on the burning glass. Karan said even a small amount might make a difference and reduce the flaming torch beneath them.

But without her weapon, Garesh would kill her in a heartbeat.

Aniri didn't hesitate. She dashed down the side of the butterfly, seeking the platform at the far side. Garesh would surely pursue her, but moving would give her a second's time to make a good throw. She rounded the corner, coming out on the far side. Edging as close to the wings as the heat would allow, she gripped the blade of her father's sword and gently lofted it into the center of the butterfly, hoping her aim would be true. It clanked against the crystal, jumped up onto one of the wings—which made her heart stop in her chest—and then rattled its way back down to the center. The jeweled hilt came to rest directly on top of the burning glass.

As Garesh pounded around the side of the platform, the hilt of her father's sword popped and sizzled, quickly melting and smoking and oozing all over the giant crystal. Garesh stared open-mouthed at the smoke now pluming up from the center of the butterfly. Aniri held her breath: it had to be working. She couldn't believe any light, no matter how powerful, could cut through that grayish mass. The wind tossed the smoke, clearing it a little.

Garesh roared in anger and slashed his blade at her neck.

Aniri ducked and fell backward. She scrambled on her bandaged hands and boots as he lunged for her, driving his blade straight down toward her heart. At the last instant, she rolled to the side, and Garesh's blade embedded itself in the wooden plank. He yanked it out and came after her again, sword raised. A deafening bang sounded off the side of the ship, and the platform rocked, sending Garesh back on his heels and causing his blade to miss her. She leapt to her feet and ran for the ladder. A wisp of gray smoke drifted up over the gasbag from somewhere below the ship.

She froze. Was the ship on fire?

Then she saw a small flotilla of paper lanterns peppering the sky all around the ship, white dots against the brown and gray landscape. As she watched, another one, too far to impact the ship, exploded into a puff of ash and smoke.

Her mother had somehow known; somehow seen them coming. *Of course.* Janak would have messaged ahead to warn her.

Aniri turned back to Garesh. "You've lost."

He was gaping at the flotilla as well.

"Your burning weapon is broken, Garesh, and my mother will bring down your skyship. Surrender now, and no more lives need be lost."

"We can easily steer around your mother's toy balloon bombs," Garesh said with a sneer. "And yours is the only life that will be lost in the process."

He lunged. She dodged, but his sword sliced the tip off her cloak. She backed to the edge of the platform, tugging off her cloak as she went. She held it stretched between her hands. Maybe she could ward him off long enough to reach the ladder.

A blade being drawn swished behind her. Garesh's gaze flitted over her shoulder, and Aniri whirled to see if one of Garesh's men had braved the climb to the top—

"Ash!" she cried. Blood marred his cheek and goggles covered his eyes, but she would recognize his face anywhere. He quickly heaved up onto the platform and stepped around her, his sword pointed at Garesh with her at his back.

"Priya said you might need some assistance." Ash kept his gaze locked on Garesh, but his words were obviously meant for her.

"I've disabled the burning glass," she said quickly. They didn't need to fight Garesh; they needed to get off the gasbag in one piece and signal her mother to stop launching paper lanterns. And she didn't want Ash to get hurt… or *more* hurt.

"Get below, Aniri," Ash said, still not looking at her.

"But the weapon is—"

Ash lunged for Garesh, who easily dodged and countered with a slash that sliced through the prince's overcoat but missed his body. They clashed swords again in a rapid-fire parry and attack. Neither gained or lost ground on the platform, but Garesh had a maniacal look on his face that made Aniri's blood run cold. He had nothing to lose at this point, and Aniri could see the mad desire to kill the last of the Malik royal house in his eyes.

Garesh feinted to one side, and Ash slashed at him, seeming overbalanced for a moment. Then another paper lantern exploded off the side of the skyship, just close enough to buffet the ship. Ash stumbled and Garesh dashed past him, slashing at him as he went, but thankfully missing. Ash growled and lunged backward, trying to reach him, but Garesh slipped between the tip of Ash's sword and the wings of the butterfly.

Garesh rushed straight at Aniri. She dropped to the platform, grasping hold of the edge, afraid he would try to simply push her off.

A familiar voice called from behind her. "Step aside, your majesty!" It was Janak, somehow alive, clinging with one hand to the top of the rope ladder. His other arm hung limp at his side, and his voice was strained, the words breathy with pain. Aniri scrambled away from the edge on hands and knees. Garesh's rush took him to the edge of the platform. Janak swung up onto it, and his legs swiped Garesh's out from under him. Garesh's sword hand flailed back. He hacked forward again, aiming for Janak's neck, but before he could land the blade, Janak wrenched Garesh closer. His swing overreached and clunked into the edge of the platform. Janak twisted his body, pulling Garesh on top of him, and the two of them rolled off the platform in one quick motion.

Aniri's heart seized in her chest. "No!" She lunged toward the edge, half-crawling on her knees. She and Ash arrived at the same time, him teetering on the toes of his boots to peer over. Janak hung from the ladder, one hand grasping it, but his legs dangling free. Garesh had grasped Janak's tinker clothes in one hand, his legs and sword-hand twisting in the wind as he stared at the thousands of feet of air below him. He tossed his sword aside, and it slowly tumbled out of sight. Then he grabbed at Janak's clothes.

Janak's dead-weight arm was no use, and his other arm was all that kept them both from plummeting after the sword. As Garesh climbed him like a human ladder, Janak twisted his legs around. Aniri thought he would try to kick Garesh free, but instead, Janak gave a guttural sound and let go of the ladder.

Aniri gasped. Janak pivoted head-down, Garesh falling with him, but then they both yanked to a stop. Janak had twisted his leg into the rope ladder, holding on by friction and the hook of his foot. It was a wonder he

wasn't pulled straight out of his boot. His hand now free, Janak pounded Garesh's face. After a terrifying moment when Aniri was sure Janak would slip free of the ship, he landed a blow to Garesh's throat that made him reflexively let go of Janak and grab for it. Garesh fell silently away from the ship, tumbling like the sword, end over end, a scream fixed on his face but no sound coming from it.

Aniri was transfixed by his rapidly disappearing form for only a second, then she hastened to climb down the ladder after Janak.

"Hold on!" she rasped through the tightness in her throat, looking down between her boots. By the time she had worked down the dozen steps to him, Janak had righted himself. He held fast to the rope with his good hand, his legs holding him up from the rope rungs below. Aniri hovered above him on the ladder.

"What exactly are you attempting, my lady?" Janak asked with a wheezed breath.

"I'm going to rescue you, Janak!" she cried, but she could see his point. There wasn't room for two on the ladder, and she might only jostle his grip.

"That's my job, your majesty." His voice was still strained. "Yours is to save our Queendom. Please make sure that you turn this infernal ship around before it reaches our Queen, will you?" That last sounded far too polite for Janak. And far too much like a goodbye.

"Janak, the weapon is disabled," she said quickly. "The Queen is in no danger. But you are not relieved of your duties." Tears crowded her vision. How could she help him down? She was afraid the fight had taken what strength he had left. "I'm wounded, Janak!" she lied, desperately. "And I'm dangling on the side of an skyship, and your sorry *raksaka* hide is blocking my path. So get thee down safely, or I'll be tempted to toss you off this ship for endangering a member of the royal household!" Aniri peered between her boots.

Janak didn't look up at her, just gave a breathy chuckle instead. "Your majesty is an extremely bad liar."

"Janak, please save your breath—"

Another paper lantern took that moment to explode near the bow of the ship, making it lurch underneath them. Aniri drew in a sharp breath and held it until she was sure Janak still had hold of the ladder. Then she looked up to Ash hovering above her, beseeching his help with her eyes.

"Janak," he called out. "Your lady needs to get below deck immediately. We need to rise above these floating mines or none of us will survive."

Janak didn't say anything, but he started to move— one jerking, heart-stopping step at a time as he climbed one-handed down the ladder. Aniri had no idea how he had managed to climb up in the first place. She descended after him, and Ash soon followed.

At the bottom, Priya was beside herself, fluttering between Aniri and Janak, trying to decide who to attend to first. Janak slumped against the railing, all energy fled, the only motion the unsteady rising and falling of his chest. His eyes were closed, and Aniri couldn't tell if he had fallen unconscious or not. She could see his wound now, a gaping hole in his chest, and his tinker uniform stained dark with blood.

Ash touched her shoulder gently. "I'm going to the engine room. We need to drop some ballast and get above these mines."

She nodded, still looking at Janak, then turned to Ash. "Do you need me?"

"No." Ash gave her a small smile. "This is a Jungali

vessel. We will negotiate a landing with Dharia shortly." He gave her shoulder a squeeze. "Attend to your guard."

She nodded, and Ash hurried belowdecks. Aniri bent to Janak.

"You saved my life," she said, quietly.

He didn't open his eyes, but the corners of his mouth quirked. "'Tis my job, my lady. Please tell the Queen that I performed it."

"Tell her yourself."

The quirk grew into almost half a smile, then lapsed into a slackness that could only mean he had passed out. Aniri's hand shook as she checked for his pulse. It was still present, but faint. She prayed it would keep beating until they could reach the ground and a proper doctor to save the man who secretly loved her mother.

thirty-five

Aniri's royal garments were even more stiff and uncomfortable than she remembered. It hadn't been that long since she had worn full, Dharian royal dress. But a lifetime of adventuring and spying had been compressed into a few short weeks, and her body had grown accustomed to that freedom.

She stood on the far side of her mother's receiving room while the Queen looked over the final treaty documents. They were smeared with fresh ink and lacked the neatness Aniri would normally expect, with several things crossed and amended. They had been put together hastily in the twenty-four hours since Prince Malik successfully negotiated the landing of a Jungali skyship outside the gates of Kartavya, the capital and heart of Dharia.

Aniri hadn't seen the prince much since then. He and Karan had been locked in meetings with the Queen and her advisors. Her sister, Nahali, had been involved in the negotiations, and Aniri imagined the prince now had more occasion to speak with the First Daughter of Dharia than the Third. Aniri had spoken briefly with her mother, singing Prince Malik's virtues as a worthy ally, but she wasn't surprised when her presence was no longer needed.

It was just as well because she wanted to attend to Janak's recovery. His injuries were grave. The court's best surgeons did what they could to stop the bleeding and repair the damage, but Janak was lucky Garesh's bullet went clean through his shoulder, missing his lungs and merely destroying the use of his arm, at least temporarily. Time would tell on that, as well as his overall recovery. He had not yet awoken from the heavy vapors the surgeons had given him.

That didn't stop Aniri from sitting at his bedside, softly telling him all he had missed while she had been foolishly off adventuring on her own. She even asked him quiet questions about her father, but only when Janak's angular face was slack with drugs and there was no hope of any answers.

She wasn't ready to hear them yet.

Her burning need to find her father had evaporated into smoke, like his sword. Someday, she would seek him out and demand to know why he was such a coward. Why he had forsaken them. For now, it was enough to know that, when it counted, she hadn't run away and abandoned the ones she loved like he had.

The Queen rubbed her eyes. Her face was heavy with lack of sleep, but she seemed finally content with the treaty papers neatly stacked in front of her. The Queen's court waited outside in her Grand Chamber to hear the details. The entire countryside had been buzzing about it since they'd arrived in the skyship. Aniri decided it was time to approach her, before the public could commandeer her attention again.

"Your Highness?" she asked, keeping her station by the door.

"Come, Aniri!" her mother said, rising and sweeping her silk dress around the side of her desk. She motioned Aniri closer. "I'm sorry, child. I haven't had much time to spend with you since you returned."

Her mother hadn't called her *child* since... Aniri stumbled on a stray bump in the stone flooring, but managed to quickly recover. "You've been busy with important matters—"

"I've been busy too long with important matters." The Queen surprised her by taking Aniri's shoulders in her hands and looking into her eyes. "It's your birthday, child, and I don't even have a gift prepared for you."

"There's no need, Mother. I have *you*, safe, and that's all the present I need."

Her mother smiled sadly. "Your father used to say the same thing to me every year." Aniri tried not to cringe under that knowledge. She hadn't told her mother yet— that she knew the truth. That there was no reason to protect her from it any longer. But the fact that her father had abandoned her, her mother, their country... the wound was still too raw for Aniri to share it.

"You've always had his eyes," her mother said, drawing Aniri out of her thoughts and stealing her breath. "But since you've returned, I've seen so much more in them."

Then the Queen hugged her. It took Aniri a moment to remember to put her arms around her mother's tightly drawn corset. She felt awkward in the movement and wished she knew how to do a better job of it. Then her mother released her and looked at her again.

"You've done well, my Third Daughter."

Words caught in Aniri's throat, but she cleared it, determined to have her say before the prince came to sign the documents and make it official. Before Janak awoke to a new Jungali-Dharian coalition and possibly new duties.

"Mother…" she started, but somehow her rehearsed lines fled her mind in the presence of her mother.

"Is there something you want to ask me, Aniri?" Her mother's smile was gentle now, as if Aniri was a child she had to coax.

"No." Aniri frowned, unsure what that was about. "I… there's something I wanted to tell you." She paused again, gathering courage. Her mother's face was lined with worry and time, having gone too long without a love in her life to ease them. She had lost the man she loved long ago and gave everything to her country instead. Aniri took a deep breath. "When father died," she said, the lie lying heavy on her heart, "I thought there could never be someone else who could take his place. That there never *should* be someone… else."

Her mother's face darkened, and the circles under her eyes became more pronounced. "He was a good man. I loved your father a great deal."

"I know." Aniri took her mother's hand and nodded to emphasize her point. "I know you did. As did I. But it's been a long time since he left us…" Aniri swallowed. "…and I want you to know you have my blessing to find someone else to love."

Her mother smiled through her surprise. "My dear daughter, I hardly need your permission to—"

"I don't mean the courtesans, Mother." Aniri gave her a knowing look. Her mother's eyes widened slightly. "I mean, you have my blessing to marry again. To someone who is not my father. Even someone who, perhaps, is not exactly from royal lineage."

A flash of fear crossed her mother's face and leapt straight into Aniri's heart. Maybe she had stepped too far. She dropped her mother's hand and affected a more casual air.

"I spent a lot of time with Janak in Jungali," she lied again, knowing it was the shortest pathway to the truth. "I've already told you of his heroics on the skyship. He's a good man, Mother, and an even better *raksaka*. But I think it is time you allowed him to retire from his active duties. Perhaps let him take a more courtly role."

"This is what you wanted to tell me?" Her mother's eyebrows lifted.

"Yes."

Her mother slowly nodded, eyes still curious, probing Aniri's face. But that was all she would say about it—all she *could* say without straying into matters of the heart that were none of her business. If her mother returned Janak's affections, Aniri would bless their wedding with her love for both of them. The Queen seemed like she might press for more, but a soft knock sounded at the door.

Her mother smiled. "I believe the young prince has arrived to sign the treaty."

Aniri ducked her head in acknowledgment and took a step back from the desk to give the Queen room to receive him.

"Come!" she called, and the door creaked open. Ash strode in, dressed in the finest Dharian courtly attire that could be obtained at short notice and tailored to fit him. He wore it with ease.

"Your majesty? Are you ready?" He caught sight of Aniri, and he checked himself in his long strides toward

the Queen's desk. He made a quick bow, hands pressed together. "Arama, Princess Aniri."

Aniri returned the gesture but omitted the words. Ash's gaze lingered on her, as if expecting a response. Then he hastily turned back to the Queen. "I apologize for the state of the documents, your majesty. But I won't apologize for the contents. I think we've crafted a fine agreement."

"Agreed." Her mother's smile was as bright as Aniri had seen in some time. She seemed quite taken by the prince. Which Aniri could completely understand. After his daring act of bringing the rumored weapon of war to the Dharian capital only to propose peace, return her Third Daughter, and defeat his own war general… if it were possible, Aniri was quite certain the Queen would adopt the barbarian prince as a son. And he was handsome too, even more so with the lack of shave shadowing his face. Given time away from treaty negotiations, she was sure his earnest heroics would win him any lady's hand he cared to claim—in Dharia or Jungali.

Her mother and Prince Malik bent over the treaty, checking the final corrections and adding the flourish of their signatures. Aniri did not miss the irony that Dharia and Jungali were signing a peace treaty on her birthday. The day she had longed to arrive now stood empty of all the things she had wanted from it. Devesh had betrayed her. Her father had destroyed her dream of finding justice for him long before, only she didn't know it. And now that her birthday was here, a simple piece of parchment on her mother's desk had set her more free than any date on the calendar ever could.

Only now she wasn't quite sure what to do with that freedom.

The treaty meant her mother did not need Aniri to enter into a peace-brokering marriage with the prince of Jungali. And the prince... he could return to his country, bearing a shiny new alliance with Dharia and an amazing new technology that would bring great things to his people.

He had no need of her either.

She had no claim on him and nothing to offer. No reason she could give for him to stay, not even a day past the signing of the treaty, and yet... her heart was heavy with the thought that this might be their last chance to speak. Courtly duties would soon pull him away. She might not even see him again before he left.

The prince straightened and bowed to the Queen, who pressed her hands together in acknowledgment. Her mother swept the papers up in her hands.

"Now," she said to the prince, but also including Aniri with a glance, "I have to freshen before we can present our new treaty to the court. I'm afraid the night's work has drawn down my energy. Will your highness excuse me for a few minutes while I have my chambermaids attend to me?"

Aniri frowned. The Queen was more than prepared to address her court and could certainly do so in any state she wished. But the prince did not appear surprised in the least. Aniri had a feeling they had arranged this little delay ahead of time. But for what purpose?

"Of course, your majesty." He bowed again. "Please take your time and let us know when you are ready. There is no rush."

The Queen smiled broadly and patted the prince's arm as she swept past him. "Thank you, dear boy."

Aniri was nonplussed by her mother's sudden exit. The room's heavy wooden door clicked solidly behind

her. That left the prince and her alone together.

"Well, that was... interesting," Aniri offered. "But I'm happy for you, Ash. You have the alliance you wanted all along."

Ash took a few slow steps toward her, seeming to choose his words as carefully as his footfalls. "Your mother has agreed to build a new rail line to connect our countries."

"Something that should have been done long ago." She clasped her hands in front of her and glanced down at them. The half-Dharian, half-Sik crest leftover from the Bajiran tinker's kindly help was oddly symbolic of the new treaty.

"And this new trade agreement we've signed..." Ash was only a couple steps away and still inching toward her. "...will include transport by skyship as well as rail."

Aniri looked into his eyes. "It's just what your brother would have wanted."

He stood next to her. "We have the beginnings of a lasting peace between our countries."

"Nisha will be so pleased. And I think your mother would be incredibly proud of you." She decided not to mention that hers would accept him as a son in a heartbeat.

He had continued to inch closer and now stood very still and close. She could smell the freshly washed garments her mother's court had given him and the faint tang of the ink clinging to his fingers.

"My business here is done." His eyes peered into hers, solemn and expectant. He was saying goodbye—she could feel it in every minute movement of his body. He had the peace he needed, and she had nothing to offer him but her thanks... and even with that, she had done a poor job.

"You're not quite done, Prince Malik," she said softly, looking up into his eyes. "I believe I still owe you a proper thank-you for saving my life."

She took his cheeks in her hands—now free of bandages, so she could feel the roughness of his unshaven face—and pulled his face down for a kiss. Her fingers slipped into his hair, and she tried to show with her lips what she couldn't put into words. He met her kiss with a tenderness that made her heart race.

She stretched the moment as long as she dared and still have the guise of it being a measure of thanks and not an offer of more. Pulling away was much harder than she expected.

But she didn't get far. Ash's hand found the small of her back and brought her tight against him. His other hand cupped the back of her head, and his lips found hers again. Only his kiss was no small press of lips, but deep and demanding. He crushed her body to his, bending it back with the fierce need of his lips for hers. She allowed it to consume her, stunned and absorbed completely by his desire.

When he gentled his kiss, retreating from the demands he had just placed, she nearly clutched at him to bring him back, even though their bodies were separated only by a whisper. When her arms didn't move, she realized they hung at her sides, shocked into limpness.

His breath was hot on her lips, still kissing her with their closeness.

"That," she said, equally breathless, "wasn't very proper."

His lips curved, and he kissed her again, soft touches this time, on her lips and cheeks. The hand that held her head skimmed forward, his fingertips drawing lines across her cheek and down her neck, sending sparks racing

across her body and setting brushfires in her heart.

When he pulled back, his eyes were blazing with an amber fire.

"Third Daughter of Dharia." His voice was softer than his kiss. "Is there any possibility I may convince you to marry me for love?"

Breath escaped her.

Images flashed in her mind. The biting winter cold of the Jungali mountains. The breathlessness of its air. The pulsing dancers and their barefooted celebration of love. The heart-breaking kindness of an old woman who saw through her lies. And their prince, a barbarian more noble than any man she'd ever known. A man who had saved her, and her people, from the worst among them.

Her heart soared. "It *is* my birthday. I may marry whoever I wish."

His eyes went slightly wide, and he ducked his head to whisper against her ear, "Name your conditions, Princess."

Conditions? Was he teasing her? She drew back to look at him. Did he misunderstand? But no, the soft mirth in his eyes was tempered with a look of disbelief, as if holding her in his arms wasn't something he ever expected, but he wasn't about to let go.

"I will need to have Priya by my side." She scrambled to think of something that would say this wasn't an alliance of nations, but of hearts.

Ash smiled. "But of course. Where would we be without her?"

"And Janak as well," she said, then thought better of it. "If he's not otherwise disposed."

"Granted." Ash trailed a finger along her jaw, then chased it with his lips. When they touched her neck, her skin inflamed once more, and her heart spasmed as if it might actually stop.

She pulled back so she could breathe again. "I reserve the right to make further demands."

Ash grinned. "I cannot even picture a time when that would not be true."

She nudged him away, then thought better of it, and pulled him in for another kiss. This time she was the one making demands: on his lips, on his attention, upon his very heart. That was what she truly wanted.

When they broke apart, she whispered, "And I insist that you never, ever, take another lover."

"Understood." This time, his look alone set her skin on fire.

"And there may be children," she said, suddenly timid under the heat of his look.

His gaze didn't waver. "And they will be as beautiful as their mother."

His words stole what breath she had left. "Then, Prince Malik," she said, her voice soft with emotion, "I agree to your proposal to marry for love."

He crushed her again with his kiss.

It felt as though their marriage occurred at that moment, as if their hearts were melded together by sheer want. It was a kind of joy she'd never felt before, so strong it nearly burst out of her body and danced around the room. All her plans, all her daydreams of escaping Dharia, had never included a barbarian prince's kiss in her mother's antechamber. Ash was something entirely new. Something she'd never expected. But his kiss made her forget everything but his lips on hers, his hands holding her like he would never let go.

The sun streamed through the windows of the captain's quarters, throwing spots of light that jittered with each bump in the skyship's flight. Each jostle felt like they had run into some physical thing in the air that made the ship rumble along like the carriage of a train, even though Aniri knew it was only the currents that caused them. She bent over the wind maps on the captain's desk, hoping to glean some understanding from them. If she was to be Queen of Jungali, and the skyship was their latest technological innovation, she wanted to understand more about it. Next to the maps sat the *Aerophysiks* book she had swung at Ash earlier—perhaps it would better serve her now. She wasn't brilliant like her sister, First Daughter Nahali, but she might manage a basic understanding. Maybe Karan could tutor her if he wasn't too busy with his duties as Master Tinker for the united Jungali provinces.

She glanced over her shoulder. Ash stared out the window. She joined him in watching the capital city of her homeland retreat into the hazy distance below.

"Do you think the flight back to Jungali will be rough?" she asked.

He brushed back a long strand of her hair, trailing his fingers through it. "It can't possibly be any worse than the ride here."

She smiled at his humor, then returned her gaze to her home. At any moment, it would be lost over the horizon.

"Are you quite sure you won't miss it?" he asked softly. "The capital?"

"The city. Your family. Your homeland. It has a way of weaving into your heart so deep such that you don't miss it until it's gone."

She smiled and slipped her arms around the military

uniform he now wore to command the skyship. "You've been reading too much poetry again."

"Perhaps." He kissed her lightly, toying with her hair, taking his time to wind the strand around his finger, then let it slip through again. "I just want you to be sure."

"I'm sure." And she was. Of all the bad decisions she had made, this wasn't one of them. It felt right in a way none of her other longings ever had. She grinned playfully and escaped his grasp. Before, when Garesh held her captive in the captain's quarters, the room had been stripped bare. Now, it was filled with all kinds of things—stacks of books on shelves, boxes of gadgets, heaps of tinker tools.

"I would like to know more about Jungali's newest technology," she said, examining the objects on the shelves. "Your alliance with Samir—"

"*Our* alliance with Samir," he challenged her from where he leaned against the window, watching her.

"*Our* alliance with Samir," she echoed with a smile, "will surely suffer now that Garesh is gone."

"I'm not exactly mourning the loss of our General. And I would willingly throw the Samirian ambassador off a skyship as well, but I hear she has already fled."

Aniri prayed the ambassador had taken Devesh with her. While he had betrayed her and broken her heart, she had loved him too much to wish him jailed. Or worse. If he or the ambassador had remained in Jungali, it would have gone badly for them.

"She won't find much refuge in Samir," Aniri said, examining the row of leather-bound volumes on the shelf. She wondered where Devesh would go as well.

"I wouldn't be too certain of that."

She threw him an arched look to match his tone. "You don't believe the Samirians when they say the

ambassador acted without authorization? Seledri is married to the prince heir-apparent. She would know if the attack on Dharia was authorized by the crown. She insists it wasn't."

Seledri had returned to Samir even before the skyship arrived in Kartavya, but her communiques said the ambassador—and Devesh—would not be welcomed back to court. And that she had no knowledge of Devesh returning to their country. It wouldn't surprise Aniri if he had lied about the Samirians planning war with Dharia, along with everything else.

"I'm sure your sister is telling the truth," Ash said softly. "But the burning glass didn't invent itself, Aniri."

She frowned but didn't reply. He was right, of course. Someone created the weapon, and as beautiful as it was, there was no peaceful use for it that she could discern. And it was certainly possible her sister wouldn't know everything that went on in her husband's court. Aniri lifted one of the many clockwork devices haphazardly set on the shelf. "Where did all this come from?"

"Karan has been cleaning out the engine room and bridge. I told him he could use this room for extra storage."

Aniri put the device back and trailed her hand along the bookshelf. "I know Karan worked with your brother on the original skyship design plans, but Samir provided so much of your technology. Will it be difficult to carry forward with your plans for the skyship if…" Her voice trailed off as she came to an ironclad box sitting on the bookshelf: a Samirian aetheroceiver, just like Devesh's. She flashed a look to Ash. "Where did this come from?"

"*That* was tucked away on the bridge," Ash said. "The captain won't give us the code, and Karan's engineers haven't the tools to break it open until we return to Bajir."

She lifted the heavy box from the shelf and brought it to the desk. She ran her hand over it, checking for the symbols. They were there, same as before. This had to be the same box that was in the ambassador's office. She pressed the three symbols all at once: a tinker, a crown, and a ship. The aetheroceiver whirred and unfolded before them.

Ash's eyes went wide. "How did you do that?"

"My lover was a Samirian spy, remember?"

"Ah. Yes." Ash seemed less than pleased about the reminder, drifting back to the window to stare out of it again, arms crossed. Aniri shook her head and ignored him.

The aetheroceiver contained the same pencil drawing of the skyship she had seen before. Now that she had time to examine it, she noticed the tiny lettering in a box in the corner.

"You know," Aniri said conversationally, hoping to distract Ash from the brooding looks he was casting out the window, "I always thought of the ship as just *the skyship*. I didn't realize she had a name."

"The *HMS Samirdi*." Ash turned from the window. "My brother named it early on. It means Prosperity."

Aniri frowned. "The skyship is named Prosperity?"

"*Her Majesty's Ship Samirdi*, but yes, Prosperity."

Aniri stared at the sketch in her hands. "Was there an earlier version of the ship?"

"No."

"Is this the only ship you've built?"

The look on her face drew Ash away from the window. "What's wrong, Aniri?"

The schematic was clearly labeled *HMS Dagger*. It

could only mean one thing, and it made her mouth run dry.

"There's a second skyship."

The Dharian Affairs Trilogy continues with *Second Daughter*!

Subscribe to Susan's Mailing List
to be notified when it releases!
http://bit.ly/SubscribeToSusansNewsletter

If you enjoyed *Third Daughter*, please leave a review.

other books by susan kaye quinn

The Mindjack Trilogy

Open Minds, Closed Hearts, Free Souls
young adult science fiction

**When everyone reads minds,
a secret is a dangerous thing to keep.**

Sixteen-year-old Kira Moore is a zero, someone who can't read thoughts or be read by others. Zeros are outcasts who can't be trusted, leaving her no chance with Raf, a regular mindreader and the best friend she secretly loves. When she accidentally controls Raf's mind and nearly kills him, Kira tries to hide her frightening new ability from her family and an increasingly suspicious Raf. But lies tangle around her, and she's dragged deep into a hidden underworld of mindjackers, where having to mind control everyone she loves is just the beginning of the deadly choices before her.

The Debt Collector Serial

Season One of *Debt Collector*
(nine-part serial)
Adult future-noire

***What's your life worth on the open market?
A debt collector can tell you precisely.***

Lirium plays the part of the grim reaper well, with his dark trenchcoat, jackboots, and the black marks on his soul that every debt collector carries. He's just in it for his cut, the ten percent of the life energy he collects before he transfers it on to the high potentials, the people who will make the world a better place with their brains, their work, and their lives. That hit of life energy, a bottle of vodka, and a visit from one of Madam Anastazja's sex workers keep him alive, stable, and mostly sane... until he collects again. But when his recovery ritual is disrupted by a sex worker who isn't what she seems, he has to choose between doing an illegal hit for a girl whose story has more holes than his soul or facing the bottle alone—a dark pit he's not sure he'll be able to climb out of again.

mature themes and content

Find all of Susan's works at www.SusanKayeQuinn.com

acknowledgments

Third Daughter started as a contest entry on Rick Daley's blog, *The Public Query Slushpile*. He wanted to run an experiment (which, naturally, hooked me immediately): given a vague premise, writers were asked to submit a query and the first five pages of a (fictitious) novel. His objective was to see which was easier to write (the query or the pages) and to prove that writers' fears of their "unique" story being "ripped off" were unfounded. He posited that each author couldn't help but craft something unique, even though they were starting with the same, basic story construct (a military intrigue). The results? I'm not sure if pages or queries were considered easier (for me, it was definitely pages), but it was clear that the stories were very diverse. And I'm fairly certain I was the only one to take a military intrigue and turn it into an east-Indian steampunk fantasy romance! Rick's note at the time:

I hope this turns into a project you can finish and sell! I'd totally show all my friends my name on the acknowledgments page.

Well, here you are, Rick!

Your spark of a story kept smoldering for two years, nagging the back of my brain, before I finally turned *Third Daughter* into a proper novel. It took another year before it was ready for publication. Shockingly, the first line remains the same, although the rest has morphed substantially. Thank you for the nudge and the encouragement—without you, this novel literally would not exist!

Further thanks are due to the wonderfully talented freelancers who helped bring *Third Daughter* into its final form: Byron Quertermous, who pinch-hit a developmental edit and convinced me this needed to be a trilogy; Sher A. Hart, who lent her sharp copyediting eye to clean up my sloppiness; Ali Cross, who made the book gorgeous on the inside; and Steven Novak, who made it gorgeous on the outside. I'm tremendously lucky to have such wonderful people bringing their talent to bear on my novel!

Special thanks go to my writer-friends and critique-partners, Matthew MacNish and Pavarti K. Tyler, for your insightful notes, quick turn around, and most of all, for loving the story. Thanks as well to Aspi Havewala for the definitive guide to Bollywood movies! That was some of the most fun research I've done to date.

Finally, thanks go to my readers for your constant encouragement and excitement about the book as I was writing it. Whether you were following my *Third Daughter* Pinterest page, or dropping notes asking when the book was going to be out, or just gushing over the steampunkery pictures I posted for inspiration—your enthusiasm is literally the steam that drives my story engines.

I hope you enjoy the result!

about the author

Susan Kaye Quinn is the author of the bestselling Mindjack Trilogy, which is young adult science fiction. The Debt Collector serial is her more grown-up SF, and The Dharian Affairs trilogy is her excuse to dress up in corsets and fight with swords. By the time you read this, there will probably be more... she always has more speculative fiction fun in the works.

Susan grew up in California, got a bunch of engineering degrees (B.S. Aerospace Engineering, M.S. Mechanical Engineering, Ph.D. in Environmental Engineering) and worked everywhere from NASA to NCAR (National Center for Atmospheric Research). She designed aircraft engines, studied global warming, and held elected office (as a school board member). Now that she writes novels, her business card says "Author and Rocket Scientist," but she mostly sits around in her pajamas in awe that she gets paid to make up stuff.

All her engineering skills come in handy when dreaming up dangerous mind powers, future dystopian worlds, and slightly plausible steampunk inventions. For her stories, of course. Just ignore that stuff in the basement.

Susan writes from the Chicago suburbs with her three boys, two cats, and one husband. Which, it turns out, is exactly as much as she can handle.

Susan loves to hear from readers!
Like her **Facebook Page**
www.Facebook.com/SusanKayeQuinnAuthor
follow her on **Twitter** @SusanKayeQuinn
or visit her **author blog** at SusanKayeQuinn.com

Subscribe to her newsletter
http://bit.ly/SubscribeToSusansNewsletter
to be the first to hear about new releases.

Made in the USA
Charleston, SC
27 January 2014